I0772048

Between Broomsticks & Beating Wings

BETWEEN BROOMSTICKS &
BEATING WINGS

MARISSA SERRAO

BROKEN WING PRESS
An imprint of Eighty-Eight Butterfly House

PRONUNCIATION GUIDE

People:
Áma- AH-mah
Angrboda- ahn-ger-BOH-duh
Bodil: BO-deal
Freyja- FREY-yah
Kari- CAR-ee
Odin- OH-dihn
Odr- OH-thur
Rayna- RAY-nah
Rune- RUE-nn

Places:
Asgard (Realm of the Gods)- AS-guard
Fólkvangr (Freyja's Meadow)- FOLK-vaun-ger
Helheim (Realm of the Dead)- HELL-hame
Midgard (Human Realm)- MID-guard
Muspelheim (Realm of Demons and Fire Giants)- MOO-spell-hame
Nidavellir (Dwarven Realm)- Nid-uh-vel-LEAR
Sessrúmnir (Freyja's Hall)- Sess-ROOM-near
Stormheim (Kari's Village)- STORM-hame
Valhalla (Odin's Hall)- Val-HALL-uh
Yggdrasill (World Tree)- IG-druh-zill

Other:
Bygul and Trjegul (Freyja's Felines)- BYE-gul and TRYE-gul

Seeress (Magic Practitioner)- SEA-rehs

Seidr (Magic)- SAY-duh

Nídhöggr (World Tree Dragon)- KNEE-hoe-ger

Ratatoskr (Squirrel)- RAT-uh-toss-kerr

Jörmungandr (World Serpent)- YOUR-mung-gund-er

CONTENT WARNINGS

This book is about a seeress who can see ghosts and a valkyrie who goes down into battlefields and collects souls from the slain, so, naturally, death plays a large role in this story. While there are cozy elements, please be aware of the following:

• Previously deceased/murdered family
  • Diminished will to live
  • Self-sacrifice
  • Mild body gore
  • On page murder
  • Corpses
  • Ghosts
  • Death

Other topics include:
  • Swarming insects
  • Sexual situations
  • Intoxication
  • Profanity
  • Light stalking

Now, grab yourself a blanket and a cup of something warm, and let's begin. Shall we?

CHAPTER ONE
BLOODFLIES AND BROOMSTICKS

Kari

My fingers molded the soft clay as if I were a goddess and the pliable substance was the foundation of my next realm. Stretching and pulling at the clay, I began shaping it into something reminiscent of a bowl. Pottery wasn't my strong suit growing up, but once my mother and sisters passed over to Hel—presumably—I'd been left to pick up their slack. I'd been making everything for myself these past few years, from wooden spoons to clothing, but that's what happened when you lived alone at the ripe old age of twenty-seven.

I wasn't fully alone, I supposed, but my only source of company typically made my life more challenging. My belongings were often found broken or torn, thanks to the orange, furry gremlin that occupied my longhouse. Thankfully, he didn't require me to make his meals—not anymore, at least.

Speaking of... Where in the nine realms is he?

Whenever I went too long without hearing from him, my heart began to tighten. My worry didn't stem from something happening to him—that longship had sailed. I worried the little bugger got into something he shouldn't have, yet again.

I pushed back my chair, its wooden legs scraping across the dirt floor as I rose from my seat.

"Tove?" I called out, careful not to let the neighbors hear. They thought I was mad enough as it was, always talking to myself as if the spirits of my family had stuck around. In truth, that phase only lasted a few months, and eventually, they disappeared, one by one, to their afterlife.

Those few months with my family were bittersweet. I often tacked "sweet" to that sentiment to dull my guilt, but most days were more bitter, knowing I couldn't join them. My sisters had attempted to cut the threads the Norns had woven for me to see that I could leave this mortal plane. I didn't think they *wanted* to kill me, but they were young and angry, and they yearned for their eldest sister to hold their hand as they ventured into their eternal rest.

Was that yet another lie I told myself? Maybe. Maybe the two young girls grew angry and resentful, watching me eat, sleep, and do all the things they would never do on Midgard again, and they wanted to punish me for going off to the market that day. Maybe they wanted to punish me for surviving.

A sinister mew pulled me out of my spiraling mind. I had no reason to be in that dark and twisted place anyway.

"Tove! How many times have I told you not to play with the cloth coverings?" I asked, rushing over to a long wooden table shoved up against the far wall of my bedchamber. I adjusted the cloth-covered mirror that threatened to fall to the knick-knacks below.

The cat simply mewed at me again and carried on with his nonsense, hopping off the cluttered wooden table and sauntering across the compacted dirt floor. I shook my head as the tips of my fingers lingered over the rough fabric, its edges now stained with orange clay and specks of charcoal soot. A daring spark lingered somewhere deep within me, urging my fearful heart to yank the cloth off the reflective surface.

Who was I fooling? I knew exactly what would await me once the fabric dropped to the dirt and revealed my cursed reflection. My eyes fell shut, memories being plucked over countless years, all haunting. As my eyes flew open, I cleared my throat and dropped my tempted hand. I stumbled backward, and I caught myself on the edge of my bed.

Nothing good would come of adding another memory to my collection. As it was, the ones I stored in my mind were beginning to fester and overflow. There was only so much the mind could forget, and I despised my ability to remember despite my best efforts. I feared one more terrible memory added to the collection may very well break me. Or maybe... No. No, I wouldn't allow myself to believe this time would be different. I wouldn't allow my mind to trick me once again into taking a peek at my cursed eyes.

Pulling my hand from the end of my bed, I traced my fingers over the smooth skin of my eyelids, feeling tiny blood vessels and the movement of my wandering eyes underneath. My eyelashes tickled my callused fingers as they fluttered. Everything about the way my eyes felt under my light touch was normal. There was no bumpy, raised flesh, no puss or goo, and surely, the tone of my skin matched the rest of my body. It wasn't an unending well of black rot, unlike what my reflection would tell me.

They were all lies, I liked to tell myself. Every single memory staring at myself in a reflective surface over the years was a ridiculous little lie. I imagined what I might look like to other people, a young woman with creamy skin splattered with freckles. I was told my eyes were blue, though I wasn't exactly sure which shade. I hoped they were the color of the deep sea; surely that would be beautiful and alluring.

One day, I would break this dreadful curse and see myself the way others did. I knew this to be true, and I hung onto that truth as I picked a leaf off my floor. Twirling the dried stem in my fingers, I carried it outside. Once I stood on the stone steps of my longhouse, I stretched my spine and crushed the fragile alder leaf in my hand, savoring each note of the music it made as it turned to dust.

Mindlessly sprinkling the remains over my dying summer garden, I peered out at where Tove chased flies in the distance and tried not to think about why there were so many in the first place. The orange feline was a ferocious little thing and would have certainly caught each of the flying pests, had his paws not passed through their tiny, winged bodies. Like a cat with a ray of light, he never seemed to mind that he rarely caught his prey. Tove simply kept at his hunt, always managing to pull a laugh from me in the process as he tumbled and jumped into the air like a mad hare.

"Morning, Kari!" Hilda Akesdotter called out as she beat a hanging tapestry in front of her longhouse. Dust particles danced around her, pulling a cough from the old woman. She waved a wrinkled hand in front of her face, her wiry grey hair gently bending with the breeze.

"Morning Hilda! Careful around that dust, my friend, or I'll need to fix you up another breathing tonic earlier than I should have to."

"Oh, always looking out for me girl." The woman's warm smile created crow's feet around her eyes. She dropped her hand and her smile as she stared off into the distance. "What are you watching today?"

Hilda tilted her head toward Tove and the flies, her curiosity hanging in the air longer than the dust. She often wondered what I spent so much time looking and chuckling at despite myself. I followed her gaze and paused for a moment as I took in the area around my beloved cat for something she may have seen with those old eyes of hers. "The flies. There are more of them today."

"That there are." Hilda's expression soured as she averted her eyes. They lingered on her tapestry, handmade despite her failing vision. "No worries, child. There are people to carry that burden for us. Thank the gods for that."

"Mmm," was all I said as my head bobbed.

The gods, I thought to myself. *There are about a million other beings I would thank first.*

Not long after going back inside, I'd finished the bowl and set the warped thing to the side to bake in the upcoming days. I dipped my hands in a pail of water, washing them clean of dirt, though they stayed mildly stained a burnt orange around my nails.

I gathered my woven basket, keeping the thin layer of fabric at the bottom, though Tove didn't need the aged scrap anymore. I'd yet to remove it, more for me than for him, though I hoped he found comfort in it too—emotionally, of course. The cat was rarely corporeal long enough to feel much of anything physically.

"My sinister boy!" I called as loud as my pride would allow. "It's time for the market."

Moments later, Tove hopped up onto the counter and crawled into his safe haven. He curled up for his routine nap, knowing the walk there would be the same as always. He needed to save his energy for the bustling market and all the wonders it held. As I lifted the basket and propped it in the crook of my arm, a pang of grief hit me upon feeling the basket's unchanging weight. It was as light as a feather these days.

Pushing the unappreciated feelings aside, I let out a sigh and said, "We really need to fatten you up. I swear, you're losing weight."

Tove opened one of his black eyes, then the other, staring at me with an attitude only he could muster.

"Oh, don't you dare look at me like that. Humor keeps the tears away, you should know that. As it is, you're the only one left to witness them."

Tove closed his eyes in defeat, and I set him down to lace up my boots before heading out the door. As I stepped out under the light of the day, I twirled a chaotic, bent curl of strawberry blonde hair around my finger, attempting to form a neat ringlet, though my hair rarely did what I wanted.

The clouds passed overhead in varying shapes, waning then reforming as I carried myself down the straw path. I was thankful for my shawl in the crisp air, pulling it closer to my chest. I tucked the ends of my green fabric into the leather strings lacing the front of my dress so I didn't have to hold it tight to my body. My mother had always told me I looked ridiculous when I fashioned my clothing in this way, and I'd always boasted about my method's practicality and convenience in response, more to annoy her than anything. While I slowly grew out of some of my childish tendencies, I still found myself wearing my shawl this way long after her death. Each time I did, it was as if I were raising my mother from the dead and hearing her bicker over my choices all over again. Amusement and familiarity would keep some of my antics alive forever, I believed.

As I rounded the corner, I averted my gaze from the sky and focused on the way the straw path bled into dirt compacted by many boots. The market was the liveliest place in all of Stormheim, filled with vikings and farmers alike. The folk of Stormheim were proud people, but not too proud to admit we couldn't do everything ourselves. That was the beauty in community—everyone coming together and stepping in where others slacked, knowing they would do the same for you.

My senses awakened as I sauntered past a cart of warm bread, my mouth watering in response. I made my own bread at home, but that didn't mean I wasn't tempted each time I came to the market and saw fresh loaves, ready to be devoured. The woman behind the cart with flushed cheeks smiled at me, and I smiled back, but I wouldn't let her pull me in.

I gripped my basket tighter and carried on through the stalls and carts. I had a list. I wouldn't stray from the list. Straying from the list was how I blew a week's worth of coin and came home with everything I wanted, yet nothing I needed. Today, I needed three things: a broomstick, mugwort, and beeswax candles. Anything else would have to wait, no matter how appealing a new crystal or a warm, woven blanket was.

"Kettlesdotter, when are you going to fill that basket of yours?" a loud voice called out into the market, pulling my attention from a whittled star resting on a cluttered table. "You carry it around every day, yet every day, it remains empty, all but that ratty strip of fabric."

"I'll fill it once I find what I'm looking for, Arnesson," I said, not looking at the man as I perused his inventory. My fingers trailed over a bundle of twigs, just supple enough to be wound into the head of a broomstick.

My response pulled a chuckle from the merchant. The older gentleman was relatively new to Stormheim, joining our small forest village after his own was raided. Stormheim was a place of survivors, it seemed. Many said it was a horrible omen for us all to be in one place, believing we were the ones the gods refused to claim. While they should have taken us too, dividing us amongst their halls, we were left on Midgard for some reason unbeknownst to us. Village folk didn't like the unknown, hence the fear that, one day soon, something much worse than the gods would come collect us all.

Arnesson shot me another smile, as if his last one had faded with my silence. This smile was wobbly, lacking charm, unauthentic, unlike the first.

Nine realms.

"I'm sorry, did you say something?" I asked, noticing the way he ran one of his rough hands down the dirt-stained cloth hanging over his shoulder.

"Don't worry about it, Kari. I've been told what was once held in that basket of yours," he said, his expression softening. "You know, a litter of kittens was just found in the old barn at the edge of the village. The black one might be a decent fit for you and your...ways of the night."

"Ways of the night? You make it sound as if I'm a scarlet daughter," I said with a dry laugh. I peered down at Tove, who looked about ready to pounce out of his basket and onto the man who suggested I replace him. "It's called being wand-wed, Arnesson. Your wife was a seeress herself, was she not?"

"My wife... Odin give me strength. She had the gift, yes. She didn't practice her talents as you do, though. She was content in the ways of trees, harnessing nature to heal our people, instead of harnessing—"

"Seidr?" I asked when the man seemed incapable of speaking the simple but loaded word.

The man cleared his throat, as though he would be struck down for standing so close to me as I said it. "Hmm, yes. Seidr."

Men like Arnesson, who traveled from the south, were not used to the ways of Stormheim, or the north in general. There was talk of a new god who hated seeresses and their magic, their seidr, punishing all who acknowledged it. Here in the north, we knew the old gods claimed domain, and seidr was welcomed—if not encouraged.

"I have no need for a midnight kitten, but thank you for thinking of me. I do, however, need a broomstick," I said, holding up the bundle of twigs.

His eyes darted from the twigs back to me. "That, I can do. Let me grab one from the back."

"It's not used, is it?" I asked, my gaze flicking back to the whittled star. My pointer finger found one of the points, and I pressed into it to test its sharpness.

"No, I just made it last night under the moon. It's safe to bring inside your home, as it's never been inside mine. I store them outside as well, friend. You're in good hands."

"Thank you, Arnesson. I can always count on your thoroughness. I have a feeling I have your wife to thank. May the gods treat her well, wherever she rests."

"That, I have great faith in. She was a good woman and a wonderful seeress. The village folk where I'm from down south, Kaldrstein, all looked up to her, almost as if she were a goddess herself." Arnesson paused, his dark blue eyes peering deep into mine. "I know you will be what she was for this village someday, even with your seidr."

I fiddled with the end of my shawl, bile rising into my throat at the thought. Yes, I loved being the village's seeress. Yes, I loved getting glimpses into the future, even if that future wasn't all too pleasant. But I didn't want a position of leadership. I wanted to frolic, make my subpar pottery, and conjure spells in peace.

I felt the color fleeing my face as he stared at me expectantly. I wanted to tell him I'd rather catch flame than have a seat of leadership in this village, but I simply cleared my throat, found a smile, and said, "You're kind, Arnesson, but trust me when I tell you, no one around here is looking at me like I'm a goddess."

Arnesson frowned, then cocked his head. "Well, of course not!" He let out a laugh so outrageous, I didn't know if I should join in or be insulted. "They may never look at you as though you are a goddess in the way the people of my village did my wife, but they do respect you and your talents. Even if they think you're a nut."

I chuckled, relaxing the tension that had been accumulating in my chest. I snatched the broomstick out of his hands playfully and tossed a single small coin onto the table.

"Listen, I'd rather them think I was a nut. It's harder to disappoint them that way."

Arnesson simply shook his head at me, his shoulders lifting and falling as if he were still chuckling but the sound hadn't yet made it out of his mouth. He raised a large hand into the air, offering me a wave as I made my way down the dirt path.

I'd choose to be a nut over a goddess any day.

I reached into my basket, attempting to give Tove a good scratch, but my hand fell to the bottom of the basket. Tove let out an angry meow, and I whispered an apology under my breath. I didn't like the reminder any more than he did. The sassy creature decided to up and jump out of the basket, leaving me in his wake as he trotted through the market ahead of me.

"Little asshole," I muttered under my breath.

The frail older woman walking close by shot me a concerned glance.

For Valhalla's sake!

My apology to her lingered in the air behind me as I hurried after Tove. That demon cat was going to pay for pulling embarrassment out of me twice in one day. I swore he stuck around the mortal realm of Midgard just to torment me. Then again, wasn't that what my sisters and I had done when they were alive, tormenting each other to show our love? When Tove turned back around and waved his little orange tail at me, my jaw relaxed, and the truth settled in. I would curse out every frail old woman in Stormheim to keep him around.

CHAPTER TWO
FOR THE LOVE OF ALL THINGS LIVING

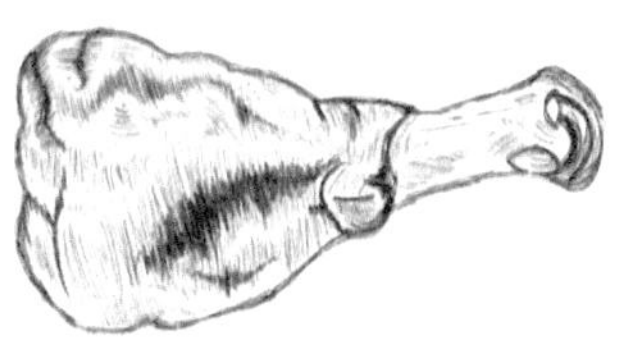

Rune

Boredom. Oftentimes, I wondered if it could ever be enough to kill a person. Sure, my life was a beautiful symphony of clashing swords and golden goblets, but all blades eventually began to dull if not sharpened, and all cups were drained if not refilled. My life was full of dull blades and empty cups, though the gods loved shoving new, shiny weapons into my hands and throwing feasts in my sister's honor large enough to fill bellies for a century.

"Dragomir," a voice boomed, pulling me out of my wandering mind. "It's about time you showed up."

The wood of my chair creaked under my weight as I leaned back in it to get a better look at the approaching man. The man named Gro towered over me, his blond locks cascading down his left shoulder. He wore a diagonal scar across one of his rosy cheeks from one of the many battles he'd fought in his mortal life.

Dragging my chin up to meet his eye, I grumbled, "Well, how could I miss tonight's feast? It's only the fifth one this week."

A hearty chuckle filled the room, shaking the round belly of the bronze man who peered down at me. I kicked my feet off the chair my boots had been resting on and lazily stood to greet him. It didn't suit my ego, having a warrior scrunch his neck to meet my eye. My ass had grown sore from sitting anyway, so when I rose, I stretched my spine and tilted my chin toward the chandelier above.

"Ah, well, that's the glory of Valhalla, isn't it? Feasts every night, celebrations grand enough to fill these golden halls to the brim, you and your sisters at the center of it all."

"You mean with Odin at the center?" I lightly corrected him, the corner of my mouth twitching.

The man chuffed, his bright blue eyes twinkling. "Would you have it any other way, Dragomir?"

My gaze darted around the feast and its guests, knowing the only appropriate thing to do was to say no, so that's exactly what I did. I was too sober to cause a scene. "Wouldn't dream of it."

"Ah!" The man scooped a goblet off the table and shoved it into my hand. He smashed it against his own, a smile cracking his perpetually merry face in two. "Isn't that the truth."

Gro stumbled away, and I watched him as he went. How many times would I have these same conversations, agreeing to unchanging sentiments posed by unchanging people?

The most exciting thing around these parts was death itself, and while I didn't wield it, I did bless these very halls with its victims. The dead brought a new life to Valhalla, unfamiliar faces belonging to unfamiliar names. It was never long before I memorized them too, even through drunken hazes and forgettable revelry. Time would do that, and here, time never lacked.

I took a swig of the mead gifted so generously by Gro. Mead. It was my cure to the bounty of years here on this plane of existence, a plane filled with bodies standing on golden floors, living for war. Even in death, vikings fought battles in search of endless glory. This place was glory personified. It lived within us all like a beating pulse.

Maybe I didn't wish for war like the rest because I was the one who cleaned up the messes left behind by mortal battles. In life, these viking men and women lifted swords and great axes, screaming out their gods' names as they fought in their honor. They ran into battle with banished fear, knowing they would live to see another day or earn a warrior's death, either outcome just as welcome. When their blood was shed, and the day's battle had ended with another setting sun, I would be there, plucking souls from the slain.

Warriors rode pegasuses into the skies, awaiting the place boasted by all since the time they were babes. My younger sisters were always caught up in the excitement of war and the newness of it all. They saw nothing but heroes, and their chests were swollen with honor for carrying the souls of warriors to their next destination—their eternal reward.

But with many battles and many setting suns, their pride and excitement too would fade, and they may begin to look around at everything those heroes had left behind. It was easy to ignore at first, the intoxication of removing a soul from its body. You didn't need a stomach of steel if your eyes were clouded by battle haze.

Every drug wore off eventually. Eyes would clear and minds would open. It was nearly a hundred years ago I finally saw a battlefield for what it was. I noticed every drop of blood, every torn family, every burning longhouse. While we celebrated nightly with warriors in golden halls, I worshiped all those they left behind in thatch huts.

There would be another collection of souls tonight. I had a feeling I would be dragging my feet yet again, flying down to the mortal realm and allowing my younger sisters to have their fill. The faster they collected, the higher on battle haze they became, and the less they noticed I was missing.

Tonight, I would take my time. Tonight, I would press the limits of a mortal body, see how long I could let its soul linger within its confines. The longer the warrior souls could wait for their afterlife, the longer I had to explore the home they were to abandon—and the people they abandoned too.

Mead swished from one cheek to the next before I swallowed it down. Elderberry tonight. At least some things changed. I refilled my goblet, not meeting the eyes of the people sharing the long, wooden table with me. They all knew I wasn't much of a talker anyway, at least not before my tenth cup. I didn't mind reconfirming words and whispers spoken as I turned my back.

I pulled a turkey thigh from the silver tray in the center of the table and took it, and the goblet, with me. Right before I left, I tucked a bottle of mead under my arm. I'd shown my face for long enough tonight; there was always tomorrow night.

Ripping meat from bone, I ambled through the great hall doors and out into the breezeway. I closed my eyes as the evening air ran over my flushed face and walked like that until I inevitably ran into someone. I mumbled my apology and opened my eyes to see where my blinded stumbling had landed me. I'd arrived just short of a balcony with strong stone pillars and a fountain carved of marble. My eyes darted from the water spewing out through little faces, then back down to my turkey leg.

Shrugging, I set my goblet and bottle on the edge of the fountain and bit down on the turkey to free my hands. I unleashed my feet from leather boots, curling my toes on cool stone. Before I changed my mind, I climbed into the fountain, the water soaking my leathers. My whole body squeaked in a ridiculous melody as I splashed about. Once I found a nice spot where the stone dipped and cradled my ass perfectly, I reclaimed my goblet.

As I ate and drank, I stared off at the horizon lit only by flame and stars. I'd never argue Valhalla wasn't the most beautiful place I'd ever seen. Its beauty was never my ailment, and I oftentimes couldn't put my finger on what exactly my ailment was. Yet, I needed to medicate for it, nonetheless.

Truth be told, I'm not sure how long I stayed in the fountain, staring off at dark and hidden mountains. By the time my fingers had pruned and my leathers were ruined, the turkey leg was nothing but picked bone. Sadly, my goblet was emptied of mead, somewhere at the bottom of the fountain.

"I leave you for no more than a few moments, and you're already getting yourself into trouble?" a woman's voice poured out into the night like spun silk.

"Rayna?" I swung my head to look behind me, but my eyes filled with fluid as the woman dumped a goblet of water onto my face. The cool water upon my dry skin sent a shock of awareness through me, my heart thumping in my chest, bringing new life to my unmoving limbs. I jerked up just as she grabbed my hands and yanked me clean out of the fountain, soaked clothing and all.

"Yes, it's me, you idiot," my younger sister said. "You're lucky I found your drunk ass before one of Odin's guards did."

"Eh, wouldn't be the first time." I shrugged, pushing off her slightly to stand on my own, but she held me firm in her grasp. As I wiped my eyes, Rayna came into focus as more than a simple, hazy figure. Her pale blonde hair was tied neatly back into braids, still maintaining strands of color from her previous mortal life. She looked as if she'd been distracted while in the middle of putting on her armor, her right breastplate strap hanging limply down her chest.

"Exactly my point. Gods, you reek of stale water. Let's get you out of here and cleaned up, alright?"

"If you so wish," I said through a string of hiccups. "I *do* have souls to collect."

"Not in this state, you don't." Rayna dragged me along, though I insisted I could walk on my own.

"I am inebriated, yes, but not a drunken fool. My feet are simply...numb and uncooperative at the moment. But as soon as my blood comes rushing back, hear me, I'll be flying to Midgard with the rest of you."

"You're no fool, but you are a drunken hazard, Rune," Rayna said as we walked. She gave me more leeway to make it down the corridor independently. Even through hazy eyes, I didn't miss the disapproving glares she shot me. "I know you care little if your behavior gets you hurt, but don't forget about the rest of us."

"You're too hard to kill, Rayna. I've tried," I said with an amused chuckle. The woman, while still young, was one of the fiercest warriors I'd ever known. The muscle in her jaw pulsed with each word I spoke.

"There are more ways you could harm me and the rest of the sisters than by simply taking our lives. You should know better than anyone, there are much worse fates than death."

My own muscles stiffened at her sobering words. I realized then she was holding my boots. Had I still been barefoot? My throat cleared, and I motioned for her to hand me the leather boots. I may have destroyed the rest of my gear, but at least I'd had some shred of decency and removed my shoes first. They were my favorite pair, after all.

Rayna handed them to me with a tight-lipped smile. Her eyes wandered my face, like if she looked hard enough, she could see if her words penetrated my thick skull. Lucky for her, they had.

"I hear you, Rayna. I do."

Her shoulders relaxed, and she silently nodded her head. The two of us didn't speak for the rest of our walk as we made our way home.

<hr>

I'd grown accustomed to the pounding headaches that followed after gorging myself on mead and meat all night. The extra blood pulsing in my temples created music for my ears only. It was special, really, when you thought of it like that. What was better than the music of your own blood to remind you that you were still alive? Because I *was* still alive.

Though my days were surrounded by the dead, I wasn't truly one of them. Sure, my mortal self had slowly faded away, as did the color in my hair, but I still lived and breathed just as I always had.

If I were like the warriors who had been flown up to Valhalla, I could eat and drink to my heart's content and suffer none of the nasty consequences. But alas, I had something they didn't: flesh and blood.

Once Rayna and I arrived at the House of Wings, she directed me to the washtub to clean up. The golden tub had done the rest for us, already waiting for me with steaming hot water. After stripping out of my sodden leathers, I collapsed into the tub without a shred of grace. My fingers were still pruned from the fountain water, but the healing waters of the golden Valhalla tub immediately plumped my skin. I only lingered long enough to scrub myself of stench, not bothering to untie each braid from my hair. Surely, my locks could wait a day or two to be washed.

When I crawled out of the tub, there was a small plate of berries and honey sitting on a wooden stool to rouse my senses. I popped a sticky raspberry into my mouth, letting the energizing flavors pull me out of my stupor.

Wrapping myself in a towel, I gazed into the mirror opposite me, trimmed with ornate patterns in precious metals. I stared back at the reflection longer than I should have, like I often found myself doing. When I first entered the Sisterhood and moved into the House of Wings, I stared into a mirror much like this one, fascinated by the idea that I would someday know every line and curve of my face. When I realized I had a lifetime to do so, I'd believed it was deeply romantic to know yourself in such a way. I'd imagined that by the time I earned my one hundredth year, I would have memorized every feature on my un-aging face.

How wrong I'd been.

I'd earned my one hundredth year a half a millennia ago, and I swore, with each year, the image staring back at me became more distant, more unfamiliar.

Sure, I could draw the sharp lines of my face in my sleep, but I'd never been able to capture what lingered beneath my grey-blue eyes. While my hair and body had changed with time, my locks white and my body stronger, my face remained an unchanging enigma.

Sucking all the honey off a blackberry, I watched the way my pink lips closed over the fruit.

Hel, Rune.

I shook myself out of the haze, knowing no good could come from allowing my reflection to hold so much power over me. I meandered over to my wardrobe, thankful to have my own after decades of sharing one with my sisters. That was how it always was in the beginning. Nothing was your own, always shared. The next thing you knew, you'd been in the House of Wings for thirty years, and you were still sharing shoes with the girl in the room next door. You'd forgotten what it'd been like to have a night's rest, or a meal on your own, because our belongings weren't the only things we shared.

I yanked open the wooden doors then scoured through my many dresses, leathers, and pieces of armor. All mine, I thought as I ran my fingers down a velvety sleeve, the texture of the fabric reminiscent of yule's past. Each piece was earned as a token of dedication.

"Rune! For the love of all things living, what's taking you so long?" Rayna called out from the other side of my bedroom door. In the olden times, I would've jumped, but my nerves had since been lost. "Are you coming or not?"

I'd wondered how much time I'd wasted as I pulled a pair of leathers from the wardrobe. "Be out in a moment!"

"I'm about to remove the mirror from your bathing chamber! Asta should have never allowed you to have one," Rayna grumbled. "You're almost as bad as Bodil with her damn boar hair brushes. Obsessed, both of you."

I climbed into my gear, then swung open my bedchamber door. Rayna stood just past it with her arms crossed, looking a moment away from removing it from its hinges. When she turned to me, her mouth gaped then shut like a breathless trout. "You look rather presentable."

I suppressed a chuckle, worried she'd think I was still drunk if I broke my frozen façade. There was no way I was being left behind tonight. "Thank you. It's from all the time I spend staring into that mirror you loath."

"We all have our vices, Ru," Rayna said with a shrug, leaning onto a thin wooden table lining the wall of our shared living space. "I just wish yours didn't make me late every night."

"There's no rule stating you have to wait for me, you know." I turned back to look at my sister as I walked past her, beginning our journey through the chambers Rayna and I'd inhabited for the past two centuries.

"I would see the ice of Helheim catch fire before I ever went down to the mortal plane without you."

"Let's go then," I said, not being able to contain my chuckle this time. "Souls are waiting. I can taste them."

CHAPTER THREE
THESE DREAMS THAT FIND ME

Kari

Crisp autumn days like today yanked me through a portal back to my curious childhood. Sometimes, the cause was the crunch of leaves under the sole of my wool-lined boots. Other times, it was the whispers of wind though the brittle branches of trees that'd begun their hibernations. Either way, this season was the source of my undying love for the scent of decomposing leaves, lit fires, and the need for additional clothing to warm my chilled flesh. It was also the source of sleepless nights and wicked dreams.

As I ladled steaming water out of my iron pot and into a clay mug, I pondered the dream that had found me last night. The twisted images my mind constructed were muddled over the past several weeks. I spent each morning sorting them as I sipped on mugwort tea I'd made from market ingredients and from what I'd grown in my own garden. I jotted down any symbols I recognized and attempted finding patterns within them.

I curled in on myself as I brought the mug to my lips and used the power within the brewed leaves and stems to help piece my mind together. Sure, the tea was meant to be drunk before sleeping to elicit clear dreams, but I figured there was no harm in a cup upon waking as well. The first few moments after rising were always the most crucial, and I kept charcoal and birch bark on the table beside my bed to prevent me from missing important details. For if I did, the meaning of my visions could be twisted into falsities. Just because future truths came to me in the night didn't mean I always knew how to decipher them. I needed to perfectly understand their meaning if I were to know what was coming for me.

Leaning back in my chair, I set the birch bark on the table, close enough so I could still read what was on it. There were drawings of a setting sun, whooshing winds, of feathers and darkness. I saw flashes of gold, death, death, and more death. The dreams that replayed in my mind were hauntingly beautiful and so very dark. I wasn't sure if there was a way to stop what was coming, and I was thankful no one lived in my mind, for they would discover I didn't know if I wanted to stop it at all.

The woven basket on the far side of the table began to shake just before Tove jumped out of it and launched himself at me.

"Tove!" I yelled out as he extended his claws. My heart thrummed in my ears at the scare, even though it would have no impact. The feline's attack was like that of his attack on the flies, and his small body passed right through my body and landed on the dirt floor behind me.

"Must you do that every day?" I asked, my voice raised a little too high. "One of these mornings, you will become corporeal and sink those claws right into me."

Tove sat up properly and gave me a slow blink as an offering of peace, but I knew better than to trust it.

"We will make peace when you allow me to have mine," I grumbled to the cat. In my mind, Tove was still an orange fur ball, he and I alike in our unique coloring. But when I took a moment to truly see him, it was only then I noticed I could see through him, that he had a blue tint around his edges, which always allowed me to tell the living from the dead.

Tove wasn't the only ghost I saw each day—far from it. Stormheim was littered with them. Many were fresh souls wandering over from neighboring villages who had been slain in battle. The valkyries were getting a little lazy if you asked me, because I couldn't go more than an hour without hearing one of their wails. Some complained about dying in rather pitiful ways that wouldn't allow them into Valhalla, and others hadn't quite realized they'd lost their lives in the first place. Sometimes, when I was alone and the spirit was close enough, I would help guide them on their way, but seeing them only allowed me to do so much. I could never deliver them to where they needed to go. That was the job of the gods and their attendants.

When Tove flopped onto his side and began grabbing at his tail, it reminded me that I had work of my own. I decided I'd spend a few more moments jotting down runes and trying to decipher what I'd seen in my slumber. By the time I was finished, my tea had grown cold, and my legs were itching for a walk. I set the charcoal down, knowing it was time to move on. I had a pinecone to collect anyway.

Once outside, I took a deep lungful of clean, crisp air. I wished I could bottle autumn air to savor for the rest of the year, but my many experiments as a child had always proven futile. There was nothing to do but simply enjoy it while it lasted.

I wandered about the land for a while, gathering natural necessities for potions and tonics. The woody scent of heather filled my nose, and my hands grew damp with dew and sap as I dug beneath exposed tree roots and through the forest's underbrush.

I got lucky, finding a few animal bones polished by time, the most pristine pinecone, and a few handfuls of pine needles. A conspiracy of ravens cooed and clicked in nearby trees, and I wondered if any of them were messengers of the Allfather. I laughed to myself. Since I was a child, I couldn't see a raven without thinking of Odin, but who was I to think he'd watch over such a small village such as Stormheim?

The sun was beginning to set already, casting shades of pink and yellow across the sky streaked with clouds. I hadn't realized just how much time I'd spent in the forest, gathering my bounty. Days when I had no patients or clients coming to see me always went by in a blur. It was impossible to know where my precious time had gone. Too much time spent frolicking and recounting visions, I suppose.

As I made my way out of the forested area, I noticed a swarm of bloodflies coming in from the east.

Great.

These vermin plagued our village—not just by infecting our food with the rot they carried on their little bodies, but they plagued our minds as well. They were our reminder that Stormheim was on the edge of collapse due to outside forces. War was closing in around us, the reason for it lost on me. All I knew was, people were dying or being pushed out of their homes, and the battle was spreading like an untreated disease—quick and out of control.

Seeing the pesky creatures, there was one last thing I needed before I could race the setting sun. *Acorns.* I searched the ground, instructing Tove to be on the lookout for perfect, unsampled ones. He tried to paw at the little round nuts to inspect them, occasionally tripping over himself or tackling one of the nicer acorns. He pulled laughs from me, unhindered by curious nearby ears, though I could feel there was a pair out there somewhere.

For the past two years, I felt eyes on the back of my head upon the exit of the sun from our sky. The sensation came in the form of a tickle down my spine, and I chalked the feeling up to creeping spirits. I couldn't allow myself to consider that the looming force was something more sinister. As I picked up the few remaining acorns of Tove's selection, I pondered if the presence haunting me had anything to do with my recent twisted dreams. I thought about my scribbles and runes, how I'd made no progress uncovering the glimpses of the future for the first time in my life.

Was I desperate enough to...

No, Kari. Don't.

I heard a twig snap in the distance, and the chills running down my neck amplified. This presence was no mere ghost.

Fuck it.

"Hello?" I called out into the night, holding my breath in between questions. "Anyone there?"

I slowed my beating heart so I could hear if there was any sort of response, be it a verbal reply or footsteps that ran off into the distance, but there was nothing except the buzz of insects and the howl of the wind. I pulled my shawl in closer, telling Tove it was time to return home.

When I turned on my heel, I caught a flash of blue out of the corner of my eye, but I had no interest in communicating with the deceased tonight. As I carried on, I ducked beneath a fallen log. I was almost in the clear, but a swarm of bloodflies buzzed around me, some bold enough to land upon my skin.

A scream ripped loose from my lips as I felt them crawling over my flesh. "Go find something dead to feast on, you rotten, no good wastes of space!"

Sunset had passed, and I hurried from the insects into the safety of the area lit by village torches. It was stupid of me to lose track of time like that, taking no fire with me to guide my way. I pulled one of the permanent village torches from the ground and used its glow to find my way home.

CHAPTER FOUR
APPLES FOR APPLE

Rune

Rayna and I snuck toward a large iron door, careful not to alert our house mother, Asta, to our late departure. Asta had been enduring my antics for over a century, and I wouldn't have had any gripes about continuing in my ways if not for Rayna. Rayna cared deeply about her duty and how people such as Asta looked down upon her and cast their judgment. She lived for praise and pride and wouldn't allow my behavior to impact her ability to become one of the most valuable soul collectors in the House of Wings.

Rayna hadn't been chosen by Odin for the Valhalla sect of the House of Wings like I'd been long ago. She, like most valkyries, was selected initially by one of the four other sects. In most cases, valkyries must provide invaluable service for decades—centuries— before they capture Odin's attention. Only then would he advocate for a transfer of houses and take them under his metaphorical wing. A house transfer was a rare thing, and Rayna had done it after only one year of service in Freyja's sect in Fólkvangr. The time it took for her to catch Odin's attention was unheard of, and the day she was sworn into his sect, she rewrote history.

Reaching for the iron door's handle, I didn't care if I alerted the whole realm. Rayna shot me a look that demanded I behave, and, just as my fingers brushed the cool metal, I reduced my strength, dragging down the handle with maddening slowness. Once the two of us were safely on the other side, into the tunnels lit by nothing but torches anchored to the wall, Rayna released a breath.

"Thank you." She squeezed my forearm, her eyes locked eagerly on the base of the tunnel—a black void that led to a field of stars.

"Same time tomorrow?" I asked, a laugh hidden somewhere within my shrouded voice. She shot me a glare, one side of her face illuminated by candlelight, the other half lost to the darkness.

Winding through the tunnels didn't take long, as our muscles memorized the way long ago. The path was a direct shortcut built under the House of Wings for emergencies, though to my younger sister, being late *was* an emergency. The rest of our sisters traveled to the fields above ground, but that required leaving the front door and walking right past Asta's chambers—so the tunnels it was.

When a sparkle of moonlight blessed our vision, we knew we were in the right place. Rayna climbed up the ladder first, leaving me alone in the darkness. Maybe I hesitated each night, my boots lingering on dirt floors, because the silence, the peace, was my hidden pleasure. When Rayna called down for me, I raised my chin, shook off my growing doubt, and ascended the ladder.

Rayna tipped back her head and audibly sucked in midnight air, releasing her breath back into the dark sky littered with twinkling stars. I joined in, expelling the stale tunnel air from my lungs and replacing it with crisp, Asgardian oxygen. I swore the air here was intoxicating. Odin's Hall was one thing, shiny and marvelous, but the rest of Asgard was glorious mountains, breathtaking fjords, and air so fresh, it rivaled berry mead.

"Let's go!" Rayna's pointer finger found the sky, and she began running as two large figures suddenly nosedived in our direction. But she wasn't running *away* from the looming feathered beings. No, she was running *toward* them.

The being with dusty charcoal feathers and hair—long and obsidian—opened its muzzle and let out an irritated chuff. She dipped down close to the grassy meadow, but her hooves never touched down. That didn't stop Rayna. Using her well trained muscles, she launched herself into the air and grabbed hold of the pegasus' harness, squeezing her calves around her midsection. The winged horse didn't wait for the valkyrie to adjust herself before she shot back into the sky.

Showoff. I muttered, then spun to see where the other pegasus had disappeared to. A white streak through the sky stole my attention. I brought two fingers to my lips and, with a loud, pointed whistle, called her over.

The creature dove to meet me. Her landing, while graceful, caused air to whoosh around her massive wings, sending a hit of oxygen up my nose, sobering me a little more. When her black hooves graced the flattened grasses, I reached up for her bridle and directed her face toward me. Her soft, putty-like chin found my palm, then her curious lips nipped me.

"I don't think so," I said. "Apples after Midgard, not before. You know the rules."

The pegasus let out a disappointed huff, pulling her head from my hands, then showing me her rear.

"Come on... Rayna and Gunhild are probably already at the Bifrost Bridge by now. You know how they get when we keep them waiting too long."

She cranked her head backward to look at me, her top lip flaring.

"You're impossible." I said, tossing an apple up into the air. She caught it with her front teeth, and as she began munching on the fruit, she adjusted herself so I could climb on. Hoisting myself up, I swung my leg over her in one swift movement. "Let's go!"

Epli, or Apple, as I liked to call her, launched herself into the sky, up through a cluster of puffy white clouds. I cursed her under my breath, yet I knew better than to open my mouth so high into the air. As punishment, I caught a bug that hit the back of my throat with the force of an arrow. With a quick cough and a sharp turn, Apple and I headed toward the Bifrost.

Apple was the pegasus no one wanted. Year after year, no one bonded to her. They said she was too unpredictable, impossible to tame, and the first pegasus in history that had no real interest in war. At a time that I, myself, cared much for war and glory, I still felt a pull toward her. Her beauty had almost caught her a few potential matches, but I was the first one she hadn't thrown off her pristine white back laced with golden feathers.

What everyone else had failed to miss was that Epli needed to be bribed. After 604 years riding together, she still required payment...in the form of apples. What she lacked discipline, she made up for it in more ways than her beauty. Firstly, she was fast. Rayna's pegasus, Gunhild, knew this, which was why she never landed and made Rayna work to mount her—not that Rayna ever minded showing off her skills. The two of them were a match made in Valhalla. Both fierce, both focused, and both wildly competitive.

As Apple and I began to approach the Bifrost, it was impossible to miss the way the bridge, made of pure, colorful light, lit up the entire night sky like an exploding star. The Bifrost shot beams of light across the sky from red to indigo, forming the perfect illusion of a rainbow. It was not created of sunlight and rain, but Odin's powerful seidr. The bridge was made for gods, valkyries, and sometimes even the dead to travel the realms at the speed of the rainbow light itself.

I saw Rayna on the back of her strong pegasus, hovering over the bridge, staring off into the trails of color that bled into the night sky. The sight was magnificent, and I wondered if her position over the Bifrost each night was the same as the moments I stole in the cool, dark tunnels beneath the House of Wings—a moment to be alone and cherish the utter silence of your own company.

Interrupting my sister's peace, I yelled out into the rainbow sky, "I imagine Bodil has already collected ten souls by now! How long do you think it will take you to double her numbers?"

"It's not about the quantity, Rune, but about the quality! You taught me that."

"I did, didn't I?" I said as Apple flew next to Gunhild. She gave her a quick nudge as we approached.

"The sisters will learn not to get caught up in the high of selecting souls soon enough. Once they figure out Odin is sending half their bounty right to Hel, they'll take a moment to ponder whose soul it is they're taking."

That was the thing about Rayna. I could teach her all I wanted, and sure, the knowledge I'd collected over the years helped her stay in Odin's good graces, despite being associated so heavily with me, but what no one but the gods and us knew was that Odin admired how picky Rayna was. He loved that Rayna only brought the fiercest warriors back to Valhalla—the ones with the most meaningful deaths. Just like the sister's got high from taking souls, I believed Odin was fueled by his halls being filled with the souls who brought him the most glory. Rayna's selections often offered him exactly what he needed most.

The difference between me and Rayna, compared to the rest of the sisters, was that we knew all you needed was a few amazing warriors each night to tide Odin over. He didn't care for the runners, the whimperers, or the ones who feared their deaths. We knew when we looked into the souls of the people on the battlefield who exactly he'd be sending to Freyja and her realm, Fólkvangr.

If I were to indulge in my nightly obsessions, it meant my efficiency on the battlefield needed to be without flaw. If I wanted to hang back, letting the souls I'd collected wait while I lingered on Midgard, those souls better be the best on the battlefield. If I wanted my passions to be hidden from the gods and my sisters, then I could never let them know I only spent a fraction of my night in the minds of the deceased, seeing their last moments and deciphering if they were worthy enough of Valhalla.

No one would ever ask, because I'd give them no reason to. No one would ever ask, because despite being drunk and late, I could hover over the entire field littered with blood and bodies and sense the few souls Odin would approve of. I didn't need to individually go into the minds of every single warrior. I could watch them all at once, like a play of a hundred humans' lives, and locate who had true, strong deaths—who risked their lives for the greater good, who went down in a blaze of unbridled glory.

When Rayna and I both nodded to each other, we descended upon the bridge. A whoosh of air laced with beams of light hit our faces, and almost as soon as it started, it was over. We were spat out into the Midgardian night, no rainbow hues to light our way, only stars dimmed by the pollution of a burning field.

Sisters of the House of Wings were already picking through the dead to find their chosen souls. Some sisters frantically collected as fast as they could, wearing the black and silver armor of Helheim or the emerald and gold armor of Fólkvangr. These were sisters from the other sects, gathering souls rejected by the Valhalla valkyries. The Valhalla sect moved a little slower, watching the memories of the slain and deciding who would come back with them.

Rayna and Gunhild dove down to meet the rest of the valkyries while I hung high above them all. I watched as the blue-tinted spirits rose from their bodies, guided by the choosers of the slain. It'd been a smaller skirmish tonight, not leaving many souls to choose from. As I closed my eyes, listening only to the sound of beating wings, I began to see images move behind my eyes: A man in leather armor tripping and falling on his own sword, a woman caught in a fire, and countless more.

I didn't stop watching the last moments play out until I came across a memory of an older gentleman, laced up in his finest armor. He'd been told to stay at home, where his family believed it to be safe, but he geared up anyway and ran into battle, despite his failing body. At first, I'd thought the man had ignored his family to prevent passing on naturally and being sent to Helheim with the rest of the villagers who died of old age. When I came upon his final moment, though, I realized the man had fled to save his family. Raiders had encroached on the small family home, and if it weren't for the elderly man using whatever strength he had left to fight off the three violent men about to attack, his family would have been lost to the night.

Apple dove down to the beacon the man's memory provided. He sat with his back against his home, eyes closed, as if he'd drifted off for a nap under the stars. If I were to move his ruby red hands that laid across his belly, this man's slumber would be seen for what it truly was: a final rest. I took a moment and listened for movement inside. When I heard hushed whispers, I knew this man had succeeded in what he'd set off to do. His wife and two daughters were alive, hiding in their longhouse until they felt it was safe to emerge. What I'd do next wouldn't help with their loss, but I hoped it would ease their transition. Apple nudged a yellow wild-flower unaffected by the flames toward me. I took it from between her teeth, and I tucked the stem into one of the man's curled hands.

When the stain on his tunic was partially covered, I placed my hand upon his chest and pulled the man free from his mortal confines. He took shape in the form of a blue orb, which I held in my hands for only a moment before bottling his essence. If anyone deserved to dine in the golden hall for all of eternity, it was him.

I gathered two more souls, wrapping all three bottles with the warriors' essences in leather and tucking them into Apple's armor. Rayna was still wandering through the scene, being particular as ever, despite the slim pickings. I gave her a few more moments to wrap up before we moved on. Valkyries didn't simply attend to one village or even one kingdom. Once we were in Midgard, we would follow the scent of blood and the energy of souls. Wherever we were needed, we would be.

When Rayna was finished, the two of us hopped back onto our prospective pegasus and flew into the night. We grew closer and closer to the village where I spent almost every night, even if no battle waged on. Stormheim was a peaceful village—for now. The surrounding areas had been hit one by one, all taken by the encroaching war. It wasn't our job to know why the war had begun or what side was in the right, if any, but this one, I found myself interested in, merely for the path of destruction it'd been taking.

When Rayna and I touched down in Toftvik, we assessed the battle scene and started all over again. I skimmed through final moments until I was satisfied with the four souls I plucked, adding to the collection I kept safe within Apple's pouches.

Leaving Rayna to her selection process, I wandered away through dying autumn trees on Apple's back until she took off into the sky. We were one village over from Stormheim now, and I feared what that might mean for my nightly routine.

Apple and I flew to Stormheim as always. Neither one of us were necessarily able to blend in with the Midgardian villagers, Apple with her wings and me with my long white hair, not to mention our armor, shiny and golden with crimson detailing. So, I always had her land on the outskirts. We walked the rest of the way on foot, careful to stay hidden within the trees.

When I heard a shout in the distance, both Apple and I froze.

"Hello?" the voice called out, as familiar as ever, though never directed toward me. "Anyone there?"

I shook my head at Apple, who dared to walk forward. My hand found her back, and I swore, it was the only part of my body I was able to move. Even my lungs had frozen at the sound of the seeress' wondrous, perpetually curious voice.

I couldn't see her from where I hid, but I could hear her ragged breathing with the help of my valkyrie gifts, the way she slowly backed away upon my silence. When the sounds of her departing quieted, I finally moved, leaving Apple behind as I lurked through the ghost-infested trees to find my little mortal. I caught a glimpse of her strawberry blonde hair, though the night never did the color justice the same way a roaring fire did.

She ducked under a rotting log, right into a cloud of pesky bloodflies. They began attacking her unmarred skin, though there were more than enough corpses in the area to feast upon. It was as if the greedy little insects couldn't wait until the Stormheim folk too had perished. Her scream cut through the night, sending a shock of ice through my veins.

"Go find something dead to feast on, you rotten, no good, wastes of space!"

My shoulders relaxed, and I held in an amused chuckle as the seeress danced away the bugs, shouting at them as she went. I didn't follow any further as she found a torch and carried it off to her village.

She and I sharing the same space was a rare thing. Over the years, I'd become addicted to her scent of wildflowers and spruce. I couldn't help but follow the identical path she'd taken, wondering if her scent still hung in the air after she was gone.

CHAPTER FIVE
A CUP OF MUGWORT

Kari

When I arrived at my longhouse, I realized just how satisfied I was with my bounty. I began separating my finds, placing the pine needles on a wooden hutch with my other tea ingredients, trying to forget all about what had occurred after collecting the goods. I carried the rest of my finds to the room where I saw clients—the room that once belonged to my parents.

I set the pinecone on a table scattered with objects tagged with my client's names. These objects, like the pinecone, would be used in my spells. The seed-bearing cone, once prepared, would be given to a woman in the village. She'd finally come to me after years of trying to conceive a child, with no such luck. I'd felt quite proud of myself the day she'd stopped by.

I was aware many of the village folk wished my mother had been the one to survive, as she was a true wielder of seidr. She'd been practicing for decades, a master in her craft. I, on the other hand, had been practicing for half a decade and still found myself fumbling around with my ingredients half the time, though I tried to never let my lack of confidence show when I was with a client.

When I was my mother's apprentice, she'd often told me stories of the days she too felt weary of her abilities. While she had difficulties seeing the future, she found confidence in her brews. I had the opposite problem. Though now, I suppose, I was having difficulties with my visions as well.

Pushing thoughts of my dreams out of my mind, I separated the animal bones into their individual vessels, depending on which animal they'd come from or which part of the body I'd found. A crow's skull, some fox phalanges, the teeth of a rabbit. They all had their own uses, some more powerful than others. Tove used to be the one to collect bones for me, but now, he simply pointed them out when he'd uncovered them.

With a yawn and a stretch, I brought the handful of acorns back over to my desk, where charcoal dusted my workspace. Pairing them with my newly-acquired broomstick, I prepared a protection spell to ward off evil in the area. Protection felt more important tonight than ever. Between the bone-chilling presence, the amassing bloodflies, and the increase in wandering spirits, war was close.

Part of me debated if I should take Tove and go, but this place was my home. People like Arnesson made it clear that no matter where I went, as long as war waged on, nowhere would be safe. It was better to stand my ground and die in my home than die on the run. Worst case scenario, I'd get to see my family again. There were worse fates.

When my protection spell was complete, I swept my front steps with the broomstick laced with string and acorns, then hung it upon my warped wooden door. Walking back inside the long-house, I felt like I could breathe again.

Another yawn tugged at my lips, so I lit a fire to boil my nightly tea and slipped into a nightdress. Tove already beat me to bed. He was curled up on the pillow next to mine, where my youngest sister used to rest her head. Haddy was a sweet child in life. She didn't speak much, which made her a great person to share a room with. She was tidy and often made me bracelets out of the wildflowers she'd find around the yard. I kept each of them hidden away in a box so she never realized how much I loved them. It wasn't until her ghost haunted our room that I dug the wooden box from my chest of clothes and showed her the dried vines twisting into delicate, dead flowers. She'd wept and wept, and when her face finally dried, she left the longhouse and vanished to her afterlife. Haddy was the first of them to cross over, and some-times, I wished she'd been the last.

Once my tea was gone, I laid back, positioning my head next to Tove. On nights like this, I wanted nothing more than to squeeze him, to have someone real in my arms. I couldn't recall the last time I had physical affection, if only just a brush against my leg from my cat. I truly believed humans needed other living beings to hold and cherish, and as I drifted off to sleep, I wondered how long it took loneliness to kill a person.

Shining gold emerged from a star-lit sky, blurring my vision with the sheer force of its glow. Black and white feathers rained down upon the ruby floor until I, too, was a shattered gem. I was a little ruby piece among the soft piles of feathers that had fallen from distorted clouds. I tried to yell out, but gems don't have lips. Gems don't have thoughts, and suddenly, neither did I. Someone had scooped me up into their hands, fascinated by my fractured pieces. I saw no face because I had no eyes. Eyes. If I had no eyes, did that mean I was no longer cursed?

I awoke with a gasp. My body shot up in bed, sending the top of my quilt rolling off my body, revealing my thin nightgown. I grabbed at my arms, feeling flesh and blood under their grip, not cool, hard stone. I touched my eyes next, but they felt as they always had.

Should I uncover the mirror across from my bed to check?

No, no.

When the blood thumping in my mind subsided, I reached for a piece of charcoal to start jotting down what I'd seen in my dream. It was so similar to the others I'd been having for weeks now, and even so, I still didn't know what the vision meant.

As I wrote down my thoughts, I didn't need to peek outside to know we were still in night's territory. Why had I risen? Usually, I slept like the dead, my visions taking hold of me too strongly to wake.

Then, I heard it. A scream. A shaking, bitter scream.

Hilda!

I threw the rest of the quilt off my body, not caring that it fell to the dirt floor. I didn't hesitate as I threw on leather boots, my fingers quick and nimble. When I flung my door open, I saw her, hobbling down the path to her longhouse, eyes wide with terror.

"Hilda!" I screamed, rushing over to the elderly woman, who dragged a heavy silver weapon behind her.

"Look, child," she pointed, and I saw it: a raider running out of the tree line, heading straight for us.

"Stay back!" I pulled the sword from her hands, wondering where she'd gotten such a violent thing. Bracing myself, I sacrificed one hand to push Hilda through the entryway to her longhouse. She protested and grabbed at my wrist, but she spiraled into a coughing attack and released my arm long enough for me to pull the door shut. I stood in front of it in case she got any wild ideas to come back outside, the sword's leather grip in my hands being squeezed and flattened under my newfound strength.

Shouts came from behind me, signaling the rest of the raiders had hit the village from another angle. I cursed under my breath, unsure if I should charge and leave Hilda unprotected, or continue to stand around like a lamb ready for slaughter. Hilda's cries from inside made my decision for me, and I dug my feet into the stone beneath my boots, ready for a fight.

The raider moved to strike, but I got to him first, slicing down his forearm. The animal skin lining his arm split in two, blood spilling. He hissed but lunged again. Yet again, I dodged his blade. This time, when I moved to attack, my sword clashed with his in a collision of silver and crimson.

As we battled, I talked myself through every step, grinding my teeth, holding my ground even as he pushed harder. I had fuel of my own, sourced from the sounds of my people fighting back, fighting for *our* land.

I. Will. Not. Let. This. Man. Win.

With one final push, I shoved the blade into the man's stomach. His mouth fell open just before the rest of his body hit the ground. There was nothing I wanted more than to let my heavy arms fall to my sides, but more raiders were coming, and Hilda still needed protecting.

A viking raider screamed as he pushed through the tree line, and a guttural yowl ripped from his throat when he raised his bow.

Before I could run, before I could breathe, he released an arrow into the air. I tried to deflect the arrowhead with my sword, but as I raised the shiny weapon, I caught a glimpse of something horrible reflecting back at me. I couldn't pull my gaze away from the black, rotting eyes in my skull, and as a reward, white hot pain coursed through my shoulder. As I stared at myself in the reflective metal, I heard the air leave my lungs and felt my knees crack against stone.

Never had I known a darkness so pure, so infinite. I was no longer sure if my eyes were open or closed, because all that filled my vision was the expanse of a starless sky. I collected bits of sounds here and there, distorted and detached, as if they'd been echoes of another realm. And then, there it was: a sound so real, it might've pulled me from my slip into the void.

"I have you."

CHAPTER SIX
OATHBREAKER

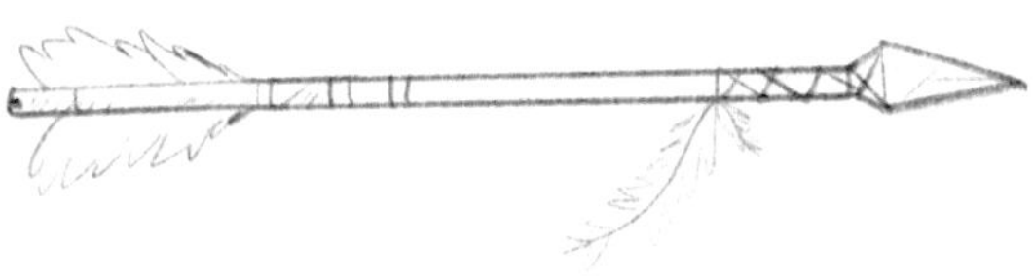

Rune

Nine realms, Rune.

I should have known. I shouldn't have let my sick curiosities distract me from every warning sign that hung in the air like a waving red flag. I'd collected enough souls in my time to know raiders' appetites were bottomless, and there was no trusting they'd stop just because one village was sacked.

My toes curled in my boots as I watched the seeress swing the too-heavy sword, slicing flesh and dodging her opponent. Apple whined at me to leave it be, to fly back to Valhalla where we belonged—where it was safe. I wasn't worried about these pathetic raiders taking down Apple or myself. No, I was terrified about what I might do if they pulled even a drop of blood from the seeress.

She was *my* mortal, not to be touched, not to be trifled with. Without her, what were my nights? Eating, drinking, and collecting? The same three things every day until I drew my last breath. She was what grounded me, what allowed me to feel connection to this realm of mortals, what reminded me what it was to be truly alive, not just living. She survived when her family and so many others hadn't. No one would fuck with something so pure. I wouldn't let them.

I lurked behind an alder tree, burying my boots into the loose dirt Apple had pulled up. My hand gripped the hilt of my sword, and Apple failed to nudge it away as I watched the scene before me unfold. Kari slid the blade into her attacker, and the man dropped to the stone pathway they'd fought upon.

"That's my girl," I began to mutter, but just as pride began to swell in my chest, she was struck.

No, no, no.

Blood dribbled down her shoulder as she fell to the ground below. The arrow protruded unnaturally from her body in a way I'd seen on a nightly basis, though those bodies held unfamiliar faces, and hers was far from unfamiliar. I'd memorized every line drawn into her uniquely beautiful face, every curve of her body, every sound she made when she thought she wasn't being watched.

I made a promise, one to end whoever pulled blood from the one thing in my life that grounded me to my mortality. The goddess of love and war wouldn't have her today. No. Freyja would have to wait.

Before I could stop myself, I pulled my sword free from its sheath and began slaying each raider, one quick movement after another, until all that remained was me and her. My own blood pulsed in my head, temporarily distorting my thoughts, allowing me not to dwell on the knowledge that I had killed mortals, that I had broken my sacred oaths.

My bloodied weapon found a home within its sheath, and I dropped to the crimson ground where the seeress lay. I pulled her into my arms, the wound from which the arrow protruded oozed blood. "I have you."

I wasn't trained in healing humans, or what to do when one was injured. I dealt with them *after* they'd succumbed to their fatal injury.

Do I pull the arrow out? Break it? Leave it in?

The woman in my arms, at first rigid under my touch, began to grow limp. She wouldn't survive my indecision.

"APPLE... EPLI!" I screamed into the night, knowing the pegasus wanted to stay far away from this mess. Even so, when her name left my lips, she came trotting out of the forest. She stepped over the fallen raiders, and when I looked up at her, golden armor and golden feathers shining under the light of fire, I'd never been more thankful to see her.

"Brace yourself," I warned. "It's not just me you're taking home tonight."

Despite Apple's protests, I hoisted Kari into the air and positioned her upon my saddle. This would not be a comfortable ride for her, but I didn't care for her comfort, just her life. There was no time to figure out a better way to accommodate her. She needed to get out of this broken place full of death, for there was a more beautiful place of death awaiting her.

"Rune?" Rayna's voice called out into the night. "Rune, where are you?"

I climbed onto Apple's back, tempted to fly away before my younger sister could see us. If there was one thing I hated, it was when my younger sisters were right. Was I in the wrong? Yes, I knew that, but I grabbed hold of the seeress and braced her in my arms anyway.

"Rune!" Rayna called again, this time in the clearing ahead. When she spotted me, she stared me down, mouth agape in horror. Her eyes wandered to the slumped woman in front of me, then to the fresh kills on the ground between us. She moved slowly, as if not to startle me. "Set her down with the rest."

"I can't." My fingers tightened on Kari's nightdress with one hand, the other gripping Apple's reins with white knuckles.

"Unless she's in one of those bottles of yours, you can, and you will," Rayna said. "I'm staring into her soul now, and there are no final moments, because she has yet to have hers. Do not deny her of them."

"You've looked into her soul, so you've seen the way she would have died, protecting that old woman! She belongs in Valhalla, and you know it."

Apple began to step forward, impatient. Gunhild blocked her by spreading out her massive charcoal wings, a few loose feathers drifting to the ground below.

"Yes, I did, but she *didn't* die, Rune! You carry a mortal along with your collected souls. A mortal seeress, not a viking. She doesn't belong where we're going. Put her back!"

"I won't," I said. "I don't want to fly away from you right now, Rayna, but I have to, before she really does die. I won't have Freyja's Fólkvangr sect showing up and taking her."

Rayna shook her head in disbelief, and how could I blame her? Centuries of service, just to end up slaying and capturing mortals. When she spoke, her voice cracked. "What's your plan?"

"I'll bring her to the House of Wings through the tunnels and find her help. Bodil was a healer in her mortal life," I said. "Now, come with me or don't, but either way, I'm leaving."

I motioned Apple forward, worried about what this interaction had already cost the seeress. Just as Apple launched off the stained dirt, Rayna screamed out, "Bodil has been trying to knock us through the ranks for years! You want to give her all the leverage she needs?"

"Fine, then. I'll make Gro help me!" I shot back behind me. If she wanted to continue this conversation, she was going to need to keep up. I heard her grunt as she mounted Gunhild.

"You want to bring a *spirit* into the house?" Rayna's voice grew closer as she gained on me. Apple slowed, working against me. She too knew Rayna was right. When Gunhild flew over us and blocked our path yet again, Apple almost came to a full halt.

"Rune, snap out of it! What's wrong with you?" Rayna was staring right at me now, our two pegasus' wings beating the air around us as they remained at a standstill. My braided and unbraided hair alike whipped me in the face from the sheer strength of Gunhild's wings, and I had to hold on to the seeress' thin night dress to hold her in place. There was only one thing left I could do if I wanted the seeress to get out of Midgard alive. I had to tell my sister my long-awaited truth.

I took a deep breath, my face settling into stone as I revealed the woman's identity, and said, "This is *the* mortal."

Rayna's face paled. She'd never met Kari, never seen her, but she'd known why I hung around this little village so often. Her mouth parted, and she closed her eyes right before she said, "Bodil it is. You're lucky I have dirt on her."

"You'll keep her mouth shut?" I asked, ready to shoot through the sky now that I had no one in my way.

"She'll keep it shut herself when I tell her I've seen the ways she keeps herself entertained on Midgard." Gunhild flew to the side, letting Apple and me pass. As we picked up speed, the mortal rocked against my chest, pulling a moan from her dry lips.

"Tell me all about it later," I said "I have to go slow with her. Now, leave, find Bodil, and have her prepare for our arrival... *Please.*"

<hr>

I was thankful Rayna stood down. How did one choose between family and the object of their desire? If the seeress passed on, she would be with all the other souls wandering the expansive meadows of Fólkvangr, or wild up in Hel. She wouldn't be able to return to Stormheim, and without her presence in the mortal realm, I feared what my nights would turn into. Who would I watch? Who would be my nightly muse?

I'd grown so accustomed to watching her through cracked doors, gaps in the walls, or even the smoke holes of her roof. I knew her longhouse like the back of my hand, and I craved to know her so thoroughly.

Apple flew slowly through the sky, careful not to send the mortal woman in my arms careening off her back. We were close, so very close to safety. When the Bifrost was in my line of sight, the knot in my gut loosened a tiny bit.

A rustle of fabric brought my attention between the seeress' legs where her nightdress gathered.

"What the Hel?" My shouts had Apple shooting through the sky like a bug on fire. I almost lost grip of the unconscious woman in my arms when I saw a blue little creature crawl out from under her dress.

Is that—

I stared at the creature tinted blue with death at the tips of its orange fur.

A cat? What in Odin's great realm is the seeress' cat doing on my pegasus?

The thing looked up at me and mewed, leaving me utterly dumbfounded. I tried my hand at settling Apple, but she was not welcoming of our new guest. On top of having no interest in war, the flying horse also feared incorporeal beings. A spirit passed through her body *one time*, and that was enough to scar her for the rest of her life.

"Just get us to the Bifrost!" I shouted. "Everything will be okay soon!"

Apple did as I asked, blasting forward without care for the seeress's safety. I held on as tight as her mortal body would allow, knowing we'd be in the clear soon. Flashes of light and color lit the sky, and the next thing we knew, the mortal realm was behind us, and we were back on Asgard. Soon enough, the House of Wings came into view, a sight so welcome, I couldn't stop the audible sigh from slipping through my lips.

The cat meowed again, though this time, when I peered down at it, the blue that once highlighted its features was gone.

Apple calmed, allowing us a smooth landing upon the long grasses of the open field. When I noticed how red-stained Kari's nightdress was, I dragged her off Apple's back and cradled her in my arms.

I wouldn't allow myself to stop moving until she was safe and in my bed. I descended the ladder into the dark tunnels, and even then, I didn't stop. The chubby cat trotted alongside me, but I didn't spare him a second glance. My eyes were locked on the iron doors ahead.

A few more steps.

I only hoped what awaited me on the other side of those double doors wasn't Asta or Odin's guards ready to steal her away from me so soon.

The iron doors groaned open, and I peeked my head through. Rayna stood across the hall, leaning against a gilded frame. She tried to look casual, as if waiting for someone to come out from their chambers, but I saw the way her thumbs twiddled. Rayna didn't fidget. Her body language always remained eerily calm, even if her voice and tone didn't. To see my younger sister twiddling her thumbs sent my nerves on edge.

I crept forward, and when we caught her gaze, her eyes widened, and she motioned us forward with a quick drag of her hand through still air. I didn't bother closing the tunnel doors behind me, beelining for the door to our chambers. Rayna pushed the door open, and I barreled through it, careful not to catch the protruding arrow on the doorframe. I only noticed the trail of scarlet following us because of Rayna's anxious yelp. She all but pushed me into the room before grabbing a rag and pulling it shut behind her.

"Quickly, place her on the bed," Bodil said. The once-healer directed me to the four poster bed with wispy, sheer curtains. Bodil had laid down rags to protect my quilts, but the seeress' blood was the least of my concerns. I'd burn the quilts if it meant she'd be saved.

Gently, I laid the mortal down upon the bed, her afflicted shoulder facing up.

"She's lucky," Bodil said. "The arrow didn't sever anything important."

The black and white haired valkyrie unsheathed a sharp blade at her hip. She looked to me, then to Kari, and said, "I'll have to cut the arrowhead out, and it isn't going to be pretty."

I cursed under my breath, my attention on the woman in my bed, soaked in blood and passed out from the pain.

"Do it quickly while she's still unconscious."

Bodil nodded, then threw herself into a healer's mindset, as if she hadn't retired from that life centuries ago.

"Help me remove the sleeve of her gown," she ordered. She must have loved it, telling her older sister what to do. Bodil had been a valkyrie for four and a half centuries, yet until her head was fully white, tonight would be the last night she barked at me.

"Take it off?" I asked, staring down at the seeress. Sure, I'd watched her. I'd even imagined how things might have been different if I were still mortal and just so happened to stumble into her village for a fresh start. But even then, I'd imagine conversing with her, learning all the things that made her tick, but never undressing her. Removing the sleeve of her gown was not sexual. It was practical, yet as my hand hovered over her skin, why did it feel so intimate?

"Yes, take it off. She's filthy. I need to clean her wound, and I need this tattered cloth out of my way."

My fingertips finally found her shoulder, and I began slowly peeling the fabric from her wound. I pulled a blade from my thigh and sliced the nightgown sleeve clean off, revealing the skin of her wounded shoulder. Bodil resumed pressure around the arrow, then ordered me to grab her supplies kit. She told me which bottles to grab and which to avoid. The two of us worked together—me as her third and fourth hand as we cleaned and prepped the seeress.

Bodil passed her blade over a candle's flame, and when it

cooled, she began her work on Kari. The seeress amazingly remained unconscious through the entire ordeal; even when Bodil removed the arrow from Kari's shoulder, she didn't wake. Bodil immediately pressed a damp cloth to her wound to stop the blood from spilling over.

When all was said and done, Kari patched up, I shifted her up on the bed so she could rest her head upon my pillow. She looked at peace now, resting, dreaming. I sat on the edge of the bed, wondering what exactly was going on in that mind of hers as her eyes moved rapidly, back and forth, back and forth.

Bodil cleared her throat, and I was on my feet in less than a second. As I faced her, I took in her sharp features. Her eyes flicked from me to the woman in my bed—not out of fear, but dangerous curiosity. Curiosity like that could get a person into trouble.

"Thank you, Bodil," I said, bowing my head. "She would've crossed on to another realm had you not intervened."

"Maybe you should've let her," Bodil hissed, aggressively collecting her tools.

"Maybe," I admitted, just to appease her. I was in no mood for a fight, and our opinions rarely aligned.

"It's not too late to send her back to Midgard. Let what will happen to her happen. It's no concern of yours, nor should it be."

"I hope we won't discuss this again," I said, disregarding her. "Go to Epli. There are bottled souls in her pouch. Take them to Odin and claim them as your own."

"That's...very generous of you," Bodil said, tilting her chin down in newfound, yet brief, respect. A piece of black hair fell into her face as she did, a reminder to us both of her age.

"Keep that in mind while you debate whether you'll rat us out."

"I'll keep this incident to myself—this once. Your little shadow has ensured that," she said with that perfected sneer of hers.

Rune, you don't want to fight. I kept telling myself that as I traced the lines of her pinched mouth.

When Bodil's sharp gaze landed beyond my shoulder on the sleeping seeress, I stood tall, casting a small shadow upon her face. The subtle movement was enough to wipe it clean of any attitude.

I lifted those black strands of hair off her face and twisted them in my fingers before sighing, "Our sister has a name. I dare you to use it next time you offer thinly veiled threats."

Bodil's throat bobbed, making me realize I'd been far too lenient with my younger sisters, especially the more...courageous ones, the ones who dared to challenge my command. I may have been a drunkard, but I was Odin's favorite drunkard, and Bodil would be wise to remember that.

"I've given you a gift. Don't let those souls go to waste."

When I dropped her hair in her face, she ducked back and made haste toward the door.

"Oh, and Bodil?" I asked, moving slowly in her direction, like one of Freyja's giant, stalking cats.

"Yes?" Bodil froze just before she made her escape.

"If I catch you uttering a word of my mortal, good or bad, you'll find yourself collecting souls for Hel."

CHAPTER SEVEN
JUST A GIRL AND HER CAT

Kari

I shot up in bed, gripping my wounded shoulder. I'd been struck; I remember it so clearly. I'd seen it coming, unable to do anything about it, as my vision was locked on my reflection in Hilda's sword. I'd screamed at myself to move, but my body had betrayed me. All I remember after that was a beautiful mix of darkness and light, and then, for the first time in my life, a dreamless slumber.

My fingers found the quilt I laid upon, feeling unfamiliar under my touch, as if my fingertips were healing from a burn, not quite able to recognize familiar textures. I still wore my nightgown, but now, one of my sleeves was gone, and my aching shoulder was wrapped in what felt like damp linen. I could see nothing but vague shapes in the dark and wondered at what point my longhouse had ever shielded so much light.

"Tove?" I called out, not seeing his light blue glow on the pillow next to mine. When there was no response, I slid out from under the covers and stumbled to the crack of light coming from behind thick cloth.

What is this?

Pulling the cloth back revealed a sheet of glass separating me from a view I didn't recognize. It was then I realized I was very, *very* far from home.

Am I dead? I thought to myself as I stared out at the mountainous view, then to the glass embedded in the beautiful stone wall. Glass inside a wall? I'd never seen anything like it. I pressed my hand against it, then spun around to get a look at the rest of the room.

Gold. There was gold everywhere. The precious metal dripped from the ceiling, drops of crystal at the end. It wrapped itself around the edges of paintings, on the cup that sat upon the nightstand.

I'm dead, surely.

Everything is so...shiny.

I pulled my chin down so my eyes couldn't lock onto my reflection. Even in death, I feared my curse would stay true. The reflection in that damned sword had gotten me killed, after all. What would happen if I glanced at any of these reflective surfaces now?

A woman appeared in the doorway opposite me, her knuckles rapping on the wooden door as she walked in.

I didn't give her time to speak before I asked, "Am I dead?" Pressing my palm against my fluttering belly, I waited for a response that took far too long to come. Her hair was white as sun-bleached bone, stripped clean of any color. Her olive skin creased between her brows upon my question, that subtle reaction sending a wave of chills up my arms.

"No," she finally said with a slow shake of her head. Her greyblue eyes watched me like I was her prey, and I didn't find relief in her answer.

"Where am I then?" I was desperate to glance around, wondering how a place could be so full of riches, but fear kept me frozen in place. Instead, I analyzed the tiny fractures in the woman's calm, stoic demeanor.

"I've brought you to Valhalla."

Everything in me stilled.

It made sense, yes, but she'd explicitly told me I wasn't dead. How could these truths exist at once?

"And I can only assume you're a valkyrie?" I spoke slowly, taking in her leathers and the way they molded perfectly to her sculpted body. She nodded in agreement, so I continued. "And you brought me to Valhalla?"

She nodded again, and that slight movement of her head made my lips twist. I stole a deep breath, trying to collect myself to avoid showing her my growing frustration.

"So, I'm dead then."

"You're not dead," she said with a sigh.

"I don't understand!" I finally let loose, my hand flying up in between us. "How did I get shot by an arrow during battle and brought to the heavens by a valkyrie, yet I'm still alive? I simply don't believe you."

"There's a lot...to understand, to explain, but you shouldn't worry about all of that now. You're still healing, and—"

"Where's my cat?" I interrupted, daring to glance around the room, my eyes scanning the floor for my orange fur ball.

"Your what?" She stared at me as if she'd never heard of such a thing. One of her brows had a scar running through it, and it slowly pulled toward its no-so-matching partner.

"My cat. Where is he?" I'd almost forgotten about the throbbing in my shoulder, but her flicking gaze toward the wound demanded I remember.

"Safe. Let me draw you a bath, and then I'll bring him to you," she said. "Alright?"

"Bring him now, and then I will bathe." I didn't know who this valkyrie was, or why she insisted I bathed before seeing Tove. Did residents of the heavens even need to bathe?

"Fine, but I must warn you..." she said, trailing off as her hand clenched and released at her side.

"Warn me of what?" I stepped forward, a pang of unease rattling me. My eyes shot to the bench in the corner, and I'd wondered if I could lean on the back of it without causing any suspicion.

"Nothing. You'll see for yourself soon enough." When she left, her words sat in my gut and festered.

What was she going to warn me of? What had happened to Tove?

She said he was safe. I played those words over and over, pacing the stone floors until she came back into the room. In trotted a little orange cat, chubby and perfect. Chubby, perfect, and...not blue?

I stared at him, and he at me.

"Tove..." I whispered, my fingers over my lips. The cat let out the loudest meow I'd ever heard, and then he launched himself right at me. I didn't scream, I didn't move. All I could do, for the first time, was beg the gods he wouldn't pass through me like he had every day for the past two years.

When claws sank into my nightgown, I dropped to my knees.

"Tove!" I wrapped my arms around him, feeling his soft fur on my cheek and along the nape of my neck. I buried my face into him, feeling the vibrations of his purrs as tears fell freely from my eyes.

"How?" I asked. "Please, I know you said you'd explain every-thing, but how can I not be dead? I need answers... *Please.*" I begged, tears rolling down my sodden cheeks. I was on my knees begging this woman, this valkyrie, for information, because what other choice did I have? My mind was spiraling, trying to make sense of everything that had occurred since I first opened my eyes. Everything I'd ever been taught about the gods, about the heavens and underworld, was spinning around my mind—unstable as ever.

All this time, had it been a lie?

"Please, sit." She motioned to the padded bench. She pulled

over a small table, on it a cup of tea I hadn't noticed before. "You like tea, don't you? Mugwort?"

I stared at the cup, then at her. The back of my hand found my cheek, and I wiped at the dampness lingering there, now embarrassed this stranger had seen me break, all while maintaining an even disposition herself. I cleared my throat, holding Tove tight to my chest as I rose.

I approached the seat, my eyes locked on the tea cup, more even and smooth than I'd ever seen a clay creation. The scent of mugwort wafted into the air, and while it should have eased me, I couldn't help but wonder how she knew I drank tea, specifically *this* tea. It wasn't the most common brew, definitely not for pleasure, as the flavor was quite bitter. It was a strange guess indeed.

"I drink Mugwort at night, yes." I eyed her as I stiffly sat, more questions swirling in my mind now than when I was splayed out on the floor.

"Good," she said with a pleased nod of her head before joining me on the padded seat. Her vision trailed down my ruined nightgown splattered in blood and mud, and then she motioned toward the tea. I guessed I had no need to fear poison, as poison had very little use on the dead. I took a sip of the warm drink, letting it wet my dry lips and mouth.

"Why am I here and not with my family? I assume they are in Helheim?"

"You're not with your family because you're not dead. I'm not quite sure how many times I need to tell you this." She smoothed her hand down her leathers, almost as if sensing her cold tone. "I understand this is all very confusing, and for that, I'm sorry. As for your feline, well, spirits are all corporeal across the heavens and the underworld."

I set the teacup down on the tiny plate resting upon the golden table, my shoulder aching with the movement. The incision site was more tender than any wound I'd ever had, but I tried not to show how much pain I was truly in. "Okay, that makes sense when it comes to Tove, but how is it that a living mortal is in Valhalla?"

"You were dying. You would have, had I left you on the steps of your neighbor's longhouse. I wasn't expecting a raid last night. I was simply in a nearby village collecting souls. I saw your act of heroism, and I couldn't let you die. I brought you here to heal, nothing more."

"You interfered? Why? I'm sure you see horrors every day; it's your job not to interfere, is it not?" I asked, racking my mind for some tale of a valkyrie saving a mortal. I only needed a moment to realize this situation was, in fact, unheard of.

She straightened her posture, staring off for a moment into the room before she focused back on me and said, "I know you have questions, but I'm not at liberty to answer them all. There are some things mortals simply cannot know."

Stubborn, self-important valkyrie.

I swallowed my frustration so as not to anger the woman who'd kept me alive. "So you saved my life from the raiders, and I'm not allowed to know why?"

"Precisely," she said with a swift nod. "I will return you to Stormheim when you're healed and ready to travel once more. These trips can be quite—"

"And Tove?" I interrupted, holding him up so she could see who I was referring to.

The woman sighed and tugged at her ear, as if my mere presence exhausted her. "The cat will remain here."

My head jerked back, and my grip on him tightened. "He will not."

"Once a spirit passes on, they may not return to Midgard without permission from the gods, and I've never heard of them granting permission to a feline," she said, her curious gaze flicking to my cat.

"Well then, I will stay too."

"You may not."

"I will."

"You can't."

"Then take me to a god! I will ask for permission," I said, my teeth grinding as I spoke to avoid raising my voice.

The woman gawked at me for far longer than what was comfortable. It wasn't until I took another sip of tea that she cleared her throat.

"Not until you're healed. You need food, and you look and smell horrid, quite frankly. Do you really think I'd let you step in front of even the weakest of gods in this state?"

I slowly rose, Tove content in my arms. I took in a deep breath —not just to steady my nerves, but also to take a whiff of myself. "Fine. We will do it your way, but let it be known, I won't leave him."

"I've taken note of this, yes," she said, standing with a stifled groan. "Now, seeress, what should I call you?"

My blood ran cold. "Seeress?" I looked down at the tea. The *mugwort* tea.

Her grey-blue eyes flared before settling into their relaxed state once more. It was so subtle, I would have missed it had I not been devouring her every move. "I can sense it in you, your power."

I let her words settle in, taking my time before making my next move. "Please, direct me to the wash bucket. I imagine I have a list of tasks I need to accomplish before meeting with the god of your choosing."

The valkyrie nodded with satisfaction, beginning to lead me out of the bedchamber. When her back faced me, I stared at her stunning hair looped with gold bands and beads, her position truly hitting me. One of Odin's valkyries had saved my life. Tove was corporeal. I was in Valhalla.

Sudden awareness washed over me, and I began to wonder if she'd been the light in my visions that my mind had been unable to process, despite all the mugwort I'd consumed. I certainly knew now what all the gold had meant.

I watched the way she walked, confident and demanding. She

could end my life before I took my next breath. She could fly me to the darkest depths of the realms if she saw fit—drop me in a land of ice, giants, and soulless creatures.

Tove and I exchanged a look, and I decided then that my sass would have to be tamed. My feet began to slow, and I awkwardly uttered, "And my name... It's Kari."

CHAPTER EIGHT
MIRROR, MIRROR

Rune

"Why do you keep bumping into things? Open your eyes, for Valhalla's sake," I said, stabilizing a vase that teetered and threatened to tip off the vanity.

"You have far too many mirrors in here. How often does a person really need to stare at themselves?" she said, her eyes glued to the floor, as if nowhere but her feet was safe to look at.

My breath caught, and I'd felt like she'd reached into my mind, plucking memories of countless moments lingering in front of any reflective surface I happened to stumble across. How vain she must have assumed I was. I wanted to explain myself, but she was a mere mortal, twenty-five, maybe? She would never understand the thoughts that plagued my mind, the curiosities and doubts.

As I watched her stare at her toes, I wondered why she'd refused to look up. Surely, she couldn't hate the way she looked that much. Yes, her current state was rather disheveled, but that was only temporary. One bath in the healing waters of Valhalla, and she would be good as new, beautiful as ever.

I did tell her she looks horrid. I suppose that could have something to do with her strange behavior.

The girl was self-conscious is all. I softened my voice as I walked over to the tub. "This soak will make you feel as good as new. The waters in Valhalla are quite healing."

"Am I supposed to go in there?" she asked, glancing at the golden tub wearily for a quick moment. She went from confident and grating to timid and meager in an instant, as if I'd beaten her. She flinched as she moved, uncomfortable unless her eyes were on the floor. No, this wasn't self-consciousness. This was fear—deep, debilitating fear.

"Yes. It won't hurt, I promise. I know you're used to a wash bucket, but we do things a little...differently here in Valhalla. Only the best for the best of souls."

"But I don't belong here, do I?" she whispered.

You do, I wanted to tell her, but I'd already said too much as it was.

"I'll have some food waiting for you when you're out. There's a robe hanging over there," I said, pointing to a hook on the wall where a crimson silk robe hung. I turned to leave her and the feline alone, stealing one last look at the seeress. She tried to gather courage to look up, and while she managed to raise her chin, her eyes remained on the floor.

The reflective surfaces. They're rendering her immobile.

"Would you feel more comfortable if I blew the candles out?"

"Yes, yes, thank you." She nodded her head quickly. "I'll find my way through the darkness."

What a peculiar creature.

I blew the candles and lanterns out per her request, leaving her alone in the dark. I shut the door behind me and then wandered through my bedroom, wondering what I should do while I waited for her. I didn't need to bother preparing food, as it would appear on my table upon my request. I could rid my bed of the bloody rags from the night prior. She'd slept upon them, and I hadn't wanted to wake her to remove them from beneath her. At some point in the night, her face had relaxed, and she looked at peace. I wasn't strong enough to take that peace from her.

Kari. Two years of watching the woman, and she had finally told me her name. I, of course, had known it already, but it was so much different when the name was offered freely from the one who owned it. The word felt right on my lips as I whispered it under my breath. I glanced over my shoulder at the door, as if she could hear me over the sound of her aimless stumbling.

As I waited, I tidied my room and scolded myself for letting too much on too soon. I blew it with the tea. Of course, I was aware she drank brewed mugwort stems and leaves each night, but *she* wasn't supposed to know that. And then there was the little slip up of calling her "seeress". She was far too quick witted to miss any of these little details. I knew it from the way her gaze trailed over me, burrowing deep into my soul with those blue eyes of hers, watchful and ever curious.

The sound of stumbling and groaning echoed from the bathing chamber. I stood and faced the door, then cleared my throat and leaned against one of the posts of my bed.

No, that's not it.

I sat upon the edge of my bed, but that too was wrong. As the door cracked open, I dropped to the floor to tie my already-tied boot, my heart pounding in my ears. The door opened, and out from the darkness stepped an orange cat and a woman wrapped in thin, crimson silk. My eyes dared to follow where the fabric dipped and hugged, and I wouldn't soon forget the trail of water from her hair that dripped down her chest. Yes, being on my knees was the only correct course of action.

My fingers forgot they were meant to be tying my laces, or pretending to at least, and there I knelt before her, staring up into those stunning blue eyes swimming with questions. Did I hate the way she looked at me with such disdain, or was I beginning to crave it?

When she noticed me kneeling before her, she took a step back, one of her dark auburn brows quirking. "Is everything alright?"

"Uh, yes," I muttered, rising from my knees. "How was your soak? Better than a wooden wash bucket?"

"Much," she said with the faintest of smiles. She wrapped her arms tightly around her chest, her confidence still not finding her.

"Good. I've laid out some clothes for you on the bed, and there's warm food and tea waiting for you upon the table in the corner."

"Mugwort?" she stared at me with a challenging expression.

"Uh, no. Sage and lavender." My face grew hot, though I'd never let her know that.

"Hmm," was all she said as she wandered over to the bed. She ran her fingers over the loose dress that lay there, then picked up the shawl next to it. "I thought it didn't get cold in Valhalla."

"The nights do grow cooler once the sun bids its goodbye, though only the living can feel it. I figured you would feel more comfortable with the extra layers. You mortals do tend to wear a lot of clothing, don't you?"

"Has it been that long since you were one yourself?" She glanced over her shoulder draped in silk.

"I don't forget what it's like to be mortal, if that's what you're asking," I admitted, glancing up at her as she began slipping undergarments on under the robe, her back still turned to me. "I'm not from a village like Stormheim as you are. I'm from a place you'd consider a distant land, one with warm waters, where different gods rein."

"Different gods?" Kari asked, her fiddling hands stilling. I wasn't sure why I was telling her all of this. None of it mattered anymore. It hadn't mattered for a long time now.

"Yes, though my civilization has since fallen. I consider Valhalla home now."

"Sometimes, I forget there are other gods."

It'd been so long since I spoke of my home, and I felt important details already slipping away. "There's so much more out there than most people will ever know," I admitted. "My people's Allfather was not Odin. His name is Zeus, and he was our King of Gods."

"Was?"

"He still lives, though his followers are scattered across his realm, no longer the strong civilization we once were. Thalassa, my original home, fell shortly after I was chosen to be a valkyrie, though unrelated, I assure you." When I spoke, Kari absorbed every morsel of information she could, soaking in every syllable, every inflection. Why was I still droning on about my past? Getting to know her, and her getting to know me, wouldn't help anyone.

She held up the dress in her hands. "Turn around, please."

I did as she asked with an amused chuckle, remembering when I first joined the House of Wings. I'd been so awkward around my sisters, uncertain about changing before them, despite sharing a room with ten other girls.

When I heard the silk robe hit the floor, all thoughts of the early days with the sisterhood fled my mind. I didn't realize how many reflective surfaces there truly were in here until they all stood before me and tempted me with their shiny secrets. I kept my eyes on the floor, much like Kari had, for fear I'd see something she'd rather me not. Even on all those nights I watched her, never once did I allow myself to witness something I shouldn't have. I would reserve that honor until she begged it of me. Only then would I fully admire her in all her very real glory. Glory that surely rivaled Odin's.

I heard Kari turn around, and I assumed it was safe to lift my eyes. The cream dress she wore was flowy and had the beauty of Valhalla's finest. I'd never worn the dress myself, though I'd been gifted the piece from Odin. I was proud to own it, even if I found that the fabric cut around the chest was far too low. I preferred my leathers, but Kari, well...she was magnificent.

Her lips wobbled, and she raised a shaking palm to her shoulder. Before she could cover herself, I noticed splotches of red seeping through the cream capped sleeve of the dress, and she said, "I, I'm sorry. This dress is beautiful, but—"

"We don't have anything more practical here, unless you want to throw on some combat gear," I cut her off, already on my way to inspect her wound. "Your bandages will need to be changed again and your wound healed. I will call for—"

"No! I'll do it," she said, already peeling the sleeve of her dress off, biting her lip as she did. "I guess those healing waters weren't so healing after all."

"Or maybe you reopened the stitches on your many tumbles through the bathing chamber," I uttered under my breath. She shot me a look that said me and my many reflective surfaces were to blame. My stomach turned at the mere sight of her, though she was not what I expected. I should have known a seeress running through forests screaming at flies and ghosts would be, well... unique, but I hadn't expected her anger. Flies and ghosts were one thing, but she had no qualms about snapping at one of Odin's attendants, even one who *saved* her.

"Let me grab a cloth."

"It's fine, I can—"

"I'm grabbing a cloth," I stated, my words stone. Her mouth gaped then shut, as if she thought better of continuing this fight I'd surely win. I riffled through cabinets in the bathing chamber, yanking a small cloth free.

What had Bodil used, and why did she take it with her?

I scanned the contents of bottled jars upon the counter, popping a few open to take a whiff, as if that would suddenly give me the knowledge I needed.

"I'm a healer, you know!" she shouted from the bedchamber. "If you insist on collecting the materials yourself, I need yarrow, vinegar, and a strip of cloth."

Her shout curdled my blood. Yes, she had cried, she had squealed, but *this* shout? She may as well have screamed out to everyone in the house that she didn't belong. If one of the sisters was a healer in their mortal life, they gave up such titles long ago. We were valkyries, nothing more, nothing less.

I stalked from the bathing chamber, cloth gripped in my fist. "Keep. Your. Voice. Down."

The door to my chamber swung open, Rayna standing in the doorway with wild perplexity. Kari stiffened, and the two women stared at each other as if neither was sure the other was safe. Rayna slowly shut the door behind her, looking from me to Kari. I didn't move as Rayna closed in to inspect the seeress. Even as she stood a mere foot before her, Kari craning her neck to look at the valkyrie, I kept my position. Rayna needed this. She needed to see this woman she'd never met yet knew far too much about.

"You're both making too much noise, especially you," she hissed, her eyes darting back to Kari. "You want to live, yes?"

"I suppose." Kari swallowed.

"You suppose?" Rayna scoffed. "What a choice, Rune."

My sister picked up a strand of Kari's strawberry blonde hair. Rayna's hair had looked similar once, when I'd drunkenly dipped her golden braids into a pot of boiled lingonberry. The white pieces of her hair remained untouched, but the rest of it had been stained all day. I tried to keep my face steady as memories of her reaction flooded my mind.

"Leave her be," I finally said, motioning to Rayna's hand still clutching the seeress' wet strands. Rayna rolled her eyes and shook her head, dropping the hair a moment later.

"This decision will be your end, Rune," she said. "If you want to keep her alive, send her back."

"Of course she's going back." My teeth ground against each other. I didn't want a fight with Rayna, but gods, she was making this all so much harder.

"After we speak to a god of Rune's choosing," Kari finally spoke, her chin lifted. Hearing my name roll off her lips did something terrible to me; a shift took place within my very core that I knew damn well would be permanent.

"A god?" Rayna laughed a horrible, twisted laugh. "This just keeps on getting better. Do I even want to know, Rune?"

"Help or don't, but don't just stand in my way. Not again," I said. "I need yarrow and vinegar. Can you fetch some? Please."

Rayna sighed, her eyes boring into me. "I have some in my chamber."

As Kari waited, she sat upon the bench in the corner, sipping her still-warm tea and snacking on foods lining a slender tray. She'd stared out the window, ignoring me the whole time as she mindlessly stroked her cat. I watched her as she took in the Valhalla sunset, pegasuses darting through scattered rays of dimming light. Only then did she say, "How long was I asleep for?"

"Almost a day. It'll be night again soon, and if I don't leave, it will cause suspicion."

"You'll leave me here in this room?" she asked. I wasn't sure if she was hurt or annoyed.

I nodded. "To go to Midgard, yes."

"I'm surprised you're not forcing me to go with you now that I'm not, you know, dead," she said, her head cocked as she tossed a walnut into her mouth.

She made herself at home upon the seat, her confidence slowly finding its way back to her.

"Not yet, you're not," I said before realizing my words betrayed my meaning. She gawked at me and choked on a piece of walnut. "What I mean is, you're still bleeding. Traveling through the Bifrost takes a toll on a mortal, a toll I'm not willing to take tonight."

Before she could answer, Rayna came into the room with a basket of supplies. "I had to tell Asta you drunkenly sliced your foot open when she saw me with this." She motioned to her basket.

"Wonderful." I let out a sigh. Another strike with Asta was not what I needed. I may have been Odin's favorite, but I certainly wasn't the old wench's.

Rayna set the basket down on the edge of the bed, motioning to Kari. "You said you're a healer, so help yourself. Rune, I'm assuming you'll still be coming with me tonight?"

"Of course." I dipped my head. Tonight would be my first sober venture down to Midgard all year. For some reason, since the seeress arrived, I'd been too on edge to take a drink, even a sip. I didn't trust the nonsense I spewed once the poison hit my willing veins.

"What do you expect me to do while you're gone?" Kari asked as she began riffling through Rayna's basket.

"I'm going to let you handle that question," Rayna muttered to me. "I swear to the gods, if you're late, I will chop your hair off, Rune. I mean it this time. We leave out the front tonight. No tunnel nonsense."

"I'll be there," I said. If any other sister had spoken to me that way, I'd have them by the neck. But Rayna's patience with me was growing thin, and I more than deserved her threats—not that I liked her dishing them out in front of the mortal.

Rayna glanced at Kari one last time before growling and storming out of my bed chamber.

"What's her problem?"

"You," I said before I could stop myself.

"Why? You said I needed to be here for a reason mortals couldn't know. I assumed the other valkyries would."

I ground my teeth; this woman was pressing my own patience. Why must she have so many questions? What was I supposed to tell her?

"Oh, I took you from the mortal realm and broke at least three valkyrie oaths to bring you to Valhalla, and now I'm hiding you,

because if Odin finds out, you'll probably be killed, and I'll be tossed out of my sect." Yeah, just perfect.

Instead, I looked at the seeress and said, "You'll remain in the room when I'm gone. I'll make sure you have food and drink before I go. Please don't alert anyone to your presence. The other sisters..." I scratched the back of my neck. "They can't know about you until *after* we speak to Odin."

The seeress pondered upon this for a moment. "Fine, I'll be quiet. Do you have any scrolls to study?"

I suppressed a chuckle as she glanced up at me. "I can grab a few from the archive. What's your preferred topic?" I asked, indulging her just this once. I figured the more distracted she was, the less likely it would be that she found herself in trouble again.

Kari made it known what she wanted to study and which food she preferred, and I summoned a platter of turkey and root vegetables before I left her. When I headed for the archive, a clearing of someone's throat brought my attention behind me. Bodil stood awkwardly, as if she had something to say but didn't know how to spit it out.

"Walk with me," I demanded, knowing there could only be one reason Bodil would want to talk. "We can speak in the archive. You can help me find a scroll of spells."

"Do you think it's wise to give a mor—*her* access to the seidr not of her realm?" Bodil corrected herself, presumably not wanting to admit to a mortal lurking around the House of Wings.

I shrugged. "She'll be going back soon."

How much could she possibly learn before I took her to Midgard? I didn't see the harm, especially since she wouldn't be able to wield seidr of another realm anyway.

"That's what I wanted to talk to you about."

I paused and raised a brow at her, encouraging her to continue. She glanced around, but tonight's feast was underway, and the halls were empty.

"I don't know why you took her. Well, I know, but I still can't wrap my head around how you let your intrusive thoughts win. Either way, I know she must mean something to you, and believe it or not, I don't want bad blood between us."

"What are you trying to tell me?" I asked.

"I wasn't straightforward with you earlier." Bodil's sigh sounded painful. "If you drop her back into her life on Midgard, she will die."

"What are you talking about? I'm waiting until she heals from her injuries so there's no reason she—"

"It's not just about her injury. It's about the natural laws of Midgard. She's tainted from the heavens now, and that doesn't just go away. Her wounds, while healing here, will cause her downfall upon returning to Midgard."

"Well what am I supposed to do with her now? She sure as Hel can't stay here, and I can't return her to Midgard just for her to meet her death," I said, my frustration seizing control of my tongue.

"Take her to Helheim before Odin realizes she's here. Once he finds her, you won't be given any other option but to return her and let the natural law take its course."

"You think Hel will feel any differently?" I asked, not imagining the goddess of Hel would be any more forgiving.

"Helheim is far less exclusive," Bodil said.

"Yeah, for the dead. Hel takes all the souls she can get, but only *after* they've crossed over," I said, running my hand down my face and showing weakness to a sister I'd prefer not to. For all I knew, Bodil was just trying to rid herself, *and the entire sect*, of me. "I can't believe I'm considering this."

She flashed me a look that told me she didn't want to be in my position, and I wondered if she'd ever been tempted to take her human playthings home with her. We both knew what she was up to on the long nights on Midgard. I wondered if tonight she'd give in to temptations or let my failures guide her on a path devoid of depravity. Either way, I let my predicament be a lesson—a warning.

CHAPTER NINE
OCEAN BLUE

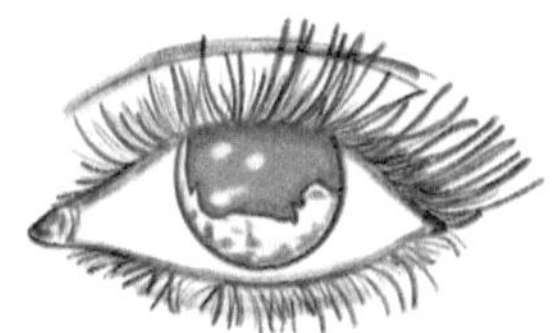

Kari

I sank into the bed as soon as Rune left to grab me a scroll, sampling the foods she'd given me. I let my head fall back to the pillow and reveled in the sheer comfort my body experienced despite the oozing hole in my shoulder. In Stormheim, we didn't have raised beds topped with thick blankets and stuffed with pristine white feathers. I sank into the mattress, wondering how I would ever return to Midgard now that I'd experienced such luxury.

Tove was curled up next to me, purring aggressively. I could feel just how much he missed having a corporeal body and having me beside him in a way he couldn't just see, but feel too.

The door flew open, and Rune poured into the bedchamber with a scowl that could've shattered glass. She closed the door and locked it behind her, running her other hand down her paling face.

"What's wrong?" I sat up in bed, feeling her angst roll through the room like a thick fog. It would choke me if I didn't help her manage it soon.

"We need to leave," Rune said, her voice hard as stone. She pushed herself away from the door and strode to the armoire, murmuring something about Rayna and how she was going to do some rather unpleasant things to Rune for this—whatever "this" was.

"Leave? To go where?" I pushed the tray of food away and scooched to the end of the bed, as if moving closer to the valkyrie would tell me what was going on inside that mind of hers.

She didn't speak for a moment while she threw her wardrobe doors open, rummaging through her belongings. Tove meowed angrily in Rune's direction, knowing she was the reason I'd stopped giving him attentive scratches.

She sighed and paused, her hand resting on a shiny shoulder plate. "We're going to have to put a hold on that little conversation with Odin, seeress. Turns out, he may not be as receptive to your pleas as I initially thought. It's best we leave Valhalla before he discovers your presence here in his hall."

"Why the sudden change?" I asked, eying her to see if I could sense any lies in her words.

No lies. But it definitely wasn't her whole truth. She was holding something back.

"Remember what I said about not being able to tell you everything?"

"Yes, but what if I don't accept that?"

Rune shook her head as she pulled her armor out of the wardrobe. Piece by piece, she began securing it over her red leathers, tightening straps and adjusting her breastplate. The brilliant golden armor was unmarred, all but for a line gouged through the chest piece. I watched as she paused to run a thoughtful thumb down the mark before she resumed getting her things in order.

I tried to ignore the reflection in her armor, but I found myself staring ruthlessly at that gouge, wondering why it seemed so familiar. When my gaze sharpened, I realized, while unintentional, that

I'd been staring right at her breasts. I should have looked away, but even she didn't move. Out of the side of my eyes, I saw her watching me, and I couldn't help notice the way the metal warped around her body so perfectly, she looked as if she'd been dipped in liquid gold.

Rune cleared her throat, and my eyes shot straight across the room—straight to the mirror hanging mercilessly on the gilded wall.

"Great gods," I screamed, clutching my cheek. "My face!"

I scrambled out of the bed, my hands shaking as my gaze locked on my eyes in the reflection.

Ocean blue.

Deep pools of ocean blue.

My knees threatened to buckle, and the only thing that held me upright was knowing I wouldn't be able to see my reflection from the floor. I could hear the blood pulsing in my head as my hands fell to the mirror, knocking on it and double checking it wasn't some cruel trick.

There was no rot, no goo, no peeling skin, no black veins—just the smooth skin I'd always known there to be from the truth of my touch. One hand was still on the mirror, the other one on my face, which shook back and forth in disbelief.

"What did I tell you about screaming?" Rune hissed, marching toward me. I could barely hear her over my own heart and the swirling thoughts filling my mind.

"My, my—" I stuttered, not knowing where to begin. How did one explain what I now saw? Or, more importantly, what I didn't.

The sound of fists pounding on wood echoed from down the hall.

"For the love of all things living," the valkyrie cursed. She ran to the glass embedded into the wall and pushed open the panes. Breeze brushed the little hairs over her face as she raised her fingers to her lips and let out a loud whistle. "Come here, seeress. Your ride is on its way."

"My what?" I asked, but she just clicked her tongue impatiently and strode over to where I stood with numb limbs. She pulled me over to the gap in the wall, pushing the bench out of her way to make room for me. Tove squirmed and screeched as she yanked him off the bed and tossed him into my arms. I held his fragile body as his nails retracted.

"When you feel the wind hit your face, jump." She pushed a bag into my chest, then motioned for me to put Tove inside so I could free my hands.

"Jump?" I said, peering out at the midnight sky. She blew her frustration into the air, sending the scent of hazelnuts and raspberries in my direction as she grabbed Tove out of my arms and did it for me. When the bag was slung over my shoulders with a small hole at the top for Tove to stick his head out of, she grabbed me by the shoulders and squared me in front of the gap in the wall.

I could hear beating wings before I saw them, and my gut clenched as the anticipation of wind on my face gripped me. With a loud whoosh, I felt pressure on my back. The dreaded feeling of falling overwhelmed me as I stumbled out the hole in the wall.

That bitch pushed me!

I only had a moment to right myself before landing on the back of a huge pegasus with white wings. I gripped it around the neck with all my strength, suppressing a scream that fought valiantly up my throat.

"Take her to the mist!" Rune shouted, and the pegasus took off into the star-filled sky.

Rune's pegasus shot through the air at a nauseating speed. Flashes of images of white feathers and the feeling of flying racked through my brain—bits of memories of my travels from Midgard to Asgard.

"You left without me! Seriously?" someone shouted from behind me, but I didn't dare turn around. Whoever it was clearly didn't intend for their words to fall upon my ears, and I wasn't so confident that if I moved, I wouldn't tumble through the clouds to my untimely death.

"Epli!" the voice called again, and only when an apple came soaring past my head and in biting range of the white pegasus did the creature slow its pace. The crunch of fruit in the winged horse's teeth vibrated through its neck and into my hands. "Rune, what are you—"

It wasn't until Rayna grew closer that she realized I wasn't her sister. No, I was just the woman she couldn't stand for some reason unbeknownst to me.

Her black pegasus soared next to me, and only then did Rayna and I lock eyes. "Did you...steal Apple? How did you manage—"

"I didn't steal this pegasus! I was thrown on top of it," I yelled out into the sky, hoping my words cut through the wind enough for the valkyrie to hear me.

"Her! Not 'it'," Rayna grumbled, having no difficulty speaking through the wind, no doubt after decades of practice, maybe even centuries. "I assume it was Rune who threw you?"

I nodded, watching the way her eyes rolled in response.

"And I assume, since you're heading in the opposite direction of the Bifrost, that you're not going back to Midgard?"

"I can assume that to be the case, yes!" I yelled; I didn't have much more information than she did.

"You have no clue where Apple is taking you, do you?"

I scanned Rayna's hardened features, knowing Rune trusted her but not quite sure if I should do the same.

"No," I said, though Rune had mentioned something about the mist, whatever that was.

Rayna closed her eyes for a moment before her pegasus pulled up into the sky and looped back around to fly back in the direction she came from.

"That's just perfect." Her grumble drifted to me as we shot in opposite directions, Apple flying farther and farther away from Rune's home. I gripped her tighter when Tove let out an annoyed mew. I could feel him rustling around in the bag, and I used his presence to ground me when I was so far from said ground.

Stone buildings soared past me, all lit up from the inside. I could hear the whispers of the wind mix with faint music in the distance, the gush of moving water through river rock. I wished the sun was shining down upon this place so I could see Valhalla in all its glory, but as we flew deeper into Asgard and away from Odin's Hall, I noticed the moon doused the trees in glowing silver.

My breath caught in my throat at the thought of spending an eternity somewhere so beautiful, so serene. I suddenly understood why so many fought to get here, as if their mortal lives were nothing but a sacrifice for eternal glory—a mere stepping stone. Something twisted in me knowing I wouldn't have come here after my death if Rune hadn't bypassed Odin's rules and broke her very own oaths. And for what? To tease me?

I wasn't sure how this couldn't all be some twisted trick put on by the Goddess of Death, as if my ancestral curse hadn't been enough for her. But what had I done? Was this punishment for going to the market that day and leaving my family behind while they all had their final moments?

Having Tove whole, escaping the pressures of my village, and being able to see my eyes for the first time in my life was all made possible by leaving Midgard. Asgard had given me the things I dreamed of for years.

I had dreamt of this, hadn't I?

I recounted the visions that had wormed their way through my mind, keeping me up and giving me a mugwort addiction in the name of uncovering its truth. Shining gold emerging from a star-lit sky. Black and white feathers raining down upon the ruby floor. By the end of the dream, I hadn't had any senses, no eyes. I thought at the time that if I had no eyes, that must've meant I had no curse. I realized everything I'd seen in my vision was now my reality.

I was meant to be here upon Apple's back, flying into the unknown mist. Tove was meant to be strapped to my back, and I was meant to see my own face without fear. If I knew anything, I knew this. No one was going to take my new reality away from me, even if it was all just a horrible trick. I would claim it, make it into something that served me instead of something that worked against me. My reality was my own, and no god, goddess, or strange valkyrie would have a say in it, not anymore.

CHAPTER TEN
INTO THE MIST

Rune

Kari screaming into the mirror was the last straw.

The second to last straw was Bodil admitting I couldn't return the seeress to Midgard without being responsible for her death. That was when I knew there was no point asking Odin for his blessing to send Tove's spirit back to Midgard, even if it was an incentive to lure Kari back to where she belonged. It didn't matter now if she couldn't return without twisted consequences.

I wouldn't put her on the Allfather's radar, nor would I admit to my mistakes—my broken oaths—if there was a risk he'd send her away despite the outcome.

Had I made a horrible mistake flying away with her that night?

No regret plagued me for slaying the mortal raiders, but maybe, just maybe, if I'd left Kari there, she would've been found by people in her village. Maybe she would've been saved. These were all "ifs" hinging on even more invisible circumstances. There was no point lamenting them, but what I *could* do was ensure my mistakes didn't cost the mortal her life now.

I rushed over to the pounding sound and swung open the door to my apartments just as Asta's fist came slamming through the air once more. She glowered at me with unmatched distaste as she held herself back from smashing her knuckles into my undeserving cheek. I cared little for the frown twitching upon her un-aging face, but all I had to do was distract her long enough for Kari to get away unnoticed.

Apple was the fastest in her herd, so I assumed my task had already been completed. She would make it to the mountains, and it wouldn't be long before Apple was back for me.

Asta had many questions for me about the screams, why I wasn't at the feast, where Rayna was, and who knew what else. My ears grew weary after she'd asked her third question without leaving room for me to speak. At a certain point, I sighed, leaned into the doorframe, and asked her if she was done. It wasn't long after that I shut the door on her and went barreling back toward my bedchamber.

I stuffed a bag full of items for both Kari and me, including that scroll she'd asked for. I wasn't sure how much it would help her now, but I was willing to give anything a try.

A tingle under my skin told me Apple had almost arrived. Looking around the room I'd given forty years to, I patted the window pane as I leaned upon it. There was a chance I'd never see this place again, and I wish I could say that didn't sting. I wish I could say leaving behind every gift Odin had given me for my service didn't feel like I was erasing hundreds of years of hard work, all for one wild decision made on a drunken night.

Saving Kari's life can't end mine.

As I jumped out the window, trusting Apple would come swooping by, I swallowed my indecision. I would live with my actions, and Hel, I'd make the most of it.

I hit Apple's back with a light 'thud', and as she darted away, I saw the glint of a tipped over bottle on the balcony below. Since Kari had arrived, I hadn't been tempted to let mead wash away my bitterness. Since she'd arrived, I hadn't stared at myself in a mirror, wondering who I'd become. Those two facts fueled me as I flew away from the only home I'd known since Odin brought me to his hall.

We flew and flew, and I could sense we were getting close when the air on my face grew sticky and thick. The mist had a warning barrier, an uncomfortable ring in its first few layers that warded off anyone who'd unintentionally wandered too close. For a moment, the humidity was so heavy on my lungs, the air felt as if it could drown me. The knowledge of what awaited us on the other side kept me going, and I wondered how Kari had fared. Apple wouldn't have let her turn around regardless. She knew better than to fear the mist.

The air lightened until it felt crisp and clear once more, the mist parting to allow our entry. On the other side, I noticed several flickering fires in the distance that warned pegasuses of the impending mountain. They would collide with it if they didn't make a swift turn to dive *through* it.

Torches lined the entrance to the gap in the mountain we soared through, and Apple took the tight quarters as a challenge as she maneuvered through rock and vines on moonlight and memory alone.

When the rock opened to a clearing, the moon cast glittering rays through rushing water cascading down from the mountain top. Apple and I flew under the waterfall, just for the fun of it, before taking a nosedive to a ledge along the mountainside.

Light emanated from the cliffside, illuminating a stone building made of mountain rock. It was covered in red ivy and had not-so-modest windows that gave us glimpses into the cozy structure. A fire roared from the hearth within, and I saw two figures lurking inside before the curtains were drawn shut by the smaller of the two.

Apple landed upon a patch of grass planted purely for pegasuses so they didn't crack a hoof as they came down. Once dismounted, I tossed an apple into the air. Epli let out an excited whinny and caught it between her pink and black lips. I patted her on her rear before straightening my bags and heading for the front entrance. My knuckles didn't rap on the door; I simply walked in and headed for the two figures sitting by the hearth.

Kari's head swung to me, and her eyes lit up when they landed on mine. An intense flutter in my stomach had my hand instinctively moving over the skin above it to quiet the excitable flurries. Those intriguing little buggers hadn't visited me once during my long stay in Valhalla. I'd remember them as a girl, a teen, and a young woman, gifted to me by various people over the years—men and women alike—but how long ago had that been?

"Look who finally decided to join us," a gruff voice followed by a hearty chuckle brought my attention to the person behind Kari. My reason for being here almost slipped my heavy mind. "Grab yourself a cup of tea and come on over, girl."

Áma.

I offered the hag a wry smile before making my way to the kitchen on the far side of the room. As I pulled a mug from the wooden cupboards and began filling it with the still steaming water from the kettle on the stove, I heard soft mummers from the women by the fire. I set my tea to brew and hung back for a moment as I watched the old woman across from Kari grab the seeress' hands.

There weren't many places shielded from Odin's vision or influence. Asgard was his realm, and as the Allfather, he had eyes almost everywhere, thanks to his ravens, but even he couldn't see beyond the mist. The seidr of the wand-wed here was too strong, and war would break out in his realm if he ever tried to take this place back. He'd accepted long ago that the valley was off limits to even him.

When I first arrived in Valhalla, I'd been young, stupid, and confused. In my mortal life, I never aimed to be a valkyrie, and there was certainly no way to plan for such a fate, but I'd found myself in golden halls with dozens of new sisters all the same. Even then, I didn't like the feeling of being watched, of having his eyes prying into my life no matter where I was or what I was doing. It had taken me years to find the valley beyond the mist, but eventually, my efforts of searching for a place beyond Odin had been successful.

"Come join us," Áma croaked, removing her hand from Kari's long enough to wave me over. Grabbing my tea, I maneuvered through the fire-lit space and joined them in the sitting room. I claimed the high back chair next to the padded bench the two of them sat upon, noticing Kari had already had time for an outfit change. She no longer wore the white and gold dress stained with blood. She wore a modest gown with a robe overtop. I didn't miss the bandages peeking out from under the light fabric, and relief washed over me, knowing Áma had brought her in without question and wasted no time taking care of her.

"Hello, Áma," I said, meeting the gaze of the crone. "It's nice to see you."

"You stupid girl." She clicked her tongue, not caring as wiry grey hair fell into her left eye. "You should have brought her here right away. What were you thinking, taking her to the House of Wings—to Valhalla?"

Kari's arms were crossed, also waiting for an answer I couldn't give—that I didn't want to. I lifted my hand and motioned to the two of them, "I'm not liking the two of you teaming up. And thank you for such a warm greeting, by the way."

"I'm sure you don't," Áma said with a huff. "You don't want to admit you were wrong. You never do. I'm still waiting for an apology regarding Apple taking a chunk out of my roof."

"I didn't bring her here so you could debate the will of the valkyrie." I straightened my spine and cast my gaze down upon both women, as if I had some secret plan they weren't privy to—

like I hadn't screwed up. "And Apple does what she pleases. Let's not pretend I have any control over her. It was your fault for leaving a basket of fruit up there."

Áma shook her head with a roll of her eyes. "Don't act like this is part of Odin's plan, girl. You wouldn't have run if it were."

"I didn't run—"

'You did!" she cut off my verbal denial, seeing right through me. "I'm four thousand years old, and you are but a child. You don't create a land away from the Allfather's eye without the motivation or the knowledge to do so. I had to know what he is to know to hide from him. And because I know him like I do, I know he would have never told you to steal a *mortal* from Midgard."

I swallowed the lump in my throat, avoiding Áma's knowing gaze for the first time since I'd sat down.

Gods, the Asgardian woman could see right through me. What did I think would happen if I brought Kari here?

"They were going to kill you," I gritted through my teeth, ignoring Áma completely. This wasn't about her, not really. She was just how fate decided to force my hand.

Kari's eyes burned into me as she said, "And?"

My lip twitched as if a fly had landed upon them. My brows pulled in, and I looked her over. "And what?"

"How is that a reason? You see death nightly. It's your entire existence," she said, the light of the fire flicking through her gaze, as if her anger transmuted into pure heat.

I stared at her, tracing the edge of her dress with my gaze as I did. My attention fixed on that little corner of the bandage sticking out, and I wondered how much pain she was still in, if any. It'd been so long since I'd had a wound of my own. My fingers pinched the exposed flesh of my neck to remember the sensation of pain, but also to wake me from this trance she always seemed to send me into.

Her words rang in my mind, sending waves of awareness through me. My life was death. If death was my very existence, wouldn't I know better than anyone that the future I altered on her behalf was warranted?

"You didn't deserve to die," I finally muttered.

"Did the thousands of people who you brought into Valhalla over the years deserve to die?" she asked.

"Well, no, but most of them died before I arrived. I couldn't intervene."

"Most. What about the ones you *did* see die? Why didn't you help them?" she asked.

A sigh slipped through my lips, and I began wishing she'd go back to her injury-induced rest. How easy she'd been under the throws of sleep. "Because I have oaths to uphold," I said.

"Yet you didn't uphold them with me, did you?"

I pushed myself out of my seat, running a hand through the loose ends of my hair. "Are you angry I saved your life?"

"Of course not. I simply want to know why I'm here. This is my life! Or, it's meant to be. I, I don't even know what my life *means* anymore, or if I still have one," she admitted with a wince. "I had visions of you taking me. As distorted as they were, I now know what I saw, though I still don't understand why. But you have the answers I need."

Visions of me?

I'd watched the seeress for years, scribbling on birch bark, stoking fires, drinking tea, speaking to spirits. What she did each time she closed her eyes evaded me, but knowing she dreamt of me sent a tickle up my spine.

"You have a life," I resigned. "I brought you here to ensure that. I took you on a drunken impulse. Is that what you want to hear?"

"A drunken impulse?" she scoffed. "If you'd let me die, I would've been with my family in a realm of death. Because you took me, I'm here without my family, and now, I must run and hide. You caused nothing but complications for me."

Her words sat with me as I reclaimed my seat, and in my heart of hearts, her speech held a truth I couldn't fight. Her complaints were valid, and were why we had rules and oaths in the first place. Rayna's complaints about me stealing the seeress' death played through my mind, but how could I regret bringing her here? She was made for so much more than death.

"I complicated things, yes, but when has 'easy' ever meant right?" I asked, and that sentiment finally ended her string of demanding questions. Her shoulders fell, and she leaned back into the bench. Even Áma grew quiet, but my intention was never to shut her up. I just needed her to see she was worth more than what she thought she was. It wasn't her time to be with her family yet, and I was intent on proving that to her.

Night after night, I watched her. Night after night, she'd proven how much she deserved not just her world, but my world too.

The silence ate at me, and I found a question rising to my lips just so I could hear her speak once more. "What's wrong with your face?"

When Kari's hand flew to her cheek in horror, I pushed out further explanation with haste, realizing what I said came out as an insult. "You screamed, looking into my mirror."

"Oh," Kari said, glancing over to Áma, as if the two of them now harbored some secret. Áma gave her a nod of approval, which rubbed me in all the wrong ways. Why did the old crone have any say in what the seeress told me?

"I'm cursed. Well, I was. Somehow, it's been lifted," Kari said, twisting her hands in her lap.

"You're...what?" I stuttered. My eyes scanned over her, wondering how I could have missed such a thing. You'd think after watching her all this time, I would have realized something was amiss. But what was it?

I thought of each time she stumbled around my bed and bathing chambers, how she grew uneasy the moment she stepped in front of a reflective surface. I thought of the cloth coverings that hung on her longhouse walls, though I'd always assumed paintings of her family hid beneath the dusty fabric. Maybe they weren't paintings at all, but mirrors.

"Why can't you look at yourself in a mirror?" I asked slowly, not completely certain I'd figured it out just yet but willing to take the risk.

"My eyes." Kari paused to take a deep, shaky breath. "They always appeared rotten. I couldn't stand the sight of them. The puss that oozed out of the rotting flesh was too much to bear, even if it was all a cruel illusion."

"Was that the first time you looked into a reflective surface since arriving in Valhalla?"

Kari nodded her head. "It was. My curse could've lifted the moment you brought me here for all I know."

"It mostly likely did," Áma said. "In the morning, I can speak to the residual traces of it in your body and use its unique signature to determine who placed it and what limits the curse has."

"I know who placed it," Kari mumbled, grabbing her tea sitting upon the table situated between us.

"Who?" Áma and I asked in unison.

Kari shifted uncomfortably before her pink lips parted, and she uttered, "Hel."

I stared at her as I took in her perplexing admission. "Hel? Why? What did you do that caused the goddess of death to curse you?" I asked.

"Not me directly. It's an ancestral curse," Kari explained. "And I wish I could tell you why. That information died with my relatives long ago. All I know is that it impacts the first-born daughters of every generation. My mother and I were cursed, but my younger sisters were not."

I nodded but remained silent, letting her words sink in, hoping Áma would have some useful information. I could pluck souls from bodies, see people's final moments, and lift things far heavier than what my body should've allowed, but I knew very little of curses, especially ones bestowed by Hel.

"Ancestral curse, huh?" Áma asked with a slight shake of her head. She pushed herself from the padded bench with a groan. "You two girls can stay up and talk about this until you're blue in the face, but his old body needs its beauty sleep, and no solution will be found until I do. We can talk more in the morning. We'll have work to do, that's for sure."

Kari said her thanks to the Asgardian who'd taken her in and bandaged her up. The woman clasped Kari's hands in hers for a moment before taking her leave. A long robe trailed behind her as she moved to the kitchen with her empty mug.

"Rune, you know where the spare bedchamber is. Use it when you're done out here. Oh," she paused to face me. "Don't you dare leave it full of crumbs this time."

"I won't," I said, an embarrassed blush forcing itself to the surface of my cheeks. Kari cast an eye over me with an amused twinkle in her gaze. "Don't ask," I warned the seeress.

Kari chuckled and played with the hem of her robe. "I'm assuming you get peckish whilst on your drunken endeavors?"

I stared at the seeress, not wanting to admit to any of my drunken memories, or lack of them, but she held a sparkle in her eye that wasn't there merely moments ago. I would swallow my pride if it meant that sparkle could remain for just a little longer.

"Quite possibly," I admitted. "Being able to transport goodies at whim doesn't help with my inability to ignore the cravings."

"That's you who's been transporting food? I'd assumed it was the seidr of Odin's Hall."

"Valkyries don't just collect souls, you know," I said with a devious grin. "We're assigned to the dead even after we bring them to their eternal resting point. I have a small connection to every soul I've collected, so once they're in Odin's Hall, I must make sure they remain content. Being able to summon food and drink at will helps in those duties. In fact, that's pretty much how I solve all their issues, now that I think of it."

"Well, that's handy," Kari mused. "What will happen to them when you're gone? Will the dead be uneasy?" Tugging on the blanket positioned over the back of her seat, she pulled the free end across her lap.

"Maybe for a little while, but Odin will simply divide the souls up amongst the young sisters who have very few souls to attend to. I might miss one or two of them, but..."

I trailed off, thinking of Gro. Sure, I'd always hated how he stood tall next to me just to force me from my chair, but never once had he asked something of me. If I'd miss any spirit, it was sure to be him.

"I'd miss my sisters more than anything," I said. My tea was now cold, but it no longer suited me anyway. Thinking of never seeing my sisters again had bile rising up my throat, so much so, I wanted to burn it away with mead. I wasn't willing to use my seidr to summon it, and I bet Áma only had odd potions stashed away instead of alcohol. I wasn't fool enough to mess around with those. Sighing, I too leaned back in my chair, realizing the only thing I had to burn away my fears of impending grief was the woman lounging across from me.

A curious look passed over Kari, and I suddenly no longer wanted to speak about myself or what may or may not happen to the relationships in my life. Those worries would have to wait for another time.

"But you..." I said slowly. "You're the one who's no longer bound by your curse. How does it feel?"

Kari thought about my question for a moment, her fingertips trailing under her eyes. "They're exactly how my sisters described them to be."

"Mmm." I nodded, thinking about what she'd said about being the eldest daughter. "Did you resent your sisters for not being cursed?"

"Gods, no. They weren't the ones who cursed me. I was just happy they didn't have to carry the burden like my mother and I did. They were the ones who painstakingly ensured I stayed away from reflective surfaces to aid in my comfort. They were the ones who drew countless portraits of me so I could imagine how I looked growing up." Her eyes grew damp, and I realized I must have said the wrong thing. In my mortal life, I'd been an only child born of two hardworking humans who were never around. My true family was the one I took my oaths with.

"You should know..." I trailed off, not knowing how to make the tears wetting her lashes disappear. Nine realms, I forgot how often mortals weep. Sure, I'd seen them cry and scream countless times on the battlefield, but we were in no battle now. No lives were at stake, blood was not being shed, so why were tears leaking from her eyes? "We will have to venture to Hel."

Kari nodded once. She wiped her cheeks, her face pink with embarrassment for letting the few meager drops fall. She sniffled and straightened as if it'd never happened, and I chose to ignore those three droplets I'd seen slip. I chose to pretend I hadn't trailed each of them with my sharp gaze, counting them as they fell.

CHAPTER ELEVEN
TAKE THE FLOOR

Kari

Setting my tea mug on the counter, I cast a look over my shoulder at the peculiar valkyrie. She'd made food appear for me, and I'd nervously nibbled on it as she briefly explained why we needed to go to Hel and why we were on the run. I hadn't been hungry, but I'd worked too hard in the mortal realm for food to turn down what she'd freely offered. Plus, the cherries had been maddeningly good.

"Odin will not accept your presence, but Hel might. She has returned beings to the mortal realm before, so if there's one god who may help you and Tove, it's her," Rune had explained.

I understood we weren't going to Hel to see if my family was there. I even understood that seeing them could disturb them more than not, knowing I'd be leaving them again so soon. Rune had said as much, though she knew nothing of my family.

I watched her as she finished cleaning our mugs, making sure to leave the place spotless after her supposed crumb incident. I too took extra care, not wanting to get on Áma's bad side. The woman was a little rough around the edges, but she'd been kind enough to take me in without question, pulling out her medicinal kit as soon as I'd walked through the door.

She said she'd smelled the mortal rot on me; as odd as that had sounded, I knew her to be wand-wed, and I wouldn't question her methods. She was four thousand years old, after all. What did I know? Before the raid, I was just trying to keep up with my client list while battling nightly trouble with my visions.

When Áma offered tea, I'd opted for lavender, forgoing the mugwort. I didn't need it anymore now that the stubborn vision had come to pass. I expected to go back to my regularly scheduled, easy-to-interpret visions.

"You must be tired," Rune said as she wiped her hands on a kitchen cloth. She peered out at the star-streaked sky through an opening in the wall with glass embedded within, a window, as Áma had called it.

"I could use rest," I said honestly. "Apparently, getting tossed out of a palace made by the gods takes a lot out of you."

She stared at me blankly, like she didn't intend on apologizing, but I could see a hint of amusement dancing at the corners of her lips.

"Come on, seeress. Let me show you where the bedchamber is." Rune didn't turn back to look at me before she made her way out of the kitchen and down the hall. She stopped in front of a polished wooden door, and only then did she take a second to glance over her shoulder at me.

She'd called me seeress again, and something about the way she watched me had me unsettled to my very core. This woman harbored secrets close to her chest, and she was old enough to know how to safeguard them. One way or another, I would uncover what she was hiding. Who knew? Maybe all it would take was one night with my head upon a pillow. In the morning, I could understand so much more of this valkyrie, of this place.

"Goodnight then," I said, brushing past her and claiming the chamber as my own. When she walked in after me and began fiddling with flint to light the candles sitting atop a wooden hutch, I stared at her and said, "I'm capable of lighting my own candles."

"I should hope so," Rune chuckled.

"Then why are you still here?" I asked. It came out more abrasive than I'd meant it, but this immortal creature had kidnapped me, thrown me from a window, and taken me to yet another mysterious location against my will. She would *not* be sharing this bedchamber with me. Who knew what kind of mischief she'd get up to as I slept?

"Unless you want me to sleep on the floor of the main room, this is where I'll be."

"This is not where you'll be," I said, my eyes darting to the singular bed sitting in the middle of the quaint room. "Do you even need to sleep?"

She released an irritated sigh, setting down the flint. "I'm alive, so of course I sleep. I may not need to sleep much, but I still need it. And I'm *tired,*" she said. "So please, let's not make a thing of it. It's a bed, not a marriage proposal."

A marriage proposal? Who said anything about marriage?

"The other side of the bed is reserved for Tove," I said, not willing to part with him for the night, not after everything.

"No, the *floor* is reserved for Tove." The valkyrie pushed her silvery white braids over her shoulder, her eyes flicking over my own. It was a power move, I could see it as clear as day. I'd been paying enough attention to realize she'd been able to get what she wanted when she subconsciously reminded people her hair was fully bleached, a sign of age, of power. If I had cared about the valkyrie's hair traditions, maybe I would've been intimidated. Unfortunately for her, I was more than happy with my strawberry blonde hair and twenty-seven years of life. Her age wouldn't force me to convince my companion to sleep on the floor.

I strutted over to the bed, yanking the covers back and stubbornly climbing inside. As soon as my head hit the pillow, Tove came trotting over. He hopped up and made himself comfortable on the pillow next to me—the pillow this valkyrie was trying to claim as her own. I cared little about whether she wanted to sleep on this mattress with me. I'd shared a bed most of my life and was more than used to it. But since my family was taken from me, the second half of the bed was reserved solely for my orange demon.

"Mortal, listen to me," she said. "You can move that cat, or I will use him as a pillow. One way or another, I will sleep in that bed."

"I'd like to see you try to make Tove do anything," I mumbled under my breath, turning on my side and pulling the quilt up around me.

She began stripping out of her armor, placing the shining golden metal on a chair in the corner of the room. The pieces clinked as she went, but I tried to ignore her noise in favor of sleep.

"How can you blame me for what's happened yet refuse to go back? You have everything you've ever wanted here, yet I'm to blame for ruining your life. Explain that to me."

I knew she couldn't see me, but I still tried to control my features. I took a long breath before I pushed the quilt back down and sat up. I wouldn't cower under the covers when I spoke my mind.

"I owe you nothing. Not an explanation, not a spot in bed next to me. Nothing," I said calmly. She may have supplied me food and healing supplies, but not actively trying to kill me earned her little.

"Fine," the valkyrie grumbled. "Have a nice sleep next to your dead cat." She removed her breastplate and placed it on the chair before stalking away, leaving Tove and I alone with her armor.

Did a tiny part of me feel bad she'd brought me out here to avoid Odin's detection, only to have me banish her to the floor in the next room? Of course not. I'm from a family of vikings, and I'm wand-wed. I have no time for such foolish grievances.

Would I be tempted to sneak out of bed in the middle of the night and share one of my many blankets with her? Maybe. But I wouldn't. I'd shown this woman too much weakness already, and if I wanted to make it out of this situation alive, or at least unscathed, I needed to navigate cleverly. Whether or not I'd still be alive was debatable, but at this rate, I wasn't sure how much that bothered me. What *did* bother me, though, was the thought of spending eternity stuck in some underworld prison, away from my family. I couldn't let this attendant of Odin ruin my life, or my death, for that matter.

"Just you and me, Tove," I whispered, settling back down in bed. He purred loudly, making himself comfortable on the squishy pillow next to mine. I swear, the beds and everything on top of them were the best things in all of Asgard.

I stared off into the corner of the room, the valkyrie's breast-plate catching my attention. Something about the groove in it itched at my mind. I'd seen the woman mindlessly stroking her thumb over it, and I had a feeling that one little mark was going to torment me until I uncovered its origin.

I laid my head upon the soft pillow, and I couldn't quite put my finger on when my reality twisted into a string of nonsensical visions.

There was stone and moss everywhere. The rocks grew distended and distorted, and I feared they would hold me prisoner within their depths if I didn't watch my step. How could I feel so huge, yet completely insignificant all in one moment? Hands gripped me, soft yet guiding, and we followed a light that beamed down from the heavens.

The visions flashed through my eyes in a series of images and sensations, and they were as disjointed as the rest. I longed for the days when they showed me exactly what I needed to see, and my future unraveled just as so.

CHAPTER TWELVE
THE WORLD TREE

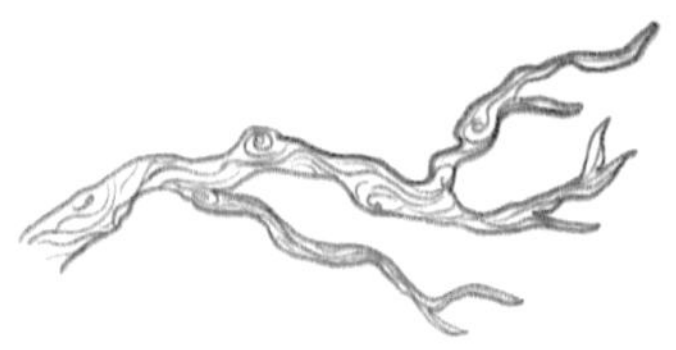

Rune

My neck was broken, I was sure of it.

The muscles along my spine screamed as I straightened myself out from my cocoon. I'd refused to sleep on the floor last night, and the biggest raised surface in the main room had been the hard, too small bench.

Pulling the warm blanket off, I allowed my numb legs to fall off the side and onto the wooden floor below with a thunk. Only then would I start to recover blood flow.

That damned cat has better sleeping arrangements than I do, I grunted to myself.

I'd been forced out of the spare room and banished to the main room without even a blanket to my name.

A blanket, I thought as I gripped the quilt that still lay across my lap. When I'd fallen asleep, I'd had nothing but the fire to warm my skin, yet I'd woken with this mysterious quilt wrapped around me.

Had Kari...

I didn't even finish my own thought, the hope creeping

through my chest too dangerous. But even then, I felt an odd clench in my heart.

"Morning!" Áma called out from the kitchen. "What did you do to get yourself kicked out of bed? I swear, if you leave, and I find that room covered in—"

"There are no crumbs, Áma." I interrupted before she had the chance to accuse me again. You eat an entire loaf of bread in some-one's spare room one time and never live it down, *gods*.

"Well, whatever you did must have been bad enough to be sent away without a blanket to keep you warm." she said, shaking her head in disbelief.

My gaze dropped to my lap. "Did you put this on me?"

"I'm not heartless, you know. You were shivering in your sleep, even with those ridiculous leathers on. Won't you wear a dress? You're not in a war, child."

"Mmm, thank you," I muttered, lifting the corner of the quilt in lazy gratitude. How could I have thought the seeress who despised me had anything to do with bringing me comfort? I'd tried to fight for hers, yet she found it so easy to rob me of mine. "And the leathers are just fine."

"Good morning, Áma!" Kari practically sang as she sauntered into the modest kitchen, a small yawn escaping her lips as her eyes avoided mine. "That bed of yours is absolutely wonderful."

"I'm so happy you had such a restful sleep," I all but sneered at the woman, not able to school my features when fatigue clung to them.

"Give me a moment. I'll fix you up something for breakfast," Áma said to Kari. "Why don't you make yourself comfortable while you wait?"

"Oh, don't you lift a finger to feed me. Rune has already kindly offered to summon all my favorite foods." The seeress beamed at the older woman before flashing me a terribly wicked smile.

"Oh, did she now?" Áma said with a suppressed chuckle.

"Well, I won't waste my food then. Rune, I'll take salmon and eggs. And don't forget the flatbread!"

Don't start a war, Rune. Don't start a war.

I sighed but reined in my emotions before I ended up needing my leathers after all.

My seidr wasn't limitless, and I didn't appreciate using it on pointless endeavors when I didn't know the next time I'd be able to fuel it. Summoning salmon and scrambled eggs for Áma certainly classified as a pointless endeavor, and Odin only knew what Kari was about to demand.

"Ah, yes! How could I have forgotten? One porridge coming right up. Áma, can you believe Kari loves it completely and utterly plain?"

"I don't—"

I cut Kari off when a bowl of porridge appeared above her, and she had to choose whether to chastise me or focus on catching the bowl so it didn't crash at her feet. She, of course, chose the latter.

If this wild creature was going to try to play games, she'd need to step it up.

Kari clutched the bowl but didn't say anything as she let out an annoyed huff and took it to the small table next to the window. She began pushing the tasteless porridge around her bowl with a silver spoon while I focused on making Áma the most fantastic salmon and eggs she'd ever had. Making the feast for her didn't seem so pointless anymore when I could use it as a reminder to Kari that I had her under my thumb.

The three of us, or maybe two of us, enjoyed our breakfasts in silence, knowing we'd have more than enough to talk about soon enough. Áma had checked out Kari's healing wound, cleaning it once more and reapplying fresh bandages. She scanned the damaged flesh for any residual traces of Hel's seidr, and, to no one's surprise, she'd found her signature mark of death despite the lifting of the curse. It was going to take a lot more than a trip to the underworld to lift the darkness of an ancestral sentence off the seeress' shoulders.

"So, what now?" Kari asked.

"Well, we have a few options, though, I admit, some of them are better than others," I said, leaning back in my chair. I crossed my arms and wondered how I'd explain the complexities of the underworld to her in a way she'd understand—preferably a way that resulted in the least amount of questions. "We're currently in the valley beyond the mist, which is close to a gateway to Yggdrasill, the World Tree. Through the World Tree, we will be able to travel to the eight other worlds, including Hel."

"Midgard is between Asgard and Hel. We'll have to travel through it, won't we?" Kari pulled Tove into her lap, a warning not to take her back to her mortal world despite all the bitter words she threw at me for bringing her here.

Before she could get even more defensive, I said, "No. We can bypass Midgard, and we will. As long as you don't accidentally wander through its gates, your precious feline will be fine."

The muscles in Kari's face relaxed.

Peering down at the fat orange animal in her arms, I summoned a bowl of white fish on the floor on the far side of the room. He leaped off Kari with a strangled meow as he beelined it toward his treat. I'd imagined it'd been quite some time since he'd eaten anything at all, and though he no longer needed to, here in Asgard, it wouldn't pass through his little teeth and mouth. He could enjoy the food for once.

I wasn't sure why I'd done it, but I imagined if Apple had gone years without any fruit, I'd want her to have a little treat too. I couldn't let my frustrations with his human cloud my judgement and allow me to take my emotions out on the innocent feline.

Kari watched as her cat devoured the contents of the bowl, a small smile forming on those pink lips. I tore my gaze away from her before I found myself lost to her features and the subtleties of their movements. I wouldn't stare at this woman. Though it felt as natural as breathing, my time watching her was over.

It had to be.

Kari tore her eyes from Tove and asked, "Tell me more about the World Tree. I want to make sure my mortal understanding isn't built off mere legends and tales. You've actually travelled through it."

I nodded and leaned back in my chair, settling in for a long conversation. "Yggdrasil is an ash tree connecting the nine realms. Its branches and trunk extend through the worlds and heavens, and its roots tap into even more locations, including Hel. Asgard is the top realm, in the branches, and Midgard is directly below it, along the trunk. There are, however, many creatures who live within the tree, and avoiding them will be our biggest challenge. They must not be ignored in our plans, as much as I'd like to pretend they're not there at all."

"Jörmungandr," Kari muttered, her lips parting.

"Yes, I'm sure you're very familiar with his story. The serpent surrounds your human world, after all."

"He's the son of Loki and the giantess, Angrboda. All three of their children were born monsters. The serpent, Jörmungandr, the wolf, Fenrir, and, of course, Hel."

"Correct, and we'll have to avoid the first two if we want to make it to the third alive. Jörmungandr won't be our only obstacle, though. Within the World Tree, there's also the dragon, Níðhöggr. Not to mention, the stags and the eagle, and of course..."

"Okay, okay, one creature at a time. Is the dragon...truly as horrible as everyone says?"

"Well, that depends on what side of the war you're on, but in Asgard, he's seen as the personification of chaos and evil and has been known to herald the end of time."

"Oh, good. Will he be hard to avoid on our way to Hel?"

"Níðhöggr is coiled around the tree, where he feasts on its

roots. We're coming down from the branches here in Asgard to travel to Hel, but—"

"Let me guess: that's where the eagle resides."

"Well, yes," I said. "The eagle remains at the very top of the tree, and that wind you feel on Midgard is due to the beating of his wings. But we don't have to worry about him, though, because we are traveling down the trunk instead of up."

I searched around for something to write with so I could better explain the path we were going to need to take from Asgard to Hel. "What I was going to say was—"

"You're forgetting about the Norns!" Áma called out from the kitchen, where she scrubbed all the dishes we'd used during breakfast.

"I didn't forget about the Norns," I grumbled. "I just wasn't going to mention them."

"The squirrel?" she called out again.

"Áma! She doesn't need to know about every being in existence."

Kari fiddled with the edge of the wooden table and said, "Okay, but now I'm curious about the squirrel."

I sighed and ran my hand down my face. I was going to get nowhere if I kept getting interrupted. "The squirrel runs up and down the World Tree, delivering tidings. Mostly, he delivers insults to the dragon, Níðhöggr. I don't know how the thing hasn't been eaten yet."

Kari held back a chuckle, almost as if she didn't want to give me credit for saying something that amused her. Her lips twitched again, but then she took a deep breath and nodded her head, as if I'd told her something as dry as why rain falls from the sky.

"Anyway, forget about the Norns and the squirrel, even the eagle and the stags. Our two main challenges will be the serpent and the dragon."

"Can't we just fly down to Hel on a pegasus or something?"

"I wish it were that simple. The Bifrost Bridge we use to fly to

Midgard would be more than sufficient for me to travel anywhere in the nine realms, but you've already experienced the strain of it once, and it's not meant for mortal humans."

"But I'm wand-wed. I have seidr," Kari said, holding her fingers in the air, her nails skyward, as if she were performing a spell. Those beautiful fingers of hers did nothing but wiggle, and I did everything to contain my laughter, to show nothing on my face but indifference. The truth was, her power was nothing.

But I wasn't going to make her feel bad about it. *Well, maybe just a little.*

"And how old are you? How powerful is this seidr of yours?"

"Twenty-seven, and I'll have you know, my seidr is... Well, I can... It's—"

"Got it. You're a mighty, powerful being," I said. "Let's just stick to the plan of using the gates, shall we?"

Kari crossed her arms and stared at me, telling me with her eyes that she thought I was the least hilarious person she'd ever met, but I'd have to disagree.

I'm funny as Hel.

Áma set a cup of tea down for us each, breaking the tension in the air. I swore, the Asgardian woman hadn't had a glass of regular, refreshing water in the past two thousand years. She lived off warm herbal blends, so whenever I came to visit, I did too. It didn't seem like Kari minded, and I guess I didn't hate the flavor. But between this, the food in my belly, and the fire, I felt too warm inside, and it was making me sleepy.

I need an ice-cold glass of mead and a shock to my system.

I grabbed the tea and flicked my gaze back to Kari's. Her blue eyes bore into me, hard and unwelcome, and that was exactly the jolt I needed. My heartbeat picked up a few more beats per minute, and I leaned forward, setting my elbows on the table.

Who needs mead when you have a fiery woman?

"You seem to have a little porridge on your face," I said, motioning to my own cheek and reminding her of her pathetic meal from earlier, courtesy of me. The intoxicating Aegean blue of her eyes flared, and I had to hold back a satisfied smirk.

"Here?" Kari said, rubbing her cheek, her skin bouncing as she did.

"Still there."

Kari took a cloth from the table and brushed it over her cheek, probably harder than she needed to. Her poor, beautiful freckles.

"Did I get it?" she asked, looking up at me hopefully.

"Nope..."

"Is it gone yet?" she asked with a frustrated huff, her skin now pink and splotchy.

I shook my head, and that simple gesture resulted in the woman looking as if something in her may very well snap.

She pushed out her chair, but I grabbed her wrist. "Let me."

Kari paused, her auburn brows scrunching. Flickers of hesitation danced through her eyes, and for a moment, I thought she'd pull away from me, but then she leaned forward ever so slightly. I took that opportunity to release her wrist, and my hand migrated to her face.

I swiped my thumb over her cheek, and when my finger made contact with her skin, I forgot all about the fatigue that had been trying to claim me a moment earlier.

"Got it," I whispered, my thumb lingering a little longer than it needed to.

Kari sat back and cleared her throat, her hand flexing in her lap. "Thank you."

"You know, seeress," I said, sucking the porridge off my thumb, "I can be quite courteous when given a reason to be."

"And what reason have I given?" she said, not taking her attention from my thumb.

"None. Therein lies the problem," I said, crossing one of my leather boots over the other. "We have a long journey ahead of us, and unless you want fights and plain porridge every day, I suggest you find it in that little mortal heart of yours to forgive me."

"Forgive you? For stealing my life?" She raised her voice, the sweet and deadly sound reverberating off the stone walls. She may have kept me awake, kept me guessing, but she was also getting on my last damned nerve.

"I fucking saved it!" My hand came down hard on the table between us, my cool façade splitting. I was her superior, Odin's favorite. Never in her life had she met a power equal to mine, yet the disrespect she fed me constantly was worse than plain barley, and it left a bitter taste in my mouth. "And until you see that, we're going to have a problem."

"There was no porridge on my face, was there?" Kari scowled.

"Of course there was. You think I just make things up for fun? To embarrass you?"

"I don't know. All I know is I don't trust a single thing that comes out of your traitorous mouth. Even if I forgave you, even if I thanked you for not letting the raiders end me, what good would that do? I'd still be here."

"Yes, you would, but we could move on. I'm tired of—"

"Oh," Kari laughed wickedly, her pink lips turning up without a hint of joy. "I'm so sorry I'm *boring* you."

"Boring me? Never," I admitted. "Testing my patience? Very much so."

She lifted her chin in defiance, staring at me a little too long before she said, "Admit it."

"Admit what?" I asked, tracing the curve of her frown with my heated gaze.

"You being there when I was shot by the arrow wasn't a coincidence."

"I don't know what you're talking about," I murmured. "I follow death. It wasn't odd for me to be in Stormheim."

"You're a gods damned liar!" she shouted, the legs of her chair scraping on the stone floor beneath us.

A traitor, a liar—I was growing weary of this human telling me what I was.

"Leave it be, seeress," I ground out between my teeth.

"Your little name for me doesn't fool me. Neither did the mugwort tea."

My blood froze.

"Fruit tart, anyone?" Áma barged into the room with a plate full of fruit tarts. She placed them down on the table between us and shot me a glance that said I owed her.

"I'd love one, thank you, Áma." Kari grabbed a fruit pastry off the plate, her fingers and jaw tense despite her sugary words. She brought the treat to her lips, and I didn't watch as she took her first bite. I couldn't give her any more reason to suspect me, and if I ogled her over the way she licked her lips between bites, I'd be in trouble.

"Well then," Áma said, a false smile working its way onto her mouth. "Kari, you and I have a few things we need to work on before the two of you head off to the first gate. Why don't you come with me to my incantation chamber, hmm?"

Kari got up, but Áma held out her hand and said, "Finish your tart here, child. No food is permitted in my incantation chamber, only ingredients. It's better that way, you see. I'll meet you there. Rune, show her the way when she's ready, will you?"

With that, Áma was off down the hall, and I was left shaking my head. Pink bloomed across Kari's face as the awkwardness got its claws into her, and a strange urge to pull her out of it took hold of me. I wouldn't, though.

Not until she no longer saw me as a threat.

CHAPTER THIRTEEN
OLD BONES AND ROTTEN SEIDR

Kari

"Rune can be a pain," Áma said, giving me a once over. She held open the door to her incantation chamber, and I ducked inside the stone room with a weary smile. "It's hard to earn her trust, no matter who you are. If you want to make it through your travels with her, you ought to focus on what she's saying and doing, not what she's holding back."

"Yet I must be honest with her?" I asked, glancing around the cluttered room. There were shelves lined with bottled ingredients, several mortar and pestles, and prepared spells. One shelf was reserved for bones and treasures of the flesh, while another wall was reserved for strung up and drying herbs and flowers.

Áma shrugged. "She can be of great use to you. The more she knows, the more she can help. Don't forget, at the core of this journey, she's the one aiding you, not the other way around." The old Asgardian pulled out two stools from under a long work bench and motioned for me to claim one.

"I'd beg to differ. I've stayed alive. She seems to have great interest in ensuring I don't find my death, even if it would've made my path so much simpler. I don't believe for one moment it's out of the kindness of her heart. "

Áma made a chuffing sound. "It rarely is with the gods *or* their attendants."

"So you agree she wants something from me?" I asked, running my nails over the wooden table.

"Who's to say?" Áma said with a shrug. "But does it really matter? If she wants to keep you alive and help you break your curse for good, does it matter if her intentions do not align with your own?"

"I guess not," I admitted, and it pained me to do so, because maybe there was truth in Áma's words. Maybe it mattered little why Rune was doing what she was doing, because the outcome was the same. I didn't have to like her, didn't have to trust her, but I could find comfort in knowing she wouldn't cause my death. That was *something.*

"But the stubborn valkyrie isn't why I invited you into my chamber," Áma said. "When I was scanning your body for Hel's signature, I could certainly feel her seidr, but it was more than that. It was more than the remnants of a curse."

"What are you saying?" I asked. When I took in a great inhale, the scent of elderflower and linseed oil greeted me.

"I'm saying, I want to spend the day with you, watching you perform your spells. I want you to tell me about your visions too, so I can understand your seidr for what it is, not for what you tell me it is, or for what I believe it to be."

"Okay..." I trailed off, glancing around the incantation room for ingredients I recognized. "Where do you want to start?"

"You tell me," Áma said, holding her hand out to the side as an invitation to select a few ingredients. I did as she wanted, grabbing elder root, a knife, and a jar of dried elderberry pigment. I came back to the table and silently began working on the totem, whittling the root, rehydrating the pigment, and marking it with finger-painted runes.

I wasn't sure how much time had passed since I entered Áma's incantation chamber, but by the time I'd finished the first spell, my fingers were aching and my butt was numb from the pad-less stool.

"Well, this is quite..." Áma trailed off, picking up the dilapidated elder root totem I'd spent way too long on. "Pathetic." The thing was meant to keep anyone wand-wed away from the incantation chamber if they had negative intentions; that way, no wicked seidr would spoil the sacred place. But I had over-whittled the roots, and the spell I had cast smelled foul, like the seidr itself was rotten.

"There's something very wrong with your seidr, child. Has it always been like this?"

"Ever since I can remember. My mother taught me her spells, and as I got older and had been her apprentice for many years, we both came to terms with the knowledge that my seidr wasn't quite like hers. It had its similarities, yes, but her spells always felt so... wrong."

"What felt wrong about them?"

"When I cast, my seidr felt very far away, tucked in my body, and I had to coax it out."

"And how did you do that?"

"By putting my own little spin on my mother's spells. I had to make some changes, or I couldn't get it to do what I needed it to," I admitted. "That's what I did just now as well. When you told me to work on a spell I already knew, I picked one of hers and then shaped it in my mind to accommodate my own seidr."

"Mmm. Doesn't seem like you need to rework the spells. You just need new ones," Áma said. She stared at me for a long time, tilting her head. "Walk around the room and choose something that calls to you. Doesn't matter what it is. Don't overthink it, just feel. I have plenty of spells cast on this place and the objects within it, and what you pick may help me understand the root of your problem."

I hopped off the stool and began meandering around the

room. Starting with the wall of dried herbs and flowers, I quickly moved on to the shelf of bones. My fingers trailed over an impressive bear skull before I had the nagging feeling of being pulled in the opposite direction. My gaze flicked over my shoulder to a low-lying chest sitting at the base of the next shelf. I lifted my finger off the old bone and made my way over to the chest.

Sinking to my knees in front of the box, I motioned toward it with my chin and asked, "May I open it?"

Áma watched me intently, squinted her eyes, then said, "You may."

I didn't hesitate to pop it open, sticking my hands inside the mounds of old scraps and odd trinkets. My knuckle grazed something hard and cold, and the instant it did, I felt a strange sense of familiarity. Áma made an odd, strangled sound as I pulled a small wooden box free. I glanced up at her, box still in hand, and she motioned for me to come forward with it. Sitting down at the table once more, I ran my thumb over the indents of the box's wood and stared at her for answers.

"How interesting," Áma mused, licking her dry lips. "Open it, and tell me what you see."

The box creaked open, and hidden within was a totem wrapped in a strip of linen. I carefully unwrapped it, and as I did, I could feel an odd pulsing in my fingertips. When the fabric was gone, all that remained was a small piece of wood carved with a series of small runes.

"That's one of the few spells in this place that was not cast by me, or in Asgard, for that matter."

"Where was the totem made?" I asked.

"Helheim, with seidr of the underworld, carved from a fallen branch of a rare pine tree grown within its soil."

I stared down at the totem for a long while, turning it over in my hands, as if I would somehow understand my own seidr more if I did. I knew what Áma was getting at. The thoughts were connecting in my mind too fast to keep up with, but somehow, I still managed to find doubt.

"With a curse like the one you have," Áma started, "it wouldn't be all that odd that your seidr would have been tainted by it. Kari, I don't believe you've been performing earthly seidr at all. That may have been why your mother's spells didn't work for you, and you adjusted them using seidr of your own. Seidr of the underworld."

"But why wouldn't my mother's have been tainted in the same way? She was talented at casting spells on Midgard. I don't see how mine would've been any different."

"I have no way of knowing, but it could have something to do with the original curse. Any word out of place or misused could change the entire spell. Or, maybe, it was something Hel wrote into her curse, and this was all intentional. You won't know until you speak with her, child."

I blew out a deep breath, trying to read the runes on the carved pine but failing. "Well, what now?"

"Now that we know your seidr may be of the underworld, why don't we try this spell?"

She pointed to a scroll, then handed me some more elder roots. The incantation looked unusual, reminding me of the ones on the scroll Rune had given me. "Do it as it's meant to be done. Don't make any changes to it."

I shrugged and read the runes of the spell a few times before I began bending the roots to my will, muttering under my breath as I went. It took me half as long to place the spell, and when I was done, there was no rotten stench. Áma took it from me with a smile.

"Ah, there you are! It only took using seidr of the underworld to get it right."

I swallowed hard, glancing back down at the elder roots I had just placed a protection spell on. The tips of my fingers felt warm, and I noticed a faint line under my nails, like I had residual charcoal shoved under them.

Áma stood and headed over to her chest. "I want you to stay with me for the week and learn more about this power of yours. I do believe it's unlike anything you've seen on Midgard, and I have the resources here to help you understand it, at least a little more than you do now. You're in no condition to travel with a wounded shoulder like that anyhow."

CHAPTER FOURTEEN
NO GOODBYES

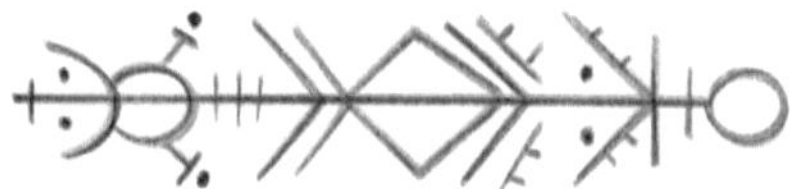

Rune

It'd been a week since Kari and Áma began their lessons, and in that time, Kari and I had managed to avoid each other for most of it. We ate meals with Áma as our buffer, since when we were alone, tension filled the air, and the two of us found some reason to bicker.

One of those days, I was feeling rather generous and put cinnamon in Kari's otherwise plain porridge. The next day, apples. I'd still given her the same meal three times a day, while making elaborate and tasty dishes for Áma, Tove, and me, but until she let me in the bed with her, cinnamon and apples were considered my kindness. She'd been lucky I hadn't let her starve, seeing as I'd woken each day with a tweaked neck and a stiff back.

I spent my days with Apple, flying around the Valley of the Mist and rejuvenating my seidr upon her back. I was using far less than I was used to, not having to cater to every whim of the souls I was responsible for. There was a deep need within me, however, one I craved to fulfill. While I'd wanted a break for so long, taking souls was ingrained in me. If you do something enough, it becomes a part of you, and a collector of the spirits of the slain was who I was, who I'd been for centuries.

Now that I was out of Valhalla, I was still in my leathers, still upon Apple's back, my white hair still in elaborate braids, but I hadn't worn my armor since I'd stripped myself of it on the first night in Áma's home. My body felt light without it in more ways than one, but today was my last day of that feather feel.

Kari had been making progress, and Áma had enough of our presence. While Kari still felt she had so much to learn from her, it was time we moved on, for Áma's sanity and for our safety. While we were hidden in the mist, we were still in Asgard, and I didn't want to give Odin more reason to find us. If he entered the mist, it would be war, and everyone hidden within the mist would pay. We weren't the only ones living under Odin's nose, but we were certainly the newest, and the ones with the most heat on us.

I'd been yearning to see Rayna, and I'd picked up Apples' reins many times to send her a message in any way I could, but I caught myself each time. She had no idea if I was still alive or where in the nine realms I was. I hated to make her wonder, and the feeling that was birthed from the lies and secrets hung over me as heavy as a storm cloud. I'd chosen Kari over my sister, and Kari fucking hated me.

Truly marvelous.

Apple swooped down through two rock houses on the mountainside before nose diving toward the valley below. Today was the day I'd go to Helheim, and I'd be collecting as much power as I could in preparation. Once we went through the Asgard gate, we'd have to go the rest of the way on foot.

The path between gates sat outside the realms. Gods ignored them in favor of the Bifrost, so they were claimed by monsters and traveled by low powered beings willing to take their chances.

I was neither.

Apple whinnied as she landed near Áma's home, and I gave her a pat on the rear. I conjured an apple and tossed it in the air for the bottomless pegasus.

"That's my girl," I whispered as she chomped on the fruit, sending apple juice spraying two feet in every direction.

"She's very beautiful."

Peering over my shoulder, I spotted a strawberry blonde standing with a basket in her hands. Tove sat within it, fat and happily eying down an insect in the distance.

"You're talking to me now, are you?" My attention was on Epli, where I scratched at the spots her armor usually covered. She too got a nice break from her gilded cage, and I'd made sure she'd gotten the most out of it.

"I was never ignoring you," Kari said. "If you haven't noticed, Áma and I have been rather busy in the incantation chamber. Doesn't leave much time for chatting."

"I imagine it doesn't," I agreed. "It's probably for the best, seeing as we'll be getting *more* than enough of each other in the upcoming weeks."

"When you'd told me we'd be traveling through the gateways, I hadn't realized it'd take so long to get to each of them. I didn't expect we'd be in a...purgatory of sorts."

With one last pat, I dropped my arms from Apple and left her to graze. My gaze wandered over to Kari, taking in the lined smock Áma had given her. It was far simpler than anything I'd ever had in Valhalla. The under bust leather supported her, cinching the rust colored fabric of her dress that complemented her hair. She wore a shawl, as she often did, the edges of it embroidered with runes. I studied them, the symbols all speaking of safe passage and blessed voyage.

Clever girl.

"Mmm...well, the trip will give us plenty of time to discover what it is you truly want."

"What's that supposed to mean?" Kari asked, following me back inside Áma's home.

"Midgard, Helheim, somewhere else. You'll need to end up somewhere when all is said and done. I assumed you'd like to be the one who chooses that location."

"Are you girls ready to leave me yet?" Áma asked.

"We'll be out of your hair shortly," I muttered to the woman. She sat upon that gods awful bench, picking pieces of lint free from it. If I heard one little comment about leaving quilt lint behind, I was going to lose it. I loved Áma, always had, but we may very well murder each other if I had to spend one more day with her. "Epli and I need to armor up."

I turned to Kari. "And I suggest you do anything you need to as well. Hooves up at mid-sun."

Meandering off into the chamber Kari all but forbade me from entering, I headed over to the chair in the corner, where my untouched armor lay. Well, it was supposed to be untouched.

How mysterious.

As I grew closer, I noticed my breastplate was askew from its original position. Had Kari tried it on? Had her chest tried to squeeze into the golden plate molded from my very form? Plucking the breastplate off the chair, I inspected it to ensure it hadn't been tampered with in any way. I wasn't sure I trusted the woman not to sabotage me.

When my inspection was complete and no sign of damage or mischief was found, I began strapping each piece of armor on until I was a warrior once more. When I was ready to go, my arsenal of weapons was next, starting with the sword I wore at my hip.

By the time I was done, I had a few more weapons than I normally carried, dipping into the collection I stored at Áma's. I wasn't new to the path between gateways, nor was I to gods and monsters. Because of these previous endeavors, I would take any precaution that felt necessary, and the double axes on my back certainly felt so.

When I stepped out into the hall, Kari stood there in her simple dress and shawl, a basket still in hand. But now, instead of

Tove, it was filled with various ingredients and glass bottles. Her bottom lip stuck out before she sucked it in. She got a good look at me, weapons and all, and said, "Well, now I'm feeling quite under-dressed."

"I think we can do something about that, don't you?" I said with a little smirk, tugging on the end of her shawl.

"You happen to have a spare set of leathers and armor laying around?"

"Don't be ridiculous," I scoffed. "Not just anyone can wear armor like mine." The red and gold metal wrapped around me like a second skin was a symbol of ultimate warrior status. Kari could never dream of getting her hands on it—even if I had a feeling she'd already tried.

She pursed her lips and rolled her eyes. "Then what *can* you do?"

"Come with me." I beckoned her into the spare bedchamber. "You know, Áma was quite the woman in her day. She still has all sorts of reminders of her time entertaining the gods. Before becoming too entangled with Odin and hiding herself away, that is."

"What happened?" Kari asked as she followed me.

"He's been known to enjoy the company of other women outside of his marriage to Frigg, and let's just say Áma knew better than to stick around when it all blew up in her face. Odin kept his ravens on her for a long time, watching her every move until she figured out how to disappear into the mist all together."

"That all sounds way too messy for Áma," Kari said with a surprised chuckle. "I can't picture it."

"That was a long time ago," I said with a sigh. "A lot can change in a millennia." Stories like these were a reminder that while I'd been alive far longer than I'd ever thought possible, I was a speck in the timeline for Áma. My life since has been a heavy dose of death clashing with untouchable life. I'd been surrounded by gods and static features, yet I carted souls off on a nightly basis. My own identity got lost in the mix so easily, sometimes making me feel ancient and invincible, and other times so utterly young and fragile.

"I suppose so," she said, running her thumb down a wooden wardrobe. "Is what you seek in here?"

"Did you do some exploring, seeress?" I asked, thinking of my armor and wondering what else she'd gotten her curious hands on during her lonely nights in this chamber when her lips were too tired to cast any more spells. The skin on the tips of her fingers were already turning black, cursed from all the underworld seidr, and I couldn't help but imagine that sight reminded her of her once cursed eyes.

"Maybe," Kari admitted with a lazy shrug. She stood before me, and while I could touch and speak to her, I'd never felt more distant from her—or the woman I'd always imagined she'd be, more like. Turns out, watching someone isn't the same as knowing them, even if that thought stung, and I had to admit, I was going to need to put some serious work in if I wanted to make things right with her.

I simply shook my head as I pulled open the wardrobe doors. Humming to myself, I slid out a copper tunic and threw it into her arms. Next were the layers of thick charcoal skirts that would swath her torso and legs, protecting her from wayward branches. "These fabrics were handcrafted by the best of the best here in Asgard. No knife can cut through them, and the skirts are heavy enough to keep you warm while not slowing you down."

"And what about my weapons? Fabric isn't going to cut it, even if it was crafted by the gods themselves."

"Are you sure you can handle them?"

"I killed that first raider, did I not?" Kari said, lifting her chin.

"Mmm, yes, I remember very clearly." A small smile snaked onto my lips at the thought.

Nine realms, I love a woman who knows how to wield a sword.

You'd think I'd be numb to it by now, but it was just the opposite. It was now my standard.

"So you *were* watching," she said, all humor falling from her gaze and taking mine with it.

"Is every conversation with you meant to be a trap?" I asked, pushing black leather straps, sheaths, and holsters into her already full arms. "There's a pair of boots in there that should be your size. Try this all on and be quick about it. And don't forget your shawl."

"Rune!" She called out my name as I headed for the door, and it was enough to stop me in my tracks, but I didn't turn around, not until I knew what she wanted. "What about my weapon?"

"You'll get one when I say so," I growled, storming off into the hall, my face hot. She almost caught me again. I let my guard down far too much around her, and it was biting me in my gods damned ass. She and I both knew I was there watching that night, and that it hadn't been the first time, but I wasn't ready to admit the real reason why.

Once I strode into the main room, I began tidying up the seating area before throwing my stuff into a bag and heading out the door. There wouldn't be sentimental goodbyes or I-owe-yous between Áma and I. Kari and I would take our leave, and one day, I'd show up on Áma's step and she'd be relieved to see me, even if she'd pretend not to be. That's how it was between us, and I wasn't about to change things.

Apple welcomed me with a flare of her lips. She demanded compensation in the form of food for robbing her of time. Little did she know, Kari and I would be occupying her time a lot in the upcoming weeks.

I summoned a pile of fresh hay and a large carrot to keep her busy while I put on her armor and loaded my gear onto her hips, including an extra weapon or two for Kari. Her having something sharp wasn't ideal until she knew she could trust me. Until then, she was just going to need to rely on me for protection. And maybe, just maybe, when I showed her my worth and proved I wasn't out to get her, she'd learn to forgive.

Kari stepped out of the stone home dressed in black, leather pieces strapped in various places on her body: one on her hips, the other around her thigh, and the final stretching across her shoulder and back. Each of these would be filled out in time. For now, she had a pouch secured to her belt on one side and a set of four vials on the other.

The wand-wed warrior look was good on her, but I wasn't about to tell her that.

"Here." She handed me her pack, and I took it without looking back up at her.

I kept my attention on the misty mountains as I attached her pack to Epli's free hip and asked, "Did you say your goodbyes?"

"I did, but apparently, you didn't."

"It's not my thing." I shrugged.

"So I've been told," she said, adjusting her stance so she was leaning on one hip.

I let her judgement roll off me as I motioned to the pegasus. "Do you know how to mount a pegasus?"

"I know how to mount a horse," she admitted. "Not quite sure where I would've picked up the skill of riding a pegasus."

"Are you going to sass me all day?" I asked, fighting the urge to cross my arms across my chest. Today, I would play nice, no matter how hard she made me work. The journey from gate to gate was too long, vigorous, and, most importantly, dangerous. If she didn't trust me, it could result in both of our deaths.

"Probably." It was her turn to shrug, but she did so indifferently, as if how she acted, how she treated me, was of no consequence.

I swallowed my annoyance and cleared my face of any emotion as I said, "Do you need help mounting her? It can be a little tricky the first few times due to her size, and, you know," I motioned to Apple, "her wings."

Kari bit her lip as she sized up my pegasus. Then, she blew out a defeated sigh and said, "That would be helpful. Thank you for offering."

I simply nodded, knowing if I made a big deal about it, I would be taking a step backward with her. "Well, come here then." I motioned her forward to where I stood next to the pegasus. She walked over, her attention secured on the challenge ahead of her.

"Do I hold her here?" she asked as she reached for Apple's modified saddle. It was suited for battle, flying, and carting around bottles of souls, not adventures on foot through the countryside, as I'm sure Kari was more accustomed to.

I hummed in encouragement. "Hold on tight, and when I give you a boost, swing your leg over her. She'll keep her wings down, but make sure you sit far enough forward so you don't accidentally kick her."

"Are you getting on behind me?" She looked over her shoulder at me with a suspicious scowl, as if trying to work out how I would possibly get on once she was up. Yes, it wasn't ideal to have two riders, but it wasn't impossible, and Apple was more than strong enough to handle us both.

"Don't worry about me, seeress. I'll get on just fine," I said with a smirk. "Now, on the count of three, you got it?"

"Yes, I got it," Kari said, focus blazing in her gaze.

My hands hovered above her waist before I grabbed hold of her. I had her permission to touch her, and she wasn't scowling at me. She looked...dare I say, excited?

My fingers tightened over the thick fabric covering her ribs, my pinky grazing the top of her black leather belt. "Ready? One, two... three!" I hoisted her up as she pulled on Apple's saddle. She swung her leg over the pegasus' back, smoothly and in control, as if she'd done it a million times. When she was sitting upright, she looked down at me with a satisfied smile, as if she knew she could do it all along. "Looks like you don't even need my help."

"Well, she did dip down for me," Kari said, patting Apple

before facing back to me. She held her arms out expectantly, and I would've had no clue what she wanted from me had it not been for the meow at my foot. I gazed down to see Tove brushing up against my boot. I scratched the feline's head before scooping him up and handing him off to his rightful mother. Kari took him from me, settling him into her lap.

I handed her a piece of leather, and she inspected it. "Is this a harness?"

"Not for you, unfortunately." The words came out before I realized what I was saying. I played it off as cool, purposeful. It was less embarrassing if I looked like I meant to say it. "It's for Tove. I already put the piece you can secure it to on Apple's armor." I pointed to a strip of leather with a metal hook on the end.

"Did you make this for him?" she asked, frowning down at the harness.

"I needed to do something to fill my time while you were off in Áma's incantation chamber," I said with a shrug, as if it meant nothing, as if the days I'd spent cutting and sizing leather and stealing Tove for measurements when she wasn't looking was nothing. "We wouldn't want him flying away, now, would we? Apple never shies away from a sharp turn. And, uh, the strap next to it is for you, in case you want it. It can be attached to your belt for added security."

"That was...very thoughtful of you," she said before strapping the harness around Tove's chubby body. The strap was just long enough for him to comfortably rest between her legs as she straddled Apple. She hooked herself to the armor next, peering down at me when she was firmly secured. "Thank you."

I nodded my head and tapped Apple's rear to let her know I was coming on next. She lowered the wing next to me, and I had to get creative, reaching under Kari to grip the front of her saddle. I suppressed my grunt as I climbed aboard, hopefully looking more graceful than I felt.

"Well then. Let's go to Hel, shall we?"

CHAPTER FIFTEEN
ON THE ROUTE TO HEL

Kari

Apple took off into the sky, flapping her wings as her strong legs pushed off the stone beneath us. I could feel not only the wind on my face, but the push of air from her wings. It hadn't been the first time I'd been on her back, but it *had* been the first time I boarded her willingly, with Rune behind me, no less.

I fiddled with the leather around my waist, reminding myself that Rune would be there if it were to fail.

She'd made this for me?

Intentions aside, I truly was beginning to believe the valkyrie wanted to keep me safe. I hadn't believed her saving me from the raiders was purely selfless, and I still held my fair share of doubts, but she didn't need to make me a security strap to aid in my comfort. She didn't need to make a harness perfectly sized to Tove's body to keep him from tumbling off Apple's back. Knowing I wouldn't be responsible for dropping him allowed me to relax my rigid spine a little.

Rune was on either side of me, my ass pressed to her front. I was more than aware of the contact we made, and each time Apple swooped or turned, I pressed more firmly into the valkyrie. At first, each movement had me gritting my teeth, but I eventually realized I needed to thank her somehow. I had a sense she was enjoying the feeling of me between her thighs. I supposed I could've tried kindness for a change instead, though somehow, this was far easier than sweet words.

Having my guard up and constantly racking my brain for snarky comments *had* been draining. It would do me as much good as her to let that front fall a little. I often found myself channeling my younger sister, Malfrid, whenever I needed something sassy to say. Malfrid was...well, she was something, and while I missed her dearly now, she'd often been the bane of my existence. I'd bet she was the one who'd convinced my other sister to try to off me during the months they lingered on Midgard, haunting our longhouse.

I tried not to think about that so much; the past would do me no good. It'd been years now, years to recover from the betrayal of waking up to see them hovering around me. Malfrid had been corporeal for a moment or two, and I'd risen to the sensation of a pillow against my face. She was a fool to think she would've stayed corporeal long enough to suffocate me. She should've stabbed me, slit my throat, but maybe that would've been too violent, even for her.

I'd been able to shove her off easily enough, and a moment later, any of her attempts at attack passed right through me. The days following her lapse in judgement were awkward, to say the least, and I walked on thin ice, hoping I didn't fall through at any given moment.

Rune shifted behind me, pulling me out of my dark, swirling thoughts. It was hard not to think of my family as we traveled to Hel, knowing there was a good chance that's exactly where they resided. I still wasn't convinced I'd have enough willpower not to see them.

My sisters were selfish when they tried to take my life so we could be taken by the valkyries together. And now, here I was, debating if I would tease them once more, to show them that while they were gone, I could keep cheating the game of death. Gods, it felt so wrong to even think about it.

"We'll be leaving the valley soon!" Rune called out behind me. "Remember to try to breathe normally when we hit the mist. If you struggle, it will only make things worse."

"Got it!" I called out, holding my tongue when I fought to yell out that it would've been nice to know that bit of information the first time around. I'd thought I was going to die. Everything in me believed I'd drown in the sky, the very last place I'd ever imagined my lungs filling with water.

The humidity had almost been unbearable, but I'd kept my eyes trained on Apple, knowing she wouldn't lead me somewhere that would get us both killed. The fact she'd kept going, without even a neigh or snort of worry, kept me going as well.

I knew what to expect the second time around, and I was ready for it. Sure, it would be uncomfortable, but I wouldn't succumb to the thick moisture in the air, and that was all that mattered.

It was daylight this time around, and when we were above the valley, I swore Apple did an unnecessary loop just to show this place off to me. The only other time I'd seen it from an aerial view, it'd been tinted silver by the moon. The water from the multiple falls sprayed mist into the air that wet my face when we flew too close. I hadn't known where we were going, or if it was safe, but now, I could fully enjoy the view.

We took a dip through the sky that had me screaming out profanities, much to Rune's amusement. She couldn't hold back a laugh as I screamed something about "savage belly bugs" as my unique way to show both her and Apple that I was less than thrilled. The sound from Rune had been pure, unadulterated joy. There was no mask, no hidden meaning or sass, just amusement, and the sound of it still rang in my ears.

How hadn't I realized how nice the sound of her laughter is?

Maybe I hadn't heard her laughing enough, not for real. With her, everything seemed like a stony façade. On this journey, I'd break her down if it was the last thing I did. I wouldn't spend weeks with someone I barely knew.

I screamed again as Apple took the sharpest turn of my life, and Tove yowled and tried to dig his claws into my impenetrable skirt. With no luck, he swung out of my lap and into the air. There was a yank on the leather strap attached to his harness, but it held, thank the gods.

When Apple righted herself, I screamed, "Cut it out!" I held on to Apple's saddle as firmly as my chilled fingers would allow, then situated Tove between my legs once more. I tried to swallow down my heart in my throat, but the effects of that little stunt still lingered in my body, as if they were there to stay. My shoulder ached where I'd been struck, even after being healed by time and various enhanced ointments.

"She's just testing you!" Rune said. "Getting all your flight jitters out before we fly into dangerous territory. You won't want to scream if something is chasing us!"

"Do you expect something to chase us?" I called back to her.

"At some point, yes! It's inevitable on this journey."

"Oh, great," I muttered, though I was pretty sure the wind stole the sound before it could reach Rune's ears.

"Just hang in there, seeress. The worst is yet to come."

"Is that supposed to make me feel better?"

"No! Just the opposite," she admitted. "You should never get too comfortable on this journey. There are too many lurking monsters, too many creatures looking to take advantage of vulnerability."

"Are you one of those creatures?" I asked before I could stop myself. She didn't answer for a long time, and I'd thought I well and truly pissed her off.

"I very well could be," she said. "But I won't prey upon you. That, I promise."

"Who will you prey upon then?"

"Anyone standing in our way," she said, and there was no doubt her words rang with truth. Rune could be vicious if she wanted. I knew it, and I hadn't even seen that side of her. She was a valkyrie for Valhalla's sake, one of the best. She'd taken down at least five raiders to save me, and she made it out without a scratch. If I was going to go to Helheim with anyone, I wanted it to be her. If I trusted her, well, that was beside the point.

Apple glided through the air beautifully as we weaved through the mountainside. We were approaching the mist, but I was ready for it. Apple dove through the fissure between two rocks, cutting off the sun's rays from our skin. The path was tight, jagged, and dark with shade, but she made it through without losing a single feather to the sharp rocks surrounding us. When we made it out on the other side, I saw nothing but an opaque haze. It felt as if I were sitting in a cloud, the air so dense, it was tangible. The pressure on my lungs increased, but I just kept telling myself it would be over soon. Just like that, it was.

When we were clear of the mist and the dense air, we noticed a flock of ravens sitting upon the brittle branches of a nearby tree.

"Shit," Rune muttered from behind me, and though I couldn't see her, I had a feeling I knew exactly where she was looking. "We need to get out of Asgard now. No distractions, no diversions. We'll head straight for the gate."

"How long until he knows where we are?" I asked, eying the ravens as we passed them.

"If they're here, he already knows. It's just a matter of time before he sends someone after us." Rune's grip tightened Apple's reins in front of me, and she sent her soaring to the right. One of the ravens launched itself from its perch to follow us, and Rune sent Apple on a wild path to lose it. We dodged under trees, above fjords, into the clouds—anything to lose the pesky black bird.

I'd used to see ravens and feel a sense of peace, knowing Odin was watching over me. Now, I had a prickle washing up my spine, knowing he was spying on us as we tried to make our escape. The raven could go anywhere we could, squeeze into much tighter spaces Apple had to slow for, take shortcuts, and weave through the land and sky like it was made for nothing else. I didn't feel safe or protected, I felt smothered and vulnerable. I realized the gods were monsters of their own variety, and Odin would prey upon our vulnerability just like any of the others.

Finally, we lost the raven thanks to Apple's unnatural speed. The raven was faster than most, being one of Odin's, but it soon tired, slowing to a point of no return. We were in the clear—for now.

We rode in relative silence, and I took that time to weigh my options, just as Rune had suggested. Helheim. Asgard. Midgard. Maybe somewhere else entirely. I hadn't chosen up until this point, because I hadn't thought what I wanted really mattered. At the end of the day, I would end up wherever people weren't either trying to have me or my cat killed. If we could live unbothered and in peace, that was where I'd go. Rune had ruled out Midgard when she said Tove couldn't return, but I hadn't given up hope we would find a god to allow his leave.

I wouldn't hate returning. I had a life, after all, with clients and people who were probably worried sick thinking I'd been taken by raiders. It was the only plausible answer, seeing as there was no body left behind. I couldn't help but wonder how long it would take for my neighbors to start picking apart my belongings, claiming what they wanted. I thought of my box of flower bracelets, my sister's drawings, runes scribbled onto birch bark, the pottery I'd spent days making. I thought of all the ingredients for spells that had been collected over decades by three generations of seeresses.

I had to focus on my environment so the grief of imagining my belongings being stolen didn't eat at me. It was then I noticed the area around us was getting suspiciously dark. We'd been traveling for a while now, but we were still a long ways away from sunset.

"What's going on?" I asked Rune.

"We're approaching the gate. Get ready to land soon," she said, adjusting her hold on Apple's reins. "We go on foot from here. I hope you like walking."

I did indeed, and I was more than ready to sink my boots into soil. I'd take a long trek on foot over flying any day of the week. I was also more than ready to relieve my bladder. I wasn't about to admit that to Rune, though. I'd been trying to ease up on her, but talking about my bodily fluids was next level comfort she hadn't yet earned.

A stone archway appeared in the distance, the area around it drenched in darkness. I had to squint to make out its details.

"Why is it so dark by the gates?" I asked.

"It's a warning we're about to leave Asgard," she said, leaning in so close, I could feel her hair tangle with mine in the breeze. "A signal to turn around and go back the way you came. We'll be landing here. Hold on."

Rune pushed her hands forward, and Apple began to descend, thankfully more graceful this time. No screams were ripped from my lips, even if the tingles in my belly were still present.

When Apple's hooves hit the grass beneath us, I let out a little sigh of relief. Before we could get moving again, I detached Tove and myself from her saddle and leapt off her back. Not caring if we were meant to ride the rest of the way there on her, I experienced far too much relief to have my feet on the ground once more.

"Where are you going?" Rune called out as I strayed from her and her pegasus.

"Uh, I need to do...mortal things," I admitted, trying my hardest not to feel embarrassed by something so natural that quite literally all animals did, humans included. Being reliant on something always felt like a weakness, and I still wasn't inclined to show her mine.

Rune's lips quirked, and she motioned her head to a cluster of nearby bushes. "Go ahead, mortal." As I began walking toward the bushes, leaving Tove behind on the lush grass, Rune spoke from behind me, her tone tainted with amusement. "You should know... it's not an act exclusive to your kind."

My embarrassment grew, and I felt ridiculous for believing otherwise. I didn't respond, resuming my walk to the bushes shrouded in shadow. Crouching behind them, I took care of matters while trying to fight the eerie messages of the biting wind that seemed to be getting more intense by the minute. The whispers in the wind wrapped around my connection to universal energies like a waking vision. They warned me to turn back, to forget about this place. As I searched for a clean leaf, I secured my mental wards to block out the unnecessary warnings. They were there to ward people away from unintentionally leaving Asgard, but there was nothing unintentional about our journey.

When I finished, I wandered back over to the others, darkness falling upon my shoulders like a heavy blanket. We hadn't even made it to the path between realms, and an uncomfortable prickle already ran up my spine. My gaze landed on Rune, where she brushed Apple's gorgeous mane as the winged creature refueled on oats.

I guess I wasn't the only one around here with weaknesses— not that I would ever harm the pegasus to get at the valkyrie. Animal abuse was a hard line for me, and I was kidding myself if I even thought I was a match for Apple. She would stomp on me for looking at her wrong and happily feast on the snacks I'd smuggled from Áma and stashed in my pockets. The woman had been secretly feeding me in her incantation chamber so I didn't fall ill after living on nothing but hot barley for days. We'd both let Rune think she was still punishing me for her sleeping arrangements, since she'd never believe Áma would allow food in her sacred room. I'd managed to break the Asgardian within three days.

"Ready?" I asked as I approached Rune. She glanced up from Apple's mane and nodded swiftly. "Good. I'll be walking from here on out."

Rune nodded once more, not fighting me like I'd expected. I wonder if she did that for Apple's sake.

"Just don't listen to the whispers," Rune said, remounting her companion.

"Oh, I can't hear them anymore," I said with a shrug as I started walking toward the gate.

Rune glanced down at me with a furrowed brow. "You can't?"

"Nope. I enforced my mental shields to block out universal messages," I stated simply, tuning into the hollow space within my mind once more to ensure they hadn't weaseled their way back in.

Just me and my internal voice.

"You...can do that?" Rune asked.

"Yeah. Can't you?" A leaf crunched under my boot, bringing a soft smile to my face—the sound reminded me of home.

"No," she admitted with a frown.

"Well, did you try?" I asked.

"No, but I think I'd know if I had the ability to block them out. Even my seidr has its limits."

I was honestly surprised she owned up to having limitations at all. I thought she had far too much pride for such admissions.

"Hmm, well, you don't need to worry about me. I'm not about to turn around any time soon," I said.

Rune frowned again. "Is this something Áma taught you?"

"No. Why?" I asked.

"Because your Midgard seidr shouldn't work here. It's of another realm, and I didn't think your power was strong enough to stretch across the worlds."

"The gods' seidr can," I pointed out.

Rune snorted. "Are you comparing yourself to one of the gods?"

"No," I chuckled. I was growing more confident in my new abilities, but I was no goddess. It would be blasphemous to pretend otherwise. "I'm just pointing out that it's possible. I've been reading that scroll you gave me on seidr of the underworld.

It's quite fascinating, and I find the spells written across its pages far easier to craft than the ones in my notes on Midgard."

Rune remained quiet for a moment as she took this new information. I debated not telling her, but she was proving to be a worthwhile travel companion so far, and it might bite me in the ass later if I keep my growing skills from her. If anything, her knowledge of my seidr may make her take me more seriously, make her look at me like I was more than a simple village girl.

Rune broke her silence and said, "If our conversions with Hel go well, I'll seek permission to enter the area where she keeps her history. If we can copy some spells over from her scrolls, it may aid in discovering what else you're capable of."

"There's a big 'if' within that plan," I pointed out. "But, I'll admit, I'd love to get my hands on her scrolls. I can't imagine the spells she has access to. Sure, she's the Goddess of Death, and I may kill myself attempting her spells, but could you imagine if I were capable of achieving even one of them?"

"Her curse does live within you. Maybe it's not so far-fetched to believe you have a larger tie to Helheim than we originally thought. You were born with her curse, a seed of her power growing inside you over the past three decad—"

"Two decades," I corrected. "And seven tenths." I muttered the last part under my breath.

"For almost three decades," Rune said, shooting me a look. I suppose she viewed age as a positive, a source of power. For mortals, on the other hand, getting older meant failing bodies and decreased power, even if our place in society was more secure. "Anyway, you may find her hold on you increases when we enter Helheim, so be prepared for that possibility."

I thought about it, wondering how it would feel to be under the goddess' thumb in such a way. I guess I had been my whole life, fear of my own face keeping me from living a standard way, not to mention the spirits that haunted me over the years. The least I'd ever felt Hel's curse was in Asgard, but that only made sense, seeing as her seidr was weakened in a place ruled by the Allfather. Who knew what would happen when we reached Hel.

Rune was right, though, because I had to be prepared for the possibility of my curse returning upon my exit from Asgard. Who knew—once we made it to Hel, I could very well acquire more symptoms of the curse than merely rotting eyes and the ability to see the dead. My stomach knotted at this knowledge, but as I stared at the stone gates quickly approaching, I forced my fears down, crushing them under my boots.

"We're here," Rune breathed. I glance up at her, a mix of anticipation and curiosity fighting for space within my body to replace the fear I was trying to banish.

"Well, here goes nothing," I said, swallowing hard as I took one step under the stone arch. I reached up toward the swirling iron gates, yanking on one, then the other, until there was a space large enough for Apple to walk through. Gripping the cold metal in my clutches, I waited for Rune to enter first. It was so dark here, I could see nothing on the other side of the gate, and I wasn't so sure about stepping into the unknown first.

"If you want to remain on the ground, take this," Rune said, handing me Apple's reins. "Give me Tove. It's best if we all stay together, and you're about to lose all your senses. You won't be able to feel it in your hand, but whatever you do, don't let go."

I handed Tove to Rune as I processed what she'd said. She placed the squirming boy between her legs and clipped him to Apple's armor.

"I'm going to lose my what?" I asked, but Apple stepped forward into the darkness before I got my clarification. I felt a tug on Apple's reins as she was lost to the abyss, and if I didn't want to fall behind, I needed to take that final step with her. With a final deep and steadying breath, I submitted to the nothingness of the beyond, getting swallowed by a false night.

CHAPTER SIXTEEN
A STEP INTO THE ENDLESS VOID

Rune

There was always something so disturbing about hearing nothing but your own endless stream of consciousness. All sensation was lost to me the moment I stepped through the gate into the void beyond. The contact my ass made with the saddle beneath me was of no consequence, and I could no longer hear Kari's nervous inhales. The void was much like the mist—a warning, but I'd pushed through it before, and I knew the scariest thing about this place was what you allowed your mind to tell you.

Kari was too stubborn to turn back. She could have been losing her mind to the darkness, but I fully intended to see her beside me, holding Apple's reins as we emerged on the other end. If she could easily block out Asgard's whispers, she was more than capable of not letting this illusion dissuade her.

One more step, and I was squinting from the sudden blast of light assaulting my eyes. A flood of sound filled my ears, and the familiar feel of Apple beneath me greeted my body. Before I took in my surroundings, I glanced down to where Kari should have been standing.

"Seeress?" I asked, tugging on Apple's reins hanging limply on the left side of her neck. Rustling leaves weren't the only thing I heard, the sound of my own beating heart growing louder.

"Over here!" Kari said, waving her hands above her head from where she sat on a boulder in the distance. "It took you long enough." She stood, dusting her black skirts off and stretching her legs as if she'd been sitting upon that rock for ages. She held a stick in her hands, the bark half peeled off.

"Took me long enough?" I asked. "It's only been a few moments."

"Moments?" Kari barked. "It's been far longer. I thought you abandoned me here."

My blood ran cold.

My brain racked with all the possibilities for why we would've travelled at different speeds. The only thing I could think of was her ability to be seemingly immune to the whispers. Maybe I *had* been crossing through the gate far longer than I even realized.

"Why did you let go of Epli's reins?" I asked.

"I hadn't meant to. When I appeared in the light, I looked down, and they were no longer in my hand. I guess I dropped them when I could no longer feel them on my skin," she said. "Has it really only been moments for you?"

I gave a slow nod, looking her over as she tried to swallow her annoyance. She'd thought I'd abandoned her, and she'd been here for who knew how long, waiting for me to arrive, not sure if I ever would. We were both lucky she hadn't given up on me and decided to take this path alone.

"I didn't abandon you." She knew this already, but I wanted her to hear it from my lips in case seeing me wasn't enough. She blew out a breath, and her shoulders relaxed as she dropped the twig in her hands.

"Alright then." She straightened her posture and wrapped herself tighter in her shawl, the ends oddly tucked into her leather belt. "We should get going. I'm not sure what time it is anymore, but I'd imagine the sun will be setting soon, and we have a gate to get to."

I glanced up; no sun or moon hung in the lavender sky of the path between realms.

"This way," I said, pointing with my chin to the flattened ground littered with crispy brown samaras. Kari scooped up a handful of the seeds, tossing them into the air and watching as they all twirled toward the ground like a disoriented flock of finches. The laugh that slipped through her defenses reminded me so much of the woman I'd thought I'd known. I always loved her fascination with nature's simple treasures that I often over-looked. Over the years of death-filled nights on Midgard, I'd begun to lose connection to anything that wasn't strapped in armor.

As we walked, I couldn't help but watch her. She knew nothing of this place, but she looked at home within this path carved through Yggdrasil. I wasn't sure if it was because of her curse, or because being in a forest again reminded her of Stormheim. Either way, I had to keep my eye on her to ensure she wasn't getting too comfortable in this place.

We walked in relative silence for what felt like half the day, but it was hard to say without the sun to indicate how much time had passed. A yawn tugged at Kari's lips, and Apple's strides began to slow. I was growing weary too, and my stomach screamed at me for food. We'd never stopped for lunch, though I'd seen Kari chewing on something after digging around her pockets. She'd either been taking a chance on something she found along the path, or Áma had given her something for the road. I hoped it was the latter.

Up ahead, I spotted a freshly fallen branch thick enough for us both to sit on. It looked like Tove had the same idea, sprinting forward to claim a spot before we could. I swear to the gods, if Kari banished me to the forest floor because of him, I wouldn't give him fresh fish for a week.

"I guess we're stopping for a bit," Kari said as she watched

Tove claim the very end of the branch where it split off into smaller ones.

"We need to eat and make a camp for the night," I said.

Kari looked around. "Here?"

"If you're looking for a plush bed, you're not going to find one," I said, my words coming out too sharp from fatigue.

"No, it's just... I thought we'd find somewhere with more coverage." Kari glanced at the fallen log, then out into the hazy wooded distance.

"It's best to stay clear of the grooves and crevices within the tree. They've already been claimed."

"Right. Monsters. How could I forget," she said. "Um, listen..." she trailed off, her hand finding her stomach.

Before she could say anything, I created two meals. Instead of giving her a bowl of barley porridge, I created two of what I was craving: nettle soup, a couple of pieces of flatbread, and a large portion of berries to finish with something sweet. The bowls sat upon the log for us, and as we approached, Kari licked her lips hungrily. She walked slowly toward it, as if she may scare it off if she approached it too desperately.

When she finally stood above it, she stared at me, asking for silent permission. I dismounted Apple, summoning a bucket of water and a stack of hay as I patted her on the rear. She snuffed and snorted, and I placed an apple on top of the hay with a small smile. She more than deserved a treat for the work she put in today. Apple wasn't used to having anyone other than me on her back, and the fact that she hadn't thrown Kari off earlier was a testament of her trust in me.

"It's not an accident, and I'm not going to take it away from you," I said. Her eyes lit up, and she descended upon the bowl of soup as if she'd been starved for weeks. Guilt flickered through me as I watched the way she slurped it down with little worry for its temperature. As satisfying as depriving her of variety in her food had been at the beginning of the week, I'd begun to wonder if what I was doing was the right move. I did want her to enjoy my company eventually, and all we'd done was sour the blood between us.

I took a seat upon the log next to her, and my back slumped, my elbows resting on my knees. As she shoved a piece of flatbread into her mouth, her eyes met mine, and she moaned a "thank you". I chuckled in response and said nothing as I popped a berry into my mouth.

When the two of us were finished with our meals, Kari leaned back on the log, stretching out her belly. She glanced at me nervously under thick auburn lashes and said, "I don't want to push my good fortune with you...but I would love some tea. Do you mind—"

"What kind, seeress?" I said, cutting her off.

She bit her lip and put some thought into my question. A smile lifted the corner of her lips, and she finally uttered, "Lavender chamomile?"

My fingers tingled, and two cups appeared, one in each hand. I offered her one of them, and she took it gratefully.

"Hopefully, this will help us both sleep. It's been a long day." I glanced around at the log and the fallen leaves surrounding it, wondering where the best spot to retire for the night was.

Kari simply nodded as she took a sip. Tove trotted over from the other end of the log and found a nice, warm spot in Kari's lap. She mindlessly stroked him as she enjoyed her tea and stared off into the lavender sky.

"How come the sun hasn't set yet?" she asked.

"There's no sun here, no moon," I admitted. "There's nothing to rise or set, but the sky will turn a deeper purple as the tree goes to sleep and its energy dims."

"Once it dims, will we be able to have a fire to keep us warm while we sleep? Or do we need to worry about what the flames might attract?"

"We'll have a fire tonight, but as we get closer to the next gate, we'll have to go without."

"Why's that?"

"Well, we're on the right side of Yggdrasil."

"Dammit. Why didn't I think about that?" she murmured. "I suppose as we get closer to Muspelheim, it's best if we don't lure demons and fire giants from their realm."

I offered her a weak grin. "We'll still need to worry about one fire giant in particular, but let's get past Midgard and its serpent before we start stressing over the creatures who guard the gates of the other realms."

"Deal."

"Speaking of..." I trailed off. My eyes focused on the ground in front of me for a moment before I glanced back up at her.

"Speaking of what? Deals?" she asked, and I slowly nodded as I assessed her. "You want to make one with me?"

"I do."

"I don't have much to offer," she said, glancing down at her borrowed clothes and the pack resting against the side of her calf.

"I don't think that's true, seeress," I said in a low, drawn out tone. Her eyes trailed over me, squinting as her fading guard, the one I'd chipped at all day, solidified once more.

"What do you want?" she asked, her tone sharpening.

"I will get you to Helheim alive and advocate for you once we arrive. I imagine you've been thinking about what it is you want as an outcome?"

"I have."

"Good," I said, pausing to take a sip of tea. "Well, whatever you land on, I will fight for you and your desires, whether that's returning to Midgard with Tove as your spirit companion, or something else. What I want in return is... Well..." I swallowed, not allowing her to see how nervous I truly was. "Your—"

"You better not say body."

I snorted a laugh, feeling the tension in my chest ease. "No, seeress. Your body is something to earn, never to barter for."

Her mouth parted, and her eyes glinted with something unfamiliar before her lips met once more. She said nothing, waiting for me to spit out what I wanted from her, but I was testing her patience as I drew out the silence. I should have thought more about the wording of my request before I'd mentioned the deal, because now, she was staring at me, waiting for an explanation, and I didn't know how to put what I wanted into words. What I wanted wasn't some tangible thing she could offer me in trade for my protection; it was a constant effort, an invisible task.

"You know when we first emerged into the light and began our walk? You picked up a handful of samaras and tossed them into the sky with a smile on your face, as if we weren't on a journey to the underworld. I want more of that. More of that Kari."

"That's not something I can turn on or fake," she said. "But is that truly all you ask of me?"

"I'd know if it was fake anyway," I said. I knew her body language too well to believe some false mood she was putting on just to appease me. It was the same thing as when she pretended to respect me and my position whenever I reminded her who I was. I hadn't earned her respect, but she'd still pretended to give it to me when I demanded it of her, and somehow, that was more of a slap in the face than nothing at all. "But if you can find it in yourself to trust me, to let down your walls and be the version of you I know you're hiding, we could have a much better journey ahead of us."

Kari sat up on the log and set her tea down next to her. "Just like my body, I won't barter my happiness or trust. I can't force myself to trust you or want to be out here with you." Her sentiment sounded unfinished, like there was something else she wanted to say but wasn't quite sure how. I remained silent and waited, hoping the next word was "but".

"Though, I will see your point about potential...improved

travel conditions," she finally said, and I couldn't help but smirk. I nodded to seal the deal before I rose and shook out my legs.

"Well then, I think that's a start," I said. "Now, if you excuse me, I'm off to do the thing that *all* living beings do."

I walked off into the trees before she could say anything else, but I heard a snort of laughter as I went. There was no one like her, no replacement if I couldn't get her to break her walls for me. The life of a valkyrie could match that of a god. I could die, yes, but not of sickness or age. Only battle could end me. Thousands of years could pass before that day.

My skin grew hot at the knowledge I'd never have a reminder like her again. What kind of life was that? What was the point of living for millennia if you didn't cherish life itself? Kari understood her life could end any moment, and I honestly didn't think she'd be particularly devastated if she met that end prematurely. Even so, I fell in love with the way she decided to live years ago.

There'd been a raid in Stormheim, and I'd descended upon the land when the sun bid its farewell. Fire burned in the distance, and not even the wails in the air, nor the tears of the villagers, could smother it. Helheim and Fólkvangr valkyries were already present, picking the souls they wanted most, leaving the rest behind. Not all souls were taken, though. Sometimes, they stayed on their mortal plane, refusing to believe their time was over.

There was no one worth bringing to Odin that night, and I'd been angered to be the singular valkyrie from my sect sent there while the rest of the house was sent to clean up a far larger skirmish in a distant land.

Mutterings of apologies had caught my attention before I mounted Apple. I'd expected to stumble upon someone holding their slain loved one, like I'd seen so many times, asking for forgiveness for any number of things they may have done. But the woman I'd seen with hair like a rosy sunset wasn't on her knees. She was standing, face to face with the spirits of her family. She begged for forgiveness for not being there, for going to the market, for not dying with them, but they all remained silent as they watched her. My gut had tightened at their confused stares. I wasn't sure if her family was disappointed she wasn't moving on with them, or if they were all stunned into silence. Either way, the tears tracking down her face hit me harder than most. I hadn't been sure why, but I didn't want to leave that woman alone.

I'd sat there all night outside her longhouse, watching her cry, watching as the spirits of her family lingered in their home, as if they were still among the living. This wasn't unusual, but what *was* unusual was the woman's ability to see them, talk to them, even. I'd watched her interact with them, wondering if she could touch them in their incorporeal states, what her limits were.

Over the following weeks, I discovered all the best gaps in her longhouse, when she took her nightly walks, and how often she had visitors. One night, I'd heard her screams ring out, and I'd peeked my head into one of the gaps in the walls to let light in.

Kari was tucked into bed, thrashing about with closed eyes.

A nightmare.

Part of me relaxed, knowing her mortal body was safe, but something else within me, the part getting far too curious about this woman, tightened and twisted, knowing her mind was in pain. I'd pushed aside the curtain that covered the gap in the wall, and I'd crept inside. A bluish orange creature had yowled at me, but the feline wouldn't have been able to tell the woman she'd had an unwelcome visitor in the night, so I carried on. The spirits of her slain family, on the other hand, were still something I'd needed to avoid.

As the woman tossed in her bed, her eyes scanned back and forth, as if she were watching a play within her mind. After a few nights like this one, I'd begun to realize what she was experiencing weren't mere dreams.

They were visions.

I'd begun finding myself too tempted to sneak back into Stormheim during the day to see how her routine shifted when the sun reined the sky. My interest had begun getting too dangerous, and I was getting sloppy. It didn't take long for Rayna to catch me, and when she did, I'd received chastising every day for a lunar cycle. She'd also ensured I came back with her to the House of Wings each night. She claimed I couldn't be trusted on my own. During that time away from my little seeress, I'd begun to itch for her presence, even if she hadn't known I was the one keeping her company.

Eventually, I'd pulled rank on Rayna and told her to fuck off so I could resume my nightly obsession. She hadn't taken it well, but she'd listened to me after I'd braided her hair the way I'd used to when she was young and had just been transferred to my sect.

A little yelp pulled my attention back to where Kari and I had set up camp for the night. I left her alone, and I hadn't even armed her yet.

What was I thinking?

My palm found the hilt of my sword, and I crept through the trees toward the source of danger.

CHAPTER SEVENTEEN
LAND OF BEASTS

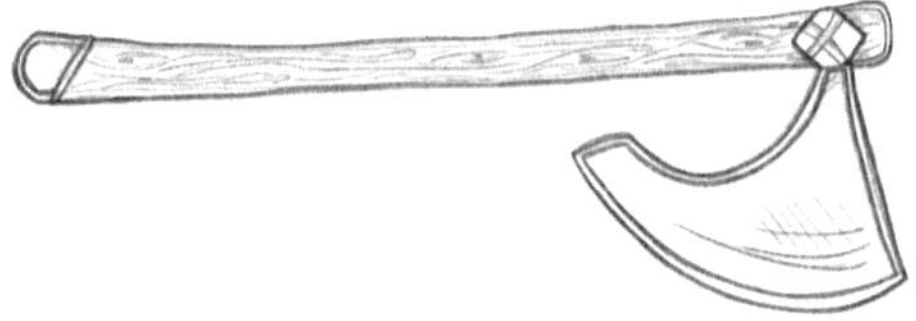

Kari

"What is that?" I hissed as Rune appeared from behind a tree, sword in hand. I pointed to a ginormous hairy beast that moved in a chaotic rhythm in the near distance. Rune pivoted to face the creature, her face set in stone cold concentration. When she turned on the creature, her mask cracked, and she blew out a breathy laugh. She lazily slid her sword back into her sheath.

"What are you doing?" I asked, motioning to her sword. "Take that back out!"

Rune gave me an infuriating smirk, turned to the copper colored beast, and let out a whistle. My eyes widened as the creature turned on us, and I realized what I'd been looking at was merely its bushy tail.

How big is this thing?

A whimper escaped my lips as the creature charged toward us on all fours, crushing bushes under its paws as it scampered across the forest floor. My jaw slackened as I stared up at a ginormous red squirrel.

"Is that—"

"The shit-talking squirrel, Ratatoskr? Yes, it is," Rune said, amusement lacing her tone. "And utterly harmless to us, might I add."

I worked on a swallow as Ratatoskr watched us with curious, glassy eyes. He was quite cute when I ignored his size, my eyes trailing over the braids in his tail as if he were a viking warrior.

"Hello there, Ratatoskr," I said, my throat still dry from fear. My clenched fists slowly released as even Apple turned her rear to the squirrel in an obvious sign of being unbothered.

"Rune Dragomir and Kari Kettlesdotter," the woodland creature squeaked. "State your purpose."

What the fuck?

I stared between the talking squirrel and Rune, wondering if she was hearing him too, or if I was losing it.

"We're traveling to Helheim and no further," Rune said, and my jaw all but fell from my face. I wasn't losing it. She could hear him. "Feel free to tell Nídhöggr his scaly ass is stinking up this entire path, and we haven't even made it into the roots yet."

"I'd love to do nothing more. That limp-winged worm has it coming. You're not the only valkyrie I've collected sweet, sweet insults from today," the squirrel said, his tail twitching with excitement.

"How interesting," Rune murmured. "From which sect?"

"Yours. Odin's. One and the same," he said. The hair on the tips of his ears stood tall and brushed the underside of the canopy of leaves above us. "She called the root munching dragon a brainless lizard."

"Shit," she muttered, and I wondered if she already knew who he'd seen. "Thank you, Ratatoskr."

"Good health to you, Rune," the squirrel said as he turned away. "Better health, now you don't reek of wild revelry."

Rune cursed under her breath as Ratatoskr darted away at breakneck speed.

I guess no one is safe from his insults.

"Do you know who he's talking about?" I asked.

"I have an idea," she admitted, picking up a few thick branches. "We just need to make sure she doesn't find us."

Rune used one of her axes to begin chopping the branches, building the base for a fire. I helped by finding some kindling as she grew the woodpile.

"Is it Rayna?" I eventually asked, thinking of her extremely intimidating younger sister who stared at me as if there was nothing she wanted to do more than drop me over Midgard from a bone-shattering distance in the clouds.

"Quite possibly. She's called me brainless on more than a few occasions," she said. The fire base sparked, and Rune took the kindling from me as she began feeding the small flame.

I nodded and then tilted my head up to the purple sky. It was as dark as I thought it might get, and sleep tugged at my lips as I fought a yawn. Tears pricked in my heavy eyes, and I looked around at our surrounding area for something to lay upon to steal a few moments of sleep.

Away from the fire, hay began pouring from the sky like dry rain, and soon enough, there was a mattress-sized pile next to the log we'd eaten dinner upon. Tove sprinted forward and dove into the pile with a delighted meow, and Apple began walking over as well, her tongue lolling out.

"Don't even think about it," Rune said as she held her hand up to the pegasus. "This is mine. You have your own." Apple let out an irritated snort and retreated to her much smaller pile of hay, munching on it once more. Rune began unhooking the second axe from around her back and the sword from her hips, but I didn't doubt she still had weapons hidden all over her body.

She set her more obvious lines of defense down, leaning them against the log for easy access from her position upon the hay. She didn't look at me as she said. "This is no bed. There are no pillows or sides, no feline to steal my spot. You may join me if you wish."

She nestled down into the hay, distributing it upward to support her head and neck. Yellow pieces clung to her hair, and she surely wouldn't enjoy picking them out in the morning. But as I watched her, my gaze flicking to the damp forest floor beside her, I figured I'd take my chances by her side.

Lowering myself onto the dry pile, I motioned for Tove to take a spot between my legs. He voiced no complaints as he laid upon my skirts, saved from the blades I laid upon. As I got comfortable, I tried not to think about the fact that Rune Dragomir, favorite to Odin, was right beside me, the metal of her armor pressing into my arm with nothing but a shawl to protect me from its cold bite. I was thankful my shoulder had healed nicely and I no longer had to dress the wounds, for I had little energy to do so.

"Try to get some sleep, seeress," she said, her voice hollow with fatigue. "We have a long day ahead of us in the morning."

"Rune?" I asked, adjusting my position so my eyes could trail across her profile. Her eyes were closed, but her jaw was still tense, and one of her hands rested upon the hilt of a dagger hidden within the armor on her thigh.

"Yes?" she asked in return, her eyes remaining closed. The light from the fire lit her features, and I stared at them for a moment before I spoke.

"I'm sorry I can't give you what you want."

"We'll see about me getting what I want. I'm quite skilled at it, if you haven't noticed." The side of her lips hooked up, and her jaw relaxed in the process.

I released a deep sigh, enjoying the feeling of the fire on my back. I wasn't so sure about her getting what she wanted, but some part of me hoped she did, for what she craved was my happiness, and why would I stand in the way of her getting it?

"I won't fight you as you try," I confessed. Something about that admission made me feel like Rune very well could succeed.

"Goodnight, Kari."

"Goodnight, Rune."

We walked for two days until we came across the first gate.

Midgard.

It was right in front of me. There was nothing stopping me from walking right under those stone arches and returning to Stormheim, returning home. I pressed my hand into the stone arch, staring at the iron gates that taunted me. Rune stayed quiet behind me, keeping her eyes out for the scaly serpent that protected this realm.

My eyes dropped to Tove, where he rolled around on his back in a rare patch of grass. I blew out a sigh, lifted my chin, and pushed myself off the stone.

"Let's go," I said before I could change my mind. Rune dipped her head and followed behind me, not saying a word. As we began to distance ourselves from the gate, I caught an eerily slow movement in the distance. Rune and Apple froze, ushering me to do the same.

"Is that a tail?" I whispered, my eyes scanning forest green scales so large, I couldn't believe what they were telling me. I thought the squirrel had been big.

"It is," Rune said. "And we need to stay very quiet as we walk past it."

"Well, we should be in the clear! Tails are on the opposite end of heads," I said, stepping forward into the clearing with a relieved smile on my face. Branches cracked under my weight as I did, but I paid them no mind.

Rune caught my arm with a ferocity I'd never felt from her. "Not another step."

My body froze as I took in her stoic expression.

"He sleeps with his tail in his mouth," she whispered, almost inaudibly. She no longer had to hold me, because those eight words stewed in my mind until my limbs became stone. If he was asleep, his head could be lurking around any tree.

A large dragonfly flew past us, and Tove couldn't resist. I tried to call after him, but my throat was closed shut. My demon cat chased after the flying insect as if it had been his very own toy, and he scampered closer and closer to the beast. The serpent's tail was a natural wall, with scales like stone that stretched into the cloudless sky. There was a *thud* as Tove threw his body against it, clawing the dragonfly, raking his nails down one of the serpent's scales.

Tove! NO!

My eyes widened as the creature he'd thrown himself against began to quiver, as if he was beginning to wake from a deep, dreamless sleep. Tove began taking steps backwards, his movements silent, but it didn't matter now; the damage had been done.

"Shit," Rune cursed, her unease less than comforting. "We need to get to the next gate, now!"

"But the next gate has a gods damned fire giant guarding it!"

"We'll have to take our chances!" she shouted as she grabbed my waist and hoisted me onto Apple's back. She scooped Tove up and threw him at me as if he'd been plaything. When Rune was behind me, the pegasus took off with a nervous whinny.

Her hooves were loud against the underbrush of the forest, and my gut tightened each time a branch snapped, though Jörmungandr already sensed our presence.

The next gate led to the realm of fire giants and demons, and somehow, that seemed more comforting than the serpent that outgrew the ocean, that outgrew the entire world. I became a little faint as I pictured all the drawings and coal sketches I'd seen of him growing up. He was a monster, through and through.

A loud hiss made the ground beneath us tremble, and Rune gave Apple a nudge with her boot to urge her faster. The gate to Muspelheim was close, way closer than Asgard to Midgard. My hope was that if we got close enough to the fire giant who guarded it, he'd secure his territory and ward Jörmungandr off. Sure, even the giant was no match for the world serpent, but they coexisted long enough for me to believe they'd leave each other alone and not steal each other's prey.

"How long of a flight would it be?" I asked, the wind from Apple's speed rushing into my mouth as I opened it.

"It's easier for Jörmungandr to snatch us out of the sky than off the ground. The trees protect us down here."

"But Apple's faster up there!" I shouted. "And we need speed."

Rune was silent as she debated it. The sound of cracking trees echoed around us as the serpent slowly shook itself out of sleep.

"Rune!" someone called out. "This way!"

When I swung my head to see who the culprit was, I saw Rayna on the back of her charcoal pegasus, waving her arms in the air to catch our attention. She was about twenty yards away, though we had a clear shot to her through the trees. Apple pushed herself harder as we picked up speed, and Rune made promises of red fruits as she went.

"Rayna, what are you doing here?" Rune barked as we grew closer.

"Saving your sorry asses," Rayna muttered in that chastising tone I'd remembered so well. "Follow me. There's a groove up ahead I've been traveling through. It's too small for Jörmungandr."

Her pegasus ran off into the forest, and Apple didn't hesitate to follow. I hadn't had time to secure myself or Tove to Apple, so I gripped him tightly with one hand as I held the horn of the saddle with my other. Rune's breath skated across my neck, battling with the chilly wind. I appreciated the reminder we were still alive and breathing as Apple lunged into a crevice within the wood of the World Tree. The purple light of the day dimmed as we were cast into shadows from the tunnel monsters surely had already claimed, but anything was better than being prey to a serpent the size of the world itself.

"What're you doing here?" Rune asked again, now that we were in the protection of the tree.

"I came here to find you," Rayna grunted at her older sister as she dismounted her pegasus in favor of walking next to her. The ceiling within this place was low, and I was thinking she was onto something. I wasn't in favor of smacking my head on some wayward bark. Shifting my position on Apple, I turned enough to be able to look at Rune. She dismounted Apple and offered me a hand before I even had the chance to open my mouth. "All Hel broke loose when you left. Did you really think Odin wouldn't notice your absence?"

"Of course I knew he'd notice. His ravens spotted us as we were leaving the mist. He must know I'm in the path between realms. Did he send you here?"

"What do you think?" Rayna said with crossed arms, a scowl painted across her face.

"Well, what are you going to do?" Rune asked, the two women stopping in their tracks to face off, despite the fact that we really couldn't spare the time. The serpent may have not been able to slither his way in here, but he could certainly crush this entire tunnel in his jaws if he wanted us badly enough.

Rayna and Rune stared at each other with enough tension to walk on.

"Pretend I never saw you," Rayna finally said with a heavy sigh. She dropped all pretense and slammed her armor into Rune's in a hug that was all metal and anger. "Gods, I'm just glad you're okay. But seriously, fuck you for keeping me in suspense."

"I'm sorry," Rune said, clapping a hand over Rayna's back. "I wanted to send you a message so many times."

I stood next to Apple, the two of us watching the encounter. My eyes scanned over Rune's back and the look of pure relief on Rayna's face as she embraced her sister. They weren't related by blood, but that mattered little when I saw the love between them, rivaling that of my blood sisters.

At least they don't try to kill each other, I thought to myself for a bitter moment.

It was hard not to be completely enraptured by the look Rune wore, love painting a beautiful smile on her face. Tove pawed at me to be let down, making me realize I'd been staring, not that either of the valkyries were paying me any mind.

Clearing my throat, I set Tove down and said, "We, uh...should probably get going."

Rayna's attention fell on me, and I expected a grimace that matched that of an angry god, but instead, she looked me up and down, then agreed with me with a simple nod.

"This tunnel will take us past Muspelheim," Rayna said. "I've been traveling through it for days now, long before Odin's ravens spotted you near the gate."

At least we can avoid demons and fire giants, I thought to myself as Rayna asked Rune a slew of questions. We all walked through the tunnel made from Yggdrasil itself, the darkness keeping me vigilant of all noises that echoed off the bark wall. Apple and the other pegasus, whom Rayna called Gunhild, walked with their wings tucked, one in front of the other, down the slender path. This left me and Tove sandwiched between the valkyries and their pegasuses, and I'd wondered a few times if they'd forgotten I was back here.

Rayna mentioned she'd slept in this tunnel on one occasion but was woken by a group of demons who'd been looking for trouble, and by the looks of it, they certainly got it. We had to step over their bodies as we passed them, and Rayna looked pretty damned pleased with herself.

The three of us had used the tunnel until it filtered back out into the forest, and by that point, the sky had dimmed to a deep plum. We were far enough away from the fire realm that we felt we could warm ourselves as we made camp. Rune summoned food for all five of us, muttering something about needing to go for a ride as she did. We all ate in relative silence after a day of talking and strategizing. Rune had filled Rayna in on our plans while Rayna tried to poke holes in it. Each time she did, the two worked to fix those holes. Meanwhile, I had some nice quality time with two pegasuses and an overweight feline.

Rayna had her own bedroll and set up for the night with Gunhild on the other side of the fire while Rune, Tove, and I created another hay bed for ourselves. Tomorrow, we'd be halfway to the realm of dwarves, otherwise known as Nidavellir. That meant we were one stop away from Helheim, and I could all but taste Hel's power in the air like a beacon calling out to me. I hadn't had the courage to look into water or a reflective blade, going back to my old ways of being terrified to look at myself.

But no more.

"Do you mind if I borrow your dagger?" I asked Rune, though her breaths were heavy, and I feared she may have already found her rest.

"You're not going to stab me in my sleep, are you?" Rune murmured, her back facing me.

"No. Rayna would gut me before I had the chance, I think." I let out a disappointed sigh, which pulled a chuckle from the valkyrie. "I just wanted to... I don't know. I want to see something." I stared up into the sky, in awe of its unique beauty, trying not to overthink what I was about to do.

I heard Rune's armor clink as she rolled to her other side so she could face me. Next came the distinct sound of a metal blade sliding out of its sheath. She stared into my eyes, her blue ones swimming with the fire blazing behind me. Rune offered up the dagger, hilt first, and I grabbed it with a slight wobble of my hand.

"You know," Rune started, still pinching the blade between her fingers. "No matter what you see, your eyes will still be beautiful to me."

I tried to swallow the lump in my throat, but my mouth had suddenly gone very dry.

"Can you stop flirting with the mortal? I'm trying to sleep over here," Rayna called out, breaking the growing tension. Instead of getting annoyed or embarrassed, Rune simply smiled and released the blade. I gave her a soft grin in return, then steadied myself, dagger in hand.

No matter what you see, your eyes will still be beautiful to me.

Her words echoed in my mind as I turned the hilt in my hand so the flat edge of the blade was facing me. It wasn't a large weapon, and the surface area of the reflective steel was rather insignificant, but I could see myself all the same. Rune had been right about one thing—my eyes were beautiful to me too.

A sigh of relief left me, and I lowered the dagger after taking a long look into it.

"No screaming. I'm taking that as a good sign," Rune whispered, as if not to disturb her cranky sister.

"A good thing indeed." My chest was light as I handed the weapon back to her. I'd wished I'd had the courage to look into it sooner.

Rune held her hand up and said, "Keep it. I have more than I know what to do with."

"You trust me to have this?" I asked, holding the deadly thing up so the firelight glinted across the blade.

"I told you I'd earn your trust, and that starts by giving you mine," Rune said, her white hair cascading over her shoulder like freshly fallen snow. The stubborn lump was back, rendering me speechless once more. I wrapped my hands around her gift, keeping it close to me, feeling secure for more than one reason.

Rune Dragomir trusted me.

CHAPTER EIGHTEEN
DWARVES OF THE NEW MOON

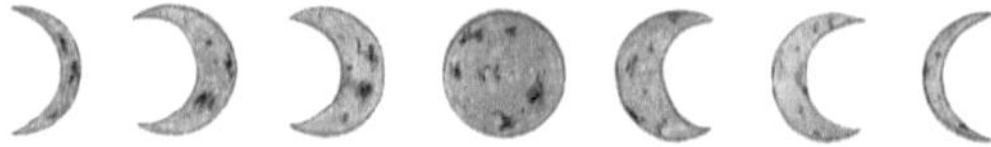

Rune

We all stood in front of the gate to Nidavellir. There were no serpents, fire giants, or a creepy black nothingness threatening to swallow us whole, because unlike the first few gates we encountered, the entrance to the realm of dwarves was quite discreet. Kari had walked right past it, thinking nothing of a large, curved branch from which vines cascaded.

Pulling the curtain of foliage to the side to show the iron gate hidden behind it, I held them in place and said, "After you."

Rayna took it upon herself to stalk in front of Kari, Gunhild right behind her, muttering something about how insufferable I was being. Kari offered me a sheepish smile as she and Tove snuck under the branch next. Apple and I followed shortly after, and I took one last glance into the dimming sky before stepping through the gate, pulling it closed behind me and securing it with a *click*.

There was no use spending another night in a pile of hay when there were perfectly good inns in Nidavellir, even if you had to push two of the beds together. I hadn't visited in a few years, but Rayna, a couple of other sisters, and I had taken the Bifrost on our respective pegasuses more times than I could count over the centuries.

Once we walked through the gate, we weren't met with unnatural whispers or man-eating snakes or demons. What we *were* met with was music, sweet, earthy music. It was dull and rhythmic, emanating from somewhere underground. It'd been a long time since I'd come through the Nidavellir gate.

I glanced around at the mountainous region to get my bearings, pretending I didn't see Rayna and Kari watching me out of the corner of my eye. Striding forward, I followed the music, something scratching at my brain, telling me to remember. I let my feet take me, as if the muscles held memory. The others followed me, glancing up at the new moon as they went. Kari was in for quite a treat tonight, and anticipation crept up my spine at the prospect of what may come out of our time here. Nidavellir wasn't named after the new moon for nothing.

When we approached the base of the first mountain, I said, "This is as far as the pegasuses can come." My gaze locked on Apple, then on Gunhild. Kari turned to find Tove, and when she did, a shriek escaped her lips, her hands flying to her mouth.

"What happened to him?" she asked, motioning to her once orange cat, who was now incorporeal and tinted blue.

I placed my hand on her shaking arm. "It's okay, seeress. Nidavellir is not of the heavens or the underworld, much like Midgard. Once we leave, he'll be his orange, solid self again, I promise. While you've been getting used to him seeming like he's living once more, you have to remember, Tove is still a spirit."

Kari stared at her companion and then nodded her head.

"He'll be safe here with Epli and Gunhild. If he tries to run off to find you or get into trouble, they'll know what to do."

Kari let her head tilt to the side, then let out a sigh. She blew a kiss to Tove as he released a loud meow, seemingly unbothered by his slip back into ghosthood.

I left more than enough food and water behind for the pegasuses so there would be no battles over resources. It wouldn't be the first time. When the second half of our traveling party was secured and comfortable, I led the rest of us through a passage of rock until we came upon a granite slab jutting from the soil.

I placed my palm upon it and ushered Kari and Rayna to do the same. Once we did, the granite sank into the soft ground, swallowed up by the realm itself. I hopped over the mud from where it disappeared and landed on the start of a stone path. The path was a staircase that descended into the depths of Nidavellir, and as we descended, the music grew louder. There was nothing to guide our way but the eternal flames mounted upon the stone walls every few paces, casting shadows across rock.

"What's going on?" Kari asked as we were funneled into a large cavern. Dwarves were everywhere, dancing, singing, and drinking horns of ale. Lanterns were strung up from stone wall to stone wall, bathing the dwarves in an orange glow. Someone bumped into Kari, spilling frothy ale down the front of her. She let out a shocked hiss in return, but the dwarf who'd bumped into her didn't seem to notice over the flutes and lyres and the people cheering around us.

Light typically filtered into the cavern, designed specifically for the moonbeams to reach the depths of the cave. On a night like tonight, when the moon was hidden, the lanterns had to work double time. In the center of the high stone ceiling, there was a large gap where the moon would be shown only during a precise time of the night. When the new moon morphed into the faintest crescent, beginning the lunar cycle over once more, the joyous occasion turned wild.

Kari's hand on my arm brought my attention to her, her forehead creasing. I realized I'd ignored her. "Sorry, seeress. It's hard not to get distracted on Nidavellir. As you'll soon understand, there's never a dull moment in this realm," I explained as I began maneuvering us around the outskirts of the cavern to avoid the crowd and stay out of ale-spilling range. "Tonight is the new moon, and the dwarves worship said moon. Each lunar cycle, sometimes even twice, the dwarves will celebrate the presence of their source of power. When they bask in the darkness of the new moon, it refuels their seidr levels, like how I need to ride upon Apple. Seeing as the new moon is the start of the lunar cycle, it represents new beginnings, and the dwarves believe that's something to be celebrated."

"And they celebrate...hard," Rayna added, her lips tilting up at the corners. I swore, if Rayna had to reside anywhere in the nine realms, throwing away her life as a valkyrie, she would settle here. She left the drinking to me most of the time, but the woman knew how to indulge when the weight of her Asgardian duties lifted from her shoulders. Between the ale and the world's finest smiths, she'd get on here no problem.

I caught Kari watching Rayna as if she'd noticed she was a person with actual emotions for the first time. Her attention then shifted to me and the hand that still held my metal-coated arm as I directed her to a network of underground tunnels. Only when we crossed the threshold into the first tunnel did she let me go. I didn't bring any attention to her desire for guidance, hoping if I acted as if it hadn't filled my stomach with butterflies, she might do it again upon reaching another crowd. And tonight, we surely would.

Rayna's favorite tavern was up ahead, lanterns mounted onto either side of the stone façade. Dwarves funneled in and out, a drink in each hand, some freshly topped up with an amber-colored ale and others drained, leaving nothing but foam to tell you what it once held. My younger sister pushed her way to the front of the tavern, where a granite bar top glistened with sticky substances, and I found myself hoping it was all ale and nothing more potent.

When I noticed Kari trapped behind a group of drunk dwarves who'd decided they'd start an arm-wrestling challenge right in front of her, I grabbed her hand and pulled her toward me. One of the dwarves shot me an irritated glance when they were shoved to the side to make room for her, but when they spotted my armor, their bearded jaw fell slack, and all they could do was admire the craftsmanship. That tended to happen here, which gave my sisters and I a little leg up around these parts. Quality metalwork would never cease to catch the attention of a dwarf.

"What was that about?" Kari asked, glancing at the dwarf, who now was gathering the attention of their companions.

I gave her a shrug and said, "They can't help themselves."

"What, you think you're just that attractive?" she asked, holding back an eye roll.

I snorted, giving her a once over to understand the harsh edge in her tone. I couldn't tell if she disagreed with that logic or simply didn't love the idea that a group of people were fawning over me. "You jealous, seeress?"

"Hardly." Her jaw was set, and she stared after Rayna, where she secured our spot in line.

"Well good, because it's not me they like. It's what I wear."

Understanding flashed in Kari's eyes, and maybe I was imaging it, but I swore, an embarrassed blush crept over her cheeks. "Your armor. Of course. I presume a dwarf seeing what you have on your body is the equivalent of a viking running into a battle."

I chuckled and nodded my head in agreement. Kari smoothed a hand down her skirts until she remembered she was covered in some strangers' abandoned beverage. She grimaced, but Rayna waving her arms above her head to catch our attention quickly stole Kari's annoyance. I hadn't realized Rayna was no longer standing next to us; somehow, she'd managed to secure a table for three amongst the chaos.

"How did you get so lucky?" I asked once we got close enough.

"A couple dwarves asked if they could touch my armor, and well..." Rayna glanced at the table. "I told them I'd do a trade."

"Nice work," I chuckled, and even Kari seemed quite happy with my younger sister.

The three of us took our seats and, shortly after, a dwarf with deep, brown eyes and braided auburn beard greeted us. "Ah ha! Many happy greetings, valkyries! Why do I have the pleasure of seeing you again so soon?"

"Alvion," Rayna said, clapping the back of our old friend. "I was hoping you'd be joining in on the celebrations tonight, not working."

"My duties will expire within the hour. I'll catch you out there for a dance or two, don't fret," Alvion said with full cheeks and a toothy smile. "Who's this you've brought me?"

"Greetings Alvion, and merry moon. This is Kari, our…" I trailed off, searching my brain for an appropriate title for her.

"Hi, Alvion! It's nice to meet you," Kari cut in. "Rune and Rayna have brought me from Asgard. I've never been to Nidavellir. Can you believe it?" Kari said, far more enthused than I expected.

"Well, nice to meet you, Kari. Welcome to the greatest of the nine realms. If you don't believe me now, you will before the night is up." Alvion offered Kari a warm welcome, then turned to me and Rayna. "Look at you girls, making friends outside the House of Wings. Proud of you."

"You're a…friend outside the House of Wings," Rayna pointed out.

"Well, I always thought I was your very special exception," Alvion said. "Who we spend our time with aside, I'm happy to see you all. Can I grab you all some food, or are you just celebrating with ale tonight? There's no wrong answer."

"We'll take three of whatever the stew of the night is, plus three ales," Rayna said, slipping more coin than necessary into Alvion's apron. As responsible as Rayna was, she cared little about being smart with her coin. If she loved something, she was going to spend her coin on it. If she cared for someone, she had no limits on showering them with gifts or paying extra for something as simple as stew. If she valued you, she made it known.

Alvion patted his apron pocket, then brushed his hand over

Rayna's shoulder. "Oh, how I love when you come to visit," he chuckled. "Three horns of ale and three bowls of boar and mushroom stew, coming right up!"

Alvion left us, calling to someone behind the bar. "Ay! These ladies are our first priority, hear me?" Alvion's work companion nodded over to us before they resumed hastily filing mugs of ale.

"He seems nice," Kari pointed out. Rayna agreed, and as we waited on our food and drink, she began telling Kari the story of how we'd met the man many years ago. It'd been Rayna's first time leaving Valhalla since she'd transferred to our sect; traditionally, sisters weren't permitted to travel within their first five years of service. I, on the other hand, didn't want to wait another four years to take Rayna out into the realms. Sure, she'd seen Midgard, and she'd spent more time in Fólkvangr, but Midgard was our work, and Fólkvangr was still in Asgard. Rayna had needed to loosen up more than anyone I'd ever met, and the only place I'd thought might make her more tolerable for the rest of the sisters was Nidavellier.

Alvion came back with ales and stews, and we sipped and ate while Rayna recounted that first night in this very tavern from her point of view. Sure, some of the details were a little hazy, and her recollection was slightly different than mine, but I didn't think either one of us would ever forget the sight of Rayna attempting to dance.

She's always been the more disciplined of the two of us, but after a few too many tankards of dwarven ale, she'd been grinning like a fool, spinning in circles with wild abandon. Unfortunately, she hadn't quite had the hang of it. At one point, she'd tripped over her own boots and sent a table full of dwarves scattering with a mighty crash. The room had fallen silent for a heartbeat, but then the dwarves burst into raucous laughter, cheering her on as though she'd been the victor of the night.

Kari laughed so hard, actual tears came streaming out of her eyes, and she had to put down her half-empty cup to avoid the choking hazard. I watched in awe as her entire face lit up, and I couldn't help feed the spark of joy within me, finally seeing the two women get along. Somewhere along our night, Rayna had stopped acting like Kari was the biggest inconvenience to her otherwise perfect life, and once she had, Kari seemed to have no issue enjoying Rayna's company. By the time the mortal's second cup was gone, she even seemed to be enjoying *my* company.

When our bellies were full of stew and bread, I settled into my stool and sighed, listening to Rayna and Kari chatting away. I didn't think Kari would win my sister over so quickly, but maybe Rayna was starting to see why I've been so enraptured by her. Maybe not entirely in the same way as me, as Rayna preferred her lovers to be more muscular and much hairier, but I hoped she understood me better now.

"Rune? Is that you?" A small dwarf pushed through the crowd, her dark chestnut hair braided down to her waist. Her short beard was textured and wispy, and she ran her fingers through it as she grew closer. "Ah! It is. I'd know that head of white hair anywhere."

"Nori!" I shouted, hopping out of my chair. I brought the woman into my arms before pushing her back out again to get a good look at her. She wore a layered green gown with mock armor detailing her chest and bodice. Her warm, brown hands were still calloused and stained with soot, even if she dressed up for the occasion. "What are you doing here?"

"You know I always come back home for the new moon. You should've told me you were coming. We could've travelled here together," she said.

"Nori," Rayna called from behind me, not bothering to get out of her seat, offering a respectful salute all the same. "This was a rather spontaneous trip," she admitted.

"Ah, well, next time," Nori's brow crinkled, and her pointer finger moved up to my chest. She pressed it into the gouge in my armor. "You've got to let me fix this. Come by my shop when you get back to Asgard. Can't have you walking around like this. My reputation can't handle it."

"Your reputation will be just fine. You're the best smith in every realm," I laughed. "I think I'm going to hang on to this for a little while." I motioned to the mark on my armor.

She clucked her tongue in disappointment, and I knew full well I was practically refusing her life's work. She was recruited by Odin to fashion armor for his valkyries, and even if she knew Odin wouldn't be pleased by this act of rebellion, this armor that wrapped me was her art, and it must have pained her to see it damaged.

"Suit yourself, but when you change your mind, you know where to find me." Nori squeezed my hand before getting lost in the crowd once more. She'd left before I could even introduce Kari, but I had a feeling her pride was wounded. If I could ever return to Asgard, I'd be sure to make it up to her.

When I sat down at the table once more, Kari asked, "Why don't you want her to fix your armor?" She pulled her shawl over her shoulders, and her eyes sparkled in the lantern light.

"Ask me again after a horn of ale," I said, my throat a bit rough.

"Why after a horn?" She leaned in, her curiosity getting the best of her. I almost wanted to place my hand over my chest to block the mark from her view, but then again, I didn't mind her staring.

"I'll be drunk by then, and the truth will find me easier," I admitted.

Over the next while, I fought between slowing my pace to delay the inevitable and taking greedy gulps to get on the same level as my companions. I wanted Kari to know me, to understand me, but I also feared how she might look at me when I bore myself to her.

One more ale down, and Kari flicked my empty mug.

"So tell me," she said with a wobbly voice. "Are you drunk yet? What's the gouge in your armor from?"

Rayna straightened and her face dropped. I may have not explicitly told her how I acquired the groove in my armor, but she'd seen me before I'd gotten it, then shortly after, and she was smart enough to put two and two together. My sister squeezed my knee under the table, then excused herself in the name of having too much ale in her too small bladder. When she made her escape, I had a feeling I wouldn't be seeing her for a while.

"I'm getting there," I admitted with a tentative smile. Part of me wanted so badly to tell Kari my truth, and this seemed like a nonthreatening start. There were the facts, and then there were the emotions beyond them. Kari would get the facts, and depending on her answer to them, I'd determine if telling her the emotions behind them felt...safe.

I took a big swig of her amber ale, savoring the flavor and the mere fact that it had been different from my nightly mead. "Interacting with mortals on Midgard is frowned upon, to put it lightly. We collect their souls, interact with their last moments, but we should never linger to see the loved ones left behind, the survivors. We have a job and shouldn't waiver from it. And we certainly should never, ever harm the mortals in any way, because not only would that be interaction, but it would be inter-ference."

"Okay..." Kari said, encouraging me to go on. She laced her fingers through each other and sat them on the table, as if I had her full attention. Kari was locked in on me, taking in every word, and I found the level of interest in her blue gaze to be frighteningly distracting.

"I was, of course, nearby when you got attacked. We valkyries aren't supposed to take sides, but let's just say, raiders have never flown up to Valhalla with me. So, when I saw you get struck with that arrow, something just...broke in me. I was tired of seeing good people get hurt, and yes, I could sense you were good, through and through," I tacked on so she didn't accuse me of knowing things I shouldn't. I felt the alcohol working its way through my veins, but not enough to slip up. I was paying too much attention to my words for that.

"I acted when I took oaths not to. There were six raiders emerging from the trees around you, not including the one you'd already taken down. Despite being a warrior, I've never been in a true battle. Sure, there are mock battles in Valhalla every day to give the residents a taste of action and glory. The valkyries take turns fighting in them to keep our skills sharp and give the souls a challenge. But when I swung my sword at the raiders, they would not get back up, unlike those I'm used to fighting. I think something about knowing I'd be causing their true death had distracted me enough to allow one of the raiders to land a blow on my chest piece. My armor is much stronger than any raider weapon, but it still left its mark on me, in more than one way."

Kari nodded her head in understanding, her brows pulled in as she did. I stole another sip of ale, feeling raw and exposed, though I hadn't even reached the deepest layers of my feelings yet.

"Were those the first people you killed?" she asked.

"No," I admitted. "Though it'd been a bit. Sometimes, people come after us while we collect souls, whatever their reason. I know better now to see it coming, but I didn't always. Self-defense never breaks oaths, though."

"Was it the first time someone had managed to damage your armor?" she asked, and I understood the reason behind these questions. She didn't just want to know how I got the mark. She wanted to know why I'd kept it.

"You don't live as long as me and fight as much as me without acquiring damage to your armor along the way. We have dwarves living on Asgard, like Nori, who mend our gear, be it weapons or armor," I said. "The reason I didn't have it mended, well..."

Gods, why is this so difficult?

Kari stared at me with her big blue eyes, and I couldn't tell anymore what she wanted. Would she run when I told her the truth? Grab my hand in understanding? I had no clue, and the ale-induced haze around her was starting to play tricks on my mind. Was she smiling at me? Or was that just my desire?

"It reminds me of you."

"Of me?" Kari's hand found her chest, and she held it there as if to stabilize herself.

Is that a look of horror?

She hiccupped, then laughed, then said, "Rune, why do you need a reminder of me? I'm always around you."

Not horror.

Relief spilled through me, and I let out a long exhale as I watched her. She stared at the groove, and I wondered if she thought I was being ridiculous, or if a small part of her was flattered.

"Can I touch it?" she asked.

"Touch it?"

Kari bit her lip and nodded. She tapped the hand closest to me on the table, already impatient for my permission.

"You may."

Kari leaned across the table, her hand inching forward. I couldn't feel as her fingers traced my armor, but I was acutely aware of the sensitive skin that lay beneath, the same skin that craved to be shed of layers of leather and metal, to be touched by warm flesh and curious hands.

I tried not to hold my breath, but her hand lingered far longer than I ever expected. Was I expected to say something? Even if I believed I should, that didn't mean I was capable of forming speech.

"Why do you want to be reminded of me, Rune? I'm right here," she whispered. "Are you expecting me to leave?"

"I hope not," I confessed. "But I always want to remember the oaths I broke for you, because that day fundamentally changed me. *You* changed me."

Kari tucked her chin inward, her eyes cast down before dragging them back up to meet mine. A small smile played at the corner of her mouth, and nine realms, did honesty feel good. She wasn't screaming at me or storming away; she was fucking smiling, and that smile was directed toward me, of all people.

"I don't see how I could've done that," she said. "Maybe breaking your oaths did, but not me."

"Yes, you. You make me yearn for something different than what I have, and I don't know if I love that or hate that about you. I suppose I haven't been content for a long time now, but you have both been the bandage on that pain and the source of it."

"How have I been the source?" she asked "Wait, no, how have I been a bandage? It could be the ale, but I don't understand you, Rune Dragomir."

"Iris Ariti," I said.

"Is that...your real name?"

"It is. I haven't spoken it in decades, but I wanted you to know it. It's not something we're supposed to share with our sisters. Anything that pulls us back to our past lives, our 'dead lives', is not to be discussed."

"I-I don't like that," Kari stuttered, her eyes watery, seemingly from the ale working its way through her. I would never assume she'd get emotional on my behalf, but she *was* two and a half horns deep into dwarven ale, and, well, her mortal body was surely feeling the effects.

I should probably slow her down before she forgets everything I tell her and we have to have this conversation all over again, I thought to myself, eyeing her mug.

"You shouldn't have to hide who you were before Odin made you into what he wanted you to be. You and your sisters were all people before him and Valhalla. You had lives, mortal lives, families, lovers. He can't just take that away overnight."

I chuckled, casually sliding her mug to the side in a way I hoped she wouldn't notice. "No lovers, and the family was questionable, but I certainly had a life, one that didn't include plans to be a valkyrie. But it happened one day, nonetheless, granted by a god ruling a distant land and people who were not my own."

When Kari went to take another swig, her hand fell onto an empty spot on the table. She looked down, frowned, then glanced around for her missing drink. When she looked up, she wobbled on the stool, and I shot forward to grab her arm so I didn't lose her to the sticky floor.

"What do you say we find a room for the night, hmm?" I cooed, knowing she wouldn't make it much longer if we stayed in this tavern.

"But we didn't even get to dance!" she gargled, the alcohol hitting her hard, making me fear what the rest of the night was going to look like.

"You're right," I said, my grip loosening on her. "How about you show me your favorite move? This song is beautiful. It'd be a shame if we wasted it."

"I'm not dancing *for* you," she said. "I want to dance *with* you!"

"Alright, alright," I chuckled, and it probably was for the best that I stood beside her in case she went down like a sack of potatoes.

Kari leapt off the stool and crashed into a nearby dwarf. He didn't even seem to notice, because while shorter, dwarves were sturdy, and it would take a lot more than a wand-wed mortal with below average muscle mass to knock one over.

Kari mumbled her apologies, righting herself on our makeshift dance floor. She started off strong with a few sways of her hips, but when she attempted a spin, I grabbed her hand and pulled her close to me. Her feet were tangled, and all that held her up were my arms.

"Careful, seeress," I spoke into her hair. "I'd hate to see a perfect apple bruise."

CHAPTER NINETEEN
A VALKYRIE IN MY BED

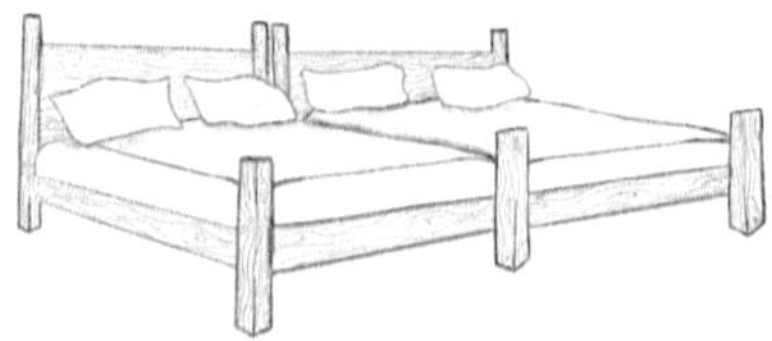

Kari

"But how does it glow?" I said, poking at the moss growing out of the cracks in the wall. I could barely hear the music now, but this moss seemed like it was still enjoying the celebration.

Is this moss blushing at me?

Rune grabbed my hand and held my fingers up. They had faded to their usual color after taking a break from practicing the last few days. That'd been weird. Charcoal-dipped fingers. It'd never happened to me on Midgard, but then again, my spells sucked there, and the spells on the scroll Rune gave to me spoke to the seidr that lived within me.

"How can you cast spells?" Rune asked, still holding my fingers in the air.

I shrugged as she led me up the stone steps of the inn, bidding farewell to that flirty moss. "I have seidr. I'm fancy like that, I suppose."

An odd sound came from Rune, and when I looked at her, she pressed her lips together to silence it. "The moss is fancy too," she said with a smile.

"That makes sense." I nodded in response, seeing more moss ahead as it lit our path up the stairs. I quickened my step to meet it.

Hello, fancy, flirty moss.

Rune pulled me away from this one too, and I felt a pout on my lips as she did. The shiny valkyrie held a brass key in the hand that didn't hold mine, and she tapped in on the stone next to her as we went.

When we reached the next floor, there was a circular room with a cluster of chairs. On the outskirts of the room were doors embedded into the rock. Rune moved me four doors down and began wiggling the key into a hole next to the knob.

The next thing I knew, we were in the room, and she was dragging two beds together. They were wide beds, big enough for two people, but they were too short for either one of us. Once pushed together, we had one standard sized bed, big enough for a seeress and a valkyrie.

"Where's my cat?" I asked, my head swinging around.

"He's with Epli and Gunhild, remember?"

"Oh yeah," I sighed, sinking down onto the bed. It was quite soft; I'd assumed they'd be made of stone. We were under a mountain, after all. As my back hit the bed, my heart ached for my sinister boy. "I've never slept alone."

"You won't be alone," Rune said as she began unlacing my boots. I didn't stop her; my feet were sore and my belly was so full, if I folded to take them off myself, I wasn't sure what would come out of me.

"But you're not going to curl up by my head and purr all cute," I sighed. She really couldn't compare. "You're very hard and shiny. That's not very cuddly of you."

"I won't purr, but maybe if you're lucky enough, I'll snore," she said. "And I'm not hard once my armor comes off."

"Yes, you are."

Rune cocked her head, and I rolled my eyes. Didn't she know what she looked like?

"Your muscles are so hard. Not cuddly at all."

Rune barked a laugh, and I propped myself up on my elbows to watch her face light up. I liked that laugh.

"I won't be flexing them in my sleep. I can be soft for you if you wish."

"Okay, okay, I accept. You may sleep with me, and I shall cuddle you."

"Whatever you wish, seeress," Rune said. She began removing her golden shell, but she wasn't like a snail. She wasn't very gooey inside. She was strong, with muscles that rippled when her hands clenched. I hadn't seen her without her leathers very often, but I couldn't help but peek at her exposed olive skin.

She knew I was watching her, but she didn't seem to mind. It was only fair, because I knew she watched me too. She had been for a long time.

"I like you better when you're not lying to me, you know," I admitted as I laid my head back on the bed. I was sideways across both mattresses, but that was the only way I could lay without my feet hanging off.

"It's hard to tell you the truth," Rune whispered. I kept my eyes shut to give her privacy, but I could hear her thumping around as she changed into her night attire. The poor woman hadn't had anything but leather and metal on her body in days. I wondered if my warm skin next to hers would feel good. I wondered if she was deprived of touch, of comfort.

"Why?"

"There's no point talking about it now, seeress. That's a conversation for another night."

"There she goes again, evading questions like a fly avoiding a palm," I mumbled into my arm.

Rune chuckled as she climbed into bed next to me. "Some answers require sobriety. When I tell you this truth, I want you to remember it."

"I could tickle your secrets out of you."

"You could try, but I'd hate to break both your wrists."

"You're violent."

"And you're persistent."

"Thank you." I smiled proudly. "Gods, we fucking stink," I moaned.

"That we do," she said with a chuckle. "There's a tub in the bathing chamber, but I don't trust you not to drown."

"What if you hold my head above water?" I asked with a wobbly smile. Surely, my charm would convince her. She simply smiled, as if she thought I was being silly, not sincere. "I mean it!"

"That would require me to be in there with you." she pointed out, and I felt her shift next to me.

"And?" I asked, propping my head up on my arm.

"And...you'll be naked."

"And?" I asked again, not sure why she was resisting my perfect plan.

"Well, I don't think you'll feel as passionately about this plan in the morning," she said. "Why don't we have one night where we reek of ale, and then we can both bathe in the morning? Separately."

"Sounds sticky, but fine," I sighed.

We both turned to face each other, the blanket pulled up to our necks. My fingers ached to touch her under the thick quilt.

Did I want to scratch her? I must, because my hands kept balling into fists every time the urge struck me. She wasn't a cat. Valkyries weren't for petting.

"You're thinking about me not being a cat, aren't you?" she asked.

"I am."

Rune let out a long sigh. "You and Tove have an unhealthy relationship, you know that, right?"

"He's all I have."

"No, Kari." She shook her head, her face serious. "You have so much more, if you want it."

CHAPTER TWENTY
THE SUFFERING MORTAL

Rune

I'd claimed the bath before Kari could open her eyes. When I'd gotten back from grabbing us breakfast and meeting up with Rayna and saw Kari was still sound asleep, I'd decided it was time to check on her pulse. As soon as my fingers touched her neck, she jolted awake, sitting straight up, as if she'd been revived from the dead.

I'd lurched back as she'd yelled, "Never wake a sleeping seer-ess!" Her hand clutched her chest, as if her heart had threatened to stop.

When she'd risen and began bathing in the other room, I'd sat with my back pressed up against the stone wall next to the doorless chamber entrance, listening to her as she'd recounted her vision the night prior. She'd spoken of a large, snarling wolf, thick iron, and a woman with hands as cold as ice, and I'd had a pretty good feeling we would wind up in Helheim before the day was up.

Rayna had gone ahead to check on Apple, Gunhild, and Tove, and I'd told her we'd meet her there as soon as I could get Kari ready for the day. She seemed to be in no rush, and I had a sneaking suspicion the nasty effects of the ale from the previous night weren't the only things slowing her down. The seeress had also seen Hel in her dreams. She'd felt the goddess' frigid skin, seen the hound that guarded her gate. Maybe Helheim wasn't as fearsome as certain ignorant mortals made it out to be, but the entrance wasn't exactly welcoming to anyone who wasn't escorted by a god or one of their attendants. It was in Niflheim, after all.

I was a valkyrie, yes, but I wasn't from the Helheim sect. I couldn't stroll in there like I belonged. Kari had every right to be nervous, but I'd hoped she knew I'd never let anything happen to her.

When Kari finally stopped dragging her feet, we met Rayna by the gate. My sister's face was bright and refreshed, as if she'd had the best night's sleep, though I didn't think she'd gotten much sleep at all. I'd seen her dancing with Alvion as I'd swept Kari off to the inn. She'd been laughing, light, and *gods*, I loved coming here with her. She deserved the happiness she found, and she deserved Alvion.

"Good morning, everyone!" she chimed with a smile as bright as the sun. Her blonde streaks sparked in the sunlight, a reminder of how beautiful she'd looked when she first arrived in my sect. She was nineteen at the time and hadn't even gotten her first white hair yet, even if her first strand was stripped of its color a few days later.

Kari's gaze darted from Rayna to me before she grumbled a greeting and proceeded to shield her eyes from the sun. When we walked through the gate back into the path between realms, she dropped her arm and sighed in instant relief. It was darker here, with a purple-tinted sky that was even across the sunless expanse, unlike the cloudless Nidavellir sky.

Now that he was solid once more, I scooped Tove up and placed him in her arms, knowing she hadn't wanted to go the night without him. She pulled him in close, a smile creeping onto her face despite being ale-ill.

Helheim was the next root over, and unless we ran into any

trouble, we'd be able to make it to the gate by the end of the day. Sure, we'd be worn down and dirty, but maybe we'd be granted rest before an audience with the Goddess of Death.

Kari spent most of the day on Apple's back, sleeping or pretending to so she didn't have to entertain the notion of conversation. Rayna and I weren't going to try to force the suffering mortal to participate in idle chit chat with us. I only hoped her silence had everything to do with her state of wellness and nothing to do with regret. We'd finally been able to break some walls down between us last night, and I held my breath the entire walk that she wasn't sitting upon Apple wishing it had never happened.

I replayed what she'd said to me far too many times as we laid face to face under that quilt. I thought too often of the way she'd drifted off to sleep as if I was a suitable replacement for her favorite companion, even if it was just for one night.

When the iron gate of Helheim finally appeared in the distance, Rayna slowed. I stopped in my tracks and cocked a brow at her, not needing to say a word. She knew I was asking what she was doing, why she was slowing.

"This is where Gunhild and I leave you."

"What?" Kari said. "But we just got here!"

"She can't be seen in Helheim with us," I said, catching on. Why hadn't I thought about this before? "Rayna wasn't sent here to aid us. She was sent here to capture us, to bring us back to the Allfather."

"I never would have betrayed you," Rayna said. "But—"

"But I'm not going to let you ruin your life by appearing to have betrayed Odin. You'll already be going back to him empty-handed. The last thing you need is to have Hel or one of her valkyries report back that you were found here with us."

Rayna nodded gravely, but I strode over to her, bringing her head into my shoulder like I used to when she was just a girl. I held her there for a moment, not saying anything but expressing everything we needed to. Kari and I owed her our lives. If any other valkyrie had been sent here, we'd be back in Valhalla, chained on the floor of Odin's Hall. Because of her, we were paces from the Helheim gate, moments from speaking with Hel. We'd have our answers soon, and we owed her for that.

Kari dismounted Apple and walked over to the two of us. I released the back of Rayna's head, and she pulled back with a small smile before turning to Kari. The two of them exchanged a hug, Kari whispering her thanks, Rayna telling her she hoped to see her again someday.

When Rayna mounted Gunhild and flew off to find the Bifrost, Kari and I were left to face what was on the other side of those massive black gates. When we began creeping forward, a howl rippled through the air that made my bones ache.

Garm.

CHAPTER TWENTY-ONE
LEAD THE WAY, GARM

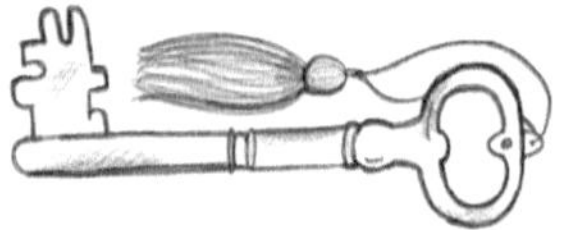

Kari

I smelled Garm before I saw him. There was no denying his presence, even being on the other side of Hel's thick gate. Rumbling howls disrupted the false night, and the stench of rot permeated the air. If Hel wanted to create a better reputation for her realm, a good place to start would be by getting rid of the giant wolf in front of its entrance.

Kind of a bad first impression, if you ask me.

Rune led the way, and Tove hissed and spat in my arms the entire time, knowing we grew closer to the creature that could very well gobble him up. I tried not to think what would happen if things got out of hand and Garm decided he wanted a tasty treat. Tove might have not been alive, but he was still a soul, and here, in Hel, even souls could be destroyed. If the Norns had woven such a fate for Tove, there'd be nothing I could do to reach him again.

Cut it out, Kari. I begged myself, my heart beating far too fast in my chest as Rune used the gate's knocker to alert our presence.

As if the wolf didn't already know we were here.

Unlike most of the gates we traveled through, Helheim had a

guard on the *inside* that didn't let just anyone in. The Goddess of Death was notorious for being protective over the souls in her realm. If she took you in, you were hers, and she wouldn't let any outsider get a piece of you.

Garm let out another skin-quivering howl before the gate creaked open. A voice, mighty and demanding, reverberated through the air. The sound came from the blood-stained wolf, though he'd never opened his massive jaw to do anything other than lick his jowls upon spotting the hissing cat in my arms.

"State your purpose."

Rune stepped forward and spoke, her chin pointed high. "I come from the House of Wings' Valhalla sect, with a mortal who claims to have been cursed by Hel."

The white-eyed wolf stepped forward before I could say or do anything, and when he did, he left a paw print behind in pure white snow larger than my entire body. My throat worked on a gulp as I tried not to take in his foul stench. Tove thrashed in my arms, and I was suddenly very thankful for the impenetrable fabric of my skirts as his nails flared in warning.

The guard of Helheim drew in a deep breath through his nostrils, right at the side of my face. My teeth were clamped tight, and when my eyes darted to Rune, she held my gaze in a way that was so soft and warm, I couldn't help but settle my nerves.

Garm's tongue rolled out before it slid up my neck and the side of my head in a slow, hot greeting. This wasn't a friendly hello, but a test. He was tasting me, my emotions, my lies, but I'd spoken none, and neither had Rune.

The wolf let out a low growl in his throat before turning his hind legs to me, his tail almost knocking me over. My knees wobbled, but I held my chin up just like Rune, using every speck of restraint I possessed to not wipe the foul saliva off my neck.

He uses that tongue to fucking eat people. What happened to a dog's mouths being cleaner than ours? I ranted to myself, because I couldn't out loud unless I wanted to join whoever was surely already in the pits of his belly.

"Follow me," the air around Garm seemed to say. Rune moved first, Apple right beside her. My feet felt frozen, as if the ice of Helheim had wrapped around my ankles and refused to let me move. Rune glanced over her shoulder when she realized I wasn't with her, and held her hand out to me as an offering. I grabbed it without thinking, and only when her warm hand was in mine did I realize I'd been endlessly grateful to have been given her steady presence.

With our palms pressed together, I took my first step through the gate. I kept my eyes trained forward, not wanting to appear nervous by looking around, even if everything in me was curious about this place. For some reason, unlike being in Valhalla, I felt as if I was cheating by being here in Helheim. I would have never ended up in Valhalla upon my death; I would have been carried here by valkyries in black. Gold would have never found me, but the cold of Hel would've.

Rune squeezed my hand as we walked across a bridge made of ice and stone, reminding me I was still alive, and just because I was here didn't mean I needed to stay.

Was I horrible if I left my family here? Could I stay in this place, be twenty-seven forever, all because I didn't want to say goodbye to this fur ball in my arms that should've passed on years ago?

Rune stared at the side of my face, and I truly felt as if she knew everything going on in this chaotic mind of mine. She knew my fears, and I think I was beginning to understand hers too. I also had someone I didn't want to say goodbye to, and I understood how stubborn we can be, how much we can hold on to what has given us comfort, even if it was holding us back. Just as much as Tove was holding me back from living, I was holding Rune back from her destiny.

Garm snapped his salivating jaws in our direction, and I dropped Rune's hand so fast, it could've been on fire.

"What do you need, Garm?" Rune asked, unbothered by this monstrous creature before us. I imagined she'd seen worse. Maybe the true monsters didn't look like Garm, instead the old men who lived in golden castles.

"Give me the mortal," the air said as he let out a low growl.

"She's not mine to give," Rune said, because I wasn't an object to be had, and she knew that. "I'll be staying by her side, nonetheless."

"She won't like it."

"She'll get over it," Rune said. I held my breath as she talked to Garm as if he was beneath her, and I guess in the power structure, he was. Garm may have been a direct attendant to Hel, but Rune was a direct attendant to Odin, and he was the Allfather. Rune would always have more power than the attendants of any other hall or realm, even if they were ginormous and stained an ominous red.

Smoke rolled out of Garm's nose, but he didn't fight Rune on the matter. As we continued walking through the cold expanse, I tucked my shawl into my belt. I folded my arms against my chest to try to retain the heat within me that bled freely into the frigid air. If only fire wasn't immediately extinguished in this realm.

I suppose there are other ways of keeping warm.

My gaze wandered over to Rune, and now, it was my turn to take in her profile as she stared off at something in the distance. Before I sought what she was focused on, I stole a moment to observe her features, trying to piece together last night. I felt as if something lingered in the air between us. There was something to be said, but I couldn't remember what. Whatever it was, I kept trying to work it over in my mind, because even if the memories weren't all there, it still warmed me from the inside out.

Up ahead, I finally spotted the haze of a palace. I wasn't sure if it was made of black stone, or if the distance was playing tricks on my mind.

"We're here," Rune said. "Are you ready, seeress?"

"Seeress?" Garm echoed, his front paw hovering in the air instead of taking its next step onto the snow-covered stone.

It was my turn to speak now. I couldn't expect Rune to fight this battle for me, because we both knew Hel would expect to hear from me.

I may as well start now.

"Yes," I said to the light grey wolf. "Part of my curse, I assume."

"I see."

Neither Garm nor we spoke for the remainder of the trip across the icy bridge to Hel's Hall, and it soon became apparent that the palace we walked toward was, in fact, carved of pure onyx.

"Your pegasus companion may take flight. She is not welcome inside Hel's Hall," Garm finally said.

Rune patted Apple on the rear, and the pegasus trotted down the bridge before leaping off the side into the air. Her wings snapped out and caught her gracefully, and she became a blur of white across the snowy sky.

When she was gone, Garm continued the rest of the way down the bridge until stopping before its impressive entrance. While eerie at first, the second I stepped into the building, I was surrounded by an otherworldly warmth, as if the stone on all sides of me whispered everything would be okay.

My fear slipped away with each step I took, and as I glanced over at Garm, I realized he was cleaned up, no longer tainted and splattered with the evidence of violence. I wasn't sure if what lay outside this place was the illusion, or if something about Hel's Hall made me see and feel what I wanted.

"Will we be taken directly to Hel?" I asked, peering down at my skirts with little leaves clinging to them. The words Rune spoke to me about looking presentable when I'd first arrived in Valhalla played in my mind.

"She is expecting you now. She won't like it if we make her wait much longer."

Great. I look like shit, and I probably smell like it too, I thought to myself, though I'd been relieved I was given the chance to clean the ale off my skin and clothes earlier this morning. I'd rather look like I was rolling around outside as opposed to the floor of a dwarven tavern.

We rounded a corner, and I spotted a wide-set double door. I steadied myself with a deep breath, telling myself I was ready. Hel was a goddess, *the* Goddess of Death, and in moments, I would be standing before her. I'd thought a million times about what I'd say to her, but it felt as if all the preparation I'd done was fading into an abyss in my mind, leaving me with nothing but "Hey, you cursed my family. Undo it. And give me my cat back while you're at it."

Garm halted in his tracks as we approached the stunning black doors. They split down the middle, a sliver of light exposing what was on the other side.

"You've got this," Rune whispered as the doors ground to a stop. Garm directed us inward with his snout, and I offered Rune a weary smile, grateful she'd demanded to be here with me.

"Thanks, Garm," I said as I passed him, noticing how beautiful his big brown eyes were. Out under the light of the moon, his eyes looked like nothing but white orbs. I was once again left wondering what was real and what was a mere fear-inducing hallucination, a warning to turn around and never come back.

Walking through the double doors, Garm stayed behind, but Rune was firmly at my side. Hel was waiting for me on a high backed throne crafted from the same onyx as the floor, as if it had risen from the base of the palace in the shape and size perfect for the goddess.

I didn't meet her eyes as I approached her, but I kept my shoulders squarely in her direction at all times. When I stood before her throne, I bent the knee, chin pointed to my ribs.

"Rise, Kari Kettlesdotter," Hel said, and I didn't wait to follow her command. The soles of my boots found the floor once more, and I raised my gaze to finally look upon the goddess of death and ultimate ruler of the underworld. Half of her hair was ash blonde, the other half as black as the stone she sat upon. On the side of her hair that was black as death, the skin on her face was peeled back to the bone. She was one of the three monsters born of Loki and the giantess, Angrboda, and because of that, I'd imagined her to be far more frightening. The skeleton part to her face was not gory, reminding me of finding a beautiful skull in the forest of Stormheim. Runes were carved into it, but I was too far from her to read what they said.

I realized I was staring at her, and I wasn't sure if it was my turn to speak, or if I should wait until she told me to. Or maybe she knew exactly why I was here and was about to go on a long tirade about my horrible, curse-worthy ancestors.

"Why have you come to see me, mortal? Why come all this way?" she asked, and that knocked a few theories off my list.

"Greetings, Hel." I dipped my head again out of respect. "I have travelled across the realms to ask that the ancestral curse placed upon my family be lifted so I may return to Midgard. And... I would like my companion to come back with me." I held Tove up, and he went limp in my arms when he came face to face with the goddess.

"You defied all odds to stand before me, and I admire that," she said. "But what you speak of is not a curse."

"It... With all respect, it feels like a curse," I said, trying not to let her words rattle me. This was a curse, and I wasn't leaving until it was fucking lifted.

Hel sighed, flicking black hair over her shoulder. "What you speak of is my gift. And clearly, it has gone to waste on the ungrateful."

My fists clenched at my sides, and I bit my tongue before I said something I'd regret. I could sense Rune watching me, and I wondered if she was expecting me to lunge at the goddess any minute now. I wouldn't.

I won't, I told myself again so the idea would stick.

"A gift?" I asked, keeping my voice light and pleasant. "How so? Maybe I have misunderstood."

"I did not curse your ancestors to have rotting eyes, as you seem to believe," she started, and I suddenly grew very weary of this goddess and the knowledge she held. "I can't place curses. I can bestow gifts. I gifted your ancestor, Norfrid Bosdotter, with eyes of the dead. With this gift, she was able to see the dead as I do, or similarly enough. No one will ever truly see them as I do, but it was as close as a mortal could get. I was kind enough to allow this gift to be passed to each first daughter from thereon. Norfrid's daughter was born with the same abilities, though I made a minor revision so only she could see the true nature of her appearance. Norfrid rejoined me far too quickly due to her...challenges with the village folk."

"Was she killed because of how she looked?" I held back the fact that Hel made her look that way. She had caused her death.

"It was unfortunate, yes. I rather did like her, but I suppose she's here now, isn't she?" Hel gave me a proud smile. "I quite enjoy having your line here with me."

"Why did you bestow this...gift upon her?"

"She made an offering for it, of course. I believed it could be quite useful to have a witness to the dead on Midgard. Their eyes are my eyes." Hel's singular white eye flickered, and for a moment, it looked just like mine. I stumbled back, and a strangled scream left my lips against my will. "Don't fret, child. It is not just your eyes I see from, but all eyes of the gifted ones."

"Fuck that!" I yelled, spit flying from my mouth as I did. Hel's eye returned to its white, blank slate. Rune grabbed my arm, muttering something, but I couldn't hear her over the pounding in my head. All this time? I'd thought the worst thing about my curse was the superficial look of it, but that was nothing compared to the privacy stolen from me. Sure, she was a goddess. She had more important things to do than watch my boring life every day, but what had she seen? What moments had she sat in on without my knowledge or consent?

"Watch yourself, mortal. It's best you don't forget where you are. You don't plan on staying in my realm, do you?"

My jaw ticked as I held it shut. The being I just yelled profanities at was the only one in all of existence who could permanently destroy my soul, and I didn't know where she drew the line. Maybe all it took was a displaced mortal screaming in her face.

"No, I think I've made that pretty clear," I grunted.

Rune groaned beside me, but she didn't try to correct me or do damage control.

"So you have," Hel sneered. "Despite your lack of gratitude for the power I have given you, I will not take back what has been given. My power lives within you now. Separating you from it would surely destroy your soul, and, well, that would be quite the waste."

"It's a good thing my line will die out then. You'll hold nothing over my family anymore," I said, the bitter, petty words dripping off my tongue like poison. If more cursed spies was what she wanted, I'd be the last person to give them to her.

"It will die out, yes," Hel said before turning her attention to Rune. "You haven't told her yet, have you?"

Rune's mouth parted, and then she looked at me with regret on her face I'd never forget.

"No, I suppose you haven't." Hel emitted a smooth laugh that chilled my flesh. "You may not return to Midgard. That is, unless you'd like your life to end. If that's the case, I will happily host you here."

I didn't look at Hel as I asked, "What do you mean?" My eyes were locked solely on the valkyrie who'd been keeping this from me. If I couldn't return to Midgard, I was as good as dead. I'd never see Hilda again, never see my longhouse, never lay in my horribly uncomfortable bed, prepare a spell for another client, or open the box of wildflower bracelets given to me by Haddy.

"Kari…" Rune said before squeezing her lips together.

"You gave me the illusion of choice. I was never returning to Midgard, was I?" I asked, my hands trembling with the untapped energy within me.

Rune flinched, her hand tightening on the hilt of her sword. When she opened her mouth, her words pierced my very soul. "No, seeress. You weren't."

CHAPTER TWENTY-TWO
TO SHED YOUR ARMOR

Rune

Kari stared at me as if she would've loved to do nothing more than crush me under her wool-lined boots. I deserved any punishment she yearned to give; not just for the truth she'd heard, but for everything she had yet to uncover. There we stood, in front of Hel herself, and I could do nothing but stare back at her, my mouth parted with nothing to say.

Kari shook her head furiously, and I chanced one glance at Hel, long enough to know she was growing bored by our silent display. While amused at first, the only expression she wore on her half-flesh face now was annoyance. It was evident Kari and I needed to have this conversation later. Alone. I only hoped I could get the seeress to move past this for now, for all our sakes.

I cleared my throat and tried to ignore the shaking in Kari's hands when I said, "Kari—"

The woman next to me spun to show me her back, leaving my drying tongue frozen in its place, cutting off any words I would have spoken. "Hel, what do you want from me? What can I give you other than my eyes? I know that's the deal you bartered with my ancestor, but I agreed to no such terms. I accepted no such gift."

I bit my bottom lip, not wanting to show fear in front of a goddess, but did Kari really just ask Hel what she wanted from her? Would she really give Hel other pieces of herself in replacement of her eyes? I suppose this was about so much more than what she saw in the mirror; this was about the blatant breach of privacy. Hel had been spying on her and her family for decades, for fuck's sake, and even in death, she would hold control of Kari's own vision. When would she know peace away from this fate?

Hel hummed as she assessed Kari and leaned back in her throne. Her black hair hung over her partial skull face, and she brushed it back to show the runes carved into it once more. "You cannot give me anything more than what you already have, but someone else can. I just so happen to know they're in need of a seeress. Though, nothing comes free, you know. Or you should by now," Hel laughed despite herself.

"Who?" I jutted in. I wouldn't let Kari agree to being some low tiered god's seeress under false pretenses just because she wanted to get out of this position with Hel. Hel wanted something Kari couldn't give her, but the goddess of Helheim could still barter Kari like a stack of golden coins.

Desperation never led to anything good, though, and things could always get worse. I would help navigate Kari out of this mess, even if she hated me with everything she had. I wasn't expecting her forgiveness for what I did, but I would only accept the very best terms for my mortal.

Kari shot me a horrible glance that screamed to stay out of it, but her eyes were never scary to me, so I didn't flinch. Her brow softened for half a second before it hardened once more and refocused on Hel, awaiting her answer.

"Freyja."

My head cranked back.

Freyja?

Freyja was wand-wed, just as Kari was. No, not just like Kari—insurmountably more powerful. Why would she bargain for a seeress from Midgard? Something wasn't right.

"The goddess of seidr is looking for a mortal seeress? Why do I find this incredibly hard to believe?" Kari asked, saying exactly what I was thinking.

"What you believe is of no consequence. The truth remains as it is all the same," Hel said. "But I will indulge your mortal mind. Dear Freyja shares Asgard with Odin, and with that comes its...consequences. See, Odin has a love for anything and everything that can bring him glory." Hel turned to me. "Rune, you would know of this. You were once a shiny little mortal and he just had to have you, didn't he? And when your sister's talents grew too great in Freyja's sect, who transferred her to his?"

"Odin," I said, though no one really needed me to answer her question. We all knew where she was going with this.

"Mm, yes, he did. So, you can imagine, any talented attendant of Freyja's tends to be taken from her in time. It's hard to have a glorious hall when anything that supplies you with it is removed, now, isn't it?"

"Why does Freyja need a seeress when she herself is wand-wed?" Kari was asking all the right questions, and I had to hold back a grin as I watched her speak with Hel. Maybe I hadn't been giving her enough recognition. Maybe she was more capable of taking care of herself in a realm such as this one. She'd been alone for a long time before I came to take her life away. At some point, you learned not to rely on anyone, and me wanting her to need me changed nothing.

"We all have our limitations, though we hate to admit it." Hel sighed. "Freyja is my opposite, if you will. She rules over a portion of the heavens, whereas I rule over the underworld. She has no connection to this place, try as she might. But you...you, my little creation, do. She has been missing something for a long while now, and she's running out of ways to find it. She hasn't yet tried seidr of the underworld, however."

"I'm not your anything," Kari growled just as I thought she was making progress. Hel was surely going to steal our souls.

"And even so, your seidr is *mine,*" Hel sneered. "You're my creation, as much as Rune is Odin's. Your options are limited, dear Kari. You can go back to Midgard just to die and return to me, or you can allow me to trade you, and you may take your feline with you."

"And what about my eyes?"

Hel blew out her annoyance, waving her hand at Kari dismissively. "Yes, yes. Your eyes shall be yours, just as they were in Asgard previously. Odin and Freyja would never allow me to have such a privileged view into their realm."

"What will you be getting from Freyja in return?" I asked.

"That doesn't concern you."

It did, actually, because what did she want so badly that she was willing to give up her spy? Because even if Kari hadn't known it, that was exactly what Kari had been for Hel all these years. Who knew how many mortals Hel had out there with cursed vision, being able to take over their sight at any given moment without them ever knowing. It was creepy, and it was damn time she got out of Kari's head.

I didn't like the thought of her being used for a trade between goddesses, but returning to Midgard wasn't an option, and the only way I'd ever be able to go back to Asgard was if I had Freyja's protection. Maybe this was what was best for the both of us.

"I'll do it," Kari blurted out, and I wondered if she'd come to the same conclusion as I had.

Hel pushed herself out of her onyx throne. "Lovely. Assuming Freyja accepts my terms, I'll give you until the next new moon before you begin your travels back to Asgard. You may both reside here in my realm until then."

Kari shot me a look, and I couldn't tell if it was excitement or relief, but she soon remembered who I was, what I'd done, and she robbed me of that stunning gaze of hers.

"Oh, and Kari?" Hel said as she stepped forward off her dais. "Your family dwells within Helheim. When you're ready to see them, Garm will take them to you."

Kari's eyes went wide before she slowly nodded. "Thank you."

"Yes, well, I'm quite tired of this conversation and must be on my way. Garm?" When Hel snapped her fingers, the double doors swung open, and the grey wolf came prowling through. I turned back to Hel, but she was gone.

"Come with me." Garm didn't wait for us before he exited the room just as quickly as he'd entered. Kari went first, and I hated that wherever he took us, she wouldn't want me to be there with her. I followed shortly after, remaining quiet as Garm took us through Hel's enormous hall. There were endless halls with endless doors leading to endless rooms. Garm stopped before one of these doors and spat a black key onto the stone floor. It had a red tassel on the end soaked from his saliva. I stooped down to pick it up before Kari did. If she got her hands on this key, she'd lock me out of our room, and I'd never have the chance to explain myself.

Kari turned to Garm expectantly. "Where's the second key?"

"There's only one," he growled.

"And how many beds are inside this room?" Kari asked with skin as white as snow.

"One." The air encasing Garm emitted the number like an echo. Before Kari could ask any questions or demand alternate accommodations, Garm showed us his bushy grey tail and walked down the black hall lit by torches.

"Well then." Kari smacked her lips. She looked down at the key, and she knew better than to expect me to hand it over. I said nothing as I jammed the key into the door and pushed it open.

As I entered the room, I shoved the key into a hidden spot in my armor where she wouldn't dare reach.

The room was softly lit by candles, as if it'd been expecting us.

There were rugs lining the black stone floor and colorful tapestries lining the walls. It wasn't dreary, but warm. My room in Valhalla was all whites and golds, but this one was black and shades of red. They were vastly different, but Hel could have supplied us with much worse accommodations than this. After hard benches, forest floors, and dwarven beds, I was relieved to see the massive bed in the center of the room, a wispy canopy strung up around it.

Kari blew out a breath to tell me how unhappy she was with our situation, but at least that loaded sigh hadn't been a scream in my direction.

"When were you going to tell me?" she finally asked. I turned to face her then, and my stomach lurched when my eyes met hers. I didn't want to see her anger, her distrust.

"I should have told you sooner," I said, unstrapping my sword and leaning it against the wall. The double axes secured to my back came off next. I didn't want to have this conversation strapped to the chin in weapons.

"You didn't tell me at all. Hel did." Kari ground her teeth. "You tell me nothing. You never have. And you wonder why I keep my distance, why I have such strong walls. You built them! They're there for you and you alone."

"I know." I swallowed, running my fingers through the loose strands of my hair. This white hair of mine had gotten me out of so many confrontations over the years, I'd forgotten what it was like to have to work for what I wanted with words, to be the one expected to grovel.

"That's it? You know? Great. I guess this is all worked out then." Kari laughed bitterly, throwing her hand up in the air. Tove came out of nowhere and hissed at me as he trotted by to use his human's leg to scratch his sides on.

"It's not worked out, seeress. Far from it," I said, wanting badly to reach forward and grab her, but I wouldn't until she begged it of me. "I take responsibility for those walls, and I'm sorry for giving you a reason to build them. My intention was never to hurt you, though I understand intention means very little when the outcome is harmful all the same."

Kari crossed her arms, fighting an eye roll as she said, "So tell me then. Would you have confessed the truth?"

"I would have," I admitted. "I was waiting for the perfect time, but I realized there was no perfect time far too late. I wasn't holding back out of malice, but I was trying to spare you grief. You'd already had far too much of it for someone your age. For anyone, really. You've lost so much, had so much *taken* from you, and I didn't want to take that option away from you too. I figured if you chose another path, that would have truly meant something. You wouldn't have just chosen it just because Midgard wasn't an option. And selfishly, I was worried you might have chosen Midgard anyway so you could have been taken to Helheim to be with your family prematurely."

Kari stood before me, her arms by her sides, showing me she was hiding nothing. She was open, expecting me to do the same. "You selfishly didn't want me to leave you."

"Yes," I sighed, admitting just one of my many hidden truths. I removed my boots, one at a time, never taking my eyes from her. "It was selfish, yes, but not entirely so. Kari, you don't deserve to be here just because I took you to Valhalla. At the time, I didn't realize I wouldn't be able to bring you back. I never meant to steal the mortal realm from you."

"When did you find out I wouldn't be able to return? And what if I'd chosen Midgard? What would you have done then?"

"Bodil told me. The, uh, healer. You may not remember her, but it was your second night in Valhalla. If you had chosen to go to Midgard, I would have done everything in my power to ensure you survived once there. I would have gone to the gods, struck a deal, anything."

Kari remained silent for a while before she retreated to the sitting room by the windows, her shoulders slumping with notable fatigue. "As soon as we walked through those gates, I could tell I wasn't ready to be here. I feel Hel's seidr so strongly here, it calls to me like never before. I feel it scraping its way under my skin, trying to crawl back to her, like it was never truly mine to begin with. I can't stand the feeling, and I will go anywhere to get away from it. It seems like anywhere I go, her *gift* follows me, but being on Asgard was the best I've felt in my entire life, even with a hole in my shoulder." She gave a bitter laugh, as though her heart wasn't truly in it, and that, I could understand.

"You're happy to return to Asgard? Truly? Not because it's just the better of two options?"

"Truly." Kari nodded with a crooked smile. "And maybe working under Freyja, being her attendant, will be the best thing for me. She's the goddess of seidr, after all. Who better to learn from?"

I slowly nodded my head as I came to sit with her. I kept my distance so as not to spook her, but I didn't want to pace the room or hover either. "Seeress, I have so many things I need to tell you. More apologies, more veiled truths."

"I wasn't sure if I'd ever hear the words I've been yearning to. I'm still not," she said, shifting her weight so more of her was sitting on her seat. She rested her elbow on the arm rest and stared down at her nails, as if what I was about to tell her was of no importance, like she hadn't screamed at me to tell her my secrets.

We were in Helheim now, and I couldn't keep this knowledge from her any longer. If her family saw me, they'd know my face. I'd tried to be careful on so many nights in those early days, but spirits have a funny way of sneaking up on you, and there were five of them I'd been trying to keep my involvement hidden from. I should've known Haddy would find me lurking around their longhouse eventually. She was even more curious than Kari, always wandering around the longhouse, never spending much time within it. She was quiet, kept to herself, and seemed to enjoy my presence instead of being scared by it. I'd told her not to tell the others, and she'd agreed not to if I'd promised her one thing.

Haddy and I played hide and seek every three moons. She would be the one to hide, and Apple and I would wander through the forest to catch her. I'd let Apple find her most of the time, and Haddy would fall to the dirt laughing her little butt off as soon as she was caught.

Staring at Kari now, I could see as clear as day what she would have looked like at Haddy's age. My heart twisted, and Kari's expression did as well, as if she was reading my mind, though her imagination would have never been able to fabricate these memories. I needed to start talking before she got up and walked away from me, but gods, the words on my tongue had grown so heavy over the weeks.

"I will tell you everything you yearn for and more. Anything you want, seeress. Not to appease you, but to finally give you what you've long deserved."

"How long?" Kari asked, her chin pointing up and her elbow falling off the armrest. "How long did you watch me before you swooped in and took me to Valhalla?"

"Two years."

"Two years... So you..." She shuddered. "You were there that night? The night of the raid."

"I was. It hadn't been the first time I'd been to Stormheim, but it had been the first time I saw you." I thought back at the memory, pain spreading through my chest like a wildfire. "I was sent to see if any of the souls taken in the raid were worth bringing back to Valhalla with me and—"

Kari ground her teeth before interrupting me. "You went back empty-handed."

"I did. In truth, I'd been annoyed Odin had sent me at all and not one of my younger sisters. It was a small raid led by rouge raiders, and only a handful of people were killed. I hadn't understood why he would send me, of all valkyries. I'd lingered longer than I should have, trying to understand what my purpose was in your little village. And then, I saw you."

Kari's eyes widened, her hands on her chest. I wanted to skip this next part, to spare her of it, but I couldn't lie any longer. Keeping it to myself wouldn't help her. I truly believed the only thing she wanted from me now was my truth, so I'd give it to her, untainted.

"I watched as you found their bodies. Your mom, dad, three sisters, and Tove. I hadn't believed there'd been any survivors. I thought you were merely a neighbor coming by to see what all the fuss had been about, but when you fell to your knees, I knew otherwise. I didn't take any of their souls, and I stopped all valkyries who came by each time from taking them either. I wanted to give you more time. I promised Haddy I would give it to you."

"Haddy? You spoke with her?" Kari slid to the edge of her seat, and, as if her unrest called Tove forth, he jumped up onto her lap. I told Kari about my time with her youngest sister, the conversations we would have about Kari and what was going on inside the long-house I couldn't see.

"It wasn't until Haddy told me about what your other sisters had done that I decided it was time for someone from the Helheim sect to collect them. Haddy asked to go first. She didn't want to watch the others go."

Kari let out a soft sob, and all I wanted to do was pull her into my lap. My hands twitched and balled into fists so I wouldn't reach out and disrespect her wishes. There was nothing I could do to comfort her except tell her all about the good moments too.

"She loved Apple. I'm sure she'll be happy to see her. The two of them always got along so well, and oftentimes, I had Apple distract her after too many rounds of hide and go seek so I could see what you were up to. It was wrong of me, I know, but..."

"You played with her? Haddy? You kept her company?" Kari asked with a sob of release.

"I did. I wanted to tell you so many times, but I didn't know how to explain how I even met her, or why I was at your long-house," I said. "She's sweet. I look forward to seeing her again."

"Thank you," Kari whispered.

"Why are you thanking me, seeress?"

"Thank you for keeping her company when it was too painful for me to do so. She deserved, still deserves, to be happy, and you helped give that to her until her time on Midgard was over. I know she's playing around here somewhere, collecting flowers that poke out from beneath the snow, but I just wish she could've grown up first, you know? I guess I never will either—grow old with someone, and...I don't know, it's stupid."

"Far from it. When Odin brought me to Valhalla, I was eighteen. After my first decade in Valhalla, I stopped aging all together, other than my hair, of course. My face has remained the same for so many years, and it can be unsettling seeing the face of a twenty-eight year old when you've been alive for over six centuries. We expect to grow old someday, to have the people around us grow grey and wrinkly too."

Kari looked over at me and gave me a weird, hiccup-y laugh. "I guess all my favorite people," she hugged Tove tighter, "and creatures won't be aging with me."

Favorite people? Surely, she couldn't mean me.

Her eyes lingered on me for a long time, and then she finally said, "I've had a few weeks now to sit with the knowledge that you've been watching me. We both know this isn't news, just new that you're admitting it. Truth be told, I sensed someone watching me long before I met you. There was always a strange presence in the forest at night that I could tell wasn't a spirit. Sometimes, it was an odd thump on my roof, or a flash of white after I'd woken from a horrible vision."

I shifted in my seat, exhaling as I began unfastening my armor. My heart was hidden under far too many layers, and this woman before me deserved to have it close to the surface, raw and bleeding for her. Kari watched me as I went, but I didn't rush what I was going to say next. I didn't wait to tell her, only to butcher it now.

"After discovering Hel had been seeing through your eyes, I'm ashamed to admit, she wasn't the only one watching. The months after your family was taken to Helheim, you were so alone. I was the only one there to know you were laughing at Tove and not the bloodflies. I was the only one dabbing the sweat off your brow when your visions took hold of you. I was the only one there to see you falling to your knees and breaking down on the 8th of every lunar cycle."

Kari's mouth opened then shut, and she pushed her curly, strawberry hair over her shoulder.

"I always felt so alone, like no one understood me. No one *saw* me," she choked out. "But you did, didn't you?"

Dry tears remained under her eyes, and the salt in them sparkled like crushed crystals in the candlelight. Nine realms, she was beautiful. I wanted to kiss away those tears and savor the taste of them. It was a privilege to have her raw like this in my presence. It was an honor to sit here with her, even if I'd been the one to pull forth those tears, even if there was someone else she'd rather be sitting with.

I nodded, my gaze burning into hers.

I made a promise to myself long ago that I would protect her, and my will to do so had only ever grown. She could despise me, she could fear me, but I would never give up on her, my sweet mortal.

CHAPTER TWENTY-THREE
DOUBLE THE SOCKS

Kari

Once again, I was left with a valkyrie in my bed. This time, we were freshly bathed and swathed in black silks we found in the room's wardrobe. Rune's was long, but it dipped low, and the damned mesmerizing material of the nightgown made her look as if she could take Hel's spot upon her throne. I wasn't used to seeing her outside of her leathers, and this dress was a dark sea of temptation.

Snap out of it, Kari. I squeezed my eyes shut as I tried to clear the images of her climbing into bed from my mind.

"What are you thinking about, seeress?" Rune's voice called to me in the dark room, smoke still lingering in the air in swirling patterns from the candles we snuffed out. "Your breathing is heavy."

For the love of the Gods.

"I was just starting to fall asleep," I lied, my back facing her as we laid under the luxurious sheets.

"How have your visions been?"

I sighed and rolled over, feeling awkward having her speaking to my back. When I faced her, the side of her mouth curled upward. I ignored that slight movement, or tried to, at least. I caught my eyes darting to her faint smile twice more before it faded.

"Ever since I started dreaming of you, of Valhalla, and leaving Midgard, my visions have been so distant, foggy," I said, hating to admit she'd found a way into my visions.

Her hair was free of war braids, and she looked softer than ever as her head rested upon the lush pillow. I wanted to run my fingers through it, show her I cared little for the status it brought her, but something about that still seemed like it'd be a win for her. I wasn't in favor of giving her the upper hand any time soon.

"Have you been reading the scroll I gave you?"

I snorted a laugh. "At least twice. I read it in its entirety when we were staying in the Valley Beyond the Mist with Áma. I snuck in moments here and there along our travels when my visions were keeping me up, but what I really need is mugwort and something to write my dreams upon."

"All you need to do is ask, seeress. There's a cup on your side table," she said with a tired smile. She looked as if she'd love to do nothing more than to fall asleep in this incredible bed, and I wondered if her seidr was starting to wane.

I peeked over my shoulder to see a steaming cup of tea sitting just a few feet away. I sat up, using puffy pillows to prop me up, and murmured my thanks to Rune. "I'm going to stay up for a bit to drink this. Why don't you sleep? You look exhausted."

"I think I've had enough vulnerability for one night," she chuckled. "I can wait."

"You're going to stay awake, watching me drink tea because you feel too vulnerable being asleep next to me while I'm not sleeping? Do you think I'm going to stab you with the dagger you gave me?"

"Well... I..." Rune stuttered with scrunched brows. Did she

really not see what she was doing? "I suppose when you put it like that, it sounds rather ridiculous."

"It does. Go to sleep, Rune. I could use a little alone time anyway, some time when I'm not being observed for once."

"I can give you that," Rune nodded, her eyes boring into me. "You deserve peace, Kari."

"Thank you," I said, allowing my gaze to trail all over that beautiful hair and the contrast of it against her olive skin. This valkyrie was one I could get used to, the one without the armor. "Sleep tight."

"Sweet visions, seeress," Rune said with a yawn. I thought she would turn her back to me to drift off to sleep as she usually did, but tonight, she simply closed her eyes.

As I sipped my tea, I spent far too long doing to her what she did to me for years: watching. I knew that was exactly what she was afraid of, but at some point, she needed to have the favor returned. At this rate, I'd need to watch her sleep each night for 730 moons before we were even. As I sat there, sinking into the mattress, I wondered if that fate would be all so bad.

When I woke, there was no warm body next to me, not even Tove. He sat by the window, staring off into Helheim's landscape and pawing at the glass whenever a snowflake blew past. In the place Rune once slept now sat a leather-bound collection of pages. Sitting up in bed, I grabbed the mysterious object and dragged it onto my lap. There was a string keeping the pages closed, and I unwound it to see a note scrawled on the first page in runic writing.

The morning is yours.
- Rune

I found myself smiling as I read those simple words. My fingers found Rune's markings, and I rubbed my thumb down them. As soon as I did, it triggered something in my mind, a vision fragment from the night prior.

Iris. Iris Ariti.

Something in my mind itched, screamed, and clawed; it wanted me to remember that name, who it belonged to, the story behind it. I wrote the name under Rune's note and found my hand and fingers working on their own accord, crossing out the four letter word spelling out Rune.

Iris and Rune are one in the same. As soon as I thought it, Rune's story from the night in Nidavellir came rushing through my memories. Heat rose to my cheeks as I recalled our conversation and the secrets she'd shared with me, the name she hadn't spoken in years, the reason behind that gouge in her armor. The damn dwarven ale had almost robbed me of everything beautiful from that night.

The past wasn't the only thing I dreamt of, though, and I began to sketch out everything I'd remembered: faint lights, draping cloth, flashes of olive. So many details felt hauntingly familiar but too distant to reach out and grab. I needed to master these visions if I was ever going to be a seeress worthy of Freyja.

I hummed to myself as I scrambled to find the teachings on seidr of the underworld. As my stomach growled, I wished Rune was here to summon me some tea and a nice little breakfast.

I spent the morning studying everything I could, getting lost in a world of runes and spells. The ingredients I brought with me were limited, and I wondered if I could collect more, or if Hel would frown upon me practicing my seidr in her realm. She did give it to me, after all. Why let me have it if I wasn't allowed to use it?

My fingers zinged with power, and I felt unknown spells forming on my tongue. They came to me as if they'd been carved into my skull, always there, always meant to be spoken by me. I hadn't realized the sun had dipped into its afternoon position until I heard a knock on the door.

"Come in!" I called out without looking up, lazily waving the visitor in with charcoal staining my nails. I was locked in, dedicated to my craft.

"Someone's been busy." I heard Rune's chuckle before I saw her. My fixed gaze broke, and I finally glanced up at her from where she stood at the end of the bed. Her eyes scanned the texts covering the bed, scattered bottles I'd brought with me, a few items I'd found in the room, then finally landed on my fingers.

"Iris?" I asked.

Rune cocked her head, blowing out a large sigh. "I was worried you didn't remember."

"Our night in Nidavellir? I remember...most things," I said. "Something about moss, Rayna smiling for once, and your armor. I remember why you didn't have it fixed," I confessed, memories coming back to me even more now as I spoke them aloud. I reached for the runic scribbles I'd jotted down, running my thumb over Rune's crossed out name. "I'll admit, I'd forgotten most of it, but I had a vision last night, and I heard the name Iris Ariti."

Rune glanced down at my work, no doubt seeing the charcoal smudge where I rubbed my thumb down her name. "So, you do remember."

I nodded slowly, then tilted my face to look at her. "Do you want me to call you Iris from now on?"

Rune looked taken aback, as if she'd never even considered this option, before finally saying, "I haven't been Iris in a very long time. The name 'Rune' reminds me of my rebirth, of who I was destined to become, not who I once was. I'm glad you remember me sharing that piece of myself, though, and while I don't ever intend on going by 'Iris' again, I never want to forget it, or where I came from," she said. "Will you hold on to this memory with me?"

"I will," I promised, meaning it with every fiber of my being.

"And if you want to add more memories to it, I will listen to stories of your past life and keep them alive in my mind too."

"Thank you, seeress," she said with a genuine smile. When she found herself smiling at me for a moment too long, she cleared her throat and ran her hand over her leathers. "Have you eaten?"

I shook my head, and, within the next second, there was a feast waiting for me on the table by the window. I didn't hesitate to push the spell work off me and crawl out of bed. Rune, Tove, and I ate together, and as we did, I caught Apple soaring through the snowy Helheim sky. Rune told me about taking Apple out for a ride and refueling her power stores, and I had to say, I could tell the difference in the food she'd been able to summon for us. Everything was far fresher and more flavorful than it had been the past few days. The berries were so sweet, I was pretty sure I could die happy.

"Would you like to visit them today?" Rune asked, and I'd been wondering when she'd bring my family back up. Knowing when I finally saw them again, I'd have Rune by my side made it all the stranger. Haddy would be happy, I was sure, but would my parents be disappointed in me for arriving with the immortal presence that had haunted us all? On the other hand, she was a valkyrie, an attendant of Odin, and my parents were dedicated and loyal to our Allfather. Her visit could be seen as the ultimate blessing. She was as close to Odin as they would ever get.

Trying to guess what they'd think would surely drive me mad, as I hadn't yet determined how I felt about the situation myself. Rune could be sweet when she wanted. She could pull complex feelings out of deep and hidden places within me. But she'd also been alive far longer than me, and I couldn't help but feel like she always had a secret plan up her sleeve, and letting me in on it was her last priority.

"What are you worried about?" Rune asked when I didn't answer her question.

"I didn't expect to still be alive the next time I saw them, and selfishly, I'd hoped it wouldn't be for a long time, not until I had a full life."

"That's not selfish. I'd say most families hope for the same thing for their living loved ones. I was there the night following the...pillow incident, you know. Your sisters were the selfish ones. I hope you know souls start souring the longer they stay on Midgard without their bodies. I think you'll be surprised by the change you'll see in them when you decide to visit. A change for the better."

"Really?" I asked, thinking back to the feeling of the pillow over my face, the fabric that puckered in my mouth as I'd tried to take in a restricted breath. My hand instinctively found my lips, and I forced a smile when Rune caught my gesture. "Okay, I'll see them today. I have no idea what I'm going to say to them, but I can't hide away in this room forever, knowing my family resides in the same realm as me."

"That's my girl," Rune smiled. She smacked her knee excitedly and brushed crumbs off her lap as she stood. "I'll leave you to change and prepare. Dress warm. Double up on socks, okay? The dead may not be able to feel the cold, but we certainly can."

Rune saw herself out, and I began getting myself together. There was a bubble rising in my chest, one of fear, of apprehension, but also of excitement. I may not have planned to see my family until I was old and grey, but being here in the same realm was a gift I wouldn't be taking for granted.

When I was dressed and as mentally prepared as I could be, Rune rapped on the door once more, as if she could sense I was ready to go. I tucked Tove under my arm, knowing he'd be happy to see the family again. He hadn't moved on with them like he should have, and I often wondered if they worried about where he'd gone. If I could address their concerns and squash them, I would. My sinister boy was not only okay, but he was thriving.

Rune took us through Hel's Hall, winding down torch-lit corridors, through snowy courtyards, dining rooms, and sprawling fields to find my family. Eventually, my arms grew tired, and I put Tove down. Turns out, I hadn't needed to worry about his ability to trudge through the snow. He walked above it, leaving little paw prints behind but not sinking inches into the perfect powdery piles like Rune and I had been.

Finally, I saw a streak of golden hair, followed by the sound of infectious laughter I could never miss.

Haddy.

I ran toward the girl, leaving Tove and Rune behind. I didn't care if she wasn't expecting me, or if I scared her. The second I saw her sweet face, there was nothing I could do to stop myself from picking her up and twirling her around. She was heavier than I expected, assuming she'd be ghostly light, and the two of us tipped over into the snow.

A yelp slipped out of her as I avoided falling on top of her legs, but when she saw my face, she broke out in another bout of laughter.

"Kari!" she shouted, her voice full of joy but also a little fear. "What are you doing here? You're not...dead already, are you?" She reached up and placed her hand upon my cheek. Her skin wasn't warm, and it wasn't cold either, but I didn't care how unnaturally tepid it felt. She wasn't passing through me, and that felt incredible.

"No! No." I reassured her with a shake of my head, pressing my hand on top of hers so I couldn't lose the feel of her on my skin. I didn't even mind that my boots had filled with snow, the double lining of socks keeping my ankles dry for now. I had my sister right here in front of me. What else mattered?

Rune came up behind me, and Haddy peeked over my shoulder to take a look at my companion. "Rune? Tove!" Haddy scrambled away from me, kicking snow in my direction as she did. When she got to Tove, she picked him up and spun him around, much like I'd attempted with her. Tove meowed loudly and rubbed his little orange cheeks all over my sister, occasionally opening his mouth to scrape his teeth against her hands. I could hear his contented purrs from where I sat in the snow.

Rune reached a hand down to me, and I didn't hesitate to take the support she offered. "You're not going to last very long out here with that snow in your boots," she said.

"I'm from Stormheim. You really think I can't handle the snow?" I scoffed with a teasing eye roll, though we both knew she was right. Haddy and Tove may have been fine out here, but once the snow melted from the warmth of my boots, I was going to be in trouble. "Haddy, where are Mom and Dad? Malfrid and Odel?"

"Oh! They're eating lunch by one of the great hearths. Let me take you to them, and then you can explain why you're here with Rune," Haddy said, nuzzling Tove one last time before putting him down. Tove promptly began using his tongue to smooth out any area Haddy ruffled up, which was pretty much his entire body. My sister shifted her attention to Rune. "Where's Apple?"

Rune chuckled and pointed to the sky, where Apple was flying in loops in the distance. "Want to go for a ride?"

"Yes!" Haddy squealed. "You never let me before."

"You know how she is with ghosts," Rune said before blowing air through her first two fingers to get Apple's attention.

"But I was always her exception. She played with me, after all."

"Well, now it doesn't matter, because you're nice and solid." Rune pushed Haddy in the shoulder so hard, my sister fell into the snow. My mouth popped open, but Haddy simply laughed and told Rune she was going to get her back. I guess my mouth was still hanging open when they both faced me, because Haddy's head was cocked, a subtle smirk over Rune's lips.

"It's okay, Kar." Haddy reached for one of my hands, her tone soft. "She won't hurt me, or you. You don't need to be scared."

"I'm not scared." I shook my head.

"Are you mad at me?" she whispered. "For asking Rune not to tell you I knew she was...spending time near the longhouse?"

"Spending time near the longhouse?" I scoffed. "You mean watching me?"

"Well..." Haddy shrugged. "She never did tell me what she was up to, did you?" Haddy asked Rune.

Rune blew out stale air and looked between the two of us. "No."

The sound of Apple's wings beating above us broke the tension. She hovered for a second, making sure Tove was out of the way, then landed several feet left of us. Haddy squeezed my hand and backed away from me, still not facing Apple, though I knew she wanted to. She wanted to make sure my face softened, that I wasn't mad. She always hated when I was anything but happy. Was I seriously going to waste the little time I had with her by holding on to old weight?

I offered her a small smile and pointed my chin to Apple, signifying I was fine. I wanted her to enjoy Apple's company. I wanted her to ride upon her back and do wonderful things she was never able to do in her mortal life. It made me believe that being in Helheim wasn't all that bad for her. I wanted to believe this place could offer her everything she needed and more.

As Haddy ran her hands down Apple's mane, Rune shot me a glance. How could one look be so loaded? It held questions I didn't have the answer to, ones I wasn't ready to admit I already had.

I let my rigid shoulders fall, releasing my fears and hesitancies for once. I was tired of maintaining my walls, and if Rune was shedding her armor and showing me what was beneath it, maybe it was safe to start doing the same. She'd seen me vulnerable on more than one occasion, and I'd beaten myself up afterward for being too open, for letting her see me for who I really am. Being reunited with Haddy made me realize I was tired of not being seen, of not being known. Maybe, just maybe, I'd give this valkyrie what she'd been craving for years now.

Maybe, I'd give her...*me.*

CHAPTER TWENTY-FOUR
GREAT HUGS BY THE GREAT HEARTH

Rune

Kari and Haddy flew on Apple back to Hel's Hall while Tove and I walked through the snowy landscape. The reintroduction went well, all things considered, but I thought about the odd expression Kari wore right before Apple took off with her on her back.

A gust of breeze brushed my hair across my forehead, and its cool touch reminded me of a spirit right after being separated from its body. I craved that sensation and the high that accompanied growing my collection of souls. My tongue ran over my teeth, as if hungry for that type of hunt.

As I stared out at the mountainous expanse, seeing souls littering the area, I wondered which of them I'd passed up. Which of these mortals had I watched the final moments of and decided against taking to Valhalla?

I'd never worked at the Helheim sect, but I imagine the job was vastly different than what I'd been trained to do. Here, it didn't matter if you were a viking. It didn't matter if your death was glorious. All you had to do was not drown in the sea and not be a horrible person. There were other halls for those individuals, ones valkyries never saw.

In my early days, I took far too many souls, loving the feeling of them buzzing through me. It was hard to forget those nights, and even so, the number of souls I collected on my least picky nights couldn't come close to the number the Helheim sect took each night. I presumed they were high every time the sun hid from the sky, losing their minds in pure intoxication, just so these souls could find their eternal peace.

When I glanced around at the happy families, I wondered if a fate such as theirs would be all so bad. I thought of Kari's family that I was on my way to meet. Once we left Helheim, the next time Kari saw her family again, she should be older than her mother. She should have more grey hair, don wrinkles on her hands and under her beautiful eyes. I would give anything for that future, a future in which she lived.

I'd been in the underworld long enough to know living wasn't all it was cracked up to be, and only in death could you find happiness. But what I thought was irrelevant, because if Kari wanted to grow old, I would find a way to make that happen.

As I took my first step into Hel's Hall, I shook the snowflakes from my hair and rubbed my hands together. The warmth of her castle instantly found me, and I breathed a sigh of relief as I regained feeling in my fingers and toes. If I had known we were going to stay in Helheim for almost an entire lunar cycle, I would have packed different clothes. Sure, there were some in the wardrobe back in our bedchamber, but the only thing that fit over my thighs were the dresses, and they would hardly do.

"Rune!" Haddy called out, waving me over to where she sat next to Kari. She stood, leaving her empty seat for me, finding a place on a fur rug next to the hearth. No fire roared in the stone opening, but false orange tendrils did lick up the sides. The spirits couldn't feel the difference between a fake flame and a real one anyway. It was more about the comfort of familiarity over anything else. Even though the residents could eat, fuck, sleep, bathe, the one thing they couldn't do was feel temperature.

I shot Haddy a smile and then took my seat next to Kari. She was draped in furs, and when I took my place, she shifted so she could share, covering my lap. The hide was warm from her heat, and it sent prickles up my arms, thinking of a future robbed of the sensation she gave me. My skin was too covered for her to see the effect that gesture had had on me, but when she gazed down at my lap, I had a feeling she didn't need to see my pimpled flesh to know.

"And who is this?" a gruff voice called out, and I lifted my gaze to the man sitting across from me.

Kettle Ulfson.

Kari's father was a large man with a thick, red beard. He wore a permanent scowl and had deep grooves running parallel across his forehead to prove it.

"This is Rune," Kari began. "She's the valkyrie I told you about, the one who brought me here to visit you."

"Hmm," he grumbled, not satisfied with her explanation. I figured I wouldn't open my mouth until I was asked a question. It was better to let them all digest what Kari was saying before adding my own explanation to the mix. Not only that, but I didn't know how much truth Kari planned on spilling.

Kari's mother, Sigrid, smiled at me wearily, then said, "Rune, why did you bring our darling girl back to us?" I stared into her deep blue eyes, thinking of the curse that followed her into death. Was Hel watching us now? Was she staring at me through Sigrid's eyes, trying to gather information on us? Was the woman even aware that the goddess was using her, that she had been her entire life? I certainly wouldn't trust her with any sensitive information, though it was no fault of her own. This was all Hel's doing.

"It's nice to finally meet you all," I addressed the woman, then let my gaze scan over Kettle, Haddy, Malfrid, and Odel. "I'm sure Kari has told you why she's here?"

"Indeed," Sigrid said, her smile fading. "But what I want to know is, why would a valkyrie take interest in a living mortal? So much so that she was willing to bring her to her deceased family in Helheim?"

I was hoping for a little bit more than "indeed" to work with in determining what Kari had told her family. Haddy knew more of the truth than anyone, but was she still holding it close to her chest? I wasn't sure what she had to gain by keeping it from her own family. I had nothing left to offer her, and neither did Kari, outside of her continued presence. I suppose that was enough of an incentive. That, and Haddy didn't like her other sisters enough to betray Kari.

"It's okay, you can tell them," Kari whispered to the side of my face. I shifted to meet her soft gaze, an encouraging smile lifting the corner of her lips.

Tell them what? Tell them I watched her for years? Tell them I think the world of her still? Tell them I stole her death?

What was it that she wanted me to tell them?

I cleared my throat. "Kari is a very special seeress. She caught my attention a few years ago, and I kept watch over her to ensure her safety and the safety of the seidr within her. When she mentioned having a connection to Hel, I thought that bringing her here would bring the Goddess of Death much satisfaction, and Kari agreed to come with me willingly," I said with a practiced smile. "I have to admit, I did not bring her here to be reunited with her family, but it is a pleasant addition to the trip."

"You're not an attendant of Hel. Why would you do this for her?" a girl I assumed to be Malfrid asked.

"Because a happy Hel is a happy Odin. The Allfather wants all the gods and goddess across the realms to be satisfied and at peace. Odin takes no issue with my trip here with Kari." It was bullshit. I knew it, Kari knew it, and Haddy probably knew it too. I only hoped the rest of her family couldn't taste my lies.

Kari's father grumbled something to her mother, and Odel

stared at me with unsettling blue eyes. Her lips twisted, and she said, "Special how?"

Before I could open my mouth, Kari said, "You know Mom and I have the sight. While her seidr was strong on Midgard, mine is stronger here. I can wield seidr of the underworld because of the curse Hel placed upon our ancestor, Norfrid. I've talked to Hel herself, and she's confirmed this. She—"

"You've talked to Hel?" Malfrid sputtered, her cheeks sunken from the pucker in her lips. "And how did you know your seidr is stronger here before you left Midgard?"

"Rune sensed it," Kari lied, her jaw ticking as she did. Apparently, I wasn't the only one who didn't trust her family with the truth. "She sensed my power."

"Well, how—"

"So many questions!" Kari laughed, her posture tight despite trying to come across as casual. "It's been two years since I've seen you. Does how I got here or why matter more than the fact that I am? I want to know how it's been here. Are you all doing okay? Are you... happy?" Her brows pinched as she peered into each of their eyes.

Haddy didn't bother responding, as we already had the chance to catch up with her, but Odel and Malfrid exchanged a loaded glance. They went to speak at the same time, then paused and grinned awkwardly at one another. If I didn't know any better, I would have thought they were twins in the way their mannerisms matched and the evident similarities in their features, down to the same shade of hair and eyes.

Malfrid, the older of the two, placed her hand on Odel's knee. "We're good. It's quite nice here, and there's even a hall that mimics each of the seasons if we get tired of the snow." Her voice wavered, and she twisted her hands in her lap. "But Kari...we've had a lot of time to think, and Odel and I are really grateful you're here, because our hearts have been feeling quite heavy knowing what we, uh, tried to do to you." The sass Kari described her sister as having was leached from her tone as she stared at Kari with unblinking eyes.

"We don't know what we were thinking! Truly, we never want to see harm come to you," Odel chimed in, the heel of her palm pressed into her chest, as if her heart were splitting and she was staunching the bleeding. This wasn't the first time I'd seen spirits seek forgiveness for the actions they took after spending too much time roaming Midgard. Staying on Midgard without a body was unnatural. It ate at your soul, and the more time one spent in a place they didn't belong, the more that place teared at you.

It wasn't my place to forgive them, but I hoped, for Kari's sake, she saw their words as pure. I knew how much their actions ate at her, despite pretending she was fine.

"What did you girls do?" Sigrid asked.

Kari ignored her mother as she said, "I hold no grudge over what happened. Well, not anymore at least. Rune told me what happens to a soul who spends too much time separated from their body. By the end of those few months, none of you were acting like yourselves. To be honest, I'd been happy when you finally all moved on. Lingering in a home that is no longer yours is no way to spend your afterlife. You all deserved more, and I deserved to try to move on. I'm more than happy to wipe that morning from my mind if you are."

"What did you girls do?" Sigrid asked again, more aggressive this time. Odel and Malfrid ran over to Kari and threw themselves onto her lap, and I slid to the side to avoid the flailing limbs. But then Odel turned to me and threw her arms over my shoulders, giving me a big kiss on the cheek.

"Thank you! Thank you for bringing our sister back to us." She let me go and wiped at the tears that streamed down her face with an embarrassed grin.

I cleared my throat and shifted on the furs beneath me. I was used to taking people away from their family members and the tears that caused. Every once in a while, I would see relatives or loved ones reuniting in the halls of Valhalla, but this was different entirely. "Uh, you're welcome," I forced out, because what else was there to say? I'd be taking Kari back to Asgard again soon enough, and they would have to say goodbye all over again. At least this time, they got their closure.

"I swear to the gods, if one of you doesn't answer your mother right now, I'm going to lose it," Kettle growled. Odel and Malfrid's faces paled, and I knew this conversation was about to get really awkward. I debated sneaking away, telling them all I had important valkyrie matters to attend to elsewhere, but Kari would know otherwise. I didn't want to abandon her for the sake of my own comfort, so as Kari's sisters uncomfortably began explaining what they had done, I remained next to her, a constant, unwavering presence.

"YOU WHAT?" Kettle bellowed, shaking the stone walls around him with the sheer might of his roar. Even though Kari wasn't the one receiving the brunt of his anger, she still winced. My hand found its way to her lap under the furs, and I pressed my palm into her thigh for comfort. I caught Haddy staring at me as their father yelled, and the two of us shared a silent conversation of our own.

Malfrid and Odel began to sob, their story lost in their blubbering. I couldn't tell who was saying what, but I could make out a string of coherent words, such as, "She wouldn't have done it herself!" and "We didn't want to leave her behind!"

Sigrid looked as if she didn't know which of her children she should comfort, if any. On one hand, two of them tried to murder her remaining daughter. On the other hand, if they had succeeded, the entire family would've been able to travel to their afterlife together. I tried not to hold any anger for Kari's younger sisters, because I too would do just about anything to keep those I loved by my side. If Kari chose to forgive them eventually, that would be her decision to make, and I'd respect it.

It took about an hour, but eventually, things settled, faces lost their redness, and voices lowered. The conversation was lost to funny moments they'd experienced in Helheim, including a moment when Haddy was off collecting flowers when she caught Garm, of all creatures, doing the same. Apparently, he had a mate out there somewhere and didn't spend his entire existence guarding the gates of Hel with a snarl on his dripping lips.

By the time Kari and I made it back to our chamber, our bellies were full, and Kari's heart was as well.

"Thank you," she whispered as her eyes grew heavy with fatigue. I never got the chance to ask what exactly she was thankful for, because the seeress drifted off to sleep propped up against the pillows, her head resting crookedly on her hand. I chuckled to myself and didn't think twice as I pulled the quilt from under her and adjusted her head on the pillows so she didn't wake with a kink in her neck. She didn't wake as I laid the quilt down upon her, but she mumbled something inaudible and turned on her side, the sheets gripped in one of her hands.

The skin under her nails was already a smoking charcoal from the spells she'd performed this morning, and I was left wondering what toll Hel's power was going to have on my little mortal one lunar cycle from now. Whatever happened, I wouldn't let the seidr of the underworld hold her. Stained fingers were one thing, but the blackening of her heart was another. If she wasn't careful, Hel's power could consume her, and I would do anything to prevent that day from coming.

Anything.

CHAPTER TWENTY-FIVE
CAVE OF WHISPERS

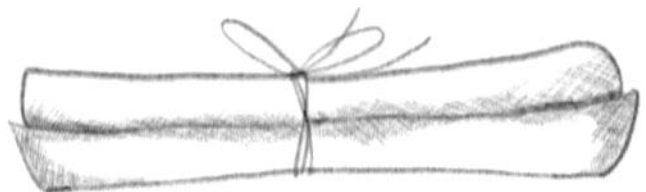

Kari

Vibrations from the hums living in my throat echoed out into the room as I worked. My fingers tingled with seidr and my eyes focused on nothing but what I had in front of me. The scent of crisp spruce hit my nose when my hands raised up to my face and the aroma of the oils coating my palms wafted through the air.

Rune walked into the room, the broomstick I'd made clattering against the door. "Looks like you made some improvements to the broomstick. Care to explain?" she asked.

I didn't look up from the spell I was working on, and I didn't want to break my chant to acknowledge her, but she stood before me, watching my moves intently, and it was enough to shatter my waning concentration.

Huffing, I dropped my hands onto the table I worked upon and finally met her gaze. "While Hel is supposed to take any wicked spirits off to Niflheim for punishment, I'm not naive enough to believe there haven't been any who've slipped past her detection. I know we're only here for one more week, but I thought it was worth the practice if nothing else." I glanced over at the door to our sleeping chamber as if I could see the broomstick hanging on the other side of it.

What a power that would be.

"Fair enough. Those souls don't pose as much risk to the residents of Hel, but you're quite… alive," she said, looking me over, and letting her gaze linger on my collection of ingredients on the table. "Seeress, I hope you know you're safe with me. Even with wild spirits roaming. I've fought much worse."

I took in her black and silver leathers which had been dropped off by the House of Wings Helheim sect, along with a few other items specific to this realm. She'd promised Hel she would lead a few training sessions with the valkyries here in exchange for some ingredients I could use for my spells, and the ability to harvest anything I wanted from the snowy realm. With the exception of the onyx of her hall, of course.

"I believe you, but you're not always around. And I want to be safe with *myself*," I admitted. Wiping my hands clean of the residual powders on them, and leaning back in my chair. My back had been growing sore from being hunched over this table for the past three weeks. I really needed to practice sitting with a straighter spine, but as soon as I started humming and chanting, all thoughts of healthy posture escaped me.

"You're very good at relying on yourself. You have been for a long time now. Why not rely on someone else for a change?" Rune asked, coming to sit by me, but thinking better of arranging any of the bottles and tools I had laid out, even if it would give herself more space.

"I can do both, you know," I said. "I'll humor you when you're around, but when I'm alone, I'm responsible for myself. Plus, Hel isn't going to trade some no good seeress to Freyja. I need to take all of my spells to the next level, and I wanted to try something new with that protection broom."

"Oh yeah?"

I nodded and excitedly began explaining how I harvested

pollen from the yellow snow blossoms and mixed it with melted icicles to make a sticky paste to secure pieces of black tourmaline to the base of the broom. The paste was meant to glow in the presence of negative energy and would attract a swarm of blood bats any time that presence got too close to our door. If we were nearby, it would surely cause a commotion loud enough to alert us to the incoming intruder.

My favorite kind of spells were the ones that mixed the natural wonders of nature with seidr. I always found them to be more effective than spells that relied on seidr alone, even if they required more time for harvesting and preparation.

Rune just smiled and listened to the other steps I'd taken in preparation for any unwanted visitors, including a few considerably more drastic measures in case they got past the swarm of bats at the door, and gods forbid, got close to the canopy bed. When I concluded my explanation, she provided me with a proud slow clap, shaking her head and chucking.

"Well done, seeress. Let's just hope none of your spells mistake one of *us* for a negative presence, or we'll be in a world of hurt. I'd rather not be covered in bat scratches, or have the tendons in my ankles severed by swinging axes."

I shrugged with an amused grin that said she needed to act right if she wanted to avoid the wrath of my seidr. "Anyway, how did training go? Are the valkyrie's here showing to be less useless than last session?"

"I never called them useless, I—"

"You might as well have," I muttered under my breath. I may have been paraphrasing, but when Rune called the group of women the "soil of the House of Wings", she couldn't have expected me to believe she thought of them highly.

"All valkyries are impressive regardless of their sect, and all of them are my sisters. Useless could never be used to describe them. Without the valkyries here, your family would still be wandering Midgard, as would many others. When I called them the 'soil of the House of Wings' I was referring to them as our foundation."

"Sure," I said, which pulled an eye roll from Rune but she continued anyway, not feeding into my commentary more.

"They need to work quickly with the amount of souls they're bringing in each night. They have the longest shift, and it doesn't leave much time for training, or practicing their seidr. Many of them barely know how to use their own strength against their opponents, or how to summon something as simple as barley porridge."

My face paled, and my stomach churned, "Don't you dare bring porridge into this conversation."

Rune laughed, breaking the serious face she'd been donning after she'd been accused of looking down on her sisters of Hel. "What? You don't like porridge?"

"Don't even start with me." I held up a finger in warning.

"Let's not pretend that Áma wasn't secretly feeding you in her incantation chamber." Rune crossed her arms.

"How did you know that?"

"I had a hunch, but you just confirmed my suspicions," she said with a shrug.

"Yeah, well, unlike someone, she wasn't going to let me starve."

"Oh stop. Do you know how long it would have taken for malnutrition to kill you? So dramatic," Rune scoffed.

"I was more likely to die due to mouth boredom."

Rune raised her scared brow. "Mouth boredom? That's a new one. But seeress, if you wanted something to keep your mouth busy, I could have given you a task or two."

Heat rose to my face, and there was no hiding the blush that surely reddened my cheeks.

"Why are you getting all flustered?" Rune smirked demonically. "There's nothing naughty about singing your valkyrie captor a little song. Or were you thinking of something *else* you could've been doing with that pretty mouth of yours?"

I cleared my throat and pushed the hair off my clammy forehead. "Singing, of course. What else?"

"Mmm." Rune hummed. Her deep blue eyes were hooded, amusement hooking up the corner of her lips.

"Anyway," I said, pushing out my chair, its legs scraping against the stone floor. "Tell me more about training." I distanced myself from the valkyrie, standing by the end of the bed where Tove was curled up with one of my used socks.

"My sisters did well, but they have a long way to go," Rune said. I thought that's where she was going to leave it, but after a pause, she went on a long tangent about her plans for teaching her sisters, and I swear there was a twinkle in her eye as she did. I wasn't going to bring it up because I knew she would deny it, but I saw past her grunts of disapproval, and her crossed arms when she referred to the lack of structure their current house mother led with. Before I could get much of a word in, Rune sucked in a large breath and then said, "The training wasn't the most exciting thing that happened today though."

"Oh?" I asked, trying not to sound too interested, as I lazily played with the end of Tove's white-tipped nail.

"I spoke with Hel to report her sect's progress after training. While I had her attention, I asked her if we could use more of her resources than simply being able to harvest natural materials around the realm," Rune said from where she still sat at the table, legs crossed at the ankle.

"And?" I asked hopefully, wondering why it took her this long to tell me. Why were we wasting time talking about porridge and soil?

"And she agreed it would be in all of our best interests to be given access to her Cave of Whispers." She wiggled her brows.

My jaw slackened, and I stared at her before I found it in me to blurt, "*The* Cave of Whispers?" My eyes widened with excitement.

"The one and only."

"What are we still doing here?" I hastily dropped Tove's tail and darted toward the wardrobe where I'd left my heavy outdoor gear. After I wrapped myself in midnight furs and wool gloves, I began jamming my feet into my boots and tying up the laces.

"Hold on, hold on," Rune said. "You need to eat first."

"Fine, but let's do it quickly!" I all but growled, motioning my hand in the air to demand she hurry it up and summon something already. She cleared some space on the table, and within moments, there were bowls of berry soup, rolls of bread, and glasses of ice-cold water.

I scarfed down every morsel of food she gave me and then looked at her expectantly. She finally gave in and began lacing up her own boots. The excitement that bubbled up in me was unrivaled as I imagined all the knowledge that was awaiting me. The Cave of Whispers was a thing of legends and I never would have imagined being able to tap into such an incredible resource while still living. I thought only in death would I be awarded in such a way.

"Are you ready yet?" I moaned as I walked in a circle by our door. Tove woke amidst the chaos, but the sleepy cat looked like he had no interest in following us on our adventure today, and I didn't blame him. He'd been on more adventures over the past lunar cycle than he had in his entire lifetime. He was due for some rest, and I wasn't going to steal it from him by making him follow along. While corporeal, he was still a spirit, and with the traps I'd set both inside and outside our chambers, I trusted that nothing could harm him, himself excluded.

When Rune finally finished strapping on her armor in the most meticulous way possible, I swung open the door, the broomstick rattling against the wood as I did. The two of us walked through Hel's Hall, and then out to the fields, where we spotted Apple in a patch of grass free from snow and ice. She offered us an excited whinny, then flared her pink and black lips at Rune in anticipation of an Apple. Rune chuckled as she tossed her a red fruit, and Apple received it happily.

She wasn't wearing her armor, but she still had a thin leather saddle to protect our asses from the intense bones of her spine where they connected to the base of her wings. We climbed aboard, Rune giving me a boost, even though I'd figured out how to mount the pegasus by myself weeks ago. I wouldn't tell her that though, because I know she liked feeling useful. And maybe I didn't mind the feeling of her strong hands on my waist, even through the furs and all my other layers. Her hands still gave me a tight squeeze, and the feeling of them made me forget there was any fabric between us at all.

When we were both on, Apple shot into the sky. The jarring movement pulled a scream from my lips, causing a group of spirits to turn our way. I gave them a wave as we took off, Rune chuckling softly from behind me.

The view from the sky was beautiful, and the two of us soon fell silent. It hadn't been the first time I'd flown upon Apple's back while in Helheim, but it'd been the first time we'd traveled in this direction. From way up in the sky, we could see ice bridges curving from one onyx building to another in a delicate network that reminded me of the crystalline structure of a snowflake. It was easy to remain silent when there were so many incredible details to feast my eyes on.

It took us an hour on Apple's back to make it to the Cave of Whispers, and every so often, she would swoop down to get a better look at something interesting we'd come across. Not even pegasus' were immune to beauty, and one could argue that they appreciated it far more than even we did.

Apple landed upon a cliffside, her hooves slipping on ice for a moment before righting herself. When Rune felt we were stable, she dismounted and then offered me a hand. The stone of this place was unsurprisingly black, though it didn't look as deep and endless as Hel's Hall. It was matte, had charcoal grey hues, and was lightly dusted in snow.

Rune asked with her eyes if I was ready, and I gave her a swift nod of my head. She gave Apple a pat, a bucket of warm water, oats, and a pile of hay to stand upon to protect her hooves from the rough stone. I swear Apple was the most spoiled pegasus in all nine realms.

When our companion was content, the two of us strode toward the opening in the mountainside. I couldn't help but imagine it like a hungry mouth ready to devour the knowledge of its prey. But even so, I was hoping I'd come away from this trip with more knowledge than I ever could have imagined, and my pack was full of charcoal and journals made of thin hides. I had one chance at consuming as much information as I could, with an entire day to do it. I only wished I hadn't tapped myself out practicing spells this morning.

If I had known I was coming here, I would have reserved every last drop of my seidr. While Rune could simply fly through the air on Apple's back to rejuvenate, I wasn't sure how my stores were refilled, or if I simply needed rest and time like my mother and most seeresses had.

"Up ahead," Rune said, pointing her chin to where faint lights light up the entrance to the cave where the sun had been unable to shine. I didn't hesitate to enter the cave, taking one long stride after the other. Once inside, I felt the nip of the breeze go still, and I instantly felt much warmer. I hoped that once I was in the belly of the cave that my fingers would be warm enough to cast.

Sconces with fake flames were mounted to the walls, and we followed them as we went. "I'm so close to being able to make a flame illusion," I admitted, feeling the burn under my nails as my body itched to try my new spell. I'd never needed to create false fire before seeing as I could simply light a torch, but here in Helheim, the bitter cold of the realm wouldn't allow for flame to exist outside of an illusion.

I passed my hand through one of the orange lights, and I felt no heat, only a slight tingling where my skin passed through.

"That's good, seeress. You'll want that skill if you get caught out here in the dark," she said, gazing at one of the torches as we walked by it. So far, there wasn't much else to look at. "Not that I ever suggest exploring Helheim at night."

I suppressed a chuckle because even I would never do something so stupid. I didn't want her to mistake my laugh for an admission to her humor though, so I hummed in response, and carried on.

The long tunnel opened up into a broad cavern, and we funneled into it, me first, and Rune following shortly behind. As we walked deeper into the empty cavern, I noticed out of the corner of my eye that she'd place her palm on the butt of her sword.

"Hello?" she called out into the echoing chamber. We walked along the outskirts of the cavern, but saw no additional tunnels to the one we'd come in through. "It's a dead end. That can't be."

I stopped in my tracks, this whole place feeling utterly wrong.

Is it? I asked myself, because something about her words rang false. I swear I could feel the vibrations of other beings in this place.

"Rune... summon a strawberry."

Rune cocked a brow at me. "Hungry seeress? Didn't I feed you before we left?"

"Just do it!" I tried to hold back the edge in my voice, but I was too anxious to uncover the secrets of this place. Rune rolled her eyes and held her hand out, muttering to herself.

A red berry fell into her palm, and she sliced it between her front teeth in a dramatic effort to show me that I couldn't have it after my snarky remark. But that was fine, because I had little appetite for food. My only craving was the secrets this place held, and I had a feeling I knew just what I needed to unlock them.

"Again, but more this time. An entire basket full." I said. Something clicked in Rune's mind, and she bobbed her head in understanding. This time, when she summoned the berries, my hair began to swirl around me, and my vision went dark. When light flooded my vision once more, the air went dead still, and I no longer found myself in an empty cavern.

"The key is seidr," Rune whispered, peering down at the ornamental rug we now stood on. "Of course."

My lips parted as my eyes darted all around the room. There were people, tall shelves, and tables with stacks of journals. Where there was once immovable stone, were now gaps in the walls that led into additional tunnels. I wondered how many of them there were and how many hidden chambers full of secrets we could uncover in one day. There was little time to waste.

"Let's go!" I said, already walking to the closest living being, hoping for a skald. They were the next best thing to Mim, the god of knowledge, who was beheaded to be carried by Odin as his personal source of wisdom.

Skalds kept our memory and history alive by reciting stories. We had one in Stormheim too, but the skald in my village wasn't an expert wielder in seidr. And while they spoke stories of our gods, they weren't tasked by the gods themselves. The skalds in the Cave of Whispers held infinite knowledge and were considered attendants to the gods, their age preserved through the millennia, as long as they upheld their duties.

Being in their presence was a blessing, and I was beginning to realize that Hel had indeed given me a valuable gift, it just wasn't the one she'd originally claimed.

"Hello?" I whispered as I rounded a shelf and caught a glimpse of grey, wiry hair. The being stopped abruptly and turned to face me.

"Ah, so you *can* see me now. Come along then, and bring your shy friend with you," the skald said. I glanced over my shoulder at Rune, flashing her a smile and lipping the word "shy" at her. She just shook her head and followed even closer than before. If there was one thing Rune wasn't, it was shy. She wasn't shy when she betrayed Odin, and she certainly hadn't been when she'd talked about my mouth as if it was her favorite toy.

"You're not a goddess, or even a demi-goddess, so I assume Hel sent you?" The skald asked, their tone neither feminine or masculine.

"That's right. She's obviously a valkyrie," I motioned to Rune, "Odin's sect. And I'm a seeress."

"A mortal one at that," they said, arching a thick brow at me. "Why did Hel send you to us?" The skald led us out of the main cavern and through a tunnel hidden behind one of the shelves. With one wave of their hand, the entire wooden structure slid to the side, revealing a corridor lit by false flames. I didn't hesitate to follow them through it, too excited about the prospect of what was on the other side. That, and skalds were known to be peaceful people, unless they got an unwanted visitor, that is. And seeing as Rune and I were sent by Hel herself, I had very little reason to believe we would get into trouble within this cave system.

"She has... interest in ensuring I fully come into my power," I started, trailing my fingers over the cool stone wall. "My seidr seems to have strengthened upon coming to Hel, though my visions are still foggy. I have a long way to go in a short amount of time. And Hel needs me ready when the time comes."

"How much time?" They asked, peering back at me.

"One week. Though, I'm not sure if she'll permit us to return here."

"She will. I'll speak with her dear," the skald said, directing us into a smaller cavern than before. There was a long stone table that sat in the middle of it, and they ushered me to take a seat at one of the wooden chairs around it, lined with a thin red pillow. Rune pulled a chair out for me and I smiled at her as I sat upon its cushion. She and the skald took their own seats, the skald not taking their eyes off me as they did. "One week isn't much time, though, I suppose Helheim is the best place for you to learn to wield your talents."

"You can already tell that?" I asked. Maybe I should've been uncomfortable that they were able to see into me so clearly, but I was more amazed than anything. I hoped to have that level of acuity some day.

"Seidr has different signatures, and yours is not of Midgard. It is of Hel. It's no wonder your spells were so weak in your previous life in the mortal realm." The way they said "previous life" made me shift in my seat, because that term was usually used to refer to the dead. And I supposed I had to get used to the reality that my time on Midgard had come to an end, and that version of me was effectively gone.

Rune found my thigh under the table and gave it a quick squeeze before returning it to her own lap. I glanced over at her, my gaze soft and appreciative, because she'd yanked me from that spiraling thought. She knew the skald's comment would get to me, and I was thankful to be known in such a way. I was thankful she was here with me, and my heart squeezed for this woman that I once claimed was my captor, a horrible sentence. But all she truly was, was a bleeding heart. And I knew by now that it bled for me.

CHAPTER TWENTY-SIX
THE POWER SHE WIELDS

Rune

"What does it feel like?" I whispered, my voice surprisingly sultry. The sound coming from my mouth shouldn't have been all that surprising, seeing as I'd been all but drooling at Kari since the moment she raised her hands to perform her first spell. Within these caves, she came to life. It was as if her spot in this world suddenly clicked into place, and her seidr flowed from her in a way that seemed so right.

Once upon a time, I too needed to get a hold of my power, and while some skills were easier to master, some took decades. But unlike Kari, I knew my place was in Valhalla, among the fallen warriors and the gods. I knew my task, my purpose, and had teachers to guide me, ones who had been attendants to Odin for thousands of years.

Kari was only now uncovering her place, her destiny. Once she was firm in this knowledge, she would be unstoppable. But for now, I would help guide her until she had no doubts. This was not something that could be forced. She had to choose a path for herself, and even my guidance would only do as much as she allowed.

"Kari?" I asked when she took too long to respond. I didn't blame her, though, because I too alternated between being hyper present, focusing on every detail of her spell, and being lost in my mind, in a world of hopes and memories.

"Oh!" she said finally, glancing up with an embarrassed grin, a ball of fire blazing between her palms. "Sorry. This one takes a lot of focus. I can't believe I'm able to do this at all! I never would have been able to cast a spell this strong on Midgard. It feels warm, even if I know it's just an illusion. The false flames may emanate no actual warmth on the outside, but I swear, I have the heat of a true flame burning inside me."

Before I could respond, the skald clapped once and said, "Very good. Let's move on." The attendant showed little reaction each time Kari performed one of her tasks, moving through a list in front of them and checking each skill off as we went. Kari had completed eight of them by now, and each time the skald told her to move on, I could sense her pride growing. The spells the skald had been having her practice were way more advanced than anything Kari had been doing with Áma, or even alone in our chamber here in Hel. "One more spell, and then we will focus on those foggy visions of yours."

Kari nodded eagerly, dissolving the false flames and facing her palms down on the stone table. I'm sure the chill of it felt nice on her skin after maintaining that illusion.

"Now, this time, I want you to summon your favorite meal," the skald said, focusing on Kari very intently. Their gaze shifted to me for a moment, telling me not to open my mouth, and I pressed my lips together in compliance. This test was for Kari. I wouldn't let my knowledge of seidr influence her decisions.

"I can't," Kari said with a shrug.

"What do you mean you can't?" the skald asked.

"I've tried about a thousand times. I can't create organic

matter. When I try to summon anything living, or anything once alive, it feels as if I were to tell myself to suddenly be pregnant with little pegasus babies. It just won't happen. It feels like nothing."

I tried to hold back a laugh, but it slipped from my throat and echoed in the room. Kari shot me a smile, but the skald just scowled.

They have no fun here, damn.

"Good. You're discovering your limits already. Summoning food would be a very unusual gift for a mortal seeress, and a part of understanding our seidr is knowing when to stop wasting our time on a spell that will never work for us. Just like you cannot summon food, Rune cannot have visions. There are different types of seidr for different people, and that is the way of things."

"You knew I wouldn't be able to do it?" Kari asked with interest.

"I did."

"Did you?" Kari shifted to assess me, her lips pursed, more in curiosity than annoyance.

"I had a strong feeling, seeress," I admitted. I had a feeling if she was able to summon food, she would have done it by now, especially during our days at Áma's.

"So, I guess I passed your test?" Kari asked with a proud smile tugging at her lips.

"I guess you did," the skald said with a satisfied grin. "Now that I know the bounds of your seidr, what you can perform with ease, and what needs work, I have an understanding of where to begin. Next, are you comfortable sharing your most recent visions with me? And when did they start getting harder to decipher?"

"Sure! My visions always used to be strong and accurate. Unlike my spells, I never had to work hard to understand them, even as a child. It could have been because they were all relatively simple and only a day or two in the future," she said. "They started getting more complicated a few weeks before I was taken to Valhalla. It wasn't until I arrived in Asgard that I understood the symbolism behind them. There'd been one that plagued me repeatedly, though, and its appearance was the first time I had the same vision multiple nights in a row."

"Ah, and each time you have had difficulty with your visions, were you, by chance, planning to travel somewhere new in the distant future?"

"Now that I think about it, yeah, I was, even if I didn't know it at the time."

"This makes perfect sense. You cannot have a vision of a realm you have never been to. You can see glimpses and symbols, but not the place itself. Once you do more traveling around the nine realms, you shouldn't have this issue."

"Really? So it's not a permanent problem? Nothing is wrong with me?"

"No, Kari, nothing is wrong with you."

"I can't tell you how relieved I am to hear that!" she beamed. "So we can focus more on my spells then? I need to master as many as I can if Freyja is to consider allowing me to join her council." Kari had admitted the truth to the skald shortly after performing her first spell. It'd become difficult to explain why we were here, what we wanted, and why we were in a rush while also maintaining that little morsel of information. Plus, the skald would know better than anyone what type of skill Freyja may be looking for. Hiding the truth would've only done Kari a disservice.

"We may, but while you're here, I want to discuss dream symbolism with you. Just because you haven't been to a realm and your visions are fuzzy doesn't mean you should be totally helpless deciphering them. A good seeress can decipher any vision, no matter how unclear. Freyja greatly appreciates someone with clear and useful visions, especially if they help her find what she seeks most."

"Well, you lead the way. If you want me to learn it, I will. I trust you know best," Kari said, clasping her hands upon the table.

"If only you'd had that attitude with me," I grumbled under

my breath. Kari rewarded me with an elbow to my side as she mentioned something about stalker-kidnappers not deserving the benefit of the doubt. I couldn't argue with her, but I could scowl and pretend anyway.

"I'm going to let the two of you sort that out. I'll be taking a walk, but call if you need me. I won't go too far," I said.

"You're really leaving?" Kari asked, a hint of disappointment in her tone.

"Unless you don't want me to."

"No, it's...fine. I just thought you might want to see me perform a few more spells. I'm improving so much, and—"

"Go!" the skald said with a wave of their hands, practically shooing me away. "You're just a distraction, and we have far too much to do here."

I mouthed "sorry" to Kari, but she just shook her head and gave me a straight smile.

She wants me to stay. She wants to show me her spells. Gods, she's so fucking cute.

Part of me felt bad for leaving, despite knowing she didn't want me to, but from the look of it, I was no longer welcomed by the skald. It sounded like they had a lengthy lesson on symbolism to get through before getting back to spells anyway, and I could think of a few better uses of my time.

I wandered away, exiting the small cavern in favor of finding one of a little more interest. I followed the tunnel we'd come down but took a left through an opening in the wall about halfway through. Once inside, orange flames licked up the walls, as if the room was on fire, but when I ran my fingers through them, I felt nothing but a small wave of seidr. The fact that Hel was able to have false fire going all throughout her kingdom was more than a little impressive. The amount of power that would require was immeasurable, but she was a goddess, after all.

Hel reigned over death, ice, and darkness, but it was also her duty to protect the dead, and part of that was the sanity of her residents. The people here died of old age, disease, accidents, and violent acts inflicted upon them. They didn't deserve punishment; they deserved a home. After family, a home started with warmth and comfort. These may have not been things the ice queen needed for herself, but she would certainly provide it.

Glancing around, I found a large rug covering the stone ground, upon it a few padded seats and wooden tables. The space was cozy, and a big part of me wanted to cuddle up with a glass of mead and settle in. I craved relaxation. I craved true rest, the ability to drop all masks and armor. It was exhausting being strong, being knowledgeable, being dependable all the time, even though these were things Kari needed of me. They may have not been things she *asked* for per se, but we were living in this uncertain existence, and I feared if I wasn't all these things, I would lose Kari to her own doubts and worries.

I knew Kari could handle way more than I was giving her credit for—she proved that today more than anything—but maybe I wanted to be strong so she didn't have to be. Maybe I wanted to be confident so she wouldn't have to second guess. Maybe I wanted to be dependable so Kari would see me as more than her captor, as more than the stranger who stole her death.

I sank into one of the seats, summoning a chalice of mead. When I took my first sip, I heard a faint whisper coming from the hall. I paused and listened for it again, wondering if I was going mad. When I heard nothing, I let out a sigh and released the tension in my shoulders as I took another sip. The fruity flavor tingled my taste buds, and I relished the familiar feel. I'd had no intentions of giving up my revelry, but since I'd met Kari, I felt I couldn't indulge due to the sheer weight on my shoulders. Maybe I didn't feel the need to as much as before.

"Rune..." the voice whispered to me again, and again I straightened, listening for where that sound had come from. Before, it had been a faint noise, but this time, I distinctly heard my own name

echoed through the cavern. I set my chalice down and swung around to look behind me.

"Who's there?" I asked into the empty room.

"Don't pretend you don't know." The distorted voice laughed wickedly, sending a wave of chills up my arms. I stood, no longer craving relaxation. All thoughts of letting loose fled my mind. I faced the back of the cavern but quickly chanced a look over my shoulder, debating if I should turn back and find Kari.

Do I really want to lead the voice to her? Maybe they've already found her.

The hairs on the back on my neck rose, and I placed my hand over the hilt of my sword.

"Oh, now, now. You don't need that silly little weapon. It won't do much good," the voice called, followed by an odd fluttering sound. When I realized the voice was coming from the tunnel, I darted into it, but there was still no one there. I followed the sounds of the mysterious beacon, wondering if I was an idiot for potentially falling into an obvious trap.

When I rounded the corner and made it back to the main cavern, I realized the sound had dissipated all together. A few skalds with scrolls in their hands looked to me, then to my sword, and I retreated with a grunt.

When I was back in the cozy cavern, now tainted by the unsettled feeling inside me, I began running my fingers along the walls to look for a hidden compartment or room. It wasn't until I reached the back that I noticed my hand sliding right through the stone and false flame.

Looks like there's more than one illusion around here.

I walked through the false wall, and I found myself in an ornate bedchamber, gold clinging to every surface. By the bed sat a wooden arch, and perched on that arch, a raven.

Fuck. Fuck. Fuck!

"Oh, relax," the raven said with a devious laugh. "I'm not here for the mortal. I'm here for you."

"Show your true form," I said, my chin lowering slightly. It wasn't a bow, but if I was going to demand anything of him, I certainly wasn't going to do it looking down upon him.

"Only because you're my favorite..." The bird began to shimmer. "Or so you were." When it finished its sentence, the figure was no longer a bird, but a man. A god.

"Odin," I breathed, my knees bending in respect. The stone bit into my armor, but I wouldn't rise until he released me. I had a feeling he was going to keep me down here for as long as he liked. It was the mildest of punishments he could inflict on me, and I'd be lucky if it ended there. The chances of that were slim to none.

"Look at me," the Allfather demanded, and I didn't hesitate. He was draped in white and gold, as always, his beard impeccably groomed, his white hair flowing behind him as if it had a life of his own. A black eye patch was tied around his head to hide that he'd sacrificed one in the pursuit of knowledge.

He wasn't a beautiful man, but he had an aura that made the air in my lungs flee. The very sight of him made me want to bend to his will, do anything he said, and thank him for it. It was the only reason I wouldn't rise, not until he asked me to.

"Ah, there you are. I have to say, Rune, I haven't been *this* disappointed in one of my attendants in the past century. Stealing a mortal? What were you thinking?"

"I'm sorry, Allfather."

"I'm sure you are. However, that isn't much of an explanation, now, is it? What is your plan with the mortal? Why did you bring her to the mist? And why are you here now?" he asked in his familiar, booming voice. He rarely directed this tone at me, though, and I had to hold back a flinch. I'd show him my respect but never my fear. "Have you been hiding from me, my sweet soul collector?"

"I couldn't help myself," I said through gritted teeth, because he'd know if I was trying to deceive him. "I didn't want to see her die, because I knew if she did, she'd be taken to Helheim, not Valhalla. It was a selfish lapse in judgement, not something I'd planned out in rebellion against you. And yes, father, I took her to the mist so your ravens couldn't follow."

"Mmm..." He contemplated my words, all true. I wouldn't give him any more reason to mistrust me. There was far too much to lose. "And after sparing her to avoid Helheim, why are you here now?"

"When we were in the mist, I discovered the mortal was given a morsel of Hel's seidr upon birth, as were her mother and various ancestors. I brought her here to better understand why."

"I see," he said with a slow nod, stroking his perfect beard. "The mortal is free to remain here, if that's Hel's wish. That's her concern, and I will not intervene. You, however, are *my* concern. It greatly pains me to take this action, but I can no longer trust your instincts, and if I cannot trust you, you have no further use for me."

My heart all but stopped, and it felt like millennia were ticking by as I waited for his next words.

Is he going to kill me? Banish me from Valhalla? Turn me into a horse?

"Rune Dragomir, you shall keep your life, but not your title. You are hereby stripped from your position within the House of Wings. You are no longer a valkyrie, and you are no longer my attendant. Enjoy your mortality, and may it be swift."

The armor secured around my leathers began to heat, parts of it already dripping to the floor. I looked down at myself and back to Odin, his singular eye glittering with satisfaction as he destroyed the only thing left of my title.

No, no, NO!

I didn't move, didn't scream or try to strip down out of the melting metal. I stood frozen despite the heat, staring at the god I'd once thought was everything.

Liquid gold pooled at my feet, and I watched as every detail Nori had painstakingly crafted turned into unrecognizable blobs. There was nothing left of the armor on my body, save for the shimmering residue trailing my ruined leathers. Even the weapons I'd strapped to my hips, back, and thighs were but a memory, and I grit my teeth as I saw the leather grip of my favorite dagger on the floor.

I'd never been so hollow, so raw, and the overwhelming feeling of nothingness was almost enough to distract me from the immortality leaching from my bones.

CHAPTER TWENTY-SEVEN
THE GOLDEN RAVEN

Rune

Please be there. Please be there.

As my legs carried me down the tunnel as swiftly as humanly possible, I begged the gods to find Kari at the long stone table, receiving lessons on symbolism. Odin told me he would leave Kari's fate to Hel, but I didn't trust that sentiment for a second.

As I ran, my muscles felt so weak, I moved at an unbearably slow speed. I didn't need to cast to know my seidr was gone. My title wasn't the only thing the Allfather stripped from me, but I could live with it, as long as what I truly needed was right where I left her.

When I busted into the cavern, the skald rose to their feet with a feline grace I would never have again. Kari spun in her chair, catching her sleeve on the wooden arm and cursing as she tried to free herself.

"Leave us!" I called out, and the skald's eyes widened in fear as they hurried out.

"Rune..." Kari said as she slowly rose from her seat. "What's wrong?"

I rushed over and pushed her chair out of the way so I could stand before her without any obstacles in my way.

She's here.

An overwhelming feeling of relief flooded me, and the next thing I knew, I was grabbing the back of Kari's head and winding my fingers through her hair. She yelped in surprise, then nestled into my hand, her eyes locked on mine. Kari grabbed my wrist to take some measure of control, but she didn't pull my hand away from her.

Leaning in, I ran my lips over hers in a teasing kiss, craving nothing more than taking her right here against the stone table. For now, tasting her on my lips would have to do, and oh, did it do everything for me, because *she* was everything.

Kari pulled her head back to look at me, a frown playing on the lips I'd just claimed.

My stomach tightened, and I blurted out, "I...I'm so sor—"

Kari interrupted my apologies with her mouth as she kissed me back far fiercer than I ever would have dared. I wound my fingers tighter in her stunning strawberry hair, pulling a gasp from her, but she only kissed me again harder this time.

The woman of my dreams was in my arms, and I vowed to myself right then that I would continue to protect her until the last sun had set. No god, not even Odin, could have her.

Kari placed her palm flat against my chest, lightly pushing me back. "What was that for?" she asked breathlessly. She still gripped onto my wrist, seeming unsure if she was going to let go yet, and nine realms, I hoped she didn't.

I stared deep into her beautiful eyes, pulling her slightly closer as I said, "I'm so relieved to see you're okay."

"Why wouldn't I be? Were you worried the skald was going to beat me with a scroll?" she laughed, and I wished I could join in on her humor. Alas, I had no laughs to give. I took in her facial features intently, memorizing the curl of her lips and the way her eyes fluttered mid laugh. A big part of me had feared I wouldn't see them again.

Kari's brows pulled together in concern when I didn't laugh with her. The truth was, she had every right to be concerned, because I sure as Hel was.

"I just spoke with the Allfather," I whispered so no lingering skald could hear.

"What?" Kari shrieked, a little too loudly. "How? How did he find you? How are you still here?"

"He let me go. He won't kill me, but...I'm banished from the House of Wings. He stripped me of my title as a valkyrie, took my armor and sword," I said with my teeth scraping my lower lip. The back of my throat was burning, but I wouldn't cry. I couldn't. Kari stepped back just enough to take in my bare leathers, as if she couldn't believe what I was saying. "He melted them down right in front of me."

"Melted? Oh my gods, that fucking bas—"

I covered her mouth, whispering into her ear, "He could still be here, listening. You're lucky he's not hunting you too. I don't want to have to make any drastic decisions if he changes his mind."

Kari nodded, her eyes widening. She kissed my palm when I tried to pull it from her mouth, and then she gripped my hand. "What about Apple?"

"He can't take Epli from me. She won't fly with anyone else, so she's useless to him. But he stripped her of her immortality too, so she's no longer his attendant."

"And neither are you," she said with a sharp inhale. "Fuck. You're over six hundred years old. Are you about to turn into a shriveled old woman and die?"

My chest swelled as I realized she was horrified by that prospect. "No, I still have a lifetime ahead of me, but not as a valkyrie. My human years won't catch up with me all at once. I will age like a mortal once more."

Kari's throat bobbed as she reached forward and ran her

fingers through my hair. She pulled a strand away, showing me a single brown hair. My heart plummeted, and I yanked it from my head, though I knew it would change nothing. My new fate was woven by the Norns, completely sealed.

"We need to get to Fólkvangr. You are Rune fucking Dragomir, and Freyja would be lucky to have you as her attendant. Sure, her sect may be less shiny, but she's also not a fugly ass old—"

"Do I need to cover your mouth again?"

She blew out an angry sigh. "What I'm trying to say is, this isn't over. He's not the one and only god, and he doesn't have the power to ruin your life like this. You were miserable in his sect anyway. Maybe this is the biggest blessing he ever gave you. You're free of him. You can make your own decisions now. If you want to grow old, then grow old. Live a life, Rune. It's yours again."

Kari's arms were held out to her sides, her fingers twitching with power as she began casting two spells, one in each hand.

"You have never been as sexy as you are right now," I blurted, seeing ice and flames lick up her arms simultaneously. I wasn't sure she was even aware she was doing it. I reached to grab her face, and when her arm grazed me, I hissed back in pain. I peered down to where the pain seared, finding an angry red welt on the back of my hand.

A burn.

"That's not possible," I breathed. "Kari, that's not a false flame. You summoned real fire. Real fire in Helheim, the place where flame has never been."

"I'm so sorry," Kari said, shaking her hands out and diminishing the flame. "I hurt you."

"You magnificent creature," I whispered. "My flesh will heal, but your seidr will change the nine worlds forever."

CHAPTER TWENTY-EIGHT
VESSEL FOR THE GODS

Kari

"What are you going to do?" Haddy asked, nervously biting her lower lip as she digested Odin's appearance in Hel and all that had come with it.

"I don't know, but we can't stay here for much longer," I said, glancing over my shoulder to see her reaction. My younger sister paused, an icicle in her hands. She pressed her lips together for a moment, and I thought she might start crying, the way she had when she left Midgard. After everything that went down yesterday between Odin and Rune, I didn't think my heart could take her tears too.

"I understand, Kar," she said. "It's not very safe for you to stay here, but do you think it will be safer for you in Fólkvangr?" She looked from me to the basket in my hands I'd been using to collect odds and ends around Helheim to use as anchors in my spells.

I sat with her question for a moment, wondering if there was a safe place for me and Rune anywhere in the nine realms. I sighed in defeat and said, "No, not unless Freyja accepts me as her attendant and allows me to sit on her council."

"And if she doesn't?" Haddy asked.

I shrugged, swallowing thickly. "I can't think about that, Had."

"Is returning to Asgard what you truly want?" Haddy asked, but I didn't blame her for her concern, or the stream of worried questions she spat my way. She wanted to make sure the decisions I was making weren't going to end up with me killed by a god, and at this rate, there may be more than one competing to make the final blow.

"It is," I answered honestly, twisting the handle of the basket in my hands as that knowledge, my ultimate truth, stared me in the face.

Haddy nodded, twirling the ice in her hand, as if the frozen thing were a toy. "Then you've got to figure it out. If Freyja has a test for you, you have to crush her, and everyone else's, expectations. And I know you will."

"You're not mad I don't plan to stay in Hel with you and the rest of the family?"

"Of course not! I didn't expect, *or want*, to see you for a long time anyway. I had so many old woman jests prepared and everything. For when you finally got here, no sooner."

I snorted a laugh, nudging her with my elbow. "Of course you did."

"But seriously, Kari, if you want to go, you should. Anyway, if you go to Asgard, you can visit me! If you stayed on Midgard, you wouldn't have been able to. We would've gone a lifetime without you."

"Something tells me Odel and Malfrid would have been fine with that," I said, the words sour on my tongue.

"That's not true! They love you, Kar," Haddy said with a little pout on her cute, pale face.

"Is that why they've been avoiding me like I'm a raider for the past three weeks?"

Haddy sighed, dropping the icicle she held, watching as it

pierced the powdery snow. Her hand should have been frostbitten by now, but her skin was entirely unmarred. "They just...feel really bad about what they did. They're embarrassed, so I think sometimes it's easier for them to not see you at all. They'll get over it, though. They'll have to. You're their older sister. Plus, it's been giving us more time to chat." She nudged me with a little smile playing on her lips, and I couldn't help but smile back, despite my obvious disappointment the turn my relationship with my other sisters took.

"Speaking of, this is the chattiest you've ever been. You were so shy when you were alive. What happened?" I asked, shifting my weight, my thumb rubbing the wicker of my basket as I watched her expression harden.

"Yeah, well, there's no point in being shy now, is there?" she said with a shrug and a straight smile. I hadn't realized that comment would strike a nerve with her.

"Why's that?"

"I wasted time on Midgard trying to figure out who I am. I stayed quiet and listened to what everyone else had to say because I thought it was more important than anything I could think up. It wasn't until I met Rune that I started talking more. She started calling me 'little mouse', and I didn't like that much. She told me I was dead, so what was the point in caring what people thought? She said it was no way to spend my eternal rest. And while I ran away from her and cried the rest of the day, I realized she had a point."

"She made you cry?" I said, my fist tightening on my basket. I took a step toward her in the snow, as if to physically guard her.

"Oh, stop," Haddy said. "Stop looking for things to be mad about. Can't you just admit the truth to yourself already?"

"What truth?"

Haddy gave me the side eye.

"What?" I asked again, louder this time as my annoyance shifted from Rune to my sister.

"You're fighting just to fight. I've known you long enough to know you carry your anger, or pretend to, at least, far longer than you need to. You hate that awkward forgiving stage. It's the same thing happening with Odel and Malfrid."

"And that has to do with Rune how?"

Haddy rolled her eyes and blew out a dramatic sigh once more. "You don't want to forgive Rune for taking you, because then you'd have to go through the awkward phase that comes after. You'd have to admit you forgave her before you even came to Helheim. I'm not sure when it happened. Only you know, but you must be tired of pretending."

My teeth unclenched, and I just stood there, basket in hand, staring at my sister. She'd seen through me, but she'd known me her whole life and then some. Had Rune been seeing through me this whole time too? The thought of that was far more embarrassing than admitting I cared for the valkyrie. I knew she cared for me too; it was written all over her face when she found me in the Cave of Whispers. She'd proven it the day she'd broken her oaths and took down six raiders to save me, and when she'd refused to send me back to Midgard because she'd known it would've brought my death if she had.

"Haddy, I have to go," I said, feeling my heartbeat quicken.

Was I really about to be honest with Rune?

The thought made me want to vomit all over myself.

"You sure do," Haddy said with a big, knowing smile. I hoped she knew how much I loved her, because even as I gave her a big hug and kissed the top of her head, I still felt it wasn't enough.

Bounty in hand, I headed toward Hel's Hall. I stared down at what Haddy and I had found, but our options were limited. Here in Helheim, there was a whole lot of ice and stone. Maybe it was time I started focusing more on the spells that required nothing but my own natural seidr. After summoning ice and fire, I was beginning to believe I didn't need to rely so much on bounties anyway.

Someone bumped into me, sending the contents of my basket all over the snow.

"Oh, I'm so sorry!" the woman exclaimed. "Here, let me help you with that."

Before I could get a good look at her face, the woman began collecting my sprawled items and returning them to the basket.

"Thank you," I said as she handed me the woven handle. She looked up at me and smiled, and I swore, it was like looking in the mirror, though her hair was black and grey instead of berry blonde.

"Do I know you?" I asked.

"I don't believe so, but who knows. Maybe we're related!" The woman threw her arms up and laughed. "You must be new here. You'll soon find ancestors dating back throughout time."

"What's your name?" I asked, scanning her features, the deep blue of her eyes, the freckles on her pale cheeks.

"Norfrid Bosdotter. It's nice to meet you, Kari."

"Norfrid Bosdotter?" I asked, my face numb with the cold but also the shock of running into my ancestor like this. The number of souls here was unfathomable. Out of all of them to run into me, it was the person Hel had given her "gift" to? The one who inadvertently passed it to my mother and me? I didn't believe in coincidences like this. "How do you know my name?"

"Oh my, did I already slip up? I'm a seeress like you, dear. I can sense these things."

"Except your seidr wouldn't work in death. It dies with you and passes to your ancestors. It passed to me."

"Um, yes. You caught me again," Norfrid said with an awkward chuckle. "Hel may have told me you were here, and I may have been looking for you."

"So why didn't you just say that instead of running into me and pretending you didn't know who I am?"

"Hel says you're not very trusting," she said with a wonky smile.

"For good reason. You started this conversation with a lie. Why are you here, Norfrid?" I asked, shifting on my frozen feet.

"Hel was curious about what you were up to, and I had no complaints about meeting my descendant."

"She sent you to spy on me? Is she in there right now, watching me? You know she's looking out of your skull with her creepy dead eye, right?" I asked, aggression lacing my tone, but I couldn't help myself.

Norfrid laughed. "Of course I know, silly! It's hard to make a deal with someone without knowing what you're trading." She slapped her hands on her frock, as if this whole situation had been hilarious, but I wasn't laughing.

"You, you did it willingly?" I could've lunged forward and strangled the woman. I didn't care if she would pop back up unharmed a few moments later. She did this to me, my mom, and countless others without caring how her greed would impact her descendants for centuries to come.

"It seemed like a fair trade for power. We weren't seeresses naturally, you see. The gift didn't run in our family, but Hel was willing to change that in return for something equally valuable: our sight."

"You're despicable," I spat. "I hope your years on Midgard wielding gifted seidr was worth an eternity of being Hel's spy. But from the looks of it, your time was cut short. The other villagers didn't like your rotting eyes too much, did they?"

It was the first time Norfrid showed a crack in her creepy front, and she pursed her lips in retaliation of my words.

Before she could speak, I asked, "Why are your eyes normal once more—free of rot? I know she still sees through you, so what's the deal? Did Hel reward you for your service?"

Norfrid turned up her nose, and for a moment, I didn't think she would respond. "A reward of sorts. When Hel first gifted me, the words she spoke made it so the death-laced eyes would only be visible on Midgard. That way, while we'd still be servants in death, we could enjoy our afterlife without the shock of our own reflection. Haven't you looked in a mirror? Or are you still scared of what you may find?"

"I was only ever scared of what I might find because of you," I hissed. "You are a selfish—"

"Selfish? Unlike you, I enjoy loyalty. I am a vessel for the gods to do with what they will. Hel is my supreme goddess, my queen. You're lucky she hasn't stolen your soul for this utter lack of respect you've shown. You think she's just going to let you keep your seidr and stop seeing through you?" she laughed, sickly and sinister.

"Let her try to take it," I spat, not able to revel in this positive news when this wretch stared back at me. Fire sparked in my palms, the flames reflecting in Norfrid's traitorous eyes. My self-serving ancestor took a step back, horror in her gaze. She knew I couldn't hurt her, but I sure as Hel could set this place aflame. There were two things her precious goddess hated more than anything: life and light.

I pushed Norfrid with a fiery hand, and she instantly caught flame. She stumbled and fell into the snow, the fire scorching her. She sat there from her spot on the ground, staring up at me with terror glazing her darkened gaze.

"Enjoy your afterlife," I muttered as I walked away from her. "And let it go wrong at every turn."

CHAPTER TWENTY-NINE
HER GREATEST SACRIFICE

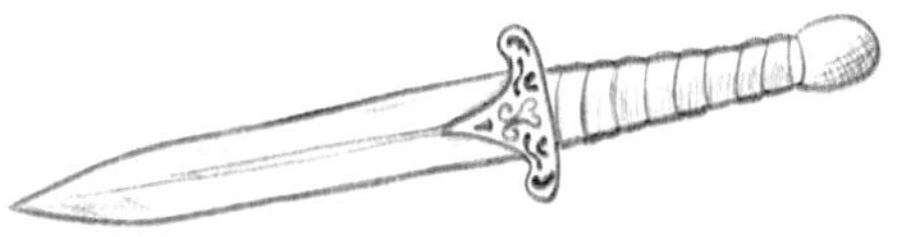

Rune

My foot thrummed against freshly fallen snow, the powdery substance compacting more and more with every passing moment, though it never grew dirty, always white and beautiful.

Yet another illusion.

I huffed out a breath, the air around me turned foggy, as if I had a fire burning in my lungs. I was armor-less, seidr-less, and my heart was torn open and exposed to the raw, brutal elements of Hel.

The only shining light in any of this was a strawberry blonde seeress with lips so soft, it was maddening. I stared at the Bifrost Bridge and replayed our kiss over and over in my mind. I wished it'd been under different circumstances, that it hadn't been the fear of losing her that'd made me finally kiss her, but I'd never take it back now. The new and wonderful feelings budding and blossoming within me were all the more volatile after having to leave her. It was too soon, but warnings needed to be sent and actions needed to be taken if I was going to keep everyone I cared for safe.

Odin knows.

He knew everything, and the columns holding up my life, my entire existence, were crumbling faster than I could rebuild.

I'd been standing across from the Bifrost, waiting not so patiently, since sunrise. The rainbow hues of the Bifrost had long since burned itself into my eyes, so even when I blinked, I saw it. I wasn't sure if my plan would succeed, or if I was putting far too much faith in an attendant of Hel I'd bribed with a stunning dagger from Nidavellir. Well, technically, it was made by Nori on Asgard, but the troll didn't need to know that.

The Bifrost flared, and I jumped to attention. Two figures were spat out before me, and clearly, there was such a thing as being too eager, because my close proximity to the landing area meant a hairy troll screaming profanities knocked me down.

Groaning, I pushed him off me and muttered, "It's about damn time!"

The troll rose to his feet, straightening out his dirt-stained tunic. He grumbled something about a nasty pegasus and held out his hand for payment. I brushed right past him and offered a hand out to Rayna, who laid on the ground in a heap. When she didn't move, I nudged her with the tip of my boot and called her name.

Nothing.

I whirled on the troll, dagger already in hand. "Your payment will be a knife to the gut if you don't tell me what happened to her."

The troll put his hands up. "I did what you're payin' me for, you crazy bitch. You asked me to bring her, and I did. She's alive, isn't she?"

I lowered the dagger for a moment, just long enough to kneel beside Rayna and check for a pulse. When her lifeforce thrummed against my fingers, the tightness in my chest eased. I pushed the whitening hair out of her face and took in her closed eyes.

"What happened?" I asked the gruff looking man, his grey hair matted with mud. "Did she not come willingly?"

"Didn't give her the chance," he said with a shrug, his

lengthy nose twitching. "Once I got past that homicidal pegasus of hers, I took matters into my own hands. Don't hire a troll if you don't want a proper kidnapping. She should be awake by high-sun."

"Fine. Why did it take you so long? I told you where she'd be," I growled.

"And that would've been helpful if she'd actually been there. I had to grab her in Sessrúmnir, which was no stroll in the field. You're lucky I'm not charging you extra for that."

"Sessrúmnir?" I repeated, looking down at Rayna. "Why were you in Freyja's Hall?" I whispered to the valkyrie, though I knew she couldn't hear me.

"Payment," the troll barked out.

I gritted my teeth and tossed the dagger by his feet. If he wanted his payment, he'd have to dig through the snow for it. "Get out of here."

I turned my back on him, knowing that even without the speed or strength of my valkyrie gifts, I would sense any attack if he chose to be brave enough. As I shook Rayna, I heard the man retrieve the dagger and be on his way.

I wasn't strong enough to carry her all the way to our room, but I also couldn't leave her here in the snow to freeze. With a whisper of apology, I reached my pointer and thumb into her nose, gripped a collection of short hairs, and yanked as hard as I could. Rayna shot up right with a gasp, clutching at her face.

"What the actual fuck!" She glanced around for the culprit, and when she saw me, she instinctively punched me in the shoulder. My eyes bulged at the pure strength her punch packed, and I failed at holding back my wince. Rayna took a quick glance around to assess the area, the snow dusting her body. Then, she noticed it. Her eyes locked on my hair, her gaze trailing from my roots to my tips.

"Rune..." She trailed off, her eyes softening. "I didn't think your hair would turn so fast."

"You already know?" I asked, my throat betraying me as my voice cracked.

Rayna nodded, reaching forward to clasp my hand. "Odin summoned me. He tossed a piece of your distorted armor at my feet. For a moment, I thought he'd killed you." Rayna paused, swallowing deeply. She shook her head, as if doing so would hold back her tears, but one slipped past her defenses anyway. That single tear rolling down her face shattered something inside me. Rayna didn't cry, not when she realized she could never see her family again, not when she'd witnessed a mortal die by her hands, and not when she'd had her heart broken for the first time.

"Rayna," I whispered, pulling her into a hug. "I'm here."

She nodded again, this time with a hard resolve locked into her features. She leaned into me, her fingers brushing the tips of my hair streaked with deep brown. I held back my own tears as my sister touched my mortality, it seeping into her fingertips, reminding us both that we were now a world apart.

"You once told me Helheim would have to be set aflame before you went to Midgard without me. It's now happened, and you will, in fact, go on without me. You must."

Rayna pulled away from me, her eyes wide. "What are you talking about? Fire? In Hel?"

"Kari's seidr is...more than I ever expected. She's magnificent. You should've seen her when she found out I was stripped of my title," I said, a small smile carving room for itself upon my face.

"Kari *summoned* the fire?" she gasped. "Nine realms, Rune, we have so much to catch up on. Get me out of this snow and tell me everything."

"She did," I said, lifting myself out of the snow and pulling Rayna up with me. "Fire in one hand, ice in the other."

"Great gods," was all Rayna could manage as she dusted snow off her red leathers. "Even so, Ru, I can't live an eternity without you. You are my mortality, much like Kari is yours."

"That's not true." I shook my head. "You have Gunhild,

Alvion, and Nori too. You are more than my sister. You're Odin's best now. *You* will be his favorite. That's not nothing."

"Fuck no, I'm not."

"Stop being modest, Rayna."

"I'm not being modest. I'm nothing to Odin now. If he won't have you, he doesn't have me either. No discussion."

"Rayna...what did you do?" I took a step back, looking her over and assessing a deep change in my sister I'd been too distracted to see earlier, but now, it was all I felt.

She stared at me, her chin raised, her dark eyes hardened.

"Why were you in Fólkvangr?" I asked.

"I'm Freyja's now, and you will be too."

"For the love of all things living, you did not!" I strode away from her, not able to look upon her foolish face. My ass was frozen, my heart broken, yet my rage was more potent.

"What, Rune? You couldn't have expected me to stay in Valhalla with that monster!" she yelled.

"Monster? Rayna, being a valkyrie is your life. You worked so hard to get to Valhalla, and you threw it all away for what? Me?" I scoffed. "I'm not worth your future."

"You're worth my life!" She shoved my shoulders, and I couldn't keep my footing in the snow. I tumbled backward, my sister's screams in my ears as I fell. Tears welled in my eyes at the weakness in my bones, the defiance in her voice. My bare hands gripped the icy snow, and I stared down into the endless white, the last remaining pillar of my former life in pieces before me.

Hands swept under my underarms, and the next thing I knew, I was standing once more. My hands were freezing, but I didn't move to warm them. Rayna rested her chin on my shoulder, a shaky sigh leaving her lungs. We stood there for a moment, two sisters on opposite sides of the same war.

Finally, my resoluteness broke, and I turned to meet her gaze. Before I could speak, she said, "Freyja is pleased to have me back, Rune. I don't feel like I'm taking a step backward, truly. I feel like

I'm taking a step forward. Maybe not in my career, but in my *life*. You know more than anyone what life in Valhalla can do to a person. I want to find my own happiness, to be content. During my year in Fólkvangr, I was so focused on being promoted to the Valhalla sect, I never looked around and was grateful for what I *did* have. I don't want that life anymore. What better place to do that than the hall designed for nothing but peace and tranquility?"

"You did this for you? Not just me? You mean it?" I asked, scanning her all too familiar features. Her blonde and white hair was messy, flakes of snow clinging to the braids that swooped up and out of her face. Her dark eyes softened, and in them, I sensed her truth.

"I do," Rayna said, and that admission had my clenched fists relaxing. "And...I told her I wouldn't re-join the sect unless she took you too."

I took a step back, pressure building in my widened eyes. "What? You did? What did she say?"

"A chance to take in Odin's traitorous favorite, are you kidding me? The goddess can't wait to swear you in," Rayna said with a mischievous smirk. "You, of course, still have to take her test of loyalty and go through the whole attendant ritual again, but after that, we'll both be hers."

"Kari will be too," I said, glancing out at the rainbow hues reflecting over the snow-covered hills. When I next looked at the Bifrost, it hit me—Kari was now strong enough to travel *through* it. No more dangerous treks through the path between worlds. "Hel is trading her in return for something from Freyja."

"What does she want from Freyja? Wait, no, what does Freyja want with Kari?" Rayna asked, and I met her gaze once more.

"I don't have the answer to either of those questions," I admitted, but hope surged in me for the first time since I saw my armor as molten gold upon the rocky floor of the Cave of Whispers. "What I do know is, Fólkvangr has another thing coming."

After walking back to Hel's Hall, Rayna and I split up. She went off to the House of Wings to warm up and make use of one of our sister's baths, and I headed back to our room to see if I could find Kari.

When I entered the room, I heard splashing water, so I called out to her from behind the bathing chamber door. "Kari? It's me."

"Come in!" she called out.

Come in? I asked myself, because she was in the bath, wasn't she?

I stood beyond the door, my hand hovering over the knob until I finally found the courage to twist it. The heavy wooden door creaked, and I spotted a head of berry blonde hair poking out from a pile of sudsy foam. I wasn't quite sure if I was relieved or disappointed to see she was all covered by the bubbles that clung to her back like fragile armor.

She shifted in the tub until she was facing me, and I had to fight the hardest battle of my life to keep my eyes upon her face. Her cheeks were flushed and rosy from the water's warmth, and I wished I could strip out of my winter gear and crawl under the suds with her. She rested her head back on the bath's rim and looked up at me with a glint from the candlelight in her eyes.

"I had the strangest afternoon," Kari began. One of her feet poked out of the water, reminding me I still had my boots on. As I nodded at her to continue, I stooped down to begin untying my laces. "I was with Haddy, collecting my bounty, when I ran right into Norfrid Bosdotter, and let me tell you, that woman was nasty."

"You just happened upon one of your ancestors?" I asked, pausing on my second bootlace to focus on her twisted features.

"I thought it was too convenient as well, so I began talking with her more, and it turns out, the little creep was sent by Hel to watch me. She went on a whole rant about being loyal to the Gods and how she loves being Hel's vessel," Kari said with distorted lips. Her whole body shivered, as if the water had suddenly grown cold, but I knew better. The look on Kari's face said it all.

"Nine realms," I muttered. "We need to get out of the underworld."

"Why don't we? Why don't we leave for Fólkvangr tomorrow?" Kari said, sitting up in the tub, sending a few bubbles rolling over the side as she did. "I've collected what I need for the journey, and I'm ready. Sure, I may not know what Freyja will want me to do, but—"

"You don't need to convince me, seeress," I cut in. "We're not meant for this place, and the longer we both stay, the worse off we'll be. I worry you're absorbing too much of Hel's seidr too quickly, and we don't know what will happen if you stay much longer. And for me, well...I'm becoming more mortal by the day."

"How will that change when we leave?" Kari asked, her voice soft.

I stared at her for a while, my heart aching from her words, though I knew she meant me no harm. There was nothing I could do in the moment to make her words untrue. Even when we left Hel, there was no guarantee I could stop the slow spread of rich brown upon my head.

"Well, I suppose I had the strangest afternoon too," I said. I slipped out of my boots and left them by the door, then made my way to the tub. Kari swallowed as I ran my fingers over the bubbles, a few of them popping under my touch. I wanted so badly to stick my hands under the surface and trail them over her soft, warm skin, and as I met Kari's gaze, she looked as if she wanted that too.

"Sit and tell me," she said, and I didn't hesitate to do what she asked of me. I stripped out of my furs, placing them next to the tub to use as a cushion against the hard floor. Once I was seated and my back was against the bath, she reached out of the water and placed her bath-warmed fingers over my temples. My eyes closed as I melted under her touch.

"Lean your head back," she said. I tilted my head, not caring that some of my hair fell into the water. Kari began taking the intricate war braids out, as well as the golden pieces adorning them. I wasn't sure if she was simply trying to help me wash my hair, or if she was purposely taking out my braids so I didn't have to suffer that fate. Either way, I felt my heart swell as she began diligently working, taking care of me in a way I hadn't realized I needed until this very moment.

"I hired a troll to kidnap Rayna, and she—"

"Wait. Go back," Kari said, her hands pausing in my hair. "You had Rayna kidnapped?"

"Well, yeah. How else was I going to speak with her in person?"

Kari chuckled in disbelief, and I imagined her shaking her head at me with a cute little grin. "Okay, go on. I imagine you had a lot to catch up on. How did she take the news?"

I told her all about my conversation with my sister and what transpired since, and she patiently listened.

"So, there's a chance you could become a valkyrie again?" Kari whispered, like if she said it any louder, it may not come true.

"There is." I swallowed a hard lump in my throat, and the two of us sat in relative silence. When my hair was free, she had me tip my head back so she could wet my hair and lather it in soap. She worked quietly, keeping water out of my ears as she went. By the time my hair was free of soap, the water had already turned cold and my neck had grown stiff, but it was all worth it when she leaned over me and pressed a soft kiss to my forehead.

Kari used her hands to squeeze the water free of my brown and white strands, then handed me the towel she'd brought out for herself. She began wrapping my hair up in it so no chilly water could dribble down my neck. When I was able to sit up and face her, I placed my hand over her cold cheek. She cupped the back of my hand with her palm and leaned further into me.

"Let's get you out of this water," I whispered, because for some reason, anything else felt like it would be too loud, too abrasive after the tenderness I'd just experienced. Kari simply nodded, so I walked over to a little wooden chest in the corner and grabbed another towel for her. When I was back standing in front of the seeress, I moved my furs out of the way to make room for her. I held up the towel, locking eyes with her as I did. There was so much I needed to say to her, so many important things, yet when I looked at her, every word drifted away, and I was left with nothing but her stunning eyes on mine.

She rose from the tub, hidden behind the towel I held. Once she was standing before me, I wrapped her up and then lifted her from the bath. She gasped as I did, but it was now my turn to take care of her.

Kari felt so perfect in my arms, and though my muscles could feel the strain of her body more than they used to, I wouldn't set her down because of it. She molded perfectly into me, as if she'd been a part of me all along, and I wouldn't be so quick to give that all up.

My perfect mortal stared up at me, her lashes full, water clinging to them. I carried her to the bed, not caring that water dripped off Kari and onto the floor as I did. She didn't seem to mind either, too engrossed in whatever she saw within my eyes. She had her arms wrapped around my neck, and as I approached the side of the bed, she rested her head in the nape.

"What do you plan on doing with me, now that you have me?" she murmured into the sensitive spot above my shoulder.

"Do I? Have you, I mean?" I asked as I set her down upon the bed. Kari didn't adjust herself as the towel rose up along her thigh and parted for me over her hip.

Kari was silent for a moment, her eyes boring into mine. I'd sworn my life had been coming apart, but when she finally answered me, everything felt right in the world once more.

"Rune Dragomir, you have me. In every way, you have me."

CHAPTER THIRTY
THE THING GODDESSES FEAR

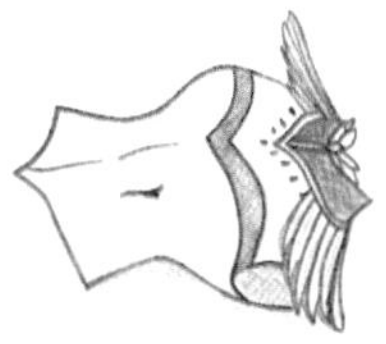

Kari

id I really just admit I was hers?
My hair dripped onto the quilt I laid upon, and my skin rose with little goosebumps all the way to the exposed flesh of my hip. Rune stared down at me, her leathers covering far too much.

Always a tease. Always hiding from me.

Despite the leathers, she was armor-less, and while that cracked something apart deep inside me, right now, I only cared about what she was wearing, not what was missing.

The way her eyes blazed with heat, I knew she wasn't going to waste this opportunity. I wanted to tell her I wouldn't change my mind, that this wasn't just for the moment, but as she wet her lips and bowed her head, my mind went blank. Whatever I was about to open my mouth to say was long gone. Nothing else mattered in this moment outside of her hands trailing over her leathers to find their seams. I reached forward and gripped Rune's forearm, pulling her closer so I could help her get out of what kept me from what I craved.

Piece by piece, I peeled the leather from her skin, revealing parts of her I'd never had the honor of exploring. Rune gasped as my cold hands found her warm flesh, and then she let out a low chuckle, like I was going to pay for that costly mistake.

My head dropped to the mattress as she hovered over me, feet still on the floor. My fingers gripped the back of her head, and none of my gentleness from before remained as I pulled her in until her lips were on mine. Our mouths moved in impatient synchronicity, and the taste of her had me groaning between our lips.

I wanted more—no, I *needed* it. Why was she not on this bed yet?

I tried to pull her up, but she just clicked her tongue and smirked down at me. A frustrated growl left my throat, and I all but whined her name.

"Not yet, seeress," she hummed. "We have one last night in Hel, and if I get to have you in the underworld, I'm sure as fuck going to take my time."

I cursed under my breath. "You're going to torture me, aren't you?"

"No, Kari." She shook her head. "I'm going to worship you."

I scoffed and gripped the remaining shreds of fabric clinging to her. "I'm no goddess."

"You're worse: you're the thing goddesses fear."

At that, I smiled. I wouldn't pretend to be a goddess, but I could play at something the gods feared. If Rune wanted me to be a predator, I wouldn't hesitate. My hands found the towel wrapped around me, and I slowly pulled it aside until I was bare to her. I watched as desire flared in her eyes—now, she was the one cursing under her breath.

Rune's fingers traced the scar left from the raider who'd struck me. That damned raider was the reason I was here, and I forced him out of my mind. I wasn't about to thank that violent villain, but oh, had he done me a favor.

She trailed kisses over the scar and continued moving downward until her warm lips were on one of my peaked nipples. She took one into her mouth, and I suppressed a groan as she playfully nipped at me. The once-valkyrie wasn't lying when she said she'd take her time. She kissed and licked every part of my chest, stomach, and hips until I was begging her to move lower. I didn't want to push her head, but gods, if she didn't get to the part of me that throbbed for her, I was going to lose my mind.

Rune chuckled against my skin, then pushed two fingers inside me. I gasped as I tightened around her, shocked by the feeling after so many teasing kisses in all the wrong places. She thrust in and out with long, languid strokes of her fingers. Her skin warmed inside me, so when she slid back out and ran them over the apex of my thighs, her fingertips were hot against the most sensitive part of me.

At this rate, it wouldn't take me long to fall apart for this woman, but who said you could only break once? I groaned as I rocked against her, lifting my hips so I had more leverage. Rune Dragomir was in my clutches, and, even if I wasn't ready to admit it to anyone but myself, I would never let her go.

Rune pulled away, then dropped to her knees before me, like she really did plan to worship. I opened my mouth to protest, but she pulled my ass to the end of the bed and dipped her head to meet me.

Fuck.

She hummed praises against my sensitive skin, getting lost in her task before finally looking back up at me as if she were a damned fire demon.

"Rune?" I gasped.

"What is it, seeress?" she asked, "Can't you see I'm busy feasting?"

I bit my bottom lip, so tempted to give in and let her finish me, but I wanted my pound of flesh, and she wasn't even naked for me yet. How could I fall into that blissful state when she wouldn't be right there with me, exposed and vulnerable?

"I want you," I groaned when she resumed licking and sucking. "All of you." I used her hair to pull her mouth off me. I kept her locked in my grasp, forcing her to look upon my face, because even though she kept distracting me, I was serious. "Now."

"What did I say about patience?"

"I don't know what that is," I panted, scrambling back onto the mattress. If she wanted me, she was going to have to join me, crawl to me here upon this bed. Rune shook her head slowly, a smile playing at the corner of her mouth. I thought she would refuse me yet again, but this time, she brought her hands up to the thin fabric covering her breasts and lifted it over her head. Rune stood before me, chest exposed, her fingers tugging at the last remaining cloth on her perfect, olive skin.

She is the most glorious thing I've ever seen.

Valhalla didn't compare. All the gold, all the wonder did not compare to this creature before me. When she dropped the final scrap of fabric, bearing her last hidden spot, I lost it. My own hand found my core, and I moved my fingers over myself to quench the need she pulled from me. Rune watched my hand bob up and down as she crawled across the bed to where I was propped up against the pillows.

"You are temptation at its finest," she said as she straddled me, pinning my hand between us. "I wanted you long before you knew me, but *gods*, I could've never imagined this. No figment of my mind could've been crafted in your image, because there's nothing like you. *No one* like you."

I swallowed, staring deeply into her eyes. What was there to say that would express how much Rune's words meant to me? Any time I attempted to rein control over the situation, this woman threw me off my game once again.

With a bratty smirk, I hooked my ankles around hers and rolled us to the side. She leaned into the momentum, her slitted brow arched as I mounted her bare hips.

Running the back of my freed hand over her soft cheek, the

wild beast bit me. Instead of pulling back, I slid two fingers into her mouth, and her eyes flared as she sucked them in deeper.

"You've always been mine, haven't you?" I asked as I slipped a third finger between her beautiful lips. Rune nodded, unable to speak. With a smile, I freed her mouth.

My slick hand found that exquisite spot between her thighs, and I began torturing her in the slow, painful way she'd done to me. Rune pressed her head back into the pillow, her eyes closing.

"Hey, eyes on me," I demanded. "You're going to see the look on my face when you break for me, aren't you?"

Rune's eyes opened, and they locked fiercely on mine. I could see the strain in her, wanting so badly to get me on my back and take control once more, but I wasn't done having fun just yet.

"Yes, seeress." Her jaw tightened as she focused on keeping my gaze, and sweat beaded her brow.

I smirked as she gave in to me. I worked my hand faster until I felt her pulsing around my fingers, coming for me with a loud, breathy groan. I barely had time to adjust before Rune's hands were on me, and I found myself flat on my back once more. A laugh slipped from my lips as she leaned in to kiss me.

"I've let you have your fun, your control, but you're mine now. And I'm still hungry," she growled against my lips. As she descended, my body went still, all but my racing heart. I whimpered and moaned as she devoured me, and I wondered why I hadn't had to die to reach this perfect afterlife.

CHAPTER THIRTY-ONE
A VISION, OR WISHFUL THINKING?

Rune

I *am ruined. Forever ruined.*

Not because of my lost title or the color returning to my hair, but from a far worse fate. Maybe the word "worse" wasn't right, because maybe the woman lying next to me was the best thing that had ever happened to me. If my fate was to be forever lost to her, I suppose I was the luckiest person alive.

Now that Kari had shared her very soul with me, I knew I could never have another. She ruined me for all others, and I wanted to bend the knee and kiss her feet in thanks. Having her was no sacrifice, but the greatest gift of my life.

I stretched across the mattress, sweat beading on my forehead, my chest heaving against hers. She stared deep into my eyes, and I felt a knot of fear in my gut. There was so much we still didn't know about the deal between Freyja and Hel, or what Freyja wanted of Kari. I wanted to continue rolling around across the quilt with her, unravelling her for the third time that evening, but my mind was being pulled elsewhere.

We would leave in the morning, take the Bifrost with Rayna,

and arrive in Fólkvangr. I hadn't seen Freyja in a decade, yet it felt like just yesterday, she'd graced the valkyries for a feast in Valhalla. She'd arrived in a chariot pulled by two giant felines, and my sisters all pushed to the front of the room to see her enter.

She was grace, beauty, and love, but I wouldn't let her affinity for light allow me to forget what she was: a goddess, a weapon if she so chose, a destroyer. I wouldn't let her appeal pull me in, because Kari's life was in her hands, as was my immortality.

"What is it?" Kari asked. "Where did you go just now?"

"It's nothing," I said. "I'm right here." I brushed the hair out of her eyes and pressed a kiss to her forehead the way she had when she'd been in the bath, just after tending to me. It was a simple gesture, one I'd never given, yet I loved everything about it.

"Liar," Kari said with a teasing eye roll.

"You love to accuse me of lies," I pointed out, gently jabbing her in the side.

"And have I ever been wrong in my accusations?" Kari asked with a raised brow and an all-knowing tone.

I smacked my lips and then blew a breath up to the ceiling, "I got lost in my mind about tomorrow. But I'm back. I'm here now."

Kari snuggled further into me, pulling up the quilt so it hid her bare body from my view. It mattered little, though, because I still had my hands wrapped around her, and I didn't intend on moving them any time soon.

She kissed the side of my neck and whispered against my skin. "I'm nervous too, you know. But I also know my seidr is strong, strong enough to do whatever it is Freyja will ask of me. And you'll pass your loyalty test and become a valkyrie once more. All will be right again."

"Is this a vision you had, or just wishful thinking?" I asked.

"I've never been to Fólkvangr, so I haven't seen anything useful, just flashes and symbols I've deciphered mean peace, but I don't know whose peace I'm seeing," she said. "And it's not just wishful thinking. I believe in us, Rune. I believe if we stick together, there isn't a single thing we won't be able to accomplish. I mean, look how far we've come. Look at all we've done in the past two lunar cycles."

"You may have a point."

"Always do!" Kari hummed against me, which finally pulled a smile to my lips. I leaned forward and stole a kiss, then two, and then she was pressed tight to me once more.

Fuck, she's magnificent.

Until tomorrow, when I had to face my fears head on, I would banish any thought that wasn't of my sweet seeress.

CHAPTER THIRTY-TWO
ACROSS THE RAINBOW BRIDGE

Kari

Hel handed me a fruit cake, her cold skin brushing mine as she did. Rune was holding the rare snow blossoms of Helheim in one hand and a jar of raw honey in the other.

"Now, what do you say?" the goddess of death asked from where she sat on her throne. The second she handed me the cake, I presented her with a slight bow and retreated ten feet in the opposite direction.

I bowed and held the cake above my head like a complete sycophant. "We have brought you gifts from our time in Helheim, sent with us by the Goddess of Death. She offers not only these delicious offerings, but me as well, a mortal seeress. I come willingly and have sensed only peace surrounding my entrance into Fólkvangr. I hope you accept these offerings and look down upon us with your loving favor."

Rune suppressed a chuckle, but Hel ignored her as she offered me a slow clap for my performance. It'd been the fifth time she'd made me practice that little routine, and my arms were starting to grow sore from holding the densest dessert I'd ever seen above my head. When I woke this morning, I knew I was in for an adventure, but I didn't count on trials by fruit cake.

"Ah, that was the one," Hel said, her teeth on display. After her first impression of me, she didn't quite trust I'd have the best sense when it came to Freyja. I tried to tell the goddess I had nothing against Freyja and wouldn't be anything but respectful, but Hel would hear none of it. I couldn't very well deny her, so I went along with her little speech and got down on my knees with a cake in hand each time she demanded it of me.

Rune had spent enough time among the gods that she was given no speech. Hel also cared little for Rune's part in all of this, for the former valkyrie wasn't the one she was trading. Rune had tried to get more information out of Hel regarding the matter of the deal, though Hel gave us nothing but stares through mixed-colored eyes.

"Now, Kari," Hel said, straightening her onyx gown that bled into her endlessly black throne. "If Freyja accepts you into her council, you're welcome to travel to my realm to visit your family once per year. If you have official attendant matters here on behalf of Freyja, I shall permit an extra visit."

"Thank you, Goddess," I said with a bow.

"I did, however, witness your little chat with dear Norfrid," Hel said, sharpening one of her talon-like nails on the stone of her throne, "and if you ever summon fire in Helheim again, you will be banished from my realm, and you can say goodbye to your precious family forever. Is that understood?"

My pounding heart rose into my throat at the thought. "It's understood," I said, because what else was there to do? If it meant I could never see my family again, I would go an eternity without practicing fire seidr. It wasn't worth it.

"Well then, I believe it's time for your departure. For *all* of your departures," Hel emphasized as she peered over Rune's shoulder to where Rayna stood, looming in the shadows. Rayna bobbed her head in answer, her hands clasped behind her back. We offered the goddess one last bow before taking the offerings for Freyja and finally exiting Hel's domain.

"I'd survive never seeing another fruit cake ever again," I muttered as our boots clacked down the hall.

"Don't you dare say that," Rayna said with the faintest of gasps. "It might just come true."

Rune laughed, looking between us, and I offered them both a lazy smile.

We caught Garm in the hall as we made our way to the great hearth to bid my family farewell. Tove hissed at the giant wolf, but Garm paid him no mind as we passed.

"See you later, Garm." I nodded, since I didn't have a free hand to spare. "Oh, and I hope they liked the flowers!" I tacked on once I was out of biting range. I wasn't sure if the love he'd found was a secret, but I certainly wouldn't risk getting eaten over my knowledge of it. Still, if I could get the misunderstood wolf to smile, even a little bit, I was going to try.

"I don't know what you're talking about," he barked. I hummed as though I knew better, and then suddenly, the air around me grumbled out, "He loved them."

I gave the wolf a big smile and strode off down the corridor, Tove in tow. Rune and Rayna were right there beside me too, and the three of us stayed quiet as we headed toward the place I'd told my family to meet me. It only felt fitting to say "goodbye" in the same spot where I'd finally been able to say "hello again".

I spotted my mother first, sitting upon a high-back chair. When we approached, she seemed too busy staring off into the false flames to notice us. Seidr didn't travel with a person to the underworld, but I couldn't help but wonder if she still had a sense, a knowing about her. I hoped so, for her sake. I couldn't imagine living a lifetime with seidr at your fingertips, just to die and never be able to wield it again.

Instead of pondering on it longer and growing sad for my mother, I smiled broadly at Odel and opened my arms to embrace my sister. Malfrid was next, and while she was a little shocked by my tender touch, she leaned into me all the same. Haddy came barreling over, throwing her arms around both Malfrid and me before our sister could pull away.

"I'm going to miss you so much!" Haddy said with one final squeeze.

"The Goddess of Death visited us, my dear child," my father's voice boomed. I turned to see the bearded man now standing by my mother, a brilliant grin upon her face. Whatever she was once distracted by in the fire was now gone, as she was wholly focused on me. "I have to say, I never expected to meet the goddess, but there she was, standing before us. It seems you've made quite the impression on her. Our daughter, can you believe it?" My father lightly nudged my mother.

"I knew you had greatness in you, Kari. Your visions were always so strong and clear. But why is it that Hel mentioned this may be our final goodbye? At first, I thought she came to us as a warning, but then I realized it wasn't threats she offered."

"What was it then?" I asked. Rune and Rayna stood far behind me, giving me all the room I needed to speak with my family. What I don't think they realized was, I didn't mind them here. It felt right somehow to have them included in this conversation.

"I think it was a message. For you," she said with a weary smile. "I know she asked something of you, my sweet girl. You don't have to tell us, but do whatever you have to do to get back to us some-day, do you hear me? Whatever it is she wants, you succeed in it, and you come back to us."

I stared at the woman who'd brought me into this world and wondered how much truth I could spare her, how much I wanted to. I didn't want her to know that if I failed, I would be the reason she never saw me again. Somehow, it seemed easier to lie, to make them think I'd gone back to Midgard, and then one day off into the heavens. But Hel took that option from me when she spoke with them. Her meeting with my family was enough to warn me of the severity of the situation, if the fruit cake display hadn't already.

"I will, Mother. I'll succeed in anything the gods ask of me," I said with a tight nod of my head. As I spoke the words aloud, I felt the verity behind them set into stone. I would do whatever it took to see my parents and sisters again. In any trial Freyja put me through, every challenge, I would succeed.

As I said my goodbyes, I noticed Rune laughing with Haddy, pulling her in for a hug. Odel and Malfrid were giving Tove pets as my mother rubbed soothing circles into my back, and for a moment, everything felt right. We were a happy family again, untouched by death. I'd hold on to this moment, whether I won Freyja's favor or a different fate claimed me. I had every intention of seeing my loved ones one year from now, and as I waved to them, a fierce determination washed over me.

I didn't even care that this feeling was exactly what Hel wanted. She'd known what she was doing when she'd sought out my family, and it'd been the powerful motivator she'd expected it to be.

When we exited Hel's Hall, Apple and Gunhild greeted us in the snow-clad field. Rune supplied her pegasus with pre-flight scratches, and the three of us began securing our packs to their hips. I hooked Tove onto Apple's armor with the harness Rune made him, and then Rune hoisted me up to do the same for me.

Rayna whistled as Rune and I got situated, and I wondered how she was faring with this exceptional change in her life. She was no longer Odin's attendant, but Freyja's once more. She wasn't acting as though she'd made a devastating sacrifice, though, and I hoped she'd truly made the decision for herself, not just for her sister.

When Rayna caught me watching her, she tilted her head and shot me a curious smile. "You know bringing you two to Freyja is my first official duty as a Fólkvangr valkyrie?"

"How did she give you such a task? I thought you were unknowingly brought here by a troll," I asked.

Rayna shifted her weight upon Gunhild, and her eyes flicked behind me to where Rune finished up her preparation for our flight.

"I was kidnapped, yes, but the Goddess had tasked me *before* I arrived in Hel. As soon as I was inducted into her sect once more, she gave me said duty. I was leaving her hall when I was taken."

"So why is it that you still wear Valhalla armor? I assumed as soon as Freyja agreed to take you back, she would've asked you to remove the armor of your previous sect. Even when Rune was training her sisters, here in Hel, they gifted her the black leathers of Helheim."

Rayna looked upon her gold and red armor. "Freyja thought it may be more comforting to see me just the way you remembered. She wasn't sure what Hel had told you about the bargain, or how willing you'd be to go to her hall. *That,* and my armor isn't quite ready yet. Takes even the dwarves more than a few days to create custom armor to your very measurement, you know."

"I always thought gold and emerald were your colors anyway," Rune pitched in from behind me. "And for your first official task, you can get us to Fólkvangr far easier than the way we came."

Rayna paused, then looked from Rune to me. "Kari's powerful enough to take the Bifrost this time, yes, but..." She seemed pained as she trailed off, like the words she wasn't saying burned her throat. "What I mean to say is—"

"Yes, Rayna, I understand Odin took my seidr," Rune cut in. "But surely I have enough residual power within me to withstand the bridge." She nudged Apple with her boot, and the pegasus made a chuffing sound as she walked forward through the snow. Gunhild followed her lead, the two winged creatures walking side by side within a few steps.

When Rayna could meet our eyes once more, she said, "I see how it may be enticing to risk it, but what if the Bifrost takes more out of you than you have to give? You have tests to pass, Rune, ones you can only take once. If you're not ready for Freyja when she summons you, everything we've been working on for over the past two lunar cycles will be for naught."

Rune took a few breaths to think about what Rayna was saying, but then she tightened her grip on Apple's reins. "It'll be fine. I'd only be a liability during an extended trip through the path between realms anyway."

I couldn't see Rune's face as she said it, but I heard the hurt in her tone all the same. If this had happened last lunar cycle, I would've been rubbing her lack of seidr and title in her face any chance I could get. After everything she'd held over my head, secrets she'd kept, and the things she'd done to keep me reliant on her, I would've cherished each time her smile faded as she remembered once-simple tasks she could no longer perform. Now, I only felt her pain.

I didn't want her to risk her chances of passing her tests, but selfishly, I didn't know if I could spend the next week with her as she relied on Rayna for each meal, for protection, and a place to sleep, much like I had on our way here. I didn't want her to fall apart on me, so I sucked in a deep breath and allowed myself to be selfish.

"She can handle it. Now, let's go. You have a task to complete, don't you, Rayna?"

Rayna conceded, and with a nod, she led us in the direction of the bridge.

Rune leaned into my back, brushed hair from my neck, and said, "Thank you for believing in me, seeress."

"Always," I whispered, my chest tight.

Apple and Gunhild ended all conversation as they took off into the sky. Their massive wings beat through the chilly air, flakes of snow occasionally blowing through their feathers. As we grew closer to the Bifrost, I felt my teeth clench, my mind running through possible scenarios. Last time I'd gone through the Bifrost,

I'd been unconscious, but this time, I was on full alert. Part of me yearned for the adventure, for the incredible chance to use the bridge of the gods without perishing in the process. I felt a swell of pride in myself and my growing seidr that allowed my mortal body such passage. Yet, as the bridge grew closer and stunning rainbow hues lit up the sky, a deeper feeling nagged at me in the back of my mind.

Rune pushed her chest further into me, her thighs clenching around mine. My gaze dropped to where she held Apple's reins in one hand, the horn of her saddle with the other. I didn't hesitate to place my palm over her hand that gripped the horn, and, despite my nerves, a smile crept onto my face when her thumb caressed mine.

As the colors bleeding into the clouds grew deeper, more vibrant, I repeated the words to myself I'd spoken to her like a chant.

I believe in us, Rune. I believe if we stick together, there isn't a single thing we won't be able to accomplish.

CHAPTER THIRTY-THREE
AS SWEET AS HONEY

Rune

The Bifrost spit us out into a familiar sunny field, a warm spring breeze pushing my hair over my shoulders as Apple and Gunhild whinnied our arrival. The sky was clear of clouds, snow, and the pinch of cold on my skin. I sighed in relief, taking in that sweet Asgardian air I'd been worried I'd never experience again.

"Are you okay?" I asked Kari as soon as my throat loosened and words found me. She nodded, risking a glance back at me with a brilliant smile upon her face. Her hair swirled chaotically around her head, and in that moment, all I could imagine was that she was in a torrent of her own power.

"Yes! But I wasn't worried about myself. Are *you* okay?"

I was far fainter than I had been prior to traversing worlds, and little white dots hovered in the corners of my vision, but I was alive. "Perfectly fine," I yelled through the gushing breeze. She didn't need to know about the fatigue in my bones. I didn't find it necessary to shout into the sky about feeling every last bit of immortality flee my body.

Her brows scrunched, and I swore I caught her glancing at my hair before she turned back to face a growing speck in the distance. The Valhalla sect of the House of Wings grew less hazy as we flew on, and I pulled on Apple's reins to take a sharp left away from the place. As much as I'd love to return home and gather my belongings, that sect was no longer mine, and I wouldn't be welcome within those walls. As it was, my mortality was quickly catching up with me, and I could feel the heavy toll the Bifrost had taken on my body. I wouldn't be surprised to see a full head of rich brown hair in the mirror upon our arrival in Fólkvangr. I needed to secure my spot in Freyja's sect, and I needed to do it soon. Human mortals had no place in Asgard, especially not disgraced valkyries.

Gunhild and Rayna shot in front of us to lead the way to Fólkvangr. Although Apple was faster by nature, I allowed Rayna to take the lead. This was her first official duty back at Freyja's side, and I wouldn't let any sort of pride get in the way of her job well done.

As we rode through the beautiful blue sky, Kari leaned back on me with a sigh. I wouldn't tell her my legs were sore and I was already exerting just enough abdominal strength to hold myself on Apple, let alone the strain her additional weight added. I would never allow her to think I couldn't support her, even if my muscles were now pathetic and slowly adjusting to the mortality leeching its way back into my bones like a disease. She would always be a light to me, and I was fortunate to be able to help her carry it.

Rayna pointed ahead to spires poking high into the sky and a long bridge that led from mainland Asgard to Freyja's stunning isle. Sessrúmnir sat alone upon the isle, fields behind it stretching far beyond the eyes could see. It wasn't all shining golds and brilliant whites like Valhalla, but a mix of soft grey stone with gold and silver accents. And while it may have looked understated upon first glance, Sessrúmnir had many hidden wonders.

Freyja put all her efforts in maintaining the most glorious fields. While the fields in Valhalla were for bloody battles, here, they saw no such brutality. They were grown for peace and tranquility, and as we flew above them, performing one loop around Sessrúmnir, there was no shortage of souls lounging in the sun, snacking on fruits, playing games. Fountains spewed high into the air, misting nearby patrons who couldn't feel the change of temperature against their skin but enjoyed it all the same.

Kari marveled at her surroundings as Apple and Gunhild landed upon lush grass on the other side of Sessrúmnir's long, stone bridge. Gunhild lowered one of her wings to allow Rayna to dismount, and Apple followed suit. Once we were all on solid ground, our packs slung around our backs, offerings in hand, Rayna summoned post-flight nibbles for Gunhild. I glanced from the pile of oats and bucket of water before Gunhild to the empty space in front of Apple. She would never leave me, never bond with another, but I was beginning to realize I could no longer take care of her in the way I was used to.

Rayna cleared her throat, almost apologetically, then waved her hand. I didn't need to take my gaze off her to realize she'd fed and watered Apple. I wanted to thank her, but the words burned in my throat like a poison. Kari's eyes widened, and then Rayna turned away with a newfound stiffness to her posture.

I blew out a tormented sigh and muttered, "Thank you, sister" under my breath. I knew Rayna wouldn't want me to acknowledge what had happened any more than I had. She was just as awkward and torn up about my missing seidr as I was, but what good would lamenting do for either of us? Bringing more attention to my inability to wield seidr like I once had wouldn't bring it back, but heading into Sessrúmnir and speaking with Freyja could.

With how Kari trailed her gaze over my profile, I imagined she would've reached for my hand had she not been holding the realm's most ridiculous fruit cake. I offered her a weak smile and followed Rayna down a moss-lined path.

"Does the moss glow here too?" Kari asked, glancing down the path as she walked beside me.

I knew what she was trying to do, so I didn't suppress my laugh as I said, "No, seeress. That's a Nidavellir specialty, though Fólkvangr has more than its fair share of oddities."

"I'm surprised you consider them oddities," Kari mused thoughtfully, Tove walking in stride with her.

"I didn't come from a line of wand-wed women, and I rarely saw seidr being used until I was taken to Valhalla. As soon as I was inducted into the sisterhood, I did as much exploring as I was allowed to. Everything I saw was so new and exciting, and I hardly understood how any of it worked, including my own seidr growing within me. It took me centuries before the shock of it all wore off," I admitted, thinking back on the times when I'd been just as curious as Kari.

"It's hard to imagine a time when you were giddy and learning, when you didn't claim to know everything." She spoke in a light tone and paired her mock insult with a playful eye roll.

"Yeah, yeah, well, I was young once," I said with a smirk and a wave of my hand. "And when you become one of Freyja's attendants, you'll eventually get used to such wonders too."

"What if I don't want to?" she asked. "Get used to it, I mean."

I looked her over. "Life doesn't have to be dull just because it stretches past when it was supposed to end. I know many attendants who've been alive far longer than me who live rich, fulfilled lives. Don't use me as your example, seeress. Knowing you, you'd never allow for such a routine and boring existence to claim you as I once had."

Kari offered me a soft smile and a head tilt. A shadow was cast upon half her face, the sun blocked by Sessrúmnir's tall stature as we grew closer. "I can already think up a few ways to keep myself entertained, though I have to admit, my plans will be ruined if Freyja doesn't choose us both." Her voice was deep and sultry, sending my imagination in all sorts of wicked directions. I smirked and opened my mouth to reply with something equally clever when someone else's voice filled the space around us.

"So, you two have finally fucked, have you?" Rayna called out from ahead, where apparently, she was still within listening distance of us.

Damned valkyrie ears.

"I thought you two were going to take care of that in Nidavellir. I certainly did," Rayna continued, showing us nothing more than the back of her head. I could tell by her tone alone she was having a grand old time up there eavesdropping.

"Alvion, I presume?" Kari asked, not seeming at all bothered by Rayna's assumption. Was she not worried to admit she'd been with me? It took me a moment to remember we were both mortals now, her and I. There was no difference between us, no rules stating we couldn't be together. I had no more oaths, and at the time we'd had each other, Kari had no obligations either. We were free of the gods, of any expectations to hide what we were to each other. Now was the best time to solidify— no, demand—that the world knew I was hers, and she was mine.

I couldn't help but smile at that thought.

"How astute of you," Rayna said, turning to face us.

"I thought most valkyries preferred the company of other women?" Kari asked. "Not that it's any of my concern who you're with. I, myself, have a range of preferences."

"Most of us do, yes," Rayna admitted, and she wasn't wrong. It made our duties a whole lot easier when the men we encountered didn't think they stood a chance with us, but that didn't mean we all had the same desires. "Alvion wasn't always called Alvion. Though he's always had the best beard, no matter what his name was." She let out a small chuckle, her cheeks rosy with what I could only imagine was love. Rayna and Alvion had been loosely together for half a century, though neither one of them could give up their realm, and inter-world relationships were never easy. Even so, the pair had never moved on from one another, and I had to wonder who would give in first. Knowing Rayna, my wager was on Alvion.

"Rune did mention you had a thing for the hairy ones," Kari said, and the three of us laughed at that.

Tove let out a loud meow as we arrived at the front steps of Sessrúmnir. Carved out of pale, grey stone, two large felines guarded the wide-set entrance into Freyja's Hall. Kari's lips parted as she took in their detail, and the soft pitter-pattering of my heart escalated into loud thumps against my ribs as I wondered if we were in above our heads. Kari was powerful, yes. Kari brought flame to Helheim using Hel's own seidr, yes. And she'd been taught by a four-thousand-year-old wand-wed Asgardian, not to mention an all-knowing skald in the Cave of Whispers. But even then, she hadn't been practicing long, and we had no way of knowing what Freyja wanted from her.

The Goddess of Fertility and Love was kinder and less erratic than most of the gods, but a goddess she was all the same. Kari had one chance at fulfilling Hel and Freyja's deal by using her seidr to do Freyja's bidding, and I had one chance at claiming a position in her sect. If a single thing went wrong, Kari and I would be right back where we were before Odin had stripped me of my title— opposite ends of mortality. If Alvion and Rayna had trouble in their inter-world relationship, what would become of us?

The sound of doors being swung open forced me to be present. Once impressed by the feline statues, Kari now marveled at the art brought to life. Bygul and Trjegul came strolling through the doors, their shiny coats gleaming a silvery blue. Freyja's chariot cats greeted us with slight head nods, then turned on their heels, their tails motioning us to follow them inside the home of their goddess.

"Ready?" I asked under my breath.

"I only practiced my speech five times," Kari muttered, motioning to the cake with her chin. "Maybe Hel should've made me do it one more time, just to be safe."

I chuckled and shook my head as we walked up the grand steps of Sessrúmnir. "You'll be just fine. You're my seeress, after all."

Kari's chest stilled despite the strenuous steps, and she flashed me a coy smile when she realized I'd called her mine. I'd never get over that smile. She made even the fruit cake in her hands seem bitter in comparison. Nothing matched her sweetness.

Rayna made it to the double doors before us. She made a "hurry up" motion with her hand, wearing her sternest face as she disappeared through them. I quickened my pace, a jar of honey in one hand, a slightly disheveled bouquet of snow blossoms in the other.

When Kari and I made it into the building, we wound through stunning halls covered in ornate tapestries and paintings. A harp played in the distance, and it harmonized beautifully with the sound of trickling water coming from a sunny courtyard. After being in Helheim, this place felt as far from the snowy realm as possible. Everything, from the walls to the stone we walked upon, breathed life, and it was hard not to let my guard down. Much like Hel designed her hall to provide comfort to her residents, Freyja designed hers for pure tranquility.

Bygul and Trjegul lead us into Freyja's throne room, where the goddess sat upon a grand wooden chair carved with delicate patterns. Freyja's golden hair flowed over her fur-lined shoulders down to her waist. She wore a white dress with a delicate gold rope tied around her midsection. She smiled as we entered her chambers, her eyes lighting up upon spotting the offerings in our hands.

Kari and I lowered to our knees, where we waited to be acknowledged. Rayna spoke first, motioning to where we bowed to her goddess. "As you requested..." she began with a voice that was confident but not commanding, "Kari Kettlesdotter and Rune Dragomir." Once she announced our presence, Rayna stood to the side to give the goddess a full view of us.

"Ah, and what have you brought for me?" Freyja asked, her voice as smooth as the honey in my hands.

"We have brought you gifts from our time in Helheim, sent with us by the Goddess of Death. She offers not only these delicious offerings, but me as well, a mortal seeress. I come willingly and have sensed only peace surrounding my entrance into Fólkvangr. I hope you accept these offerings and look down upon us with your loving favor."

A sweet chuckle filled the air. "Yes, yes, but what have you brought for me?"

Kari paused. She'd practiced the same lines over and over, yet we hadn't planned much for what she'd say *after* her speech. I was tempted to chime in, but we were in Fólkvangr now, and if Kari wanted to stay, she was going to have to accomplish much harder tasks than answering simple questions.

Kari finally spoke, "We have brought you fruit cake, made from the finest berries." She raised her hands into the air as she had practiced so many times. Her chin was dipped, eyes pointing to the floor. "And Rune offers the rare Helheim snow blossoms, as well as the sweet honey made from their nectar."

"How lovely," Freyja cooed. "I will be sure to thank Hel for her efforts. As for you both, you may rise. Your offerings have been accepted."

Kari and I rose, and Rayna took the offerings out of our hands, delivering them to the foot of the goddess.

"Thank you, Goddess," Kari and I echoed each other.

"Kari, I am pleased to hear you come willingly, as I have very little use for a seeress who has no desire to be here. I'm sure Hel has mentioned your purpose as a key element in a little bargain between us. And, well, it is my term that the bargain will only be sealed upon your acceptance into my council. That being said, before you can be accepted, you must perform a task for me."

"May I ask what kind of task?" Kari said.

"One all others have failed, including myself. I am the mother of seidr itself, yet mine seems to fail me when it comes to this endeavor. The thing I want most." She laughed bitterly, her kind mask slipping for all but a second. "My husband, Odr, is missing, you see, and he has been for quite some time. I have searched across the nine realms with no such luck, and all I want is to bring him home. If not for myself, then for our daughters." Golden tears ran down her cheeks as she spoke, splashing upon her chest, solidifying and clinking on the stone floor as they free fell.

"If I succeed in finding your husband, I will join your wandwed council and become your attendant?" Kari asked, making sure she specified if Freyja would make her an attendant or not.

That's my brilliant girl.

Freyja hummed. "Yes, well, if you succeed when no one else has, you will surely be the best choice as my next attendant. Mortal lives are so short, so you would be quite useless to me if you remained one. My husband is the god of frenzy and inspiration, after all. This isn't the first time he's gone missing over the centuries, and it won't be the last."

Kari nodded slowly, and I wondered what was going on in that mind of hers. If I didn't have to worry about my own immortality, I would have killed for the chance at freeing Kari of her mortal confines and being with her forever.

"But if you fail..." Freyja said, tapping her nails on her wooden throne, as if the thought of this outcome pained her. "You will not join my council, and you will no longer be welcome in my halls. I hear you've already been barred from several others, and I suspect after long, your only option will be to go back to your mortal plane to die. You have one week to give me what I desire, Kari—or you can refuse now and claim whatever afterlife is meant for you."

CHAPTER THIRTY-FOUR
HANDS LIKE CHARCOAL

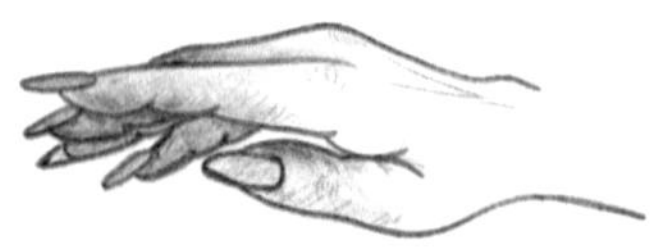

Kari

"That's it, right there," I moaned, my feet instinctively splashing through the warm, sudsy water as I writhed under Rune's touch. "Gods, that's good."

"If you keep this up, I'm going to have you moaning for a completely different reason," Rune said as she slid her thumb over the meat of my palm. She slathered more ointment over my charcoal-stained flesh, soothing the tenderness beneath. I'd given up on attempting Midgardian seidr over a lunar cycle ago, fully engrossing myself in underworld seidr, but every form of power had its own consequences.

"Well, I wouldn't say no to that," I said with a smirk, sinking further into the tub. "As long as you don't mind that I'm unable to lift my own arms."

"I'm more than capable of putting in the work for the both of us." Rune dipped her head to kiss my wrist. "But you should rest. You've been casting far too many spells since we arrived in Sessrúmnir, and you'll wear yourself out too quickly if you keep this up."

While the curse that once ravaged my reflection could no longer haunt me, the death seidr's signature was claiming the skin of my hands. I'd been casting communication spells since we arrived in Fólkvangr and Freyja had given me my task, but the only result was the spreading of the charcoal staining under my fingernails. I hadn't been able to contact Odr, and my seidr was waning. How could I not continue to try, though, when Freyja had threatened my life, my freedom?

"Resting isn't nearly as fun, but I guess you're right," I conceded, climbing out of the tub. I sat upon the side of it, water dripping to the rug below. Rune lifted me from my spot perched against the copper lip, a yelp escaping my throat as she did. Rune laid me upon a table draped in soft fabrics, then began drying me as if the act was part of a worship ritual.

I laughed as she dabbed at my sensitive, water-warmed skin and said, "My hands and arms may be useless at the moment from casting, but my legs are working just fine."

"Even so, I like taking care of you," Rune admitted with a soft grin.

"You have been for a while now, haven't you?" I peered up at her, her forearm supporting my neck. I thought of all the times she'd put me first, all the times I hadn't realized she'd been aiding me because I was too angry to see it.

"I've tried. Though I admit, my efforts haven't always... I haven't always gone about it the right way," she said. "But I intend to now. I hope I can make up for the damage I've caused."

I shook my head and sat up. "You haven't caused damage." My greying palm found her cheek, my nails, long and black, brushing her beautiful olive skin. "I'm thankful for where this journey has taken us, even if it took way too long for me to have faith in it. There's no way of knowing where we'll end up, or which tests we'll pass, but I have no doubt that whatever happens, we'll be okay. We'll make do with any outcome. Together."

Rune nodded and held a hand out to me. I took it and let her help me to stand. The floor should have been cold beneath my feet, but as I was practicing my seidr, I may have casta warming spell on the stone. As I walked across it to the dress laid out for me on a low-lying table, I spread my toes and appreciated the comfort.

The dress was almost the color of my creamy skin, though it lacked tan markings like I had splattered across my arms. I slid it on over my head and watched as the luxurious fabric rippled to the floor below. It was slightly too long, dragging as I took a step forward, but that seemed to be how all the women I'd seen walking the halls had worn theirs too. It wasn't functional, and it certainly wouldn't have worked in Stormheim, but then again, fabric as beautiful as this would've never graced my skin in my old village.

Rune walked over to help me secure thin leather armor around my waist. There was no reason I shouldn't be safe here in Sessrúmnir, but Rune didn't want to take any chances. We were too close to getting what we both wanted to have things end now. We were back in Asgard, after all, and who knew what monsters lurked around the corners to make us pay for our actions? We hadn't exactly left the realm on good terms with the Allfather.

"Rayna should be dropping off some of Odr's effects soon. The more you have of his history, the more you can understand the god," she said, handing me a light fur shawl. She was wearing something similar, as it was no longer in good taste to wear the leathers of the valkyries. She had light furs fastened across her chest, and her dress was the color of the blood moon. Her full head of brown hair was loose, cascading across her back and shoulders. She was almost unrecognizable, but whenever I found myself searching for the Rune I knew, it only took one of her smirks to see past the slow descent into Iris.

"I'm not sure how I'm supposed to find him when the gods have failed to. Freyja herself cannot sense where he's gone. It's been three decades now, and I'm supposed to be the one who ends the wait for his return?"

"You are Kari Kettlesdotter, the one who set flame to Helheim.

Finding a lost god will not be your first impossible feat, and it certainly won't be your last," Rune said, her eyes as fierce as the warrior I knew her to be.

"I did summon fire in the realm of ice, didn't I?" I asked with a smug smile, just for Rune's benefit. I feared if I let her see how uncertain I was of my own capabilities, she too would worry we were in over our heads.

"You did," she said, brushing my damp hair out of the way. She ran her fingers over a feather I'd braided into my locks and let out a soft exhale.

I stared deep into her eyes, the entrance to her very soul. "Why didn't you ask to join Freyja's sect? We were there, bowed at her feet, offerings in hand."

"I wasn't confident that our offerings were enough for the both of us, and I wasn't going to risk her listening to my pleas over yours."

"She could've taken us both. You will speak with her, won't you? We can find more offerings," I said. Iris was beautiful, but I didn't know her. What I knew was Rune's strength, her ability to make everyone in the room know she was not to be trifled with, a warrior who had honed her skills over decades, centuries, who lived in leathers and had a shock of white hair. She was not a brunette girl from a small village that no longer existed. She wasn't the one her family never bothered to love, or the one Odin had stolen in the night. Rune was not the one who would stay back and let her title be stripped from her, not the Rune I knew.

"Too much was at stake, seeress," she said, pulling me in to kiss the top of my head. "Once you find Odr, I will offer anything to Freyja to stay here in Fólkvangr with you. I will fight to join the House of Wings once more, to trade my red and black leathers for deep emerald ones."

"Do you promise?" I said, gripping her furs and pulling her into my chest so we were flush against each other.

"Don't let my hair fool you," she said with a smirk. "I'm still a warrior, still a valkyrie at heart, and I will not let anyone, not even the Allfather, get in my way of returning to the sisterhood."

"Good. That's my girl." I pulled her in for a kiss, the taste of hazelnuts and raspberries on her lips. She deepened it, sliding her tongue into my mouth like she fully intended on keeping me right where I was.

"Open up, lovebirds," a voice called from beyond the door, followed by the sound of harsh knuckles on wood.

"Rayna." Rune tilted her head back and sucked in a breath to center herself. "Perfect timing, as always."

I sighed and pulled away from Rune, placing a hand on the back of my heated neck. As I headed over to greet Rayna, I shrugged out of my furs and placed the additional layer across an armchair. When the door swung open, Rayna stood before me, empty-handed. I stuck my head through the doorway and looked on either side of her to see if there was something I was missing.

"I didn't bring anything with me," Rayna said by way of greeting. "I'm taking you to it, not the other way around."

"Oh, okay. Let me collect my things then. Come in." I ushered Rune's sister into the room. One of Freyja's attendants had chosen it for us, though I'd been hoping one of her felines were going to guide the way, much like Garm had while in Hel. The same good fortune hadn't found us.

I made my way to the bed in the far corner of the room. Sheer fabrics were strung up on a brass frame, vining plants making their way across it from the large clay pots at the foot of the bed. Tove was nestled up against my pillow, and I leaned in to kiss him between the ears. When I did, he made a soft, surprised trill, then blinked his sleep-filled eyes at me. I intended on leaving him in the comfort of the room, but when he stood to stretch, I knew he wouldn't let me leave him behind. The demon cat launched himself from his spot on the quilt to the basket by Rune's feet.

Rune jumped back, tripping on her dress and falling toward the stone floor. Rayna lunged forward to grab her arm, but the slippery fabric of her sister's dress snuck under the tip of her boot. She joined Rune on the floor, and the two women sat there, wrapped in the lunar-red dress from the gods, looking as if they had just lost their first battle.

Tove hissed as he climbed into his basket, and I lost any and all of the composure I was desperately trying to maintain. I burst out laughing, gripping at the leather armor around my stomach that didn't allow my lungs to fully inflate.

"Damn cat. You won't be laughing when I tell Apple to throw you off her back," Rune muttered, trying to collect herself and yanking the hem of her dress out from underneath a frazzled Rayna.

"You would never," I said with one final, belly-disrupting laugh. Rayna climbed to her feet, giving me space to help Rune do the same. I brushed her ass with one of my tender hands while I supported her with the other. She grumbled something about needing to find some high breeches while she adjusted her crooked bust.

Rune took a wide berth around the feline-filled basket, scowling at my sinister boy as she did. I wouldn't say anything to him now, but I *was* going to find a way to get the two of them to care for each other just as I cared for them. The constant hissing and threats used to bring me much satisfaction, but I'm not sure how much longer they could go on. I wasn't willing to lose either one of them if they couldn't figure out how to get along on their own.

Rayna sauntered away from us, completely unaffected, though I noticed Rune had a slight hobble to her step.

Maybe I shouldn't have laughed after all.

I'd forgotten Rune wasn't as resilient as she'd once been; she was vulnerable and very much human now. Muttering a quiet apology so her sister couldn't hear, I checked Rune's elbows for scrapes. I wanted to be able to laugh and know the fall did little to wound her, inside or out, but until she was inducted into the sisterhood once more, every fall, every scratch was going to be a reminder of what had been taken from her.

Before I brought too much attention to the matter, I stole a quick kiss and then made off to place some of my ingredients and belongings in the basket with Tove. When I had everything I needed, I grabbed my light furs from the back of the chair closest to the door, then motioned to the other two women that I was ready to go.

Rune and Rayna shuffled out of the room and into one of Sessrúmnir's endless halls. The moon claimed the sky, so the torches lining the halls were needed as we made our way through them.

"Where are we off to?" I finally asked when Rayna gave no indication of our destination outside of telling me we were on our way to see Odr's belongings.

"His chamber," Rayna said. I swore I could feel the color drain from my face, as if it had been my very lifeforce.

"His what?" I asked. "The god of inspiration and frenzy's *what*?"

Rayna gave me a sidelong glance.

"Oh, don't tell me this doesn't faze you," Kari said. "You may be an attendant to the gods, but I highly doubt you've ever been where they sleep. You don't offer *that* kind of assistance."

Rune chuckled and elbowed her sister. "She's got a point. Unless things drastically changed after I left."

"Okay, fine," Rayna said, straightening her spine and pushing back loose strands of gold and white hair. A smile crept onto her otherwise stony façade. "It's kind of cool."

"Admitting you think something is cool? I'm never going to let you live this down," I said with a throaty chuckle. Rayna rolled her eyes and continued down the hall.

As we drew closer, more guards and valkyries filled the halls to ward off anyone not permitted in the quarters of the gods. I took in every detail as we walked, from the tapestries and paintings to the carved statues depicting Freyja and Odr's daughters. Hnoss and Gersemi were captivating women from what I could tell, which only made sense, seeing as they were the goddesses of beauty and treasure.

"Should I be concerned?" Rune asked as she caught me staring at them a little too long, my head continuing to their statues even after we'd passed.

"Yes, you know, I've been meaning to tell you…I'm leaving you for a slab of stone," I jested, poking her side. Rune's shoulders rocked slightly, but she didn't let out her suppressed chuckle as we passed a set of guards, maintaining a level of professionalism I didn't yet have.

"Let's go, you two," Rayna said, waving us forward to where she held open a door. I entered the room first, but when Rune tried to enter, Rayna held up her arm to not let her pass. "I'm afraid Kari needs to do this on her own. Our presence will only serve to distract and confuse her seidr. It's for the best if Odr is the only force she can sense."

My mouth gaped, but I allowed my lips to close softly. My head bobbed in understanding, and when Rune found my eyes and saw my nod, she backed away from Rayna's outstretched arm.

"Kari, I'll be standing guard for the entirety of your stay. I'll only be a knock away if you need anything, be it food, drink, incantation oils, you name it. Freyja has given you full access to her husband's quarters. Nothing is off limits," Rayna said, her eyes widening slightly, as if she too had a hard time wrapping her mind around such a task.

Free roam of a god's quarters? Who knew getting struck by an arrow would allow me such privileges.

"Thank you, Rayna." I tapped my foot on the impressive stone floor a few times, and just as the valkyrie moved to close the door, I said, "Maybe…you can help Rune come up with an appropriate offering for Freyja while you both wait. You know the goddess far better than we do. If being in here aids me in understanding where

Odr has gone, we're going to need plans prepared to secure Rune's position."

Rayna glanced from me to Rune. She then nodded once, and the door shut, leaving me alone in the gilded room. The place was dusty and devoid of human touch, but I could tell it once was a well-loved space. The walls were covered in paintings and various art, even more so than the halls. Everything about Odr's quarters was over the top, as if it had been frantically put together in a burst of inspiration.

In the corner, by the window, sat a large wooden easel holding a stretched linen canvas. The painting had been interrupted, and the pigments he'd been using were now dried up. I ran my finger over the neglected boar's brush that had never been rinsed. It was hardened, with bent bristles, as if the god of frenzy had been pressing upon his canvas far too hard.

The strange strokes caught my attention as I realized they were glistening. When my fingers made contact, nothing lifted off the dried painting. I leaned in closer, noticing the unique colors appeared wet due to the opalescent pieces crushed into them. I glanced at the metal tray holding his pigments, noticing one of the jars was empty, scraped clean.

Muttering to myself, I pulled the easel into the center of the bedchamber to give me more room. I disturbed Tove as I began pulling objects from within my basket. He hopped out and dove toward a cluster of dust creatures hidden under a nearby bench. I shook my head at my little gremlin. Then, one by one, I placed candles in a circle around the easel. Once they were all set, I lit them with my seidr, forgoing flint. The tracking spell was one Áma had taught me in case I lost Rune during our travels. At the time, I never thought I'd eventually use it to find a god.

The spell would only help me locate Odr if he was in the same world as I was, but if I could determine if he was still in Asgard, it was a start. I wanted to be able to give Freyja useful information as soon as humanly possible, even if it wasn't the precise location she was looking for.

Stepping in the candlelit circle, I ensured my dress didn't become a victim of the flame. In my unclasped palm sat my favorite divination tool. I dangled the calibrated pendulum in front of the unfinished painting, the stone swaying gently from the leather strip I held. A tool just like this was used in Midgard to help me make decisions locked within my mind, ones that I may not have been completely aware of. But leaving my realm, I'd learned that through my underworld seidr, I was able to tap into the gods to get the answers I sought. Being in a place so tainted by Odr, I was hoping his lingering essence would help me understand what happened here, where he'd gone.

Testing out the pendulum's calibration, I started with a simple question I already knew the answer to. Into the stuffy air of the room, I asked, "Am I in Asgard?" The stone's swaying pattern was disrupted by a circular motion from east to west.

Yes.

Satisfied with the answer, I moved on to the harder questions. "Is Odr here in Asgard?" The pendulum maintained its rhythm, so I repeated my question with different wording. "Is Odr in the same realm as me?" The pendulum swung in a diagonal motion from the southwest to the northeast.

No.

I sighed at the response, though I had to say, I wasn't all that surprised. Glancing around at the candles I lit, I realized I wasn't going to get an exact location if he wasn't in the same realm as me. I considered going down the list of realms and asking the pendulum if he was in each of them, but I knew it wouldn't be of any use.

"Hmm..." I trailed off, an idea blossoming in my mind. I took in the easel and the brushes. "Did Odr leave in a hurry?"

Yes.

I glanced around the ornate room at what other clues I

could've missed. It was possible he hadn't planned this journey at all. "Was Odr taken against his will?"

No.

"Not taken against his will, but he left in a hurry all the same," I murmured to myself, tapping my foot on the floor. "Will Odr come back to Asgard?" I asked. The pendulum swung northwest to southeast.

Unknown.

I asked a few more variations of the same question, hoping the problem was with the way I'd asked, not the question itself, but I received the same unhelpful answer each time.

Realizing this pendulum had reached its limit, I curled it back into my fist. I left the candles lit as I left the circle, exploring the god's chamber. From his belongings alone, I could tell he was a god of chaos, and he certainly enjoyed living in euphoric splendor. I'd thrown more than my fair share of objects down after realizing what they were intended for.

Wiping my hand down my dress, I moved toward his bed. The quilt and furs were coated in a fine layer of dust, but I still lowered myself until my back hit the mattress. I stared up at the painted ceiling, depictions of ecstasy decorating it in muted colors. When I squinted hard enough, I realized the same man had been painted over and over in a myriad of erotic positions. Familiarity struck me as I recalled the tapestry of Odr in the hall.

It was him. The god of inspiration was staring down at me with his dark eyes and long, chestnut hair. His beard was trimmed to perfection, even in the depiction of another man gripping it in his fist. My brows rose, and I shuddered as I caught a glimpse of what had been painted next to it.

This man is creative, to say the least.

As I settled in his bed, I closed my eyes and tried not to think about all that had occurred below me. His presence in this place was vibrant, and I held on to that bond, strengthening it as I tried to pull history that clung to the gilded walls.

My eyes flung open just as I realized I would find none of the answers I sought while in this waking world. I hopped out of the bed, startling an exploring orange feline. I muttered an apology as I sent a gust of wind to suffocate the still-lit candles.

My knuckles tapped against the main chamber door, ready for Rayna to open it. Rune wasn't of much use to me standing around with her sister, but I had a task for her that could be more than useful.

Rayna's face appeared in the doorway, and I used my fingers to pry it open enough for me to see Rune too.

"I need you," I said to Rune over Rayna's shoulder. "Not here, but in the mist."

CHAPTER THIRTY-FIVE
THANK THE GODS FOR MOONCAKE

Rune

Riding upon Apple's back was a much welcomed reprieve after standing in the hall, discussing offerings with Rayna. I loved my sister, but *gods,* she could be utterly dry when she was on duty. She did, however, have a brilliant plan to find me the perfect offerings and reward herself in the process. Everyone knew about Freyja's love for Nidavelirian mooncakes, and we just so happened to know a tavern-owning dwarf with a generous mother who lived for lunar baking. Ale and mooncakes weren't the worst things I could offer the goddess in return for a chance to become a valkyrie again.

Apple dove toward the House of Wings, flying a little too close to the occupants of Freyja's rolling meadows. She landed upon soft grass, and not even a moment after I was dismounted, she was flaring her lips at me.

"I told you," I said with a sigh, "you're going to have to wait a little longer until I can get you some apples. Go steal some of Gunhild's." Epli snorted impatiently as she trotted away. I shook my head at the pegasus and continued down the path toward the

Fólkvangr sect. I couldn't leave room in my mind to feel badly for the pegasus' misfortune, not when I'd spent the day trying to turn the gods' favor around for us all.

After a little visit to the Valley Beyond the Mist, Áma agreed to leave the protection of her sacred home to help Kari find Odr. She asked for a few days to get her affairs in order before she departed, as it would be her first time leaving the mist in three centuries, but she would be here, and that was something. No, not just something. *It was everything.*

In the matter of days, Áma and Alvion would both be in Fólkvangr, and Kari and I would be two giant steps closer to getting what we both wanted most.

Kari had run out of ways to find Odr through spells and divination tools alone. It was time to move on to what once was her specialty but was now a great mystery, a puzzle to be solved.

Kari needed to have a vision.

There was a good chance that wherever Odr was in the nine realms, Kari had never been. She'd gained knowledge from the skald in the Cave of Whispers on using symbolism from her distorted visions to uncover the meanings behind them, which had been working quite well for her. The biggest challenge now was having a vision of someone else's past or future instead of her own.

"I sent for the washing of Odr's bedding," Rayna said, forgoing any sort of greeting, as usual. I twisted my head to see where she leaned against the entrance to the House of Wings. The building was larger than the Valhalla sect was, and the pale stone matched Sessrúmnir.

I chewed on my bottom lip as I scanned Rayna in her new leathers, so deep green, they would have looked black if not for the sun shining upon them. I grunted in a way of thanks and nodded to the front entrance of her new home. "You going to show me around? I could use the distraction," I admitted. We both knew why she'd sent for a wash service. Kari would be spending the night, alone, in Odr's chamber. If there was anywhere she would have a vision that would direct us to his whereabouts, it was going to be tucked into his very own bed.

The last thing I wanted was to spend a night without her, but I knew this was our biggest hope. Having me or Tove sleeping next to her could not only disturb her visions, but influence them. It was also why I'd been asked to leave my post outside his bedchamber, Rayna too. Kari needed a fresh perspective of the space, and she needed the room to be void of any familiar presence.

"Follow me," she said as she pushed off the wall. "It will be your home too, soon enough."

A few days later, Kari and I found ourselves in a lavish lounging area, surrounded by visitors, one expected, the other a pleasant surprise.

"I come bearing gifts!" a low, feminine voice called out. I swung to see Nori in the hall, holding a large hemp sack in front of her. I could barely make out the dwarf's face, the sack so large in front of her small body.

"Nori!" I rushed over to greet her, Kari following shortly behind. "What are you doing here?" I tried to take the sack before realizing the contents were far heavier than I anticipated. "Are you lugging around rocks? What's in this thing?" I huffed as I set it down on the floor next to me. The veins in her strong arms bulged, but she seemed otherwise unaffected by the weight of what she'd held.

"Oh, that? It's nothing you aren't used to carrying," she said with a brilliant smile. She waved over my shoulder to where Rayna and Alvion made themselves comfortable on a chaise lounge. They echoed their hellos but didn't move from where they sat, leaned against each other.

I took a step back so Kari stood next to me. Nori's eyes caught on her, and her face lit up.

"Ah, the seeress I've heard much about!" she called out before bending over her sack and pulling it open. "I brought something for you."

"For me?" Kari said, no doubt wondering why the smith she'd met while on Nidavellir had brought her something. I turned to look at Rayna over my shoulder, but she simply sat in silence with a smug grin on her face. Alvion looked quite pleased as well, and I wondered what they'd cooked up. As it was, Rayna had used one of her limited, and quite costly, spell scrolls to write to Alvion. She'd burned her note in a fire, knowing the summoning scroll would appear in Alvion's hand in Nidavellir. He showed up a day later, offerings in hand.

What are you up to now?

The sound of clinking metal caught my attention as Nori pulled a wooden box from her sack, not letting me see what else she'd brought with her. She handed the box to Kari and ushered her to open it. Kari looked almost as surprised as I felt, but she thanked Nori and pulled off the lid. Sitting inside the box were four metal rings, all carved with varying runes.

Kari gasped and plucked the first one out, inspecting it, reading the inscribed runes. She did the same with the three others, slipping them onto her stained fingers, two on each hand. She held up her hands for the two of us to see, and slowly but surely, the pinky cream color of her skin began creeping down her palms, into her fingers, under her nails. No trace of the charcoal staining remained, all gone except for the residue around her new rings.

"Nori..." I trailed off, not quite sure what to say. "What did those rings just do?"

"Ask the one who's actually wand-wed!" Nori said with a proud smile and a stroke of her thin beard, not willing to take this moment from Kari.

"They're divination bands inscribed with runes to allow the

excess seidr to flow into them instead of seeping under my skin," Kari said in amazement, her words slow and measuring.

"They will protect her against the seidr of the underworld, seeing as, well..." Nori trailed off. "It takes a toll on the human body. I'm sure you'll need more bands with the tasks Freyja ought to be giving you as her future attendant, but these were all I could make on such short notice. Once you're admitted into her council and made an official attendant, your body will rid itself of its mortality over time. These are just to help in the meantime."

Before Kari said anything, she threw her arms around Nori and let out a relieved laugh. "Thank you, Nori!" She pulled back, analyzing her hands and the rings looped around them. "As badass as my hands looked, I'm more than happy to rid myself of the stains left behind from my seidr. I've had enough of Hel's little gifts."

"You're very welcome. Rayna told me of your curse, and I figured the death rot spreading on your hands would be the last thing you'd want to see after living with such a horrid reflection." Nori shook her head, and then her eyes went wide. "From the rot, of course. You poor thing. I hope you're enjoying your very beautiful reflection here in Asgard." She emphasized "very" and "beautiful" to make up for the fact that she'd almost called my mortal horrid looking.

Kari laughed, and the sound did something odd to my chest, a warmth spreading down into my skin and around my heart.

"I am, thank you," Kari said. "These will certainly come in handy over the next several days. I assume Rayna caught you up on my task?"

"She has, and not just your task, but a test for Rune as well. Which is why," she dove back into her hemp sack, "those rings aren't the only thing I brought. Rune, I know it's nothing you're used to, but it was the closest thing to your measurements as I could find, taking into account that your muscles would be a bit, uh, smaller."

Nori smiled awkwardly as she took in my form.

Apparently, I'm not the only one who's noticed a difference in my body.

Before I could give the smith a hard time, she pulled out brown leathers and threw them at me. I gripped them, thankful for the familiar feel in my hands. They were slightly worn, just how I liked them. The best part was, they weren't the color that any of the House of Wings valkyries wore across any of the sects. They were safe to wear without causing offense, and I was already itching to put them on.

A smile crept onto my face, but Nori kept going. The next gift was a chest piece of pure silver. It gleamed in the torchlight, and while it was reminiscent of the armor worn in Helheim, it was simple enough that I surely wouldn't be mistaken for one of their sisters.

"Nori—" I started as she showed off the other pieces of armor she'd brought.

"Oh shush. Go put those leathers on. You look far too lady-like in whatever it is you're wearing," she said, peering at my clothing disapprovingly. "I'm sure you're dying to climb into something familiar, even if it might not be the best fit."

"It's all perfect, thank you. I truly mean it," I said, my face as hard as stone to keep the prickling in my eyes from turning into something much more vulnerable. I wouldn't cry over armor.

I won't cry over armor, I repeated to convince myself it was true. I turned away from Nori and Kari as I began losing my battle, but I inadvertently caught Rayna's gaze. She offered me a nod and knowing smile, and gods, my heart couldn't take this.

I cleared my throat and said, "I'm going to go try these on." I turned from the group and hightailed it toward the closest bathing chamber. I found one a hall down and slipped out of the clothing I'd been offered by some unknown attendant who'd placed them in our room. The brown leather was cool against my skin, but it quickly warmed to match my body heat. They were a little loose in the thighs and biceps, but I was expecting as much. Whoever these came from surely had more strength than what I had to offer.

For now, I tried to tell myself, because wallowing on these changes was far too pointless when they were as temporary as they were. I would be a valkyrie again soon enough, and as I looked down at myself, I knew this to be true.

When I walked back into the lounge room, something brushed against my leg, and I almost kicked it before realizing the furry creature was Tove, and he was being friendly for once. My muscles relaxed, and I stooped down to run three gentle fingers over his spine. The feline allowed for the touch, and I swear, I heard the slightest of purrs before the little gremlin darted off as if his tail were aflame.

When I stood and walked deeper into the room, I found my friends all sitting around in padded chairs, talking amongst themselves and motioning to something on a table between them.

"Thank the gods these things take forever to go bad. We don't know how long it's going to take to find Odr, and Rune refuses to make any offerings to Freyja until Kari is anointed," Rayna said to Alvion, motioning to a silver tray of mooncakes.

"Subterranean bakers don't mess around, my mother includ-ed," he said with a chuckle. "What's the point in having seidr if you're just going to let your yummies go bad right away? How else would you bake enough for the entire lunar cycle? They're *moon*cakes, after all."

"Are you sure we can't eat a few?" Nori asked, her small hand creeping far too close to the tray for my comfort.

"No one touches them!" Kari said before I had the chance. "Eating those mooncakes is considered stealing directly from the goddess herself."

A smile found my lips, and I placed my hand on her back as I reached her. I leaned in and whispered into her hair, "So protec-tive." Kari relaxed into my side, her long dress draping over my leather-covered thighs. Her face flushed at my words, as if she was embarrassed she'd gotten carried away in warning off our friends.

"Exactly," Alvion agreed, his face surprisingly stern. He struggled to maintain his seriousness for more than a moment before he broke into a pleased grin. "Which is why I brought twice as many as I thought the goddess would need! These ones are for all of you. The *real* offerings are back at the House of Wings, safe in Rayna's chambers."

Kari's eyes widened. "So we can eat these now? I've always wanted to try mooncakes."

Alvion shoved the tray toward Kari, laughing at her sudden change of mood. "Have at it!"

Nori dove toward the cakes before anyone else could, shoving three of the small, cream-colored puff balls into her mouth. Kari's mouth hung open as her hand hovered over the tray, but then she covered her amusement by pressing a cake to her lips. Her brows rose, and a muffled sound came from her throat when the sweet flavors hit her tongue.

"For the love of the gods!" she said, grabbing another mooncake before she'd swallowed the first.

I laughed as she handed me three. I'd remembered the first time I'd had one of the dwarven treats, and my reaction was almost identical, though I was pretty sure mine had included a few more profanities. Biting through one felt like eating a cloud. For people who lived under rocks, they sure knew how to make something soft.

We all ate our fair share and sipped on orange ale as we did. Kari deserved the much-needed break from searching for Odr, even if she was the only one who didn't partake in the consumption of ale. Áma would arrive any time now, and Kari wanted to keep her mind clear and ready for what came next.

CHAPTER THIRTY-SIX
BEYOND THE PIGMENT

Kari

My bare feet padded against the floor as I paced from the window to the door, which happened to be quite the distance. Gods could make endlessly large quarters for themselves, far bigger than one being could ever need. And to think, this was just one of Odr's chambers, the one meant to stoke his inspiration. I, of course, would not be permitted in the one he once shared with Freyja.

My pacing didn't cease until there was a knock on the door. I rushed over, already halfway en route. I found myself swinging the door open with little regard for who stood on the other side. There was only one face I wanted to see, and it was spotted with age.

"Áma! Thank goodness!" I said, pulling her, perhaps a little too aggressively, inside the chamber.

"Get your oily mitts off me," Áma said in her croaky old voice. "Did you dump every incantation oil you could find on yourself? My gods!"

I shrunk back, removing my hands from her shoulders and

wiping them down my fur-lined shawl. "I may have gotten carried away," I admitted sheepishly.

"Go cleanse yourself from the elbow down. I need a fresh canvas to work with, and you're far from it."

I narrowed my eyes but began backing toward the wash basin anyway, biting my tongue. I wouldn't fight with the woman after she'd come all this way. Rayna had sent Gunhild to collect her from the mist and deliver her to Sessrúmnir, and that was no small thing. I couldn't imagine seeing Áma on the back of the fearsome pegasus, and I had to stifle a laugh before the windswept woman asked me what I was going on about.

When I was cleansed to Áma's satisfaction, I met her in the center of the chamber. She stood there with a wooden bowl, and as I approached, she shoved into my chest. "Mugwort is child's play. Drink this."

"What is it?" I asked, wearily taking the bowl from her and staring at the thick, red substance.

"Don't ask questions you don't want the answer to," she grumbled, tucking wayward hairs behind her ears.

"Áma, there's no way in Hel I'm drinking whatever this is without knowing what's in it first."

She sighed and looked up at me before she muttered, "Once you know, you can't unknow, but suit yourself. I've mashed together the heart from a silver fish hand-caught in a fjord, the blessed wolf-wine drained from five humans, tea made of Yggdrasil bark, and, uh, mint, of course."

I winced and peered at the contents of the bowl. The only positive was the mint to settle my stomach after consuming raw heart and human blood. Next time she told me not to ask, I was going to listen.

"And the face you're making is why I chose not to tell you," Áma sighed. "Plug your nose and drink up. There's much to learn and not much time to learn it."

I gritted my teeth and did just as she asked. The thick, coppery liquid slid down my throat, and even after it was all gone, I waited several moments before I unplugged my nose and resumed breathing. Áma handed me a cloth to wipe my lips, and when I did, the cloth came away a diluted scarlet. My nose wrinkled, but I turned my attention to Áma so I didn't have to dwell on what I'd done any longer.

"Very good. Now let that settle into your stomach," Áma said with a smack of her thin lips, "First thing's first." Her wrinkled palm smacked the side of my face with a strength I didn't know she had. My hand instinctively found my throbbing cheek, and I stared at the woman in disbelief. "You will be an attendant to Freyja, Goddess of Fertility, War, and Love, and you will join her council. There will be many things you won't know how to do, but you will uncover the answers you seek, always. You will have a council of people to help you. You will never be alone. Even now, you're not alone. Do not see my help as a weakness. You hear me?"

"Yes, but did I really need to be slap—"

"You don't think you can locate Odr, but if you believe it, it will be so. You are young, with much to learn, but you are powerful already. Even the gods see it. Do not squander this opportunity on self-doubt."

"I'm not squandering it," I growled out.

"I heard you pacing, child. Do not lie to me. You don't have faith in yourself. Tonight, when you lay your head upon a pillow of god, you will have a vision of someone other than yourself. Say it!"

This woman is ill in the mind!

"Say it!"

I swallowed and lowered my hand from my still-throbbing cheek. My dry lips parted, and I repeated her words back to her. "When I lay my head upon a pillow of a god, I will have a vision of someone other than myself."

"When your eyes close and your mind goes elsewhere, you will see the God of Inspiration and Frenzy. You will find Odr. Say it!"

"When my eyes close and my mind goes elsewhere, I will see the God of Inspiration and Frenzy," I echoed, not just saying it to appease her this time, but feeling the words down to my marrow.

"Good. Now, climb into his bed," Áma said, her knuckles pointed toward his impressive slumber mat. I did as she said, the pounding of my blood in my ears, mixed with that of five others.

When I was tucked under his bedding, Áma stood to the side and took my hand. Her dark gaze softened as she brought her hand over my face and gently closed my eyes, humming to me as she did.

"With closed eyes, your mind opens," she sang, her voice rough. "With open palms, what you seek finds you."

My arms rested at my sides, palms up, just as Áma sang. I felt a cool wash on my skin as Áma painted shapes across the inside of my hands and up my wrists. My eyes remained closed, my mind focused. My visions usually found me in my dreams, a tangled web while I slept.

Not this time.

My chin tilted, eyes rolled to the back of my skull. I was mildly aware of the surroundings of my waking body, but the images that flicked through my mind were all I saw behind closed eyes.

Splashes of color drenched my skin as I peered down at myself. The odd pigments reminded me of the surface of a sparkling fjord when the high sun greeted the water's edge. My hands were strong, the tips of my fingers shaped in hard lines meant for wielding, creating. Upon noticing a patch of unpainted skin, I reached for my brush, only to notice the color I needed was gone.

Gone. Gone. Gone.

This wasn't right, couldn't be right, until the color I needed was mine once more. How had I not realized I was running low on the shade? It shared the pigment of the sun when cast behind the clouds, the way it lit the sky in shimmering beams of light the perfect balance between pink and blue.

My brush clattered against my tools, and I, too, was gone. A rainbow swallowed me whole and spit me back out in a land of white. This new place was one my heart beat for but my mind could not place. Golden spheres rolled upon the ground and trees bent, forming tunnels for me to walk through, a shade from the blinding sun.

I knew where I needed to go, but as I walked, walked, walked, I moved no closer. The pigment began falling from my skin, leaching into the soil below me, until I, too, fell beneath the dirt and roots of the realm. I was pulled down and down and down until I sat within the roots of the very tree that had stolen me. My hands were empty and my heart was too as I realized I was color-less, pigment-less.

My gaze fell upon my hands, memories moving across my palms much like the plays I often watched on Asgard. My home.

I stirred with a gasp, sitting up right, my arms flailing out on either side of me.

"Settle," Áma spoke in a low, steady tone. "You're here, back within yourself."

My fists clenched the damp bedding, and I took three breaths before I threw layers of quilts and furs off myself. I ran to the easel in the far corner of the room and ran my fingers over the canvas. My eyes flicked to the empty jar of pigment, and before I knew what I was doing, my finger dipped inside the jar and rubbed the sides for remaining residue. When I held my finger up, a shimmery purple coated the side of it.

"What are you looking for?" Áma asked, peering over me. I jumped to the side, not realizing she had snuck up on me.

"Where would someone go for pigments such as these?" I asked, motioning to the collection of jars and dried brushes. "I've never seen anything like them on Midgard."

Áma picked up a jar and rolled it between her fingers. She hummed before she said, "That's because the properties within don't exist upon Midgard. These are laden with seidr and rare elven elements."

"Elven?" I asked, staring down at my finger still stained the unique shade of a cloudy sunset.

The land of white.

"Alfheim!" I blurted. "Odr has to be in the realm of light elves. I think he's trapped. I-I saw him being dragged through the Earth, and I think he missed his home."

Áma slowly nodded, her grey, wiry hair falling into her face. "The light elves have underground prisons made of sentient trees to keep their prey trapped and isolated. It is very possible he went for more pigments but found himself in a bit of trouble along the way," Áma said before her mouth split into a too-big smile.

"Why are you smiling?" I asked, my stomach dropping at the odd sight.

"Because you did it."

"I did, didn't I?" I said, my hand lifting to my still-damp face. The tips of my fingers found the curve of my lips, and the knowledge of what I'd done washed over me in a wave so fierce, my knees wobbled. "I need to go tell Freyja!"

"Not so fast," Áma said, grabbing my arm before I could run past her. "It's the middle of the night. The guards won't let you anywhere near her."

I peered out the window over my shoulder, realizing she was right when I saw the glow of the moon and its glittering starry sky. "I'll wait until morning, though I can't say I'll be able to go to sleep now, not after this discovery."

"You should try. You may see something else in your dreams that could prove useful. That, and you weren't exactly asleep while having that vision of yours. How do you expect to continue practicing your seidr in the coming days without rest?"

"I wasn't asleep, you're right," I mumbled. "It was so odd. In the beginning of the vision, I was aware of my body and of your presence, but the deeper into the vision I was pulled, the less I sensed anything outside of myself. Odr and I felt one in the same, even if the vision wasn't the clearest."

"If you don't need to be asleep for a vision, that means you're understanding your mind and the workings of your seidr. It's said the seeresses on Freyja's council can have them in the waking hours, and one can even have visions on command, though I'm not sure how reliable they are."

"On command?" I asked in amazement.

"Yes, well, they've had far more time to hone their skills. Who knows what you'll be capable of in a thousand years."

I coughed on my own spittle, my hand flying to my chest to force myself to take in a meaningful breath.

One thousand years?

"Oh, I've done it now," Áma said, gently patting my back. "Yes, girl, you'll be alive for many years to come, just like that valkyrie of yours when she shows her loyalty to Freyja."

"Rune," I said with a lingering cough. "Finding Odr was the only thing keeping her from offering herself to the goddess, but now, there's nothing standing in her way."

"If they find Odr, that is. Let's not get ahead of ourselves," Áma said. "Now, climb back into that bed and find your rest. We have a big day ahead of ourselves in the morning."

I nodded once, and as I began walking over to rest my head, I caught a glimpse of the pinkish-red marks across my skin. There were open eyes crusted onto my palms, runes fingerpainted onto each of my wrists. I wondered if I should wipe them off, or if I should risk the lack of sleep to possibly uncover more about Odr and his whereabouts.

I climbed into the bed, curling under the sheets. A sigh escaped my lips, and for the first time in a long time, I wasn't worried about my future. I had every faith in Rune to show herself loyal to Freyja, and surely, after finding her husband, she would let me stay within her realm.

The immortality didn't matter to me, and neither did the fancy position on her council. What I cared about was a woman with two names. I couldn't wait to get back to her to tell her what I've done for the goddess. For us.

CHAPTER THIRTY-SEVEN
A FEAST IN HER HONOR

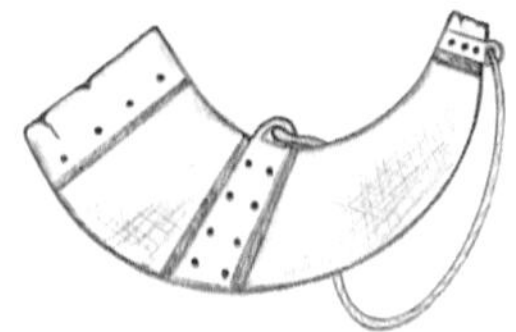

Rune

Áma knocked on my door upon daybreak, telling me I needed
to get my ass out of bed. Kari had a vision, and if I didn't
rush to Freyja's main hall, I was going to miss the goddess' reaction
when Kari told her she found Odr.

I'd never gotten dressed faster in my life. Hel, I threw a dress
over my nightgown just so I could leave the room faster.

When I entered Freyja's chamber, Kari was already bowing
before the goddess' dais. I'd missed most of the pleasantries, but far
be it for me to care about such matters of formality. I remained in
the back, not needing Freyja to notice me in my disheveled state.

I'd once told Kari she looked too horrid to stand before a god.
All she'd wanted was to keep Tove by her side, and she'd promised
to do whatever it took. I'd thought she was ridiculous, bold, and
far too human. But here I stood, in a wrinkled dress, my brown
hair tossed over one shoulder, far too vulnerable and human for
the one I'd do anything to save. I suddenly understood Kari more
than ever before.

Kari stood before Freyja, exhausted and eyes too wide, as she prepared to tell the goddess she'd found her husband. Her mouth parted, and the feeling of my breath exiting my lungs left me weak and shaking. Our future together hinged on this moment, on Freyja's reaction to Kari rising to her challenge.

"Speak, Kari Kettlesdotter. Why have I been summoned?" Freyja's voice filled her throne room, and I caught a hint of something lingering in her tone that wasn't all confidence and cool disposition. Was even the goddess nervous in this moment, her hopes living within her throat, making it impossible to swallow?

"My Goddess Freyja," Kari said with a slight bow of her head, her eyes trained on the bottom of Freyja's gown. "I have requested your presence at this early hour because I come bearing news both good and...troublesome."

Troublesome? I thought to myself as a tingle ran up my spine. Áma hadn't mentioned trouble.

"What is it? My husband, have you found him?" Freyja asked, her mouth tense.

Kari paused, her mouth ticked upward as she said, "I have indeed. He's found himself in a rather messy situation on Alfheim. I don't have all the details, but I will tell you all I have seen."

"Of course," Freyja said, showing the whites of her eyes. She rose from her throne and pulled her sweeping gown to the side as she descended her dais. "I no longer have visions of Alfheim. He should have known better than to leave without mentioning his whereabouts. Tell me, what is this mess you speak of?"

Kari shifted her stance. "It seems as though he's underground in some sort of root system. It does not look like he wants to be there, but rather, he is trapped."

Freyja blew out an exasperated breath that broke into an icy laugh. The sound had my skin pricking as my gaze shifted from her to Kari and back to the goddess again.

"I must leave to gather warriors to hunt my foolish husband down, but know this, Kari Kettlesdotter. You have given me my first shred of hope in over a decade. If he truly is where you say he is, you will have earned your spot on my council ten times over. Prepare yourself, for when I next call on you, your life will be forever altered—in one way or another. Let us hope, for both of our sakes, it is a change for good."

Freyja strode out of her throne room, leaving Kari standing before her dais with one hand at the base of her throat, the other on her stomach. She looked as if she was going to be sick, though I couldn't tell what emotion was bringing forth this sudden urge.

I ran up from behind her and pulled her frozen body into my arms. She tensed for only a moment before she released her bound muscles and fell into me.

"You did it," I whispered across her temple, pressing a kiss to her hairline. "You fucking did it."

A shocked laugh bubbled out of Kari, and she clung to me for support. Tears of relief pooled in her beautiful eyes, and her fingers tightened on me as she said, "I need an ale. Or five."

⊱──────⊰

One week later, I sat hand in hand with the mortal seeress upon the soft grass of Freyja's rolling hills. The meadow smelled of hawthorn berries and thyme, and I could think of much worse places to spend my day with the woman I cared so deeply for.

Over the past several days, she'd told me all about the foul mixture Áma had her drink, about the way she'd used the leftovers to paint Kari's skin. She was convinced she still smelled of blood despite multiple baths and even a flight over Fólkvangr to air her out.

I'd simply laughed at her reaction to Áma slapping her in the face, because I'd been there before a time or two myself. The old Asgardian woman was riddled with arthritis, but she still knew how to make a cheek sting.

Kari leaned back in the grass, a yellow flower poking up between two of her fingers. She tilted her head to the sky, her brow pulled together in a way that told me it wasn't from the sun in her eyes.

"What is it?" I asked, popping a hazelnut into my mouth.

"I just hope this waking vision I had wasn't a mere reflection of my desires. As I laid my head upon his pillow, I desired nothing more than finding him, and part of me wonders if I fabricated the whole thing. The more time that passes, the more the vision fades from my mind, I question if Freyja didn't send a handful of her valkyries on a wild goose chase because of me."

"You didn't," I said, shaking my head. "I thought the reason Áma slapped you was because you weren't believing in yourself. Now, I wouldn't dare touch your beautiful face in such a way, but if you need to shake off this self-doubt, I'm sure I could find Áma arou—"

Kari laughed and covered my mouth with her palm. "Don't you dare!"

I nipped at her hand before she could pull it away, and she yelped in shock. She toppled me over as she lunged forward, but I didn't mind being on my back for her. It wasn't preferred, but I'd take it for my mortal, my radiant light.

When my mouth was free once more, I used that newfound freedom to claim her lips. They were soft and tender against mine, but I moved like it was our last day among the living. I wanted to take advantage of every moment of her warm skin on mine.

Kari hesitated, her lips hovering over me. I was tempted to recapture her mouth, but one glance at her face had me practicing restraint. Her eyes were rolled, head tilted, as if she were one of Odin's ravens. My hands itched to shake her out of the odd haze from where I held her hips. Before I could act in haste, Kari blinked rapidly, coming back to me. But she didn't look at me— she looked *over* me. I cranked my head to see what caught her attention.

Four valkyries, dressed in gold and green, ushered a ragged-looking man up the steps of Sessrúmnir. Kari had chosen this spot in the field in case anyone of interest arrived today, and it seemed as though her connection with Odr was stronger than I ever imagined.

"He's here," Kari whispered. Her eyes went wide, and only then did she look upon me. "He's here!" She leaned in and pecked my face once, twice, before she rose off me and scrambled to her feet.

A laugh rose from my chest, though I had no doubt in her visions. Still, it was surreal to see the lost god before us, haggard and half-stumbling up the steps. I wasn't sure why they hadn't cleaned him up before his arrival, but maybe he was still in a state of frenzy, or maybe the valkyries were advised to bring him as he was—a punishment from Freyja for leaving her. Whatever the reason, I was positive Freyja didn't want us to be there for their reunion.

I rose to stand with Kari, placing a hand on her arm to ask her to stay. "Surely, Freyja will call for us when she's ready."

Kari blew out a breath of frustration, then leaned on her hip. She stared longingly at the doors to Freyja's Hall, though her feet remained where they were. "Hopefully soon."

"Gods have all the time in the world," I said. "I wouldn't hold your breath. If she summons us within the week, I'd be surprised." I didn't want to disappoint her, but I couldn't let her stand here, holding out hope she would be summoned, only to have the sun slowly replaced by the moon, day after day. When you lived forever, you suddenly knew how to take your time, and the gods often did.

"Within the week?" Kari barked.

"Is this such a bad place to wait?" I asked, motioning to the area behind me sprinkled in fall flowers. The air was crisp this time of year, but that's what the light furs were for. Fólkvangr may have seemed like spring personified, but the air could still chill the bones of the living. Even so, the beauty far outweighed any prickle of the skin.

"I suppose not," Kari said with a small smile, her disappointment still visible.

"I've never met Odr. Are you sure it's him?" I asked.

"I know it in my bones. I saw him arrive and felt it as if it were me staggering up those steps," Kari said and then added in disbelief, "Another waking vision."

"You're growing stronger, carving paths within your mind and forging homes within your heart for your unique seidr," I said, tucking a lock of her hair behind her ear. "And that only means one thing."

"What?" Kari said, biting her lower lip in a way I ached to.

"We need to celebrate this success. A first of many."

"It's too soon," Kari said with a laugh that told me everything I needed to know. She wanted this, needed the release that came from letting go with the people she trusted most, the ones who would stay by her side no matter what. And we had four of them here already.

"We're throwing a feast!" I said hastily, stooping to begin collecting our belongings from the grass below. "Rayna can be responsible for the food, and, hopefully, Alvion still has some ale and mooncakes," I said, my thoughts moving faster than my mouth could. "Of course, Tove will serve as entertainment, since there's hardly time to hire actors for a play. Oh! Did you know Nori is quite talented on the harp? Maybe we can get her to play something upbeat for us."

Kari put her hand on my forearm, and the distraction allowed me to take a much-needed breath. She let out a giggle, then nodded her head, sending her hair flying over her fur-lined shoulder, "Okay, okay! Let's have a feast, then. I expect it to be the best you've ever had."

"I've never attended a feast with you, seeress. Will you accompany me?"

"I will."

"Well then, the festivities haven't yet begun, but I already can attest that this will be the best I've ever had."

"You're such a flirt," Kari said with a giggle, swatting my arm. "Don't stop."

I looped my arm into hers, a basket in the crook of my other arm. "Wouldn't dream of it."

Kari and I laughed and planned to our hearts' content as we climbed the stairs to Sessrúmnir. We were halfway to our room when Rayna called for us in the next hall. Her voice wasn't panicked, rather, controlled with an excitable inflection. We rounded the corner to see my sister trudging toward us, a wide grin on her face.

"Have you already heard about our feast?" Kari asked. I wondered how word could've travelled so quickly, but I was happy to see how thrilled my too-serious sister seemed over the celebration.

"Feast? No," Rayna said, her smile wavering for only a moment as confusion crossed her gaze. "Freyja is requesting your presence in her hall, as is Odr."

Kari's grip on me tightened.

It really is him.

"Why so soon?" Kari asked, her face forming lines too hard for her soft features. "Is everything okay?"

"More than," Rayna said. "The God of Inspiration requests to meet the seeress responsible for finding him immediately."

"I can't believe this," Kari all but gasped. "I'm sorry, Rune, but the feast will have to wait."

"No apologies necessary. You have a god to meet. We better not keep him waiting."

Kari and I rushed down the hall, the seeress lifting her flowing gown in one hand. I hadn't expected this time to come so soon. In my many years tending to Odin, I'd learned one valuable lesson: you're always on the gods' time.

When we reached the double doors to Freyja's throne room, we slowed and caught our breath.

This is happening.

"Listen to me," I panted before the guards could open the chamber doors. "Whatever they say, I just want you to know, I'm so proud of you."

Kari's entire face lit up, and a sparkle glistened in her right eye. She didn't say anything, but she grabbed my hand and squeezed it.

"Are you ready?" I asked.

"Let's do this."

Guards standing on either side of the double doors pulled them open upon a nod of my head. Kari walked in first, and I followed behind, keeping my distance. I was here for support, but by no means would I claim to have any part in the return of the God of Inspiration and Frenzy.

Even though I stood at a distance behind Kari, I still offered Freyja and Odr a respectful bow. Kari knelt at the base of the dais, but Odr frantically motioned for her to rise. His untamed beard was crusted with dirt, his robe torn in several spots, but he still wore a smile on his face for the one who had finally located him.

"Rise, rise, Kari Kettlesdotter, and welcome to our home!" Odr said. Freyja was sitting upon her throne while her husband stood next to her, more like a guard or an attendant than her equal. Being her husband didn't make the god a ruler. Freyja was the Queen of Fólkvangr, and she may have been on to something by not allowing him to be the king. If this past week told me anything, it was that Odr was far too frantic to be a ruler of any hall, let alone a realm.

Kari stood, her hands clasped behind her back like she'd seen Rayna and I do so many times now.

"I should start by thanking you," Odr said. "I know I look rather...disheveled, but I couldn't have waited any longer to meet the seeress who was able to see through the light elves' imprisonment. The prison I was kept in is one known across the nine realms for being impossible to escape, and I had been trapped under the roots of the same tree for over three decades, completely deprived of the arts. And of my wife and children," Odr tacked on.

"It was my honor to be of service to Freyja. I'm happy to see your return to this great realm. You were missed by your people greatly," Kari said, lowering her eyes as she spoke.

"An exaggeration, surely," Odr chuckled. "How were you were able to find me, young seeress?"

"I am a mortal born of Hel's seidr. It has grown inside me, a morsel to a spark, to a flame. And now, a fire burns within me, strong enough to melt the ice of Helheim. The seidr may have once been the Goddess of Death's, but it has twisted into something entirely new. And with it, I was able to have a waking vision of your abrupt departure from Asgard. As for seeing through the wards of your imprisonment, it's not my first time being impervious to such barriers. The one imparted on Asgard's gate also has no effect on me."

"How intriguing. And, ah, yes, a departure for more pigment. The only kind worth using comes from the elves. Though, I do admit, I got a bit carried away while on my trip to acquire more. I didn't intend on staying in Alfheim for so long, you see," Odr confessed, scratching the back of his neck in the way a young mortal man might. "The light elves have an awe-inspiring collection of paintings, and if you noticed, I'm quite the collector myself."

Freyja rolled her eyes and shifted on her wooden throne.

Odr continued, his features moving excitedly, as if pulled unnaturally by string, "Do you paint? No, of course not. You have the hands of a potter. Not a very good one, at that," Odr said distastefully, but he quickly moved on as he realized he was insulting the woman who'd saved him, pottery skills aside. "Well, anyway, I was quite overcome by a stunning depiction of their enchanted forest. The painting moves you see, and I simply had to have it. All my art is still. How *boring*! When I offered to purchase it, there was no gold or jewels they would accept for such a priceless piece. It was then I decided I would have it anyway."

Odr stole a quick glance at Freyja before continuing. Even the goddess' felines looked at Odr like he should have known better.

"I was swiftly imprisoned, and well, you should already know the rest."

Kari's eyes lifted to look upon the god. "If you don't mind me asking, how were you freed?"

"The ruler of Alfheim is my twin brother, Freyr. He was gifted the realm upon the growth of his first tooth," Freyja said. "Our relationship is quite...tumultuous. He has never been one to favor my husband. We hadn't spoken in many years, not since I was sent to Asgard to secure peace between the gods. In exchange for my husband, I agreed to meet him in his realm to mend our broken relationship. He agreed to the terms I sent with my valkyries, and, in turn, I am bound by my word."

"That is quite graceful of you, Goddess. Odr is lucky to have such a dedicated wife," Kari said.

"Quite," Freyja bit. "Now, I believe it's time for my husband to depart. We have matters of our own to attend to, don't we, Kari?"

"We do," Kari said with a swift nod of her head. I couldn't tell if she was nervous or excited, but perhaps she found room within her for both feelings to place their roots.

With that, Odr was dismissed from Freyja's throne room, and Kari was left standing before the goddess. I found myself holding my breath, though I didn't understand why. This was good, wasn't it? Kari was about to be bestowed the honor of becoming Freyja's newest attendant. So why was my gut heavy with worry for what was to come?

CHAPTER THIRTY-EIGHT
EYES AS SILVER AS STARS

Kari

"Kari Kettlesdotter," Freyja announced to the room devoid of witnesses, "you have completed the task I bestowed upon you, and for that, you shall be rewarded. If you so wish, you may stay here in Fólkvangr, where you will serve as a member of my council. You are young, but I believe with the guidance of the other seeresses, you will truly find greatness one day. You have the choice to return to Midgard or try to seek refuge elsewhere. I'm afraid I simply have no room for you here unless you join me."

"I would be honored to join you, Goddess," I said with a dipped chin. My heart pounded in my ears, and I could barely hear my own voice. I hoped I was speaking loudly enough for Freyja to hear.

"I would usually host a ceremony, make a whole fuss over such an occasion, but I have spent a long while away from my husband. I'm sure you can understand why it's best to induct you sooner rather than later?" Freyja asked, though I didn't really expect that she was waiting on my response.

"No ceremony is necessary," I said. "I agree haste is the best course of action, given the circumstances."

"Well, then, there is one last matter to attend to," Freyja said, smoothing out her dress. "I have very little use for a mortal on my council. I hope you can understand. Mortals die far too easily, and their lives are but a blink of my eye. I can already see you've aged since arriving."

"Of course," I said, my heart in my throat. I had to fight a nervous laugh. Had she really thought I'd aged in the matter of a week? How odd it must be to view the life of a human as an insignificant blip in history. I wondered if one day, I would feel the same way.

"The price of immortality for valkyries is the color of their hair. Rune knew this when she took her vows, as did Rayna. They chose it anyway," Freyja said, her gaze flicking to Rune, who stood behind me as my unwavering support.

"The price of immortality for those on my council is their truth. My council is a circle of trusted advisors, but without faith and loyalty, it means nothing. Trust is earned, yes, but I cannot take my chances with something so precious. If you join my council and become my attendant, you will lose the ability to deceive me. Your actions will be your own, but your words will always hold truth when speaking with me and on my behalf. What say you, Kari Kettlesdotter?"

I swallowed hard, staring up at the goddess from where she sat upon her throne. Her golden hair gleamed in the sunlight, and my knees felt weak from staring directly into her powerful gaze for so long. It would be an honor of the highest order to sit upon her wand-wed council, but even if it weren't, I'd accept all the same. My truth was far too little of a price to earn me an eternity with the woman I was falling undeniably in love with.

"I accept, Goddess," I said, lowering to the floor in reverence of my one true queen. "It will be my honor to serve you on your council, and my truth is yours to keep."

Freyja rose from her throne, her gown a pool of the finest silks as she stepped down from her dais. I still bowed as she made her way toward me, and only when she said, "Rise," did my feet find solid ground.

I stood before the beautiful woman, and my stomach coiled into the tightest knots as she approached me. Freyja placed a hand on either side of my cheek, then pressed a gentle kiss upon my forehead. As soon as her soft lips met my flushed skin, my throat tightened, burned, and then everything went black.

I woke in Rune's arms with a gasp. My hand flew to my throat, which no longer felt as though I'd swallowed coals. Freyja still stood before me, the lighting in the room unchanged. I must have woken shortly after I fell from consciousness.

Whispering a thank you to Rune, I gently pushed off her to stand before Freyja once more. To test what she promised was true, I tried to tell the goddess her eyes were as black as night, and through my lips, I bellowed, "Your eyes are as silver as stars!"

For Valhalla's sake! Did I just scream in Freyja's face?

I stared at her in horror, my entire body as heavy as stone.

Freyja's lips quirked, and then she laughed. The goddess *laughed*, golden tears forming in the corner of her eyes. The sound was sweet as a harp, and as she wiped the escaped tear away, she said, "Previous members of my council waited until they were desperate to try to lie to me, but you did it upon waking. I love it!" she clapped. "You've learned quickly that not only can you not lie to me, but if you do, your truth will come out, and it will come for all to hear."

"Lesson learned very quickly, indeed," I said with an embarrassed chuckle. "Uh, my goddess."

"Oh, you may stop with the formalities." She waved her hand at me, spinning on her heel to claim her throne once more. "I understand finding my husband was no easy feat. Rest, recover. We may introduce you to the others after you do. Odr and I have some, well, *catching up* to do anyway. Come back to me in one week's time," she said before tacking on, "Oh, and Rune? You ought to be there as well. I believe you have a test to take, my dear."

My heart leaped into my throat, and I turned to face Rune. She was battling a look of shock, but she cooled her features far faster than I ever could. She bowed her head in response, and when she looked upon Freyja, her lips parting to speak, Freyja beat her to it.

"You really didn't think I was going to let you leave without making you mine, did you?" the goddess said. "Offerings be damned. You were a Valhalla valkyrie for half a millennia, and you were the best Odin had. If he's going to throw you away, I certainly won't waste such a brilliant opportunity. You still have to take your test of loyalty, of course, but if you pass, the position of head trainer is yours if you desire it. My girls could use a little refresher on what it means to be a valkyrie, and Hel tells me you made quite the difference in your short time in Helheim."

"It would be my honor, Goddess. I admire your sect and would love nothing more than to aid its sisters—and be back with my own as well."

"Ah, yes, I'm certainly pleased to have Rayna in my midst once more. I was so disappointed when Odin requested her transfer all those years ago. Such an intense little creature, isn't she?" Freyja's eyes flared, and her lips curved up into a bright smile. "Well, off you both go. I hear you have a feast to throw. Do keep it down, yes? This isn't Valhalla."

"Of course," Rune and I echoed each other. "Thank you, Goddess."

As it was customary, we left before Freyja did, never turning our backs to her. Just as we crossed through the entry to her throne room, her felines, Bygul and Trjegul, rose from their stations on either side of her throne. They stretched, licked their paws, and then Freyja too rose from her throne.

I caught a familiar-looking man out of the corner of my eye as he stepped forward through the back entrance to his wife's throne room. The two of them shared a look of love that spanned the millennia, and I found myself wanting to stay with them. My heart was now connected to them both, and, as fresh as these connections were, they were stronger than any faith in the gods I'd ever had on Midgard.

"Let's go, seeress," Rune said when she caught me lingering. "Or we'll be late to our very own feast."

Rune's words shook me out of the odd haze, and I gently closed the double doors behind me. I spun, then leapt into her arms. Rune's laugh mixed with mine, our chests beating against each other as I kissed her. "We did it!"

"I still have a test to pass. *You* did it," Rune said. She pecked my cheek, then my forehead, and, finally, my lips. "My beautiful seeress, you did it."

"I'm Freyja's attendant," I said, in complete awe of this moment and every one that led to this incredible twist in my fate. "And I never would have been if you hadn't saved me."

"How does it feel to be immortal?" Rune said with a waggle of her brows.

I slowly rubbed my hands together, closing my eyes to get in touch with every part of my being. My skin hummed and my heart beat rhythmically, steadily, despite the butterflies raiding my belly.

"The same, for the most part, but I do feel calm, steady."

"Well, you're Freyja's now, in her hall of tranquility. You're still you, and your emotions are yours, but this place will have a pull on you, just as Valhalla once had a pull on me."

"I still can't believe it," I said, lacing my fingers with hers as we began to walk down the sunny hall. Birds chipped and played, darting through open windows and between stone pillars. "But there's still one answer I don't have."

"What's that?" Rune asked.

"Freyja accepted me as hers, which means Hel held up her end of the deal, but what was Freyja's?"

"We'll be before Freyja once more in a week's time. You should be the one to ask her. Not only are you directly involved, but you're one of her trusted informants now. She'll know this question is not one of selfish means. If you don't have the full scope of the deal, how are you to aid her?"

"That's a good way to spin it," I said, leaning into her shoulder. "Because we both know I'm just being nosey."

Rune chuckled. "Yes, well, Freyja doesn't need to be privy to that, though I'm sure she'll find out soon enough. The truth is more flexible than most believe. You'd be surprised what all you could get away with without spinning lies."

"You'd think *you* were the one with a bound tongue for how much practice you've gotten omitting the whole truth," I said with a teasing eye roll. "You better not be using that trickery on me anymore."

Rune shook her head, her gaze soft as she said, "No. You've always seen right through me." The heat in her eyes made me gulp, and warmth of my own spread through me, inside and out.

I could hear the echoing of music from the courtyard ahead, voices from friends getting lost to chatter and laughter. I cleared my throat and said, "And to think, I was so worried about them eating all the mooncakes. You didn't even need to make an offering. You're more valuable than any treat or splash of ale."

"I guess that means there's more for us. You deserve about ten of those delicious little cakes for what you accomplished today." Rune steered the conversation back to me, and my brows knit together as I realized this wasn't the first time.

I grabbed her forearm before she rounded into the courtyard. "So do you."

She stared into my eyes, her scared brow raising slightly when she looked from my hand clamped over her arm back to my face. I didn't unhand her; I wouldn't let what she was doing slide.

"Kari–"

"You don't think you'll pass your test, do you?" I asked. "You keep making this about me when it should be about *us*."

"Odin has been my god for so long. He was a part of me, and he ripped that part out. I have no doubt I can remain loyal to Freyja, and I would be honored to remain in Asgard here with you, but the Rune you knew is the one he made. He built me, named me, and even if I pass Freyja's test and become a valkyrie once more, I will never be who I once was."

"Then be different!" I said, my thumb grazing her arm. "If this fear of change is on my behalf, don't let it be. Rune, Iris, or someone else, I will...I will care for you all the same," I said, almost letting an entirely different word slip out. "He doesn't own you, and he may always be the Allfather, but the parts of himself he gave you were of violence and deceit. And sure, maybe you were a bit of a badass, but you were also a pain in mine." A laugh spilled from my lips. "You will find yourself here, and maybe you can heal parts of the person you left behind in Thalassa, because Iris deserves love too."

"Love?" Rune asked, her voice tight. My eyes widened and my mouth dried as she waited for me to say something, anything.

"Lovebirds!" Rayna called out, stumbling into the dark maw of the hall Rune and I had crept into, out of sight from the court-yard loungers. A heavy breath escaped me as Rayna threw an arm over Rune's shoulder.

"Are you drunk?" Rune asked in surprise, steadying her sister. Something told me *she* was the one who was used to being steadied by Rayna.

"My first task was a dazzling success! Kari's here as an attendant, and I'm celebrating. You should too," she said with a massive smile upon her face. The sight was odd, but I couldn't look away. Seeing Rayna happy was like staring into the gods damned sun. "Why are the two of you lurking in this dark corner when a feast is being thrown in your honor? Well, mostly Kari's, but you'll get there too, Rune."

Rune scoffed, throwing Rayna's arm off her playfully. "How did you even know we were planning a feast?"

"You mentioned it when I came to inform you Odr had requested your presence. You were all excited about it; it was so cute. So, I told the others, and Áma made the most delicious drink. You should try it. Come on! Everyone is waiting for you two." Rayna pushed off Rune and tried to drag her into the courtyard.

Rune scanned her sister as if she'd been possessed by a wayward spirit. "Don't drink that 'delicious drink' Áma made," Rune muttered. "I think it's allowed a demon to claim Rayna's body."

"She's not possessed," Alvion said with a chuckle as he appeared between two stone columns. "She just made the unfortunate mistake of being the first one to sample Áma's potion. We've switched to mead. Come join us!"

"You don't have to ask me twice!" I said, following Rayna and Alvion into the courtyard. Something about slowly losing my mortality made me a ravenous beast. My stomach growled for food —this was a feast, after all. I planned to stack my plate a foot high with whatever Rayna summoned. I only hoped she'd done it *before* she tried Áma's potion, or the food selection could be questionable.

I turned back to Rune, who lingered between the columns. I flashed her a grin and held out my hand for her to join me. Her warm hand met mine, and I pulled her to my side. She leaned into me on a big exhale.

"We have some things to discuss, but for now, let's enjoy this celebration with our friends. When else will you be able to hold questionable decisions over Rayna's head? I'm sure she hasn't made a fool of herself since the night she met Alvion."

Rune smirked. "Trust me, seeress. Tonight, I plan to gather all the dirt on her I possibly can. She's done her fair share of mocking over the years. It's payback time."

Just as Rune's last word escaped her lips, a large crash brought our attention to the center of the courtyard. Turkey and potatoes went flying as a silver tray clattered upon the stone floor. Rayna stumbled back, her calves hitting the legs of a chair. Alvion tried to reach for her but couldn't grab her in time. The valkyrie fell ass first into a fountain, water splashing up and over the edges.

Rune erupted into laughter. "Oh, it's going to be a good night."

CHAPTER THIRTY-NINE
FOR THE WOLVES

Rune

Kari and I descended the steps lit by glowing orbs. They flared and pulsed a deep orange, creating a path of light for us to follow. Eight days after we'd last seen Freyja, Kari and I had received scrolls in our room, one addressed to each of us. Kari's was a summoning, whereas mine was an invitation.

Kari was due to meet the other councilors in Sessrúmnir's primary incantation chamber, and I had been formally requested to join Freyja's ranks and take my test of loyalty. I'd known it was coming, had even expected it a day prior, yet holding that scroll in my hand still felt as if I'd stumbled upon a chest of gold. I kept waiting for someone to come rip it from my hands and tell me it was all but a cruel jest. Though, as we traveled to the chambers beneath Sessrúmnir, it felt more and more like I truly would become a valkyrie once again.

Kari's words lingered in my mind, and whenever I felt doubt creeping in, I remembered what she'd said to me.

I will not fear change.

The person I'd become after joining the Sessrúmnir sect would be different from who I'd been in Valhalla, but that didn't need to be a bad thing. I'd stared at myself in mirrors for so long, searching for a change I'd never see, wondering at what point I'd feel like I'd truly know myself. Maybe, after all this time, I would discover who Rune Dragomir was and who I wanted to be.

Once we reached the bottom of the stone steps, Kari wrapped her hand in mine and said, "I wish I could go in there with you."

"I know, but you have exciting matters of your own to attend to," I said, tenderly squeezing her hand. "You have the honor of meeting Freyja's council and claiming your seat among them. Your family is going to be so proud."

We'd talked a few times about what it meant for Kari now that she'd be able to venture to Helheim once a year to see her family in the underworld. There weren't many people who could say the same, and visitation rights were just one of the many incredible rewards she received for being the center of a bargain between two goddesses.

Kari blushed, her lips curling up into a smile as she gushed, "I already can't wait to see my family, but knowing I have forever with them makes the ache a little duller. For now, I'll simply be happy where I am, here, with you. And listen, I know we spent so much of this past week having fun, exploring, and doing a whole lot of...*resting.*" She laughed, saying the word as if she meant anything but. I smirked at the thought. "But I want you to know I'm aware we never, um, spoke about what we'd said we would."

As much as I wanted to hear all she had to say, there was too much hanging in the balance. Once I passed the test of loyalty and we both knew we were in Fólkvangr to stay, we could have that conversation. I too had been holding on to words that wanted to crawl out of me and find a home inside her. Soon enough, I would shout them from the roof of Sessrúmnir for all to hear.

I pressed a kiss to the top of her hand. "We've had a lot on our minds, and, well, you're likely forbidden to be with me until I pass my test," I said with a smirk.

"I'm pretty sure I've broken that rule ten times over, and Freyja knows it. She's the goddess of love and fertility. I think she'd be the last one to tell anyone who to be with, mortal or not." Kari laughed and led me further down the hall. She held up her scroll, where a small map had been drawn onto the back, and took the next turn. I'd been following my own map, but we'd been lucky enough to get to travel together this far. This part of our journey would come to an end soon, as the chamber of truth quickly approached.

"It's a shame I can't be a witness for your reintroduction into the House of Wings, but I understand why Freyja forbade it," Kari said, coming to a stop. She glanced down at my map with a hesitant smile. "Just know I'll be thinking of you. I have no doubt you can accomplish anything she asks of you. You're Rune Dragomir, and don't you forget it."

I pulled her in, taking a deep breath as I did. Her earthy scent of spruce and mugwort had changed since leaving Midgard, though I found myself favoring the new, rich blend of incantation oils that always seemed to linger on her skin and in her hair. We both hesitated for a moment as I began to pull back, our faces so close to each other, I felt the warmth of her cheek near mine. We turned our faces at the same time, and our lips became one. The kiss started sweet, tender, but it quickly turned into a battle of wills, seeing which one of us would fall apart first. I didn't want it to feel like a goodbye, but somehow, it did.

Gods, I wish I could stay in her arms forever.

Freyja was waiting for me, as was my new future, a future I hoped with everything I had included Kari.

"I have to go," I said, slowly pulling away. When I dropped her hand, my palm felt cool without her touch. Before I could do anything foolish, I turned away from her and headed for the door of the chamber of truth.

The door creaked as I opened it, and I didn't look over my shoulder at the woman I was leaving on the other side, even if my tongue burned to say the words in my heart. I shut the door behind me, closing myself into the dimly lit room.

An unfamiliar man stood next to a stone altar. His moss green robe trailed the floor behind him, and I wondered if he was a council member trusted to lead such an untraditional ceremony. I'd never heard of a valkyrie getting stripped of her title, only to be inducted by another god. Usually, the women were discarded, never to be heard from by the sisters again, yet, here I stood, standing silently before the stone of truth, about to get a second chance.

The robed man pointed toward the stone and motioned for me to lay upon it. When I did, resting my unbraided hair upon the cool marble, he disappeared into the shadows. I closed my eyes and focused on my breath, trying not to think about the first time I laid upon a stone much like this one. I'd been nineteen, scared of what my life would become, but today, I held none of those same fears.

Moments later, I was being handed a chalice of honey wine, which I now knew was laced with seidr. I also knew there was no option here, so I took the chalice, draining it in three gulps. My vision began to blur, but just before I lost my hold on this reality, Freyja came into focus. She stared down at me with a smile on her face, and the way the orbs glowed behind her made her golden hair look as though it'd caught flame.

She was the last thing I saw before my vision went white.

White turned to rustling leaves and the sound of nesting birds. I stood in a forest, pine and spruce trees surrounding me, all dusted with snow. I took my first step forward, the white powder crunching under my boots, reminding me of my time in Hel. When Helheim crossed my mind, I looked over my shoulder, a prickling feeling that I was far closer to the realm of ice and death than I ought to be snaking across my limbs. I walked forward several paces until I heard a sickening snap of wood. I found myself creeping toward the sound, the ice melting under my boots as I did.

Kneeling, I peered between two trees. Ahead, there was a forest of brown, gnarled roots with bite and claw marks taken out of them. I'd never seen Yggdrasil this way before, and it was as if I were floating above it instead of walking within its dimension.

Another snap of wood, though this time, I saw a red-scaled tail leading to the thick body of the world tree dragon.

Níðhöggr.

The root munching dragon let out a bellowing roar, splinters of wood spraying from his scarlet, toothy mouth. I scrambled back, and then I ran and ran and ran until the world was on fire. Flames licked my arms, singeing my leathers, and my head swung in all directions until I spotted a sliver of white light in this world of red.

As I stumbled toward the light, I felt the love of the moon wash over my skin. I threw my head back in relief, closing my eyes and feeling the moment the sky went dark and the new moon had arrived. I wanted to stay here where it was safe, away from fire, ice, and dragons. Something in the back of my mind called to me, though, warning me this place was not for me.

Reluctantly, I opened my eyes. The moon was gone, replaced by glowing trees and a backdrop of the sunset sky. I found myself in awe of the beauty of the whispering trees. I felt them calling to me, though what spoke in my mind was far louder. I knew there was somewhere I needed to be, someone I needed to find, but every time I thought I was getting closer to figuring it out, I found myself stumbling into another unwanted destination. Some had more of a pull on me than others, but none were *mine.*

"Rune!" a voice finally called out. I saw a figure standing on the edge of a fjord, and the crystalline water glistened, inviting me in. I dove into the water to get to the other side, but my boots quickly filled, dragging me down into the depths faster than I could fight against it. It grew colder and darker as I went, until I saw a beam of light shine through the water, then another. They continued to light up the space around me until I felt an unnatural salt on my tongue, and I saw a palace gleaming below me. All I had to do was give in, take the sea water into my lungs, and allow myself to sink, but was this hall my home? I didn't think so.

As I tried to swim toward the sky and the distorted light that filtered down from the surface, I felt something grab hold of my boot. My foot was caught in a golden net, refusing me the breath I needed. I swiped the dagger from the strap around my thigh, sawing through the seidr-filled net.

The Mother of the Sea will not have me today.

The net snapped, and I shot toward the surface, as if my freedom had earned me a tail. When my face broke the surface of the water, I gasped and choked and fought for air. I wiped the seawater from my burning eyes, only to find myself sitting in a golden tub, my reflection staring back at me from the large mirror across the bathing chamber. Instant relief flooded me as I sank into the warm, sudsy water of the tub. I closed my eyes and found peace in the distant murmuring of my sisters, the sound of flapping pegasus wings coming from my open window.

Apple? I thought, realizing I had traveled so far and so long without her. I climbed from the tub, my leathers squeaking as I walked toward the window. And then, I jumped.

I landed upon my pegasus' back, and as she whinnied and shot away, I heard a name call for me once more.

"Rune!" he said, the shadowy figure standing in the window, beckoning me back.

"Epli, turn around!" I called into the air, but my voice was lost to the wind. I directed her reins back toward the window, not needing my voice to tell the pegasus what I wanted. Apple complied, and when she looped around, heading back to the House of Wings, the figure in the window came into focus.

Odin stood there, beckoning me forward. For a moment, I let him, an empty piece of myself recognizing him and yearning to be complete. But when I thought about everything that hole in my chest could be filled with, I realized there was nothing Odin could offer that would truly ever make me feel whole again.

"Apple!" I called out, and this time, my voice carried far and wide. "Take me home!"

I woke with a gasp, not in a golden tub or in a snow sprinkled forest, but on a marble altar, in a hall ruled by the Goddess of Love and Seidr.

"Welcome back, Rune," Freyja said, her voice almost like a purr. I sat up, attempting to blink away the dizziness that had its grips in me. "You've made a choice, it seems."

"I have," I nodded decisively. "I've returned home."

The heavy chamber door blew off its hinges, flying across the room and cracking to bits somewhere in the shadows. The force sent me tumbling off the altar, and my body hit the ground with a cold, hard thud.

"Home?" A horrible, wicked laugh filled the air. I didn't need to see him to know who stood in the doorway.

"What are *you* doing here?" Freyja asked, her lips curling. Odin sauntered into the chamber of truth, running his hands through one of the glowing orbs on the wall. He let out a long breath, sizing Freyja up, then me on the floor.

I didn't move; I barely breathed.

"It seems as though you have something of mine," he finally said, a strong finger pointing in my direction. Every muscle in my body tensed, and as badly as I wanted to focus on something that wasn't him, I didn't dare a glance at Freyja.

"She's yours no longer, Odin. You made sure of that," Freyja said.

"I suppose you're right. But Rune is mine no longer because she broke her oaths. She's lucky I let her live after she brought that unwelcome mortal to my realm. The girl's not even a viking." Odin cast a disappointed glance in my direction. I was unused to seeing him look at me in such a way, and even if I hated that it did, it still stung.

"That 'unwelcome mortal' found Odr when no one else could," Freyja said, her chin raised like the goddess she was. "You were swift to toss her away instead of foreseeing her potential. Rune may have broken her oaths, but perhaps you should've stopped to consider why. You usually have more foresight than that. But I'm grateful you didn't, for now I have the promise of a talented valkyrie, I filled the empty seat on my council, and my husband has returned, all because you don't believe in second chances."

"Second chances? Don't be childish, Freyja. I am an observer of fate. I'd known Rune had found interest in a mortal woman, but I did not intervene because fate had other plans. It was not my responsibility to forgive her for her indiscretions because the consequences of her actions would find her in time. And they certainly did when she brought that living mortal to Valhalla."

He'd known about Kari? I thought, my skin prickling with an intense heat.

Of course he did. Odin's ravens were everywhere. I should've never believed I could've escaped them while on Midgard. Even in Fólkvangr, he was always watching, and he'd found me once again.

"And what consequences do you see fit now?" the goddess asked. She moved toward me ever so slowly. She'd been the first to break the tension, and if I didn't know better, I would've assumed she was on the hunt, not preparing to protect.

"You will turn her over to me to handle directly. It's truly none of your concern what I do after that."

Something inside me snapped. Patience boiled over, fear fled, and I was left with nothing but molten rage. "I'm not going anywhere!" I shouted, rising from where I cowered next to the altar. "Your time dictating my life is over. You may have sculpted me into the valkyrie you yearned for, but I am so much more than the name you gave me. Everything I despised most about myself were the pieces of you instilled within me. I gladly wash my hands of you."

Freyja and Odin both turned to me, surprised in their own ways, but I wasn't sure why. I was Rune Dragomir, and my time in Valhalla was over. I was free to make this decision, and I'd be damned if Odin tried to drag me back, just to have me killed—or worse.

"I have the support of the Goddess of Love and Fertility, as well as her council. If you lift a hand to strike any of us down, I'd tell you to remember who taught you that seidr you wield so proudly," I started, taking a step closer to Freyja. "You came into the home of the Mother of Seidr and demanded she return something that is no longer yours. You may be the Allfather, but the woman you stand before is as dangerous as she is beautiful. If you want to come out of this unscathed, it's best you leave now. You're not the only unforgiving one around here," I gritted out. After six centuries serving him and entertaining his every whim, he'd done so much worse than toss me aside like Freyja had said. He'd destroyed my identity after making me feel like my title and armor were all I was. He'd stripped me raw and left me bleeding for the wolves.

The bastard smiled, and I ground my teeth together so hard, I feared a molar would crack.

Freyja stepped toward me, but she was still too far away for my comfort. I may have passed her test, but she still hadn't sealed the deal. I was a human mortal by all standards, and I could fight tooth and nail with this god before me, but we both knew if Odin wanted me dead, he could kill me without lifting a finger.

"I was sent to Asgard as part of a *peace* treaty. Or have you already forgotten about the Aesir-Vanir War?" Freyja asked, referring to the war between gods that raged long ago.

Odin almost seemed bored as he said, "Yes, yes. No one has forgotten you're a hostage here. How could we, when you bring it up so often?"

Freyja let out an exasperated breath, pushing back her golden hair, "If you act in violence against me or my council, I will consider it an act of war, and so will my people. After the last war ended in a standstill, do you truly want to head down this path again?"

"Rune is not on your council," Odin pointed out with a slight hiss. "She's your mortal guest."

"She's passed my test of loyalty, and she would've had her initiation into my sect on this very night had you not interrupted," Freyja pointed out, and I couldn't help but hold my breath as she did.

A flicker of rage shone in Odin's singular blue eye. I detested that look. I'd seen it far too many times, and the outcome that followed was always death. I was too weak, too easy to break, and I couldn't allow such a look to fall upon me.

I sprinted toward the only one who could offer me the protection I needed. I dropped to my knees before Freyja, my bones cracking against stone and splitting my skin and leathers. "Freyja, take me!"

"NO!" Odin bellowed, raising his hand to stop what was coming.

Freyja wasted no time. She bent and placed a kiss upon my forehead, sealing the deal and claiming me as her own. My scalp tingled and my vision went blurry. As darkness consumed me, a blood-curdling scream ripped through the echoing chamber.

My body went limp.

CHAPTER FORTY
SHE WHO BLEEDS FIRE

Kari

My waking vision was a cold, hard retaliation, brutal and swift.

I knew why *he* was here. I knew why he was angry, even, but none of that mattered. I would never let Odin have her. I would set Sessrúmnir aflame if it meant stopping him. He didn't deserve her; he never did.

The door flew open, and I sprinted through the exit of the council's incantation chamber. There were murmurs behind me, I heard them during my waking vision, heard them now that I was back in my body and rushing down the hall. The other council members slowly bled into the corridor, but there was no time to explain to them why I fled, not when Rune was alone on a cold stone floor.

I busted through the open entryway of the chamber of truth, wood splinters snapping under my boots. My gaze didn't scan the room for him, only her. She knelt by Freyja's feet, a smear of blood on the floor by her knees. The goddess grabbed hold of her cheeks and leaned down to place a kiss upon her.

She's still alive.

Odin and Freyja's heads swung toward me, and I only hesitated for a moment. In my vision, I'd been too late, but that future shown to me had already changed by my mere presence. There was no saying what fate the Norns would weave now.

A scream ripped out of me as I ran toward Rune. Her body was falling, slipping between Freyja's fingers, and I dove to catch her head before it could hit the floor. As I cradled Rune in one arm, my other flew up in front of me, the entire sleeve of my dress engulfed in a red hot flame. The power surged out of me in waves, the fire rising and falling like a beat, a pulse. Glowing tendrils reflected in Odin's eyes as I waited for him to make his move.

Rune stirred below me. "Kari?"

While I wanted to look upon her face, I would never lose focus in the presence of a predator.

"You've gotten what you wanted, Rune. You're a valkyrie once more, so stand like one," Odin commanded. Rune would look weak if she stayed on the floor with me, but if she stood, she'd be doing exactly what he wanted.

It was finally time to break the cycle.

Letting Rune go, I crouched like a savage beast, hands on fire, teeth barred. Rune followed suit, pulling a dagger from the sheath on her thigh. Upon her head, a single white hair glistened in the light of my flame.

The man laughed, and my seidr flared brighter.

Freyja stepped forward, white wings ripping through the back of her gown and stretching out on either side of her.

Great gods! I thought as I watched the woman materialize a deadly spear in her hands. Golden armor snapped into place across her chest and hips, the gleam of the polished metal a threat not to come any closer.

"Kari and I have both seen the violence you planned to inflict upon my own," Freyja called out. Her entire body vibrated with seidr, and it was then I realized I truly only had a morsel of what the gods could give. I may have been a powerful human, but she was the mother of seidr, and I could taste her power in the air. It sliced across my skin, mixing with my own.

The golden sconces on the wall behind Odin groaned as they twisted into sharp, deadly weapons. The gold around the god's neck began to melt, dripping down his robes in metallic trails. The man squinted, as if our will was more of an annoyance than anything.

He let out a sigh, jaw clicking as his gaze hopped from Freyja to Rune to me. "This is your mess, Freyja; do with them what you will. As their new goddess, their fate is in your hands, but I won't forget what you've done here today. There will come a time when you'll pay dearly for taking what was once mine." Odin shook his head in disgust. "You should've sent the valkyrie to Midgard to rot."

"Unless invited, you will not step foot in Sessrúmnir again," Freyja said. "Your intrusions may be excused by lesser gods, but I will not be so easily moved."

Odin straightened his robes, still covered in hardened blobs of gold. "Very well."

"Well then, get the fuck out of my hall." Freyja said, her silver eyes flaring. "You may leave through the entrance you destroyed."

Odin cleared his throat and, with a wave of his arm, transformed into a sleek, golden raven. He released an aggressive caw as his wings flapped angrily. The god disappeared into the maw of the corridor, and as I watched him go, my fingers itched to light him up. I always did like the scent of roasted bird.

Rune placed her hand on my wrist. "He's gone. Let it be."

I blew out a breath and relaxed my hand. "I guess we'd be dead pretty damn fast if we'd tried to fight hi—"

"Speak for yourself," Freyja said. "If you don't think I can take on the Allfather, you clearly haven't been around Fólkvangr long enough. My hall may be tranquil, but that doesn't mean I'm not a goddess of war and battle. Odin is only wand-wed because of me. I taught him everything he knows—but I haven't taught him everything *I* know."

My jaw fell as I stared at the goddess.

"As such, I know what battles should be fought and when it's time to hang up your weapons—or never draw them in the first place. I never would have started a war over a thing such as this. Sometimes, bringing a man to his knees is far more effective than cutting him at the ankles. Odin is a man of many things, but someone to admit when he's wrong is not one. He would have continued to meddle in your lives for as long as you allowed him to."

"I thank you for not only defending your home, but us as well," Rune said.

Freyja nodded. "As you are my attendants, it is my duty to protect what is mine. You both have shown great strength today, and I am far more pleased knowing you will remain where you are than I was when I awoke this fine day."

I took in a long breath, not sure how I felt about being called theirs by someone who wasn't Rune. But if a goddess would go into battle for us, then we were in the right place. I wanted to throw my arms around Rune and cry out in relief at seeing that tiny white hair upon her head, but Freyja looked upon her as if there was still much to discuss, and I knew there was. I kept my tempted arms by my side and took a step back to give Rune and Freyja a moment.

"Now, Rune," Freyja said, brushing back her hair and standing straighter. "This may not be the induction you wanted, but unfortunately, it's the induction you've gotten. I want to officially welcome you to the House of Wings Fólkvangr sect. I hope you find everything you need here, and you feel at home within these walls."

"I have a feeling I'll have everything I need," Rune said,

glancing back at me. My face heated, and that one look from her sent a thousand butterflies free within my belly.

"Yes, I'm sure you're right," Freyja said, her eyes slowly moving between the two of us with a ghost of a grin. "Now, will you do me the honor of becoming the sect's head trainer?"

"I will. Thank you, Goddess," Rune said with a bow of her head. I couldn't see her face, but her shoulders fell in relief, as if she'd been carrying all nine worlds upon them. A weight lifted off us both. We had each passed a test of our own, and not only had we come out on the other end more powerful, but we finally had the chance to be together, without any god, test, or fate in our way.

"Brilliant," she said, clasping her hands. "I'll have you sized for armor and leathers within the week. You'll be introduced to the sisterhood once your hair is fully stripped of color once more. We can't have a brunette telling the girls what to do, now can we?" Freyja let out a low, amused laugh.

My lungs refused to take in my next breath. I thought of how long it'd taken for Rune's hair to turn white the first time around. Even Rayna still had half her blonde hair remaining, and she was centuries old.

Rune seemed to be thinking the same thing. She shifted uncomfortably before Freyja, scratching the back of her neck. "And what would you have me do in the meantime?"

"Fear not. Once the seidr settles into your bones, the color in your hair will fade. It should take no more than a few days. Did you truly think I'd make you wait half a millennia? That would hardly be a productive use of time."

I let out an audible sigh of relief that bubbled up into a giggle. *Thank the gods.*

Or, should I say, thank the goddess? There were far too many gods lumped into the first expression, and I didn't know how many of them actually deserved my gratitude. I'd always been wary of the divine, and leaving Midgard only solidified my beliefs. As much as I respected Freyja, I wasn't naive enough to believe there were any gods or goddesses who were all good. They were all far too removed from humanity, too old and untouchable. With time and unfathomable power came scars on their godly nature, too deep to ever mend.

I watched Freyja, beautiful and deadly, and I thought about my next ten, fifty, one hundred years serving on her council. I couldn't help but wonder if those scars would find me too one day.

"Now, what should I call you?" Freyja asked Rune.

"What should you call me?" Rune repeated, her head cocking ever so slightly.

"As this is a new life, your third life, I expect you may want to choose a new name for yourself. I know Odin chose your last one, but I don't name my valkyries. They name themselves."

Rune thought about this for a moment, and I too wondered what a world without Rune would be like. She took a step back and reached for my hand. I grabbed it tight, thankful for her presence. I didn't have to think long or hard to know I didn't want to live in such a world. Whatever her name was, whatever she chose, she would be mine, and I would be hers.

"I've been Rune Dragomir for 604 years, and I plan to remain as such. Odin may have named me, but he's done stripping away my identity. I escaped him as Rune, I found my home as Rune," she paused, her gaze moving from Freyja to me, "and I fell in love as Rune."

Love.

"Well, I've never been one to fight against love. Rune Dragomir, I expect you to report when your transformation is complete. In the meantime..." she said, looking between the two of us. "Well, I'm sure you'll have plenty to do." The Goddess of Love and Fertility smiled at us in a way that told me we were going to be just fine in Fólkvangr.

Before Freyja could turn to leave, I said, "Freyja, what did you bargain for me with?"

She let out a long sigh, her silver eyes closing for a moment before she laid her hand upon her chest, drawing my attention to the massive, amber-colored jewels inlaid within her necklace.

"This is called the Brisingaman necklace, and Hel has wanted it for many centuries because of its protective forces and beauty enhancements. She was called a monster upon birth, after all, and she hoped—still hopes—that the jewels can provide her with the advantage she has never once had. It will be quite interesting to see what comes of the underworld once she finally has the Brisingaman in her possession."

"And you're truly going to give it to her?"

"I always honor a bargain. I not only had my husband returned to me, but I now have you. Truth be told, I'll be happy to rid myself of something that has caused me so much grief. One does not go about obtaining an object such as this without paying the ultimate price. I create beauty; I no longer need to wear someone else's creation upon my chest. The stones never did much for me anyway," Freyja said airily. "I will have you deliver it to Hel for me. I hear your family resides there, and you may like to see them again, let them know you're alright."

"I would love nothing more," I said quickly, my words tumbling out in a jumble.

She chuckled softly. "You know, Kari, Hel has been after this necklace for a very long time. The reason she accepted your ancestor's offering is because she knew her seidr would one day take root in one of Norfrid's descendants, and it would blossom into something of value."

"And valuable things can be bartered for," Rune pointed out with a cluck of her tongue.

Freyja nodded. "Indeed. Bartered for a lost husband and the seeress powerful enough to find him."

"Is that why she truly took control of my eyes? So she could watch me and my ancestors to see which of us would get her what she wanted most?" I asked, the thought alone making me sick.

"It is. Even if Rune hadn't taken you, Hel eventually would have. You were not meant for the mortal world. There was no escaping this fate," Freyja said. "Though, I will admit, almost all outcomes I foresaw once arriving in Valhalla, you fought against. Maybe you and Rune, here together, was something you earned, something you fought for against all odds. I do hope you continue fighting, councilor."

Freyja turned on her heel, and with that, she was gone. I was left in the broken, disheveled chamber where I had finally earned my truth. Rune turned to me, and I her. There were so many things I would have to sit with, live with, and understand with the knowledge that had been bestowed upon me, but all I wanted now was her.

I was done fighting, done pretending, and done holding back for the sake of waiting for the right time, whatever that meant. There was no right time; there was simply now, and I was going to savor it. I was going to savor *her*.

I cast a shroud of darkness in the open doorway of the chamber of truth. I hoped it would keep any curious souls from entering, but here, I could tell no lies. I knew company would do little to deter me from getting what I wanted.

Rune moved toward me like a wolf to her prey. She wrapped me in her arms, and I could feel the way every gap in her borrowed leathers had filled out. Her biceps strained against the material. Each time she'd been mine, she was mortal. Now, I had Rune the valkyrie, and nine realms, she was everything.

Rune took my face in her hands and dipped her head to meet mine. She peppered me with sweet kisses, and as I returned them, they slowly grew longer, deeper. She lifted me and placed my ass upon the marble altar, pulling back enough so I could see her wicked grin.

Across from me, a great mirror was secured to the stone wall, and I wasn't sure how it'd survived the blown out door. I watched myself in it, watched the way Rune moved in on me. She cupped my cheeks in one hand and held my face so I was forced to continue admiring our reflection.

"I want you to watch as you come undone for me. Can you do that, seeress?" she asked, her voice deep and sultry. I swallowed hard and nodded. This pulled a chuckle from a deep place in her chest, and the vibrations against my side had me burning in places she now owned.

While I once wasn't able to stand the sight of my own reflection, I now couldn't pull my gaze from the sight of us, together. She knelt, placing her torn knees onto the stone floor. I wanted to protest, tell her to stand, that she didn't need to be in pain for my pleasure, but she quieted me by squeezing my cheeks.

I swallowed my protests as she let go of my face so she could slowly slide the length of my dress up my legs. She dipped between my thighs, trailing kisses from the inside of my knee upward. I used my arms to prop myself up as I felt my spine begin to weaken.

A gasp escaped my lips when she reached the most sensitive part of me, and I wondered what I'd done to deserve her on her knees. As I threw my head back and closed my eyes, she stopped what she was doing. Her hot mouth lifted from my tender skin, and I whimpered and pleaded to the ceiling, as if that would change my fate.

"Open your eyes," Rune growled into me. I moved my hips in response, up and down over her warm, wet mouth, and I watched myself as I did. "There you go. See how good you are for me?"

I moaned at her words and continued to do so as her lips grazed mine, torturously slow. She finally gave me what I wanted, what I needed, and followed it up with one finger, then two. She slid them in and out of me, eventually moving her head out the way so I could watch her in the dim light of the room. A warm, orange glow flickered across her face as she watched herself work, and fuck, did she look good.

"You've never been as sexy as you were today, bleeding fire in front of the gods like that, showing them what you can do," Rune said, her heady voice filled with desire as she continued to pump in and out of me. She used her thumb to make small circles over my bundle of nerves, and I panted when her eyes locked onto mine in the mirror. "Tell me how powerful you are, seeress. I want to hear it from your lips."

I laughed, but I didn't dare throw my head back like I wanted. I couldn't let her stop, not again. I'd do anything she wanted if it meant she'd keep going. The glowing orbs all caught fire, and the flames danced to the tune of her thrusts.

"I'm powerful." I meant it to come out strong, but it came out more like a plea. Rune slipped a third finger into me, and I screamed out, "I'm fucking powerful!" as I tightened around her. Rune moved her mouth back onto me as a reward, using her tongue and lips to ruin me for all others. When I finished for her, my arms collapsed, and my back hit the cool stone beneath me. The flames died out all at once, leaving us with very little light once again.

"What have you done to me?" I said, my voice hoarse and raspy. My heart was pounding, and I needed water, but no part of me wanted to leave this chamber. It felt like we had carved out a piece of the world just for us, and I never wanted to say goodbye to it. She hopped up onto the altar, placing my head in her lap.

I curled into her, loving the way her body felt on mine.

"I think the real question is, what have you done to *me*?" She gazed down, pulling my bottom lip with her thumb. Her eyes bore into mine, and I could've wept for how right it felt. "For you, I am undone. Wholly undone," Rune said. "I love you, Kari. I always have."

I took her hand in mine and sat up so quickly, I saw stars. She laughed as I awkwardly climbed onto her lap, placing my knees on either side of her so I could look directly into her eyes. She pressed her palm into my lower back to support me, and I cupped her face in my hands as I said, "I've loved every version of you, and I will continue to love you until every last star in the sky has faded. You are the strongest person I know, the bravest warrior, the most beautiful soul, and I will always fight fate for a future by your side. You're mine forever."

Rune smiled and pinched my butt. "And thanks to Freyja, it seems like forever for us will be a very, very long time."

CHAPTER FORTY-ONE
THE ENDS OF EVERY WORLD

Rune

I caught my reflection in the mirror as I grabbed my dagger off the bathing chamber counter. My white hair was pulled back into intricate braids, the rest of it falling loosely down my back. I smiled at the little gold pieces Kari had pinched into it, then adjusted the wing-shaped cuff on my ear.

"Rune! Let's go! We're going to be late," I smiled, life finally feeling like it was back on course. While I loved living in the House of Wings with my new sisters, I was glad it was only temporary. At first, moving in across the hall from Rayna had felt just like old times, but having Kari with me made me crave a place of our own.

"Coming!" I called out, sliding my dagger into the hidden place within my armor. The new golden set Nori had made for me had less metallic coverage because I no longer needed something so heavy and protective during my day to day. She was still working on something on par with what I had in Valhalla, but I knew a piece of art such as that would take time to perfect.

I left the mirror behind, hustling out of our room and down the hall after Rayna. Kari and I were staying in the House of

Wings, as was traditional for valkyries; because we were committed to being domestic partners, Freyja made an exception. Council members lived in houses in the meadow, and Kari and I couldn't wait to move into one soon. We'd been staying up late, staring at the ceiling, talking about how we wanted to decorate and what we planned to grow in our garden. I tried to tell Kari I could summon anything she could ever need, but she insisted it wasn't the same. She wanted to grow her ingredients and get her hands dirty, though she never seemed to complain when I summoned her favorite dishes after a long day in one of the incantation chambers.

"There you are!" Rayna said with a satisfied grin as she pushed off the main entrance to the sect. "Just in time."

"What can I say? I'm head trainer." I smirked, walking through the doorway and stepping out into the late fall day. "I can't keep my girls waiting, now can I?"

I descended the pale stone steps, and looked out to the field filled with gold and emerald valkyries.

"Alright, listen up!" I called out to the group of women. "I know you all have souls to collect, but I called this meeting not for combat training, but to discuss soul plucking. You've all been taught to leave the most glorious warriors for the Valhalla sect, but we appease Odin no more. Do you understand?"

My sisters all began murmuring and looking amongst themselves, and then one of them, Meya, put her hands around her mouth and screamed, "HEL YEAH!" The other sisters joined in, clapping their hands or tapping weapons against their breastplates.

"And to let you in on a little secret, the best warriors aren't always the ones you expect. When you're watching their final moments, pay attention to their 'why'. Why were they in that battle? Who were they fighting for? And I don't mean the jarl or king who sent them out onto the battlefield. I mean who were they thinking of when they realized this wasn't a fight they were going to win," I said. My sisters all quieted as they listened to me with eager eyes and open hearts, no matter how much white shone in their hair.

"The warriors I brought Odin who fueled him the most weren't often the ones who went out searching for blood and glory. They weren't the ones with the most kills or brutal attacks. They were the mothers and fathers who protected their families. They were the brothers and sisters who fought to the end for the good of their people. Remember this as you fly to Midgard. Think about who you want to fill Freyja's great hall. Do you want to dine with the viking who slaughtered a thousand men? Or the elderly man who saved the women in his life from raiders?"

As I let my words sink in, I thought about one of the last souls I'd collected, the man with the yellow flowers. I hoped Bohil was treating him well and keeping his goblet full, as she'd been the one to take his soul to Odin. Kari's life for seven bottled souls. I'd do it all over again if given the chance.

"Alright, get out there," I finished. "Rayna, they're all yours."

Rayna nodded and whistled for Gunhild. While I was head trainer and ran the show in Fólkvangr, Rayna was the one who took charge on the battlefield. She flew down to Midgard with the sect almost every day, and I'd never seen her happier.

I usually didn't go with them, but today was different. My pointer and thumb found my lips, and I let out a loud whistle. Within moments, Apple swooped down to collect me. I tossed an apple in the air for her, and I vowed to never take that skill for granted again. I hadn't waited for her to ask. For once, I beat her to it.

As we flew down to Midgard, we didn't head to the same battlefield as my sisters. I had matters of my own to attend to. There was a small village on the edge of a forest, once filled with ravens and bloodflies. There was an abandoned longhouse with a broomstick on the door, and inside, each reflective surface was mysteriously covered.

I entered the longhouse, realizing Kari's scent was long gone. I began pulling the coverings off mirrors and using them to wrap up wobbly clay mugs and bowls. We would soon have a house to fill, after all, and my seeress would need her creations to make teas from the herbs she'd grow in our many gardens.

I hummed as I filled up sacks with her clothes and other belongings, including things for her to bring back to her family when she visited Helheim in the upcoming lunar cycle. Just because I wasn't able to return to the Valhalla sect to gather my belongings didn't mean Kari should be without her history too.

When I was done, I took one last good look around the place. I was about to call Apple once more when I heard a rhythmic thud, followed by the sound of coughing. I walked outside to see an older woman beating her dusty tapestry with a stick.

I smiled and waved before asking her if there was anything I could do to help. When she responded, I had to take a step back.

"You can tell me what you've done with Kari. Don't think I didn't see you take her on the back of that fancy horse you've got there," the woman said, waving her stick at me.

I cleared my throat. "I did take her. She's with the gods now, serving the Goddess of Fertility and Love. She did tell you she's a talented seeress, did she not?"

"Kari?" the woman laughed. "I loved the girl like she was my own, but she couldn't cast a spell if a seidr scroll hit her in the face."

"I think you'd be surprised," I said with a smile of my own, thinking about Kari trying, and failing, to use Midgardian seidr. How hadn't I realized she was never meant for this place sooner?

After a bit of convincing, I beat the rest of the tapestry for the woman and then was on my way once more. I didn't know if I'd ever come back to Stormheim, but I was thankful for the place that made Kari who she was.

I flew away as the sun began to set, grateful I was on my way home to the woman I loved instead of to some field full of death. There was no feast every night, no same routine every day. We had picnics in the different meadows, went for strolls along the fjord, and had sunrise flights on Apple. We were free.

When I walked through the door to our room, I was greeted by the familiar sound of a broomstick rattling against wood. Kari was standing by the bed, slipping out of her council robes and into a nightdress. I greeted her with a kiss before she flopped on the bed and began telling me all about her day learning about illusions from a man named Áki. He'd apparently been the one who'd given me the chalice during my test of loyalty, and he'd quickly become Kari's closest ally on the council.

Eventually, Kari sat up and motioned to the door, hemp sacks were propped up against it. "What are those?"

"I brought them back from Midgard. Are you sure you want to know?" I asked with a smirk, rising from where I sat on the corner of the bed.

"As long as there are no bodies in there, yes," Kari said, scooching closer to the foot of the bed.

"No, no bodies. I usually leave those down there," I chuckled as I stooped down and began untying the first sack. "This one is full of clay pottery and clothing. This next one has a bunch of random objects, like a basket with a shredded piece of fabric in it." I placed the basket on the floor, and Tove immediately dove inside. Kari let out a small, distorted noise, but I kept going. "And a wooden box full of—"

"Dried flower bracelets," Kari said, her words strained. She ran over to me, eyes misty, and I handed her the box with a nod of my head. As she unclasped it, running her fingertips over the fragile pieces of jewelry, my heart swelled. I hated to see her cry, but I knew these tears spoke of loss, change, and growth. They spoke of happiness, and sadness too, for the sister who'd stopped growing and never would again.

"Rune," she said, throwing her arms around my neck. "You went back to get this for me?"

I wrapped my arms around her back and pulled her in tighter. She was warm in my hands and felt like a life fulfilled.

"I wanted you to have a piece of your home while we build a new one for the both of us," I started. "I thought it was about time the people of Stormheim knew you were safe, but also that you were never coming back. I didn't want them worrying over your disappearance. After all the raids, it didn't feel right not to—"

Kari silenced me with a kiss, and it didn't take me long to kiss her back, deep and desperate. She was tender, fierce, and everything in between. She was curious with a dash of violence, and I couldn't have loved her more.

She may have once been a beautiful girl in a forest, whose grief I'd held onto like it was my own. I may have thought I knew her then, but I hadn't a clue. I hadn't known that the best kind of love is earned, and I would go to the ends of every world to earn hers.

ACKNOWLEDGMENTS

This book wouldn't have been written if it weren't for the support of my lovely readers! *Between Mischief & Magic* changed my life, and the readers who purchased, read, shared, and reviewed it made my author dreams come true. Since the release of *Between Mischief & Magic*, the Love X Magic family has grown. *Between Salt & Serenades* and *Between Broomsticks & Beating Wings* were created because of the love poured into the first book, and I couldn't be more grateful.

I would also like to thank my incredible critique partner, Ila Saint James, who was writing her first novel at the time I was writing *Between Broomsticks & Beating Wings*. It's been amazing growing alongside you, and I am ever thankful for your support and friendship.

Thank you to my street team for the unwavering support leading up to the publication of Between Broomsticks & Beating Wings. I hosted a little "fill-in-the-blank" challenge, and our winner was Taryn Jones! Please enjoy her submission:

She's always been the more disciplined of the two of us, but after a few too many tankards of dwarven ale, she'd been grinning like a fool, spinning in circles with wild abandon. Unfortunately, she hadn't quite had the hang of it. At one point, she'd tripped over her own boots and sent a table full of dwarves scattering with a mighty crash. The room had fallen silent for a heartbeat, but then the dwarves burst into raucous laughter, cheering her on as though she'd been the victor of the night.

My dearest husband, you have been there for me well before I published my first book. Thank you for introducing me to *Vikings: Valhalla*, which got my brain churning with ways to make Norse mythology fun and gay. Love you forever.

A special shout out to Tamsin—my original valkyrie crush. You deserved better.

ABOUT THE AUTHOR

Marissa Serrao is the author of The Seeking, a YA portal fantasy series, and Love X Magic, an NA sapphic romantasy collection.

As a child, Marissa lived in a world of fantasy, befriending mythical creatures

and building many magical kingdoms inside her mind. It wasn't until years later that she revisited her love of fantasy worldbuilding and took it to the page, where she could invite others to explore the magic with her.

You can find Marissa at home in Charlotte, North Carolina sneaking in as many moments as she can to write each day, surrounded by her husband, furry kids, and far too many houseplants.

CONNECT WITH MARISSA

@authormarissaserrao

TikTok: https://www.facebook.com/authormarissaserrao/

Instagram: https://www.instagram.com/authormarissaserrao/

Facebook: https://www.facebook.com/authormarissaserrao/

ALSO BY MARISSA SERRAO

Love X Magic

YOUR GUIDE TO THE LOVE X MAGIC COLLECTION

Between Mischief & Magic

- A drunken demon, a princess who lost her magic, and a deal to save them both...
- Vibes: Cozy Cottagecore, Grumpy X Sunshine, & Slow-Burn
- Coziness: 4/5
- Spice: 1/5

Between Salt & Serenades

- A stubborn siren, a stranded selkie, and a deal to save the sea...
- Vibes: Seaside Adventures, Natural Enemies to Lovers, & Forced Proximity
- Coziness: 2/5
- Spice: 1.5/5

Between Broomsticks & Beating Wings

- A cursed witch, a valkyrie who lost her way, and a deal that changes the underworld...
- Vibes: Norse Mythology, Quest Through the Underworld, & Light Stalking
- Coziness: 2/5
- Spice: 2/5